The Four Elizabeths

The Four Elizabeths

Mary Maclaren

Copyright © 2011 by Mary Maclaren.

ISBN: Softcover   978-1-4568-5372-3
          Ebook   978-1-4568-5373-0

All rights reserved. No part of this book may be reproduced or transmitted in any form or by any means, electronic or mechanical, including photocopying, recording, or by any information storage and retrieval system, without permission in writing from the copyright owner.

This is a work of fiction. Names, characters, places and incidents either are the product of the author's imagination or are used fictitiously, and any resemblance to any actual persons, living or dead, events, or locales is entirely coincidental.

This book was printed in the United States of America.

To order additional copies of this book, contact:
Xlibris Corporation
0-800-644-6988
www.xlibrispublishing.co.uk
Orders@xlibrispublishing.co.uk
301479

CONTENTS

DEDICATION 7
ACKNOWLEDGEMENTS 9

CHAPTER 1:   THE FIRST ELIZABETH 11
CHAPTER 2:   THE MOVE TO PORTSMOUTH 17
CHAPTER 3:   CONVICTS IN ALL GUISES 21
CHAPTER 4:   CRUELTY AND COMPASSION 26
CHAPTER 5:   THE HUMANE TURNKEY 33
CHAPTER 6:   MEET TWO MORE ELIZABETHS 38
CHAPTER 7:   LIEUTENANT RALPH CLARK 43
CHAPTER 8:   THE FOUR ELIZABETHS TOGETHER 48
CHAPTER 9:   THE LONG WAIT 52
CHAPTER 10:   JOHN HART 59
CHAPTER 11:   JOHN HART'S INITIATION 64
CHAPTER 12:   FIGHTING AND LOVING 75
CHAPTER 13:   SET SAIL AT LAST 82
CHAPTER 14:   THE JOURNEY BEGINS 88
CHAPTER 15:   SEASICKNESS TAKES OVER 94
CHAPTER 16:   JEALOUSY AND BRIBERY 100
CHAPTER 17:   BEING HAPPY IS PENALISED 106
CHAPTER 18:   REST AT TENERIFE 113
CHAPTER 19:   KING GEORGE III's BIRTHDAY 121

CHAPTER 20:	MORE JOY, TEARS AND FEARS	125
CHAPTER 21:	THE LONG JOURNEY RESUMES	137
CHAPTER 22:	LOVE, DEATH AND A STORM	148
CHAPTER 23:	ELIZABETH POWLEY'S VICTORY	159
CHAPTER 24:	CRUELTY	166
CHAPTER 25:	SIGNS OF LIFE	172
CHAPTER 26:	CROSSING THE LINE	180
CHAPTER 27:	MORALS AND PUNISHMENT	187
CHAPTER 28:	EFFORD	194
CHAPTER 29:	HUMAN NATURE	201
CHAPTER 30:	LAND AT LAST	212
CHAPTER 31:	HENRY CABLE ESCAPES	222
CHAPTER 32:	ELIZABETH POWLEY IS CONFUSED	231
CHAPTER 33:	MEREDITH AND ARNDELL ARGUE	240
CHAPTER 34:	THE GALE	249
CHAPTER 35:	THE LAST PORT	257
CHAPTER 36:	UNEXPECTED CHANGE	265
CHAPTER 37:	EPILOGUE	282

DEDICATION

I would like to dedicate this book to my late husband, Ray. His help with the initial research when he was alive, has proved invaluable and he knows how grateful I am.

ACKNOWLEDGEMENTS

I must also thank my sister, Pat, who lent me her ear on many occasions when I needed to talk about this book. And to my family, friends, and Jim, especially, I would say I owe you all so much for your support and encouragement. A big Thank You!

Also I'd like to thank the wonderful writers from all over the world that I've met online. In particular Gungalo, who writes the most exquisite poetry and supported me through each chapter; adewpearl, AliSmith, animatqua, c-lucas, Penelope, percival86jack, melyuki, Roberta Joan Jensen, goldwell, and AlvinTEthington, and so many more writers on FanStory.com

Without the assistance and patience of Rhea Villacarlos of Xlibris Publishing Co this book would still be in the drawer!

Thank you, Rhea.

The First Fleet 1787
Eleven ships

SIRIUS headed the fleet
Each vessel straining
creaking in the breeze

Eleven ships
Now well known names
The human flotsam
most pale and afraid

Eleven ships
Eleven months
Bonds greater than iron shackles
Were formed

aboard *H.M.S. THE FRIENDSHIP*

CHAPTER 1

THE FIRST ELIZABETH

Elizabeth Powley was the daughter of a prostitute and an unknown punter. She was fifteen when her mother died and already a well known girl of the streets herself. For the following nine years, she lived by her wits with a toughness bred by necessity. Never known to converse in less than a snarl she was, in this year of 1787, one of London's harlots, caring for no-one and nothing apart from where her next meal would be eaten. And the size of that meal depended entirely on her success in flaunting her grimy temptations.

She was raw-boned and had tobacco coloured hair that hung almost to her waist in unwashed disarray. But it was her lynx-eyed gaze that commanded instant attention from those who passed her. Once noted, her eyes were never forgotten and this made her an easy target for 'clients'. Other street women loathed her. In their usual style, they would rub themselves seductively against the dallying men, and it was tantamount to a bucket of freezing water tossed from the filthy rooms above for those women to be pushed aside and told, "I'm looking for that tall one with the green eyes."

Those same eyes were now coldly regarding the wagon that had just rattled through the blackened gates of London's infamous Newgate Prison. She had been arrested for trying to sneakily take a gold tie-pin from a gentleman she had accosted. The gentleman had proved to be a magistrate, and Elizabeth sentence was deportation to the New Colony for seven years. It did not worry her because the question of deportation was still being hotly discussed in Parliament, and up to then, no-one had been sent further than Newgate Prison, or to the dreaded hulk ships anchored in Portsmouth Harbour or along the Thames River. The British penal system was unable to keep abreast of its criminal problem, and prisons, as well as prison ships, were overflowing. But for now, Elizabeth was under cover and the daily meal (albeit thin gruel and stale bread) was being provided.

The weary Clydesdale horses that pulled yet another wagonload of convicts into Newgate Gaol that cold and late afternoon, scuffed to a halt. Their great hooves slipped on the moist cobblestones as the wooden barrier at the back of the cart was unshackled and then let down with a jangling crash.

New arrivals often carried something of value—perhaps a smuggled bottle of liquor, a lace-edge handkerchief, maybe even a gold coin cleverly hidden before being sentenced. For Elizabeth and her fellow inmates, therefore, scrutinizing the intake for possible conquests was a necessity, rather than an interest.

A coarse, middle-aged convict hung indolently on an open cell gate near Elizabeth. Stale scalp-oil matted his hair, his uneven nose was inflamed by alcohol, and his tattered jacket flapped pungently in the extra breeze he created as he swung back and fore. His name was William Gant and he had been goading Elizabeth all day, boredom creating sexual thoughts for entertainment.

"Garn, Liz . . . give me tail a tickle, an' I'll swap yer with some rum." He ignored Elizabeth's vicious glare in reply, and grinning with yellowed teeth he continued to swing on the iron gate. "Old Slimey is on guard duty tonight, an' I've paid 'im for a new bottle. C'mon, Liz—it won't take long, I promise."

Elizabeth pulled a weed growing between the granite slabs of the wall she was leaning on and chewed it thoughtfully, never taking her eyes from the cart.

"Looking for some new game, are yer Liz?" Gant's odour was unbearable. "Fancy anyfink?"

Elizabeth shrugged bony shoulders. "Don't look much cop from here." She spat in Gant's direction and added, " . . . and me name's Elizabeth."

"Ooh, pardun me, y'majesty!" goaded the ruffian. "You don't care what we calls yer, as long as we pays enough."

William Gant had committed murder and this crime rarely escaped the hangman's noose. By sheer blackmail and the fact that he was an expert in detecting—if not creating—corruption, his sentence was commuted to fourteen years deportation.

"Anyway, Liz," he continued taunting, "how about the young copper-top there? He looks a likely toss."

He referred to the nineteen-year old boy who looked around hesitantly before lowering his well-built frame from the prison cart. Henry Cable's complexion was white, the result of three years spent awaiting transportation in a Norwich gaol. Overcrowding there had forced the authorities to relocate prisoners due for transportation. A square-set chin, intelligent grey eyes and a crinkly thatch of reddish hair displayed none of Henry's true nature.

"Looks a bit of all right," Gant persisted. "How much d'yer reckon, Liz? Should be able to twist him for a bit . . ."

He stopped and turned away abruptly as a green-uniformed jailer approached. "What's the trouble, Powley?"

Elzabeth shrugged and spat again towards Gant, before she walked away. "Nothing."

She had only strolled a few steps when a second jailer approached her. "Wot yer doin' tonight, love?" He crowded her against the cold wall and fingered her hair.

"Leave me bleedin' hair alone," she said through tightly clenched teeth. "Any'ow, you're too late. I'm spoken for." The jailer tugged the lock of hair he'd twined around his dirty fingers until she added slyly, "By the Guv'nor."

He twitched her hair painfully then strode off. Elizabeth screamed after him, "Bastard!"

Grey clouds hung low over London that March afternoon and were a fitting match to the heavy cloud of despondency that pervaded the cold prison. Filth and degradation, privation and despair was everywhere, and as a weary apathy overtook Elizabeth, she ambled to the depths of a nearby open cell and allowed herself the oblivion of sleep.

Meanwhile, unloaded among the convicts to arrive with Henry Cable, was Susannah Holmes. A vibrant girl of twenty-two, she had filled Henry's dismal world in Norwich gaol with a tender love and bore him a son a few weeks earlier. They had named him Henry also, in honour of the grandfather who was hung the day after Norwich held its Lent Assizes in 1783.

"I was there," Henry told Susannah. "I listened to the crowd sighing like witches as the trapdoor swung away and I prayed that my father's body would be the last to stop twitching."

Susannah's eyes had rounded in horror and question. "What do you mean?"

"People get pleasure from watching hangings," Henry explained bitterly, "and they make wagers. The last body to move wins them a lot of money."

Henry's own death sentence had been commuted to seven years exile. He and his father and uncle had stolen some clothing from a rich widow's house in order to buy a hot meal. The older men had paid the full price for adding to their crime by 'leading the boy astray.'

Susannah cuddled their son close to her and led Henry to a more sheltered spot in the yard. They sat talking quietly about their new surroundings. In fact, they were so engrossed that they failed to observe yet another cart arriving, just before dark.

It was full of prisoners from Wales, and the healthy glow of these dark-eyed people contrasted vividly with the pallor of convicts who had spent years in captivity. Jailers herded them and the other prisoners in for the night and they filled the cells with a breath of Welsh lambs and green mountains.

Mary Watkins, a buxom twenty-year old, had been allocated the same cell as the young parents. She stared around at first, then spotted the baby.

She introduced herself and at first, Henry and Susannah drew back in suspicion. Then Mary's warmth embraced little Henry.

"Oh, cariads," she crooned, "he's bew-tiful." She swung a checkered woolen shawl from her shoulders, folded it in half diagonally, then wrapped it around mother and baby. 'here, have this," she said. "It will keep you both warm, innit? He's so tiny. How old is he?"

"Just four weeks," Susannah whispered. Parental pride seemed out of place in such surroundings, nevertheless, it warmed their friendship. "What does that mean . . . curry-something?"

Mary chuckled at Susannah's attempted pronunciation and settled herself on the dirty straw beside the little family. "Curr-e-ad," she detailed. "It means 'my love or lovely one.' They use it at home for the little ones, mostly." Her lilting accent soon became familiar to Susannah and Henry, and a great friendship began to be forged, transcending their captivity.

A few days later, all the convicts were awakened in the bitterly cold dawn by dreadful screams and curses. They all kept silent as the hollow stone corridors rang and were not to know that it was Elizabeth Powley. She had been taken to the punishment cell by the lecherous jailer she'd rebuffed a few days earlier. With two other burly warders, he leered as they pinned her to the cold floor.

"Hold still, y'little bitch! It's got to come orf." Maliciously, he added, "Orders from the Guv'nor."

"You filthy scum . . ." Elizabeth screamed. "You wait . . ." Her words were lost in raucous laughter as the jailer wielded a large pair of scissors and chopped away uneven handfuls of her lice-ridden hair. After her liaison with the Governor he had complained that she had lain completely unaffected by his ardent attentions and spent most of the hours scratching her head.

Women in other cells quivered as they listened to Elizabeth's protestations, unable to know exactly what it was that had to 'come orf' and imagining the worst as they listened.

"You bastards!" shouted the whore. "Don't think I'm going to be treated like a bleedin' wild goat!"

"Why not?" laughed one of her captors. "You bleedin'-well look like one!"

The early morning furore eased as the jailers left Elizabeth. They locked the cell door and their evil laughs echoed down the corridor. Moments later, all was quiet and prisoners in other cells, condemned to Newgate's unholy dampness and discomfort, slipped back into a fitful sleep.

Elizabeth's ragged breathing slowed, and her eyes narrowed as in the early light and eerie silence, a rat appeared from a hole in the corner. It proceeded to investige its familiar hunting grounds. "I'll bet that's what happens to all men when they die," she muttered. "I'll bet there's no hell really, only a place where people get turned into rats, or beetles."

It occurred to her then that maybe, for those very good people who did everything right and went to Church every Sunday, there was a place where they were turned into birds. She suddenly felt very lonely, and ran her grubby fingers through what was left of her hair. Vanity was not one of her sins, but she felt strangely vulnerable and open to attack. "Bleedin' deported—I'll give 'em hell, wherever I goes."

CHAPTER 2

THE MOVE TO PORTSMOUTH

Less than half an hour later, a disgruntled turnkey rattled the cell door then opened it with a big iron key. Startled, Elizabeth Powley leapt to her feet. "Oy, wot do you tink you are doing?" she demanded, still seething after her ordeal.

"Got to put you in with the others," he growled, and then led her to the cell where Susannah, Mary and Henry were huddled with several others. He peered at a piece of paper in his other hand.

"All right, listen here you lot. You're headed f'Botany Bay—and good riddance to the bleedin' lot of yer. Now if your name's on this paper, you're to be put on "*The Friendship*" in Portsmouth. "If yer name's not read out, then you goes on *The Charlotte*."

There was a rustle of alarm, and Susannah instinctively cuddled her baby closer into the shawl. Mary Watkins held her breath, and then her following breaths were shallow.

"John Hart," the jailer began. "Henry Lovell, William Gant, Henry Cable . . ." He called several others who were in a neighboring cell but Susannah heard none of them. She was waiting for the women's' names to be called. The jailer, however, obviously derived a lot of relish in calling just one. " . . . and Elizabeth Powley!"

Mary saw Henry flush angrily but he could say nothing, and Susannah's doe-eyes filled with tears. Her greatest fear had thrust its way into their bleak excuse for happiness. She and Henry were to be parted. No-one heard her sob because of the scuffle as Elizabeth regained her feet.

"What d'yer mean?" she yelled, bristling like a tiger ready to spring.

"That I pity the Cap'n and crew of *"The Friendship"* that's what," shouted the jailer nastily. "Now, get a move on, you lot! The carts are outside waiting, so pick up yer bits and pieces, make into a line and wait to be chained."

While they did as they were ordered, Henry put is arms around Susannah's shoulders in a vain attempt to stop her weeping. The baby began to cry pitifully, sensing his mother's distraction. Mary turned away abruptly and gathered her meagre belongings. A small sewing purse, a few cloths used for napkins, and spare baby slips she had made from one of her petticoats.

"Don't cry please, Susannah" pleaded Henry. "We'll be together as soon as we get to Botany Bay."

Susannah's usual demeanor snapped with the unknown terror of their ordeal, and anger sparked in her eyes. "If we get there, you mean."

"I'll look after them, Henry," Mary said softly, ignoring the dread in her own heart.

The convicts were to be separated for their ships once they reached Portsmouth Harbour, so the first fifteen to be led into the grey miserable dawn were loaded onto the front cart. Among them, Mary Watkins spread herself protectively against Susannah and her baby, and made sure that Henry found space beside them. The young couple sat in silence on the straw-covered floorboards, their stricken faces betraying their thoughts. Of the others, only Elizabeth Powley struggled incessantly with the two burly jailers trying to control her.

"Thought I paid you well enough to keep me off the list," she screeched at one.

"You want to try money next time, Liz," said another man and the jailers laughed cruelly. The big horses, disrupted by the noise behind them, fidgeted uneasily and clattered forward a few steps just as a young boy started to climb on board. He yelled as he tumbled to the ground and a third jailer grasped his thin upper arm. Without ceremony, he tossed the lad into the cart and then turned to assist his compatriots with the struggling Elizabeth.

Her green eyes flashed as she spotted the Governor standing a little way off. "Filth! You slimy bastard," she yelled and earned a stinging blow across her mouth. A lifetime of abuse had inured her to such blows so she continued shouting and it was minutes before she was finally tossed into the cart.

"Get rid of them," the Governor ordered. One prostitute was the same as another to him, and there would undoubtedly be more shortly to while away his boring evenings. Although he didn't doubt that he would remember Elizabeth Powley for a long time. Those eyes.

The driver's whip cracked over the horses making their huge flanks twitch. Fumes of digested hay and warm manure wafted as they scraped their hooves and slid on the dew-moistened cobblestones. They gradually took the strain of their load and the cart trundled forward. The large door of Newgate Prison with its famous black iron knocker swung open, and the first load of convicts soon lost sight of the gloomy building.

It was going to be an arduous journey to Portsmouth Harbour, some seventy miles away. Seasonal winds sliced through the cart's wooden sides causing scant clothing and matted hair to toss in frenzy. Only the bodily contact of over-crowding helped to maintain warmth for the convicts.

Crushed beside Elizabeth Powley, William Gant shifted with discomfort and leered. "Give us a kiss, darlin'. Warm me cockles, why don't yer?"

"And mess up me bleedin' hair?" she replied. The shaggy tufts added to her scorn and with high cheekbones and firm mouth, she could have been a man, if it wasn't for the femininity that stretched open her dirty and low-cut blouse.

She turned sharply when a toothless convict opposite let out a guttural laugh. "You got a hope, Bill. Liz don't give no favours, unless you can pay somehow."

Her chin jutted, but she grinned. "You shut y'mouth, too. An' me name's Elizabeth."

Gant nudged her viciously. "Who d'you fink you are—royalty or somefink?"

Elizabeth buckled him with an elbow in his ribs, and laughed as he gasped for breath.

CHAPTER 3

CONVICTS IN ALL GUISES

The cart driver made a weak attempt to hustle the horses, but he had already decided to stay overnight in Portsmouth, sampling its plethora of brothels and beer-houses. Occasionally the convicts amused themselves by shouting abuse at villagers as they passed through the little hamlets, but most of the time was spent in spiteful innuendo or lewd discussion.

"If we don't get there soon," moaned Gant, "it'll be so frostbitten, I'll have no more use for a whore."

Huddled into one corner, the frail boy who had fallen when climbing onto the cart stared at Gant's stubbled face grinning as though a picture of Satan that his late mother had shown him, had somehow materialised.

"Wot y'staring at, kid?" Gant said nastily.

"He's probably asking himself that," sneered Elizabeth withdrawing her blue ankle smartly when the lecher kicked out at her.

A buxom white-haired woman in the cart beside John spread herself like a hen gathering a stray chick. "Take no notice of him, lad. What's your name?"

"John Hart," shivered the Cockney sweep.

"Seven years in the new colony?"

The boy nodded dumbly and looked away as he crossed his arms and thrust dirty fists under his armpits for warmth.

"Me too," sighed the big woman. "My name's Amy. I was a cook for a posh gentleman, but the slut of a housemaid blamed me when some lace doilies went missing. Didn't give me a chance, he didn't, an' all because me father had been hanged for stealing. Them blasted magistrates always give in to a wink from a pretty witness, they does. Or the promise of a bit of slap 'n tickle."

John Hart wasn't listening. His pale forehead was pressed on his drawn-up knees, because that way no-one could see he was crying.

"Shut yer noise back there," yelled the driver over the clop of hooves on gravel. "Much more of your bellyaching and I'll flog the lot o'yer." He vented his suffering from the bleak wind on the huge brown flanks labouring in front of him, but the horses had no intention of speeding their pace. Drawing the green serge of his cloak across his knees, he grumbled, "Trust my luck to get this rotten job, so near to the Whitsuntide as well."

The journey wore on inexorably and the cart continued to creak past peaceful rural scenes that contrasted vividly with the discontented load. The weak sunshine that had dared to accompany the blustery day faded by noon, and clouds gathered in a glowering canopy which stilled and intensified the cold. Hunger and despair swallowed the initial ribaldry amongst the convicts. Some moaned as they stretched their stiffened joints, others dozed fitfully. For many hours the heavy silence was broken only by the sound of gravel being crunched under slow wheels and trees bending to the rising wind.

"Henry," whispered Susannah timidly. "What if we don't get there? What if your ship goes down? What if . . . ?"

"Hush now, cariad," soothed Mary. "You mustn't think about those things. God will take care of us."

Again Susannah's new maternity overrode her placid nature as she rounded on her friend. "God! Where's his mercy now? How could he let this happen to us?"

"Susannah," exclaimed Henry, scandalised. The young man gazed at the woman and child who had given meaning to his life, and struggled for words to express his love. "He brought us together."

"For what?" demanded Susannah. "To tear us apart again?"

"I promise you, Susannah. If we come through this together, I will never leave you again."

Her passionate outburst short-lived, Susannah's small chin drooped wearily to her chest as she suckled the baby beneath the voluminous Welsh wool shawl Mary had given her. Henry longed to hold mother and child in his arms but the shackles wouldn't allow. "Stay with them always, won't you Mary?"

"Don't you worry now," answered the Welsh girl softly. "I'll stick like lamb broth and dumplings do to your bones."

Roused by a change in the sound from the horses hooves, the convicts saw that the cart was pulling up in front of a thatched building. It overlooked a small garden and two wooden benches leaned against its whitewashed walls. A large elm tree overhung the squat building, and the benches were devoid of any patrons to appreciate the crocuses and daffodils beginning to show their spring favours.

The Fox and Brush Inn contrasted disturbingly with the sooty London Elizabeth and her fellow travellers knew, teeming with urchins and barrows. The only beer-houses she had experienced were noisy, dirty, and overflowing with drunken lechers and prostitutes.

"Where the hell are we, turnkey?" she yelled as he dismounted and tied the horses near the trough. "Going to buy us a pint, are you?"

"Get one f'me, too," chorused half a dozen rough voices, while Elizabeth chuckled at the jailer's shaking fist.

"Give 'em some water," he snarled at the young girl that emerged from a side door carrying an iron pot. Emptying soupy dishwater, she looked anxiously at the caged souls and promptly banged the pot against the wall. "Herby! Bring out a bucket of water and a ladle."

The cart driver didn't look back, but hastened into the Inn with the taste of ale and a thick piece of bread and cheese already in his mouth.

A weedy youngster eventually appeared. He had prominent teeth and straw-coloured hair, with texture that resembled the Inn's roof. Objecting loudly, he staggered under the weight of water which slopped from a blackened iron bucket. "I didn't come here to serve convicts . . ."

"Over here, Herby," yelled Elizabeth. "There's a luverly lad. Now then, gents—ladies first . . ."

"Yeah? Where?" Gant chuckled nastily and a scuffle ensued for the bucket and metal ladle, which had been passed up to the convicts.

"Make sure I gets me bucket back," yelled the boy. He felt secure as he eyed the convicts' chains rattling against the metal, and gave a toothy grin. "Wouldn't trust you lot if you was wearing a white collar or sprouting wings."

Gant emptied the bucket and tossed it at their tormentor. Then, with a growled obscenity, he lifted the ladle and aimed a swipe at the sandy-haired brat who scuttled back to the Inn accompanied by a chorus of catcalls and jeers. The afternoon wore on and, gradually overcome with weariness from such an early start to the day, most of the convicts dozed fitfully. Only a slowly dying wind and rumbles from empty stomachs disturbed the silence.

The turnkey took advantage of the break and prolonged his meal with what he considered sufficient ale to warm the rest of his day's labour. Several hours passed before he emerged, untied the horses and hauled himself into the splintered driving seat. He slashed his whip and stirred the horses into action while the convicts roused, and with curses and complaints they rearranged their stiffened bones as the cart trundled back onto the road.

They had travelled a few miles before Gant withdrew his hand from beneath his tattered coat and brandished the ladle he'd retained. The sign was greeted with precocious Cockney whoops that were only quietened by the wrath of the driver.

"What you think you're going to do with that?" grinned Elizabeth.

Gant waved the long-handled spoon at her. "I could sell it. On the uvver hand, y'majesty might make me a night with it." He cackled at his own joke.

Elizabeth's wits were as steely as her eyes. "I'll crown you wiv it, if that's what you want."

The shout of laughter sounded incongruous from a cartload of condemned souls, but served to hide the mixture of inevitable fear of the unknown and loss of pride that each man, woman and boy was enduring.

The driver, even more disgruntled by their humour, yelled another obscenity and flicked his horsewhip behind him. It caught John Hart viciously on the cheek and stung a sliver of flesh from just below his eye.

"You bastard!" Elizabeth screamed as the boy shrieked. "You nearly nicked his eye out."

"You'll get worse if I have to stop this cart again," the turnkey yelled back. "Now keep y'traps shut."

The motherly Amy Thompson drew the sobbing boy to her and dabbed at his wound with the cleanest part of her apron. "It's all right, son," she crooned. "You was just sitting in the wrong place, that's all." Glaring at the whore, she muttered, "Just like your sort, to get an innocent kid hurt."

Elizabeth poked out her tongue at the old woman. "Ain't none of us here innocent, missus."

CHAPTER 4

CRUELTY AND COMPASSION

Depression quickly regained a hold of the unwilling passengers and Elizabeth's thoughts drifted to more pleasant times. London was a big city and many accents from all over Britain could be heard amongst the babble of voices. Most people were drawn to the city from Scotland, North England, Wales and even Ireland by the lure of possible fame and fortune. Elizabeth Powley remembered a particular Irishman called Patrick, and a smile hovered on her lips.

Towards three o'clock in the afternoon, drizzle began to soak their thin clothing, wet metal chafed their wrists and the inevitability of their plight was overwhelming.

"How much longer, driver? We'll be bleedin' dead afore we even gets to Portsmouth, let alone Botany Bay." Elizabeth's strident yell was ignored. Cold rivulets drew paths through the grime as it ran from the convicts' hair and followed contours of smooth and stubbled cheeks alike. It lent a macabre fantasy to their expressionless masks.

"How's your face now, luv?" Amy asked the boy quietly. "Bit sore, is it?"

John nodded miserably and didn't resist when the big woman drew him even closer. He had asked for nothing more during his short life than someone to love him. But Amy's concern would end when they arrived at

Portsmouth. She had been allocated to "The Charlotte" and John Hart's name had been called with the list of transportees for "The Friendship."

Cheerless and uncomfortable hours passed but the clouds were beginning to break. The rain drifted away on a softer wind, trees showed small green eruptions and grasses sprung beneath yew hedges. Soon the cart trundled past clusters of cottages that increased in number as they approached Portsmouth. Thatched roofs behind gardens with budding crocuses, daffodils and primroses changed to rows of tall dwellings glued to each other like wasps' nests. Uninspiring buildings of bricks and mortar, they stood shoulder to shoulder craving for space, as did the crowds that milled alongside the damp roads and footpaths.

The prisoner cart rattled along Portsmouth's cobbled streets, jolting and rocking the passengers painfully, but they retained enough spirit to curse everything and everyone, from the cart driver to the Portsmouth City fathers.

"Bad as old London, innit?" scoffed Gant. "Except the women are more buxom. No wonder sailors pull in here." He leered into Elizabeth's face. "Don't you wish you could do a bit of business here, y'ighness? Bet there's plenty of money drifting around all these pubs. Wish I had as much."

"You could never have enough to buy me, y'smelly-breathed scum," she said viciously. "I've turned me nose up at better'n the likes of you."

A gasp of pain burst from her slackened lips as Gant's elbow rammed into her ribs. Amy instinctively covered the boy's ears, but her hands only served to deaden the abuse that Elizabeth screamed at the laughing men. The curses were all too familiar to the soulful lad because even London's brothels had chimneys that had to be swept by the likes of him.

The fracas evoked jeers from seamen loitering outside the pubs and along littered streets. Motley crowds bought fruit and fish from dirty street-barrows and everyone joined in.

"There's some more of England's scum."

"Good riddance, I say."

"Good job Botany Bay's the uvver side of the earth."

"Let's know if the Indians scalp you there."

"Gercha! That happens in America—this lot'll only find man-eating rats!"

Mindful that there was only another half-mile to the Harbour, the driver cracked his whip ceaselessly and threatened the exhausted horses with retirement to a glue-factory. Above Portsmouth's blackened chimneys, the masts of the tall ships of the First Fleet speared the afternoon sky and hearts plummeted. The cart rounded the City Hall and trundled on past a pub that many a sailor referred to as his 'home'.

The Mermaid's Tail had a salt-rusted sign with a faded blue sea-siren just visible. Above it, scantily clothed onlookers hung out of the windows and drunken seamen raised mugs from the doorway in salute, as the cart rattled through. One sailor shouted, "See you on board, m'darlins."

Within minutes, the expansive Portsmouth Harbour came into view. It was cluttered with warships, merchant ships, small fishing boats and wooden rowboats all anchored in one of the world's deepest sea-basins. Among the vessels were the Government assigned ships of the First Fleet—two were naval ships and three were storeships. Six more were being loaded with men, women and children from all over the country. Some of the convicts were unrepentant, even arrogant. Others were dolorous and wretched with many of them having been housed in stinking hulks for years, because the prisons were overcrowded. But all had been sentenced to exile and they moved with utter despondency.

"Look, John," said Amy, trying to occupy the trembling boy's attention elsewhere. "That's the ship *Victory* over there. She's more'n twenty years old and got a hundred guns on board her." Obviously impressed by her knowledge, Hart gazed at the imposing ship. Amy smiled, then her eyes clouded. "This old girl will never see it again."

Small groups of red-coated marines stopped chattering and converged on the cart as the jailer pulled on the reigns. The grateful horses halted and steam snorted from their quivering nostrils. The late afternoon temperature had dropped dramatically and the convicts muttered and moaned with stiffness.

"Come on, get orf you lot," yelled the marine removing the barriers. He turned to the dismounting jailer who stretched painful legs. "You're the last one. All the other carts got here hours ago. Where have y'been?"

Shrugging, the jailer drew his cloak closer and only asked where he could leave his horses. Then he headed back to the comforts of The Mermaid's Tail.

"Right," yelled the sergeant. "Those for *"The Charlotte"* over 'ere—those for *"The Friendship"* follow 'im." He waved the butt of his rifle towards Sergeant Stewart, a pleasant looking marine on his right.

"Tata, luv," Amy called to John Hart. He was meekly trooping behind Elizabeth Powley and the others heading for *"The Friendship"*. "Hope I'll see you there."

"Hold y'tongue, old woman," said the marine and nudged her roughly with his rifle, "or you won't even see tomorrow."

"Those for *"The Charlotte"* over 'ere," repeated a bored marine private.

"Henry . . ." Clutching her sleeping son, Susannah stumbled from the cart and Mary forgot her own fears as she put out an arm and supported her young friend. Henry, shackled to the line of men moving towards *"The Friendship's"* jollyboat, trembled with frustration.

"Mind the baby now, cariad." Mary spoke softly as Susannah's voice broke. She glared towards the red-coated overseers. "Don't you cry now, or they'll all make fun of you."

Once ferried to *"The Charlotte"*, Mary and Susannah clambered aboard laboriously and, with the other convicts, were checked off against a list held by a Lieutenant of Marines. The prisoners swayed with the unaccustomed rise and fall of the tide and a fair-haired Captain Tench surveyed his bedraggled consignment.

"Who's that woman with a baby?" he thundered. "We have no papers for a convict's child, do we?" His aide studied the list and shook his head. "Well, it's not coming on board here," Tench continued. "On shore with it!"

There was a stunned silence and on its heels came an incredulous fury. Screams that released the fears, despair and aggravating futility of their situation emanated from the throats of women and whores alike. Screams that pierced like shards of glass, almost deafening the crewmen and dockside labour.

"Oh, God in His merciful Heaven," appealed Amy Thompson, bursting into tears.

"You bastards!" shouted another woman. "You'd be too bleedin' evil to have kids of your own!" Her words were cut short by a savage blow to her stomach and she crumpled to the deck.

The loudest screams came from Susannah when a seaman approached and tore little Henry from her arms. "God in Heaven, No . . . no! My baby . . . oh, my God . . . Henry! My baby . . ." Her agonised cries brought the women to tears and the manacled men looked away, their helplessness weighing far more heavily than their bonds.

On the quayside was a jailer who had delivered an earlier consignment of convicts. Once they had been taken aboard, he had gone to a small eating-house nearby. His hunger appeased, he was now preparing to drive his cart back to London. John Simpson, an intelligent and kindly man in his fifties, had earned himself the nickname of "The Humane Turnkey." His love of books and gaining knowledge set him apart from most jailers, and the prisoners trusted him.

He now stared across the water at the din coming from *"The Charlotte"* and then watched in disbelief as a seaman stepped onto the shore from the jollyboat, carrying the squalling bundle. Realising there was something sadly amiss, Simpson strode across the damp pebbles as the seaman instructed a nearby fisherman to "take it to the nearest workhouse."

"Here, what's going on?" Simpson called.

"No papers," was the terse reply.

Simpson was infuriated that an innocent baby should suffer through bureaucracy. It was unthinkable. "Is there no mercy in this God-forsaken country?" he shouted. "Here, give it to me." He demanded the names of the women involved from the sailor and crimson with anger, he turned towards the ship. "I'll take care of him, Susannah Holmes," he yelled, but his voice was lost in the din still coming from *"The Charlotte."*

On board, blanched and beyond control, the young mother was prevented from falling to a faint by an outraged Mary Watkins who held on to her charge with a vice like grip. All caution and fearful reserve for the brass-buttoned authorities dissolved in an anger born of a simmering Celtic hatred as she screamed at Captain Tench. "May God in His Heaven plague you with nightmares for the rest of your life, you heathen!"

With no vestige of compassion, the uniformed officer gave a curt order to "get them all below." He turned on his black-booted heel and left the deck. His need was for rum, his senses impervious to the swell of hatred that accompanied him to his quarters.

Steering the horses back through Portsmouth's dingy streets, "The Humane Turnkey" seethed as he glanced over his shoulder to the bawling child being jolted on the straw. "I don't know what Mrs Simpson will have to say when I bring you home, young 'un. Her thinking she'd finished with babies an' all that."

It was not difficult to imagine the young mother's grief and he angrily struck his whip at the horses' flanks, urging them back to London as though distance would soften the tragedy.

Unaware of the drama on board *"The Charlotte"*, the baby's father shuffled towards *"The Friendship"*. In front of him in the pitiful line of humanity was a man who spoke softly, fearing a reprimand from the surly marine guard nearby. "We came here in the Summer, once or twice. Little urchins, orphans someone said they were, kept jumping off the piers into the mud." Momentarily distracted from the anguish of being parted from Susannah and his son, Henry stared at the man's half-turned head. "Sailors and merchants threw farthings and ha'pennies into it," the man continued. For a moment they were silent, picturing the little bodies smothered in sticky, acrid mire. "Saw somebody throw a threepenny bit once. Cor, didn't that cause a mad scramble."

"Hold your tongues," called Sergeant Stewart who then blew warming air into his hands. He'd been listening with interest and thinking how lucky his little Robert was not to have to earn money that way. His two-year old son and his dear wife Margaret would embark soon, and they were looking forward to their new life in Botany Bay.

"Take the woman and boy in the first lot, Corporal," called Stewart to the jollyboat oarsman.

"Ooh ta, ducky!" Elizabeth Powers sneered. "I'll remember you in me bleedin' Will." She raked the good-looking marine with her half-closed eyes. "Or maybe you'd like me to repay you sooner?"

Another marine pushed her into the boat with the butt of his musket. "Less of your lip, woman."

"Ow!" screeched Elizabeth unnecessarily while Gant gave a toothless grin at her performance. Female instinct made her sit between the boy and the leering convict.

"Did 'e hurt you?" John Hart queried.

Elizabeth spat into the sea. "Nah, there ain't no-one that can get t'me."

CHAPTER 5

THE HUMANE TURNKEY

By the time he approached London near midnight, John Simpson had made a decision. The monstrosity of the baby's fate had played through his mind over the miles, and he turned his cart towards the heart of the City. He knew where Lord Sydney, Secretary of the Home Office resided, having taken Mrs. Simpson sightseeing whenever he had a Sunday afternoon free. A few people wondered at the haste of the empty cart dodging along between opulent carriages and costermongers' barrows. Urchins scuttled out of its way, and a dog yapped until someone's boot changed its objection to a yelp.

He hauled on the reins until the panting beasts halted outside the grand home in London's upper-class quarter. He dismounted, lifted the now sleeping child into his arms and mounted the steps to a big black door with a brass knocker. The night capped footman's amazement, when he opened the door and saw John Simpson and his burden, was almost comical. John blurted his mission and the footman bade him stand in the foyer while he notified his master. He entered Lord Sydney's bedroom after a perfunctory knock and said, "If it pleases y'lordship, there's a man downstairs in the foyer who says he's a jailer, and that he has a baby for you."

"What are you talking about, man?" demanded Lord Sydney, still struggling to unravel from a deep sleep. "What baby?"

The equally befuddled footman dithered, not knowing what to answer. Then Lord Sydney rose to his feet and said, "Show him into the library."

A man of good humour, Lord Sydney chuckled at the audacity of the message as he donned his quilted house-gown and descended the blue carpeted staircase. He crossed the foyer to the booked-lined room where heavy wine coloured curtains excluded the chills of early spring. The jailer was on his feet contrasting the luxurious decor with that of the transport ships, and felt a fleeting annoyance. Nevertheless the inequality of Britain's class-rule was squashed in the warmth of Lord Sydney's greeting.

The aristocrat's good humour turned to disbelief, then indignation, as he listened to the jailer's story. He looked at Susannah's baby and briefly touched the infant's soft and pink skin.

"Begging your pardon, m'lord," John Simpson continued, "but I don't think the young people deserve such treatment, no matter what their crimes are. It was bad enough that the mother and baby were separated from the father, but to be torn from its mother's breast . . . why, the child is barely a few weeks old!"

Inflamed by the Marine Captain's dictatorial attitude, Lord Sydney sat at his oak desk and reached for a sheet of crested notepaper. Simpson rocked the baby, who began whimpering from hunger, while he gave the details and Lord Sydney dipped his quill to write hurriedly.

"Henry Cable and Susannah Holmes should be forever grateful to you, Mr. Simpson," he said. "I am authorising that you may return the child to its mother, and instructing Captain Tench to transfer the mother and child to *"The Friendship.*"

John Simpson's eyes moistened and his opinion of the upper-class temporarily softened. "Thank you, y'lordship. I . . ."

"That other woman you mentioned. She may as well join them too. What did you say her name was? Mary something . . . Watkins, was it?"

Simpson nodded dumbly.

* * *

To say that Mrs. Simpson was taken aback when her husband arrived with the baby at their modest home would be an understatement. She listened in awe as he described the events, and then gazed at the crying infant in her arms. "Whatever is the world coming to?" she said with heat.

"His father is Henry Cable," said John quietly. "You know the boy I used to lend books to when he was in Newgate."

"I'll get him some warm milk," said Mrs. Simpson and handed the baby back to her husband. John managed to stop the crying and rocked the child as he waited.

The milk was spooned slowly into the baby's mouth, and although most of it dribbled out again, there was obviously enough going down to placate the child.

Dawn arrived quickly. Mrs. Simpson piled the straw in the back of the cart into a small bed and placed little Henry into it. In truth, she didn't want to let him go, but her husband was obviously anxious to reunite mother and child as soon as possible. Almost as though they understood their mission, the horses sped along the road back to Portsmouth. It was early afternoon when he wearily clattered the cart to a halt at the quayside, and he hurried over to the idling boatmen.

"Take me to *The Charlotte*", he snapped to the hesitating sailor. I'll pay.

On board, Captain Tench read Lord Sydney's letter, and snorted. "As if we haven't enough trouble sorting out this scum, we're expected to be nursemaids as well." He raised his voice and boomed, "Sergeant!"

A swarthy soldier appeared in the cabin door and stared at the cloaked jailer holding the small bundle. Captain Tench gave him no opportunity too ponder the sight and commanded tetchily, "Fetch Homes and Watkins from the female quarters."

Shock still jarred through Susannah's small frame, and after a sleepless night, she could not be whiter. She did not look up when their names were called, and barely understood what was happening as she allowed Mary to assist her to her feet. Together they stumbled in front of the marine towards the Captain's cabin. Mary trembled at the thought of what was to come, unable to know just what to expect from this unexpected call to the Captain's cabin.

They were pushed unceremoniously into the room, but as soon as Mary saw the checkered shawl she cried, "The baby!"

Susannah raised her head sharply and oblivious to any need for permission she enfolded her son to her breast, and then she broke into heartbreaking sobs. "Oh, thank you, thank you," was all she kept repeating, and the baby nuzzled into her like a hungry lamb. "My baby, my baby . . ." she wept, her tears mingling with the soft down on Henry's head.

A hard lump in John Simpson's throat refused to let him speak, but Mary's dark eyes spoke volumes to the smiling turnkey.

"That's enough, Holmes," barked Tench, rising. For a terrified moment Susannah imagined he was going to take her baby again, and defensive panic flooded her cheeks. She stepped back, as if she was prepared to throw herself and the child overboard rather than endure another separation.

Missives from on high filled with criticism did nothing to lighten Tench's load, and it irked him to have his authority undermined in the eyes of his colleagues, especially those on other ships within the fleet. Transferring convicts between ships required him to notify Captain Arthur Phillip, who was leader of this expedition. He had no choice but to pass along the document from Lord Sydney and the fact sharpened his tone.

"Sergeant, escort these two over to "*The Friendship*" and give my compliments to Captain Meredith. Tell him it has nothing to do with me. Here, take this for him to read, and be careful to bring it back." With a waved dismissal, he handed Lord Sydney's letter to the saluting marine.

Now on deck and waiting for a small boat to be arranged for the transfer, Susannah reached up and kissed John Simpson. The joy in her heart said 'dance, scream, laugh hysterically' but the cold wind that caused the grey water to lap without soul against the ship's timbers, and the ever-present fear of retribution, quietened her voice.

"We will never forget you, Mr. Simpson," she said, and allowed herself and the baby to be wrapped in the Welsh shawl by Mary. "And God willing, if we all get to Botany Bay alive, I will make sure that little Henry never forgets your kindness either."

The turnkey smiled broadly. Turning to Mary he said, "Look after them, Watkins."

"That I will," lilted the Welshwoman.

* * *

On board "*The Friendship*," the ship's surgeon Thomas Arndell was waiting in Captain Meredith's cabin. They were preparing to spend the evening over on "*The Sirius*" for a meeting with the Commodore, Arthur Phillip. They looked around in surprise when the strangely jubilant convict women were brought in. Captain Meredith read Lord Sydney's letter and could only sympathise with his beleaguered colleague who must have been uncomfortable as this development occurred.

"Better check the infant over, Mister Arndell," he said. Turning to Susannah he continued, "You say the child's father is on board this ship?"

"Yes, sir," whispered Susannah. "Henry Cable."

"I'll have him informed. At least we'll have one or two happy transportees." He smiled briefly and fondled the black Labrador bitch at his side, called Lady.

Doctor Arndell could see that Susannah did not want to release the baby and he made a perfunctory examination as best he could while in its mother's arms. "Amazingly fit," he pronounced. "And seemingly undisturbed by events. I assume you are feeding it yourself, Holmes?"

Susannah nodded, watching the two officers like a startled fawn and Mary leaned imperceptibly towards her.

"Very well," said Meredith. "Take them all to the female convict quarters."

CHAPTER 6

MEET TWO MORE ELIZABETHS

An air of despondency, defiance and curiosity pervaded as "*The Friendship*" cargo was lined up on deck the next morning—males to one side, females the other. Two, however, communicated with emotional hunger in their eyes as Susannah lifted baby Henry for his father to see.

Captain Meredith's second Lieutenant, Ralph Clark, stood alongside him on the poop deck and checked off particulars of yet another cartload of prisoners that arrived earlier in the morning.

"That's the last of them, Captain. Ninety-seven on board altogether. Seventy-six males including the baby and the boy, and twenty-one females. I fear those women are going to be a lot of trouble, sir."

Meredith glanced at the familiar look of doom on his lieutenant's face and knew there would be no companionship from that quarter during the coming voyage. "Maybe so, Lieutenant. Does your list include the two women who were sent over from "*The Charlotte*" yesterday?"

"Yes, sir." Clark continued to worry at the list he held, like a dog with a bone that is far too big for him and doesn't quite know how to handle it.

Captain James Meredith surveyed the silent people swaying with the anchored ship's rise and fall on the tidal water. A kindly man in his forties and just over six feet tall, he cut a fine figure in his gold-buttoned uniform.

He dwarfed Ralph Clark, who was already earning a reputation for his lugubrious demeanor. In fact, Clark seemed intent on compensating for his lack of height and charisma with fluctuations of pomposity and romanticism. He now raised his eyes from the list, rocked on his heels, and glowered at the women prisoners.

"I sincerely trust, sir, that the marines who have elected to come without their wives, will not be drawn into bad habits by these women."

"I hardly think so, Lieutenant. From what I have seen, there isn't much to attract a man." Meredith did not remind Clark that he was one of those lone marines, then he reflected on the comment he had from the ship's master earlier.

Frances Walton was a grizzled sea-dog of many voyages and he'd referred to "our cargo of human flotsam"—and Meredith couldn't help but agree.

With no family to leave behind, Meredith was not as despondent as some of the other Marine Captains, but he too wondered what traumas the voyage would endure. Ranging over the bedraggled gathering, his eyes were drawn to those of the tallest woman. "Just look at that one with spiked hair," he remarked quietly to Clark with disgust. "Who is she?"

Clark shrugged lower into his red uniform and consulted the list. He was more concerned with retiring below decks on this chilly morning, and getting back to the diary he was determined to maintain. "Elizabeth Pully . . . or Powley, sir, according to this. Crime—larceny, sentence . . ."

"Yes, yes, all right," Meredith interrupted. "Well, get them all below again. Make sure they exercise on deck twice a day. The women first."

Preparing to leave, he noticed that Elizabeth's insolent glare was matched only by that of the convicts William Gant and Thomas Turner. Most others, including the boy John Hart, maintained the sullen and downcast look of humans stripped of pride, hope and freedom. With an instinctive trepidation, he noted the smoldering challenge in Elizabeth's stare and shivered.

"Yes, the wind is rising," remarked Clark, misinterpreting Meredith's attitude.

"The boy had better go with the men," Meredith replied, "and see they don't argue over space."

"Yes, Cap'n," answered Clark, touching his forehead in salute. He looked up at Meredith's broad frame and square jaw. "Permission to spend the night ashore, sir? I'm expecting my family."

"Sorry, Clark," was the brief reply. "I have to dine with the other captains of the fleet again this evening, on "*The Sirius*". You'll be in charge."

"Yes, sir." Clark saluted again dismally and his face darkened as he turned to the four seamen and two marines waiting beside him for orders. "Get those scoundrels below, and don't take any cheek."

The marine with the pleasant face who had assisted with the embarkation the day before was assigned to accompany the women. Sergeant Stewart had already gained a good name among the prisoners for his firm fairness. Nevertheless, he was a Marine first, and carried out his orders dutifully.

"What's y'name, soldier?" goaded Elizabeth Powley as he led them to the female quarters. "Want me to keep you warm some nights?"

"Watch your lip, Powley," he grunted. "Some of us will have our families with us." He stated the fact as though it was going to create a more solid barrier than the wooden hatch-cover they'd reached.

A devilish glint lit Elizabeth's eyes, and her full lips puckered invitingly as she thrust her chin towards him. "We'll see, ducky, we'll see."

Once the women had descended the ladder, Sergeant Stewart secured the hatchway and sighed at the wisdom of his decision that Margaret and Robert should accompany him. They were presently living with his widowed mother while he stayed at Southampton Marine barracks, and the chance to start a new life in Botany Bay had seemed attractive. It was Margaret who had persuaded him to volunteer for the voyage—already he had misgivings.

The wind increased that evening and the motion of the brig as it swooned into the swell caused several of the women prisoners to refuse their meal.

There was no fear of it being wasted, however. The loud bickering and squabbling between them caused Lieutenant Clark to leave his cabin on the other side of the bulkhead and hammer on the wall.

"That's enough from you ungrateful wretches," he barked. "Silence! Otherwise I will have you all flogged."

Returning to his cabin, he continued writing a letter to a friend in London. In it he praised the Government for the way in which the fleet had been equipped with supplies and commended the standard of food allowed to the convicts.

"But still they fight," he wrote. "I pale at imaginations of the troubles we face in sailing with a cargo. We appear to have more than our fair share of whores—the lowest of creatures."

When the women had finished their meal, there was no need to wash their wooden bowls in the bucket of water provided for that purpose. A lump of beef, a potato, gravy and a wedge of bread was a banquet to some of them who had spent up to three years in Newgate, Norwich, or other such notorious prisons.

"Gawd," said Elizabeth smacking her lips as she tongued greasy fingers. "This is a bit of all right, ay?"

"Yus," answered a perky-nosed Cockney, who was one of the women sharing the same berth. The attractive young girl flicked back a mane of dark hair and leaned on her elbow. "Wonder how long it will last?"

"Who knows?" shrugged Elizabeth. "What's your name, anyway?"

"Dudgeon."

"Dungeon?" jeered the taller girl. "What a name to go t'bed with."

"Nah . . . Du-d-geon," impressed the girl, straightening like a roused cobra. Elizabeth recognised the antagonism in her violet eyes, born of a prostitute's defensive needs. "Liz Dudgeon."

"I'm Elizabeth, too," said Powley pointedly.

"An' me," came a Yorkshire dialect from the corner of the next berth. "Beth Thackery they calls me. Me and Liz was on "*The Mercury*" together." She spat out the name of the prison hulk they had spent several years on as if that reality alone was enough of a challenge. Even a few days on these notorious and filthy hulks anchored in the harbour destroyed any vestige of self-esteem. Softness and sanity were replaced by anarchy and the need to survive.

"Are you about t'make anything of it?" Beth continued in her broad twang. "It's easy to handle the likes of you, y'know." She leaned forward into the light of a lantern that swung from a wooden beam. It lit the roof of the cramped area, and weird shadows shortened and lengthened in a macabre play across the dank walls. The Yorkshire girl's most distinguishing feature was a matted cloud of carroty hair that framed startlingly blue eyes.

Elizabeth Powley regarded the two girls for a moment. Both girls appeared to be younger by a few years, and she immediately made a silent vow to dominate the group.

CHAPTER 7

LIEUTENANT RALPH CLARK

Elizabeth Powley's catlike eyes slid down to the light-skinned woman who was sitting on the edge of the bottom berth. Her fair hair peeked out of the mob-cap she wore and formed a halo around her oval face. The widely-spaced eyes did not turn away, and Elizabeth decided the shadows beneath them were not caused by the lantern.

"I suppose you're going to say your name is Elizabeth, too," she said belligerently.

The girl tilted her head. There was a strange quality in her hazel eyes, and a stillness surrounded her as though an egg-shell facade had hardened between tears and destiny. The reply came softly. "No, my name's Sara McCormick."

Thrown off balance for a moment, Elizabeth's glance swept over the other women in the prisoner's hold. Huddled silently in their confined spaces, they all watched her with apprehension.

"Just so long as none of yer gets in me way," Elizabeth shrugged, her comment embracing everyone.

There seemed to be nothing more they could add to their revelations. Soon most of the women were either sleeping or trying to ignore the constant slap of the English Channel, the creak of straining timbers, and the acrid smell of stale bodies and vomit. The sleeping areas were no more than two tiers of almost six foot side boxes between decks. Designed for two people rather than the three that were allocated, there was scarcely enough room for the mattress, pillow, and blanket each prisoner had been issued. There was no privacy.

By contrast, in a nearby cabin, Lieutenant Ralph Clark sat alone. He laboriously entered the names of the ship's consignment of transportees, their ages, origins, and their crimes and sentences. In charge during Captain Meredith's absence, he stared at the red marine jacket that was hanging against the curtained door frame.

"Ah, Betsey Alicia, my love. What a fool ambition makes of a man. That I should have left you and our dear son, for who knows how long is surely a punishment for some unknown desire I have encompassed."

He lapsed into a brooding silence and imagined the Captain and the ship's surgeon gallivanting and carousing on *'The Sirius'*. He sighed heavily and returned to his task, murmuring, "Serious business, indeed. What can be more serious than controlling these savages we have aboard? At least the women are quiet. God knows what troubles we will endure before Botany Bay."

A hurried knock on his door-frame startled him. He stared at the marine sergeant who obeyed his summons to enter. "Well, what is it, man?"

"Trouble in the male convicts' quarters, sir. Two of them, Gant and Turner, are saying that the boy doesn't qualify for a man's space and he should sleep in the corner on the floor."

Clark threw down his quill in disgust. Reaching for his jacket he grumbled, "Am I to be a child-minder as well? Lead on, sergeant."

The rattling chains and shouted curses grew louder as the two marines neared the men's hold at the opposite end of the brig. Henry Cable, who had gained some respect mainly because he could read, had the boy John Hart pinned protectively to his bunk with a broad palm. Henry's joy at seeing his own son aboard and in the arms of the woman he loved had fostered a parental surge for the little chimney-sweep. Henry faced the unsanitary William Gant, who was trembling with fury.

"The boy has as many rights as the rest of us," Henry said with dangerous challenge. "He worked like a man, he was arrested and sentenced like a man . . ."

" . . . and he eats like man," interrupted the convict on the top bunk, as though that in itself was a crime.

"The sprat won't live t'get to Botany Bay," leered Gant. "Not if I gets me 'ands on him."

The sergeant raised the hatch and lowered the ladder which was stowed on deck each night. Descending quickly, he levelled his rifle at the men, precipitating an immediate silence. Clark appeared behind the sergeant and surveyed the scene nervously.

"Captain Meredith ordered that boy in here," Clark began and drawing himself up continued, "I don't care where he sleeps as long as there is silence! Any man who speaks again tonight will be taken before Captain Meredith and flogged. Now, snuff the light—and be aware that the sergeant here will be within earshot until the morning. I'll have no more noise."

Having delivered his version of arbitration, Clark mustered as much extra height as he could and gave orders to the sergeant. "Shoot any man who disobeys."

He turned on his heel and climbed to the deck as the men slunk into their sleeping berths. The hatch-cover thumped into place and, for a while, nothing was said. John Hart shivered with more than the cold and lay beside Henry Cable. In the reeking darkness, William Gant's voice grated quietly from the adjacent berth. "Watch him if y'want to, Cable. But me and Turner will be sharing his rations long before Botany Bay is in sight."

Back in his quarters, Clark drew out the locket he always wore next to his heart and snapped it open. He gazed on the picture of his adored wife and kissed it reverently before replacing it. "I trust the good Lord will allow me to dream of you tonight, my love."

Behind the bulkhead, only two of the women remained awake. The younger, finely boned girl of twenty-two smiled tenderly at the young baby as he suckled at her breast beneath the Welsh shawl. Tired but happier, Susannah Holmes remembered Mary's native logic when her name had been called. "Oh well, cariads. One hell is as good as another."

Elizabeth Powley lay next to Dudgeon, listening to the satisfied baby smacking at its mothers breast. She schemed ways to ensure her own gratifications with everyone from Captain Meredith to whichever seaman could supply her with extra food or liquor, in return for her services.

"Keep the kid quiet" she muttered when Little Henry began to whimper as his mother withdrew her nipple.

Susannah said nothing. She tucked the corner of the shawl underneath her son and passed opposite end around her back and shoulders as Mary had shown her. Aching for Henry, she stared into the gloom and cast her mind over events the day before. She prayed silently for the man called "The Humane Turnkey" and thanked the Lord for the return of her son. Unconsciously she spoke aloud. "God help us."

" . . . to 'elp ourselves," added Elizabeth, and grinned maliciously.

*   *   *

Several weeks later, there was much activity on water and onshore at Portsmouth, and the urchins were back diving to retrieve coins from the sticky mud.

On board *'The Friendship,'* Captain Meredith sat at his cabin desk and checked the list of supplies that had just been stowed in the belly of the brig. The Labrador, Lady, who had become pregnant during one of her jaunts ashore, laid her head heavily on the Captain's thigh and he fondled her ears.

"Ah, Lady. I'll be glad to end this preparation. No doubt the crew will too—and the convicts for that matter. What's the date?" He studied the yellowed calendar pinned on the wall beside a portrait of the King. "April 30th already. Six weeks since the last load of prisoners came aboard."

With canine sense, Lady wagged her tail and nuzzled her master's hand. Meredith was confident that, when her pups were born, he would be able to find new owners for them among the seamen. A knock interrupted his thoughts and he answered curtly. "Yes?"

The door swung open to reveal a marine who stepped into the cabin and saluted. "Captain Meredith, sir. There's another prisoner arriving."

Meredith tugged at his braided jacket and puzzled inwardly. He took the piece of paper handed over by a marine and studied it. He tossed it into a pidgeon hole in his desk and nodded. "All right, take her below with the others."

The marine turned to leave as Lieutenant Clark stepped into the cabin. "Captain?"

"Ah, there you are, Clark. Will you add another name to that record of convicts? She's a . . ." He retrieved the document and checked. "Elizabeth Barber, aged twenty-seven, born in Middlesex. She's from *'The Mercury.'*"

"Oh, no! Not another one, sir?"

"I'm afraid so, Lieutenant, but I haven't seen her. Will you go and see that she is properly accommodated, please?"

Lieutenant Clark glowered but saluted and made his way towards the female convict quarters. He arrived at the same time as the women returned from their mandatory walk around the main deck, and watched in silence as the marines bustled them back down the ladder into the prison. Between the two rows of sleeping berths below deck, and fixed to the wooden support stanchions, was a wide plank that served as a table. It ran the length of the area and on it stood three coopered half-barrels containing the water ration for drinking and hygiene purposes. Along each side, lower planks served as seating.

Liz Dudgeon was the first to descend into their cramped quarters. She was still dazzled from the Spring sunshine above on the deck and peered at the figure straddling one of the benches. She let out a jarring screech as her eyes adjusted. "Damn you, Barber! Wot you doing 'ere?"

CHAPTER 8

THE FOUR ELIZABETHS TOGETHER

The latest addition to the bedraggled group on *'The Friendship'* flashed jet-black eyes; thin lips below her Romany nose smiled cruelly. "Well, well, well," Elizabeth Barber sneered. "If it ain't Cockney Liz." The newcomer looked to the other women as they descended the ladder. "And the tart, Thackery. Thought you'd seen the last o'me, didn't yer?"

Elizabeth Powley regarded the three women who were sizing each other up like alley cats cornered in a wooden box, and she spoke with a deceiving softness. "Know each other, do you?"

Dudgeon tossed her mane which, although dark, was not quite as black as the gypsy's. "Know 'er?" she screeched. "Know 'er? If I had my way, they'd have strung 'er up years ago."

The gypsy threw back her head and filled the air with a heavy and eerie laugh. She was an awkward, gaunt woman with gnarled hands that plucked incessantly at invisible threads as though she were casting a spell. Susannah and Mary edged warily past the four Elizabeths, as did the other women.

Clark, who had followed the last prisoner into the hold, barked, "That's enough. Settle down the lot of you. Here, Barber—you'll get in this berth." He indicated a sleeping area opposite Powley and Dudgeon, which already held a buxom convict and her equally endowed daughter.

The gypsy's fingers feathered towards him and her challenge was sullen. "I can't fit in there!"

Clark bristled as he looked at Barber's tall frame and wide shoulders. Grudgingly he recognised the truth of her defiance and pointed at Sara McCormick who sat on the bunk beneath Elizabeth Powley's. "Here, you," he ordered. "You're smaller. Use this one."

Sara moved to the berth opposite, without saying a word. It was next along from Beth Thackery's and the gypsy tossed her blanket onto the vacated mattress. Throughout the tense moment, Elizabeth Powley watched the short Lieutenant with steely eyes, calculating the extent of his patience. She had already cunningly worked out that with Dudgeon beside her and Barber below her, she could monitor their movements easily and at the same time keep an eye on Thackery in the corner.

Clark drew respect from the women only by virtue of his red coat, and now they remained silent while he went through his routine of glaring at each one of them in turn, before spinning on his heel to climb back on deck. The hatch cover was replaced as he added threateningly, "Keep the noise down."

The other female convicts edged around the four simmering women to the security of their bunks. Susannah Holmes, Mary, and the baby had been allocated a smaller corner area which could not have housed another adult. The baby required little room, but Susannah tightened her clasp as Mary patted her friend's thigh.

"Wait for it," whispered the Welshwoman. "I can see what's coming."

Attention rivetted on the four Elizabeths. The charged atmosphere seemed to crackle with animosity. Arms akimbo, Powley stood in the middle of the floor looking down on the seated gypsy. Dudgeon lay on her stomach in the top berth like a cheetah lying in wait for its prey.

"Right," said Powley, as soon as she judged Lieutenant Clark safely out of earshot. "What's this all about?"

"This," answered Beth Thackery, rising to her feet ominously, "is Elizabeth Barber. A murderer and an expert at putting the blame on someone else—and a whore."

"Hah!" The gypsy's sneer as she feigned a slap at the Yorkshire redhead was evil. "Look who's talking."

Liz Dudgeon shook visibly and her eyes flashed as she butted in. "At least she doesn't steal a kid's rations then kill her when she complains to the guard. You 'ad him under your magic too, didn't yer? Thought you'd get away with blaming me when they found the kid was missing, didn't yer?" With every word, she moved her head menacingly towards her foe.

Powley stayed still, studying her smaller bunkmate. The cause of her venom was obvious and she experienced a fleeting sympathy which was quickly squashed behind self-preservation. She leaned closer to the Cockney and hissed, "And how did you get out of that one, Dudgeon?"

"By proving she'd been with the Chief Warder all night," interposed Barber bitterly, before rounding on the taller woman. "Anyhow—who are you?"

"Elizabeth Powley," came the even reply.

"Snake's belly! Not another one."

Powley waited tensely until the gypsy's maniacal laughter died away. "Yes, you cackling bitch. But this Elizabeth is different. And what's more," she surveyed the group, "you are all going to do what I say."

"Oh, are we then?" Liz Dudgeon hung over the edge of the bunk and pushed her face into Powley's. "An' who do you fink you are? Would you like us to say 'yes, y'highness,' or somefink?"

Powley paused a beat, then spat into her face. An audible gasp rippled from the watching women, then she raised her hand high and dealt the first blow of a catfight that rang with screams and curses. Dudgeon launched herself with an obscenity. Dirty fingernails scored flesh and brutally gouged eyes. Hair was wrenched out in handfuls, fragile blouses were torn and bodies flung themselves around like dice trapped in a wooden box. Seizing the opportunity to join in, Elizabeth Barber tripped Dudgeon as she came near but she wasn't prepared for Beth Thackery's flying attach in support of her friend. In a mangle of seething womanhood, they all crashed to the floor. Thuds against the bulkhead as the bitter fight continued quickly drew attention above decks, and the hatchway flew open.

"You disgusting women," yelled Clark, who had been summoned by a passing seaman. "In fact, you're not fit to be called women." The combatants stopped abruptly, simmering breathlessly and swaying like enraged circus tigers. Pointing a shaking finger at the disheveled creatures before him, Clark addressed the Sergeant at his shoulder. "Put them all in irons!"

In an electrifying silence the culprits were shackled to their sleeping berths before their captors climbed back up the steps and locked the hatchway behind them. Through the timbered and latticed barrier, Clark yelled, "Next time, I'll have you all flogged!"

An uneasy stillness settled over the prostitutes but a wealth of communicated hatred vibrated from their eyes as they glared at each other. The third woman in the berth with Elizabeth Powley and Liz Dudgeon, huddled against the wall. She had a vacant stare and appeared to have withdrawn from her surroundings.

Within the hour, the electric silence relaxed into murmured conversation amongst the other women, but apart from sly comments, the four Elizabeths ignored each other.

CHAPTER 9

THE LONG WAIT

Throughout the following week, the recently arrived ship's surgeon, Mister Thomas Arndell kept everyone occupied, including the convicts. He strenuously instilled the routine of cleanliness he expected during the voyage and for many of the convicts especially, the rules and regulations were completely foreign.

"He even expects us to wash our bleedin' hair once a week!" exclaimed William Gant to his cohort, Turner.

"Cripes!" Turner exploded. "Yours'll fall out with shock!"

"As long as all your nits fall out, I don't care." Gant said nastily and walked to the other end of the deck to spread the unheard news of hair-washing.

Already a widower, Thomas Arndell's rotund figure and thinning hair gave the impression of a man well beyond his thirty-five years of age, but his reputation in the medical service was unquestioned. And he possessed the rare attribute of compassion.

Captain Arthur Phillip, who had been chosen to establish the New Colony, issued instructions to the ship's surgeon on each ship that all quarters aboard, including those of the convicts, were to be kept cleaned, fumigated, and as well-ventilated as possible. This was by no means going to be an easy task. The fetid air of people confined for such long periods hardly had time to disperse during their daily exercise on deck. However, Thomas Arndell dutifully sorted out the peaceable prisoners that could be allocated cooking, sewing and cleaning tasks.

"Henry Cable," his marine aide called from the list Arndell had given him. "Henry Lovell, and John Hart, you've been made 'trustees' and you've got to assist Mister Arndell when he says."

"How do you mean, 'assist'?" questioned Lovell, a reticent man who avoided attention whenever he could. He was already envisioning himself having to saw off damaged limbs and bandage severe wounds.

"Mister Arndell says we have to have a lot of fish while we are at sea, and you'll be expected to assist in the fishing." The marine seemed quite pleased at his explanation. "It's so we all don't get scurvy." Having made a suitable impression of his superiority in the matter, the marine turned and climbed up the ladder before replacing the wooden hatch.

"I don't know 'ow to fish, Mister Cable," said John plaintively. "I ain't seen no-one fish before. Do they bite?"

Henry grinned and patted the boy's back. "I'll show you how, and no, they don't bite."

Obviously most relieved, John climbed back into his berth and curled up into a ball. His huge brown eyes flickered over to Gant whenever the wastrel moved, such was the fear that still filled his head.

The first morning the 'trustees' were called on, Thomas Arndell told them they were to row to the shore accompanied by a Marine Sergeant, and bring back ordered supplies. Every day they rowed over to one of the supply ships then carted sacks of potatoes, chunks of meat and lumps of salt back to the ship's cook. When they returned, their duties would continue. Henry Lovell, content now that he knew there was no blood involved, was happy to learn it was his duty to assist Henry Cable in handing out daily rations to other convicts.

"John Hart," instructed Thomas Arndell. "You are to scrub out the sick-bay every morning, and mind you make a good job of it." John nodded eagerly, anxious to please. "And refill the water barrels—fresh water every day."

John had no idea why fresh water was required every day but he nodded again.

Two weeks later, the Spring morning breeze was chilly when all the convicts were herded on deck. Thomas Arndell and Lieutenant Clark stood alongside Captain Meredith who stood tall on the raised poop-deck, then waited until the low murmuring had stilled.

"Your Government," he began loudly, looking for all the world like an impressive politician, "has provided an issue of clothing for each of you." The murmur resumed, but stopped just as quickly when Meredith continued. "Unfortunately, the women's petticoats are still to come."

He nodded to Cable and Lovell who had been chosen to hand out the small bundles of clothing to each convict. "And make sure they're kept clean and repaired."

Lovell deliberately allowed his new friend to pick up the womens' allocation. Cable handed a bundle to Sussanah, and his eyes shone when he muttered, "I love you."

Further along the line, Elizabeth Powley shook open the thin skirt she had been issued. With an insolent stare at Captain Meredith, she yelled, "What'll I do without me petticoat, Cap'n? You'll be able to see me legs right through this!"

There was an involuntary burst of laughter from the people around her, and Ralph Clark roared, "Silence!"

Meredith cleared his throat and said, "Carry on, Lieutenant." He turned to the surgeon who quickly accepted the unspoken invitation and followed him from the deck.

"She has a lot of spirit, that one," observed the surgeon wryly. "A ring-leader, no doubt."

Meredith half turned to look at Elizabeth and grunted. With an unknown venture stretching ahead of him, he had accepted there would be many different challenges. Arthur Phillip had not tried to minimise the enormity of their task, but as a bachelor and a military man, Meredith was not well versed in challenges from a female. Especially one of Elizabeth Powley's calibre and unaccountably, any contact with 'that one' left him with a confusing need for self-defence.

The following Sunday, a service and Bible reading was held on board by the visiting Fleet Chaplain as usual, and afterwards, convicts and officers spent an uneventful day. Some read or wrote letters, others dozed fitfully in the quiet of the quayside, all complained about the boredom of inaction. "How much longer?" said Turner to William Gant. They were leaning against the rope box next to the main mast and idly unwound skeins against their twist.

"Hoy! Leave them alone," yelled a passing sailor. "Or I'll have Cap'n Walton string you up!" Both convicts flung obscenities after the man, but they wandered in the opposite direction.

In the evening, Captain Meredith invited the surgeon and Lieutenant Clark to his cabin, where they were to share his meal of roast pork, vegetables, and fruit.

"Mister Arndell, Clark," he said, and indicated the tall man beside him. "This is Second Lieutenant William Faddy, who has also been assigned to us."

Thomas Arndell nodded amiably, and the two officers tucked their tricorn hats beneath their arms before they shook hands. Faddy, considerably younger than Ralph Clark, had a pleasant twinkle in his slate-blue eyes. "Pleased to meet you, Lieutenant Clark. My father press-ganged me into joining the marines when I became too big and ugly to feed. How did they acquire your services?"

Clark fidgeted at the obvious appreciation of Faddy's humor by the other two men and waited until the laughter died down. "I volunteered for the posting," he answered haughtily. He tried not to feel overpowered by Faddy's six foot frame and continued, "But already I am beginning to wonder at the wisdom of my choice."

He was still smarting from the refusal of shore-leave when his wife Betsey Alicia and their son came to Portsmouth especially to visit him. Clark glared meaningfully at Meredith, but his ire was in vain as the Captain was busy carving the pork.

"Be seated, gentlemen," said Arndell quickly, sensing the tension from Clark. "Let's try and avoid business this evening. Wine everybody?"

The two marines placed their hats on a nearby shelf and they all settled at the Captain's table. Faddy nodded to the surgeon's query, but a man of abstinence, Clark refused the wine.

"I trust your journey from London was a comfortable one?" Meredith inquired of the newcomer.

"Far more comfortable than I envisage the one to come, Captain," grinned Faddy tackling his meal with gusto. "But if nothing else, I have to thank the Good Lord for remarkable health, and that will be half the battle, do you agree?"

Thomas Arndell nodded. "I shall be quite happy to have one less patient, I can assure you, Mister Faddy. All these problems—it makes you wonder what else can delay us?"

"Captain Phillip tells us that departure dates have been issued and reissued constantly since last October," volunteered Meredith.

"True," said Arndell, pouring wine into Meredith's empty glass. "But these convicts have spent almost four months between decks now, and there's been sufficient loss of life already for my liking."

"I believe you completed your examination of our convicts yesterday, Arndell," said Meredith. "What's your opinion?"

"As far as I can observe," began Arndell, filling his own glass, "most of our convicts are in reasonable health. Only two concern me a little. The prisoner Sara McCormick has some respiratory weakness, and one woman seems to be suffering symptoms of withdrawal from her surroundings."

The following morning, when the convicts were returned after their deck exercise it was discovered that the poor woman Arndell spoke of, had hanged herself.

* * *

The daily monotony continued and a little worse for wear after one particularly bawdy evening, the officers found themselves rejoining the Captain for breakfast. They were to discuss several important preparations. Lieutenant Clark, the only one who presented himself with a clear head, thoroughly enjoyed his porridge and fresh fruit and smiled inwardly when the other three refused more than a glass of milk and a piece of toast. They listened quietly while Meredith issued instructions and Thomas Arndell was grateful that he only had one.

"I'd like a total and final list of medications in hand, and those still required, Doctor," said Meredith formally. "I have to submit this to Captain Phillip." A hurried knock on the cabin door halted the conversation. "Yes?"

"Begging y'pardon, sir," said the marine as he entered. "We have some trouble out here again."

"What is it?"

"The women, sir. They seem to have broken through the bulkhead."

Clark and Faddy jumped to their feet. "What?"

"Go and sort it out please, Clark." Meredith waved his hand impatiently. "Then report back to me as soon as you can."

Clark mopped his chin then tossed the large square of linen onto the breakfast table as his chair scraped backwards. "No doubt those whores again," he said smugly, half-pleased that his dour predictions were being proved correct. "Lead on, Sergeant."

"Go with him, Faddy," Meredith continued. "You might as well familiarise yourself with everything."

With musket at the slope and tall black hat vibrating with the smartness of his red and white uniformed march, the Sergeant led the Lieutenants. But he did not take them to the women's hold, he marched on towards the seamens' berths.

"What's going on Sergeant?" Clark demanded. "I thought you said the women prisoners . . . ?"

"Yes, sir," answered the soldier. "Five of them have been discovered in the seamens' quarters, sir."

"Not . . . ?"

"'fraid so, sir. Caught in the act."

Faddy made a valiant attempt to contain his amusement as Clark snorted in disgust and stepped ahead of the soldier. Jabbing each other with frantic elbows, five sailors tugged striped sweatshirts over their linen trousers while the four Elizabeths stood in a defiant row against the wall. The were under the watchful eye and trained musket of another marine. Sara McCormick huddled beside them, staring hypnotised by the rifle. Clark, dwarfed by most of the assembly, glared at the women then turned with unspoken question to the Sergeant.

"Seems one of my men were on an inspection round, sir, and discovered loose boards in the bulkhead to the women's quarters, so he raised the alarm. Seems these men assisted in the breakout, sir, because the women had er . . . offered their services for extra supplies of food and liquor, and . . ."

"Enough!" roared Clark. "Secure them and take them all on deck. This crime must receive immediate punishment."

The marine set about their task of moving the culprits on deck as the officers marched out and hastened back to the Captain's cabin. "This is the third time something like this has happened, sir," Clark whined. "These same women seem determined to cause as much trouble as they can. May I suggest a good lashing will settle all their nonsense?"

Meredith tapped his fingers on the table, then stood up and reached for his hat. "Follow me on deck."

The two Lieutenants did so, and with a sigh, Arndell repaired to his surgery He knew his services might well be called upon shortly.

CHAPTER 10

JOHN HART

A keen wind whipped around the deck of *'The Friendship'*. She and several other ships of the First Fleet to the new colony were still at anchor in the Portsmouth Harbour in 1787. More than four months had already passed since *'The Friendship's'* consignment of convicts had embarked, and boredom had engulfed criminals and officers like a London pea-soup fog. The break-out of women convicts had livened the atmosphere, although few looked forward to the coming punishment promised.

The wind flapped the flimsy skirts of the women who had broken through the bulkhead but the seamen who stood alongside them with their hands tied behind them, hardly noticed. They were far more aware of the coming judgment and silently cursed their own weakness when it came to dealing with the prostitutes.

Captain James Meredith surveyed the line of culprits, and his brows knitted in his black mood. The younger sailor at the end, and the only one who did not meet his eyes, lifted his head when the Captain addressed him. "Gilson, isn't it? Ship's Carpenter?"

The carpenter nodded dumbly. Normally a reticent man who was happiest when he had the smell of newly-shaved wood under his nose, Gilson had succumbed to the teasing of his shipmates, and joined their dare-devil plan for getting the women into their bunks. Meredith eyed Gilson's compatriots and recognised them as troublemakers who had come to his attention on several occasions. A fit of coughing suddenly exploded from Sara McCormick who stood in line with the other women.

"That's enough of that!" shouted Lieutenant Ralph Clark as she subsided into painful gasps. "It's no good trying to gain the Captain's sympathy."

"Lieutenant Faddy," said Meredith, ignoring his First Lieutenant's outburst. "Escort these seamen over to '*The Sirius*' and report the matter to Major Ross. The women are to be placed in irons and secured to their sleeping berths every night until further notice."

Clark barely disguised his anger at this decision and addressed the marines standing behind the lines of prisoners. "Take the women below, and carry out the Captain's orders."

The soldiers started to obey and nudged the women roughly with their guns. The gypsy Elizabeth Barber, tossed her black hair and yelled, "Careful I don't put a spell on yer!"

"Shut y'trap," said Liz Dudgeon sarcastically. "Can't you see the nice Cap'n is being kind to you?"

"Hold your tongues, you whores," fumed Clark, his pallid features flushing. In his opinion, the women equally deserved to receive the flogging the seamen would probably get at the hands of Major Ross. Elizabeth Powley spat towards Captain Meredith, and then winked at him broadly as they were led past his lofty position.

Lieutenant Faddy turned and tipped his hat to his superior. "I'll see to it, sir. Fine lot we have there, Captain. A friendly ship is the last thing we can expect, I suppose."

Meredith smiled grimly at Faddy's pun then headed back to his cabin, pondering the truth of his wit and trying to dismiss the whore Elizabeth Powley from his mind.

Hard on his heels, Clark felt obliged to remark, "I have never witnessed such arrogance, sir. Have you?" A non-committal grunt was the only reply.

On deck, William Faddy ordered, "Sergeant Stewart. Have the crew organise a jollyboat to go over to *'The Sirius'*.

"Sir!" About to carry out his orders, Stewart hesitated. "Lieutenant Faddy, sir. I understand the mail-boat is picking up letters from *'The Sirius'* today. May I collect any that our men have ready and take them with us?"

"Certainly" said Faddy. "I believe Lieutenant Clark has one or two also. You will find him with Captain Meredith."

Steward tapped on Meredith's cabin door. "Any mail to go to *'The Sirius'* sir?"

"Not this time," answered the Captain. "But make sure you bring back any waiting for us."

"I have," said Clark quickly. He reached into his tunic pocket, withdrew a blue envelope, checked the address again and pressed it to his lips. Embarrassed, Stewart barely saluted and took the envelope from Clark. The men were well aware of Clark's lugubrious nature and this example of his softer side made Stewart uneasy.

"Will that be all, sir?" Stewart asked Meredith formally. In reply, the captain waved his hand in dismissal.

"Thank you, sir."

Waiting on deck Faddy turned to the assembled prisoners and said sadly, "You sailors will be lucky to get away with ten lashes, if I know Major Ross. No doubt you'll wonder if the women are worth it? Far less painful to drink the liquor yourself without involving the women. You should be thanking your good fortune for it, not squandering it on the services of whores."

"Jollyboat's ready, sir!" Sergeant Steward directed the prisoners and their guards to the side of the ship, and Faddy joggled his hat securely onto his head as the all clambered aboard the small boat alongside.

His estimation of Major Ross proved correct, and when the jollyboat returned to *'The Friendship'* later that day, Gilson and the four other seamen were a sorry sight. He shook his head as they were led to the waiting Surgeon Arndell.

* * *

Next day, Thomas Arndell opened the door of his cabin-surgery and hailed a passing marine corporal. "Get along to the male convicts' quarters and bring the boy Hart to me."

A few minutes later, the dark-headed lad stood manacled and wary before the portly surgeon. Arndell noted odd sores on the boy's ankles, but did not realise they were due to Cable's insistence that he curl up on the floorboards beneath the sleeping berths. It was Cable's way of defending John whenever Gant became drunk from liquor he'd won by gambling with seamen.

"What's your name, lad?"

"Hart, sir. John Hart."

"How old are you, John Hart?"

"Dunno f'sure. Nine, I fink."

Arndell regarded the boy then said, "Well, John Hart, you will be working with me in the surgery from tomorrow morning."

John's eyes widened, then he glanced quickly at the surgery door which led off the doctor's cabin. His imagination of the instruments of torture that lurked behind it transcended his experiences of chains and privations. Lurid tales of the removal of gangrenous limbs fired pictures of blood-dripping saws and knives, and he swallowed hard.

"Er . . . will I 'ave to help you cut orf legs, sir?"

Arndell hid a smile and replied, "No, Hart. You'll scrape the floors and make sure my tools are ready and clean," he warned. "Is that a fresh scar under your eye?"

The boy nodded dumbly, too preoccupied with the horrors about to befall him to be concerned with those that had gone before.

"Can you read?"

Hart shook his head. "Henry Cable can, sir."

Arndell studied the boy's frank gaze. "Who's Henry Cable . . . ? Oh yes, he helps issuing rations, doesn't he?"

"Yes, sir. He's got a baby in the women's quarters, too."

Arndell leaned out of his door and summoned a marine. "Take the boy back. And see that he's brought to work here early each morning."

Back in his berth, John Hart breathlessly explained to his friend and mentor why he'd been sent for. "And he asked me if I could read?" John added incredulously.

"Well, I'll teach you," said Henry firmly.

"But you ain't got no books," scoffed Hart.

"Well, you'll have to pinch one from the surgery, won't you?" Henry looked away, stung by his truth, and then capitulated. "Ah . . . plenty of time for that. You mind to stay out of trouble and listen to the doctor."

William Gant sat at the centre bench, sneering. "Not teaching the boy bad habits, are yer, Cable?" His nimble mind had already realised the surgeon's supplies included bottles of brandy, and he was planning how to take advantage of the boy. It would take very little 'persuasion' to get him to steal the liquor, and Cable could hardly keep a lookout every minute of the day.

CHAPTER 11

JOHN HART'S INITIATION

A few days after John Hart was introduced to the wonders of a Surgeon's den, the carpenter Bill Gilson was admitted with septicaemia in one of the cuts on his back as a result of being flogged. John was busy rubbing the floor boards with a wetted cake of pungent carbolic soap, but he kept one eye on the surgeon's activities. He drew a sharp but silent breath when Arndell exposed the wound on Gilson's back. A raw redness surrounded the welt that was now oozing yellow pus and the carpenter winced when Arndell applied neat antiseptic fluid to the wound. John Hart winced with Gilson and silently vowed never to be flogged. Trembling at the prospect, he added energy to his scrubbing and tried to drown out the sound of agonised groans.

"I'll check that in a week's time, Gilson," said the surgeon at last. "Return to your duties."

The carpenter nodded tight-lipped then stood aside to allow Sergeant Stewart's entry. The tall marine had a spluttering Sara McCormick in tow. Gilson flushed, remembering that she had been his partner during the night of whoring he'd allowed himself to be coerced into. He did not know that Sara had been similarly led astray. The prostitutes had been dealt with leniently and after a week, they'd been released from day-chains. Wary, they had refrained from all but heated arguments over rations or bed space. Sara stumbled and vomited all over John's clean floor.

"Basin, boy," ordered the surgeon. John clapped a hand to his own mouth and his stomach heaved as he handed over the vessel. Then he turned away, considerably paler than normal.

"What happened, Sergeant?" Arndell eased the wan girl back on to the examination bed as he spoke and noticed she was breathing very heavily. A hoarse rattle rose from the depths of her thin chest and Sergeant Stewart looked uneasy.

"I understand the gypsy elbowed her hard in the ribs, sir," he said. "She's a wicked one all right."

Gilson had paused at the doorway but now made his exit quietly. He blamed himself for Sara's condition in part because he'd mentioned her pallor to other less sensitive seamen, and they had teased him for taking the convict's part. A final backward glance showed him how desperately ill Sara was, and he sadly headed for his cabin.

Arndell tutted and shook his head as he gave her a quick examination. "I'll give her a sedative," he said, half to himself and half to John. "You can go, Sergeant. I will send the boy for you when she is well enough to return to the hold."

Stewart studied John Hart for a moment, then seemingly satisfied that he could be trusted, he left to continue his duties. Arndell nodded to John and together they helped the frail woman into a cot. Once this was done, the lad returned to scraping and scrubbing the floor, having cleaned up Sara's vomit. Later, he sat back on his haunches silently watching the doctor who hovered over Sara. The only other time he had watched someone minister to a woman was when his mother had died. Sara was already succumbing to the sleeping draft she had been given and it was all too easy for John to imagine this pale creature was also doomed to a wooden box. John was the only one who cried when his mother died, and then mainly from fear of death. There was no ceremony, just a wooden cart that pulled up outside their hovel in London, and his uncle had helped the stranger toss the coffin aboard.

"Get a move on there," said Arndell, turning away from his patient. "There's no time for gawping in medicine."

* * *

Another interminable week had drifted by when James Meredith took a deep breath of evening air. He strolled on deck admiring the full moon that swept a silver path across Portsmouth Harbour. Then a breeze made him shiver and his Labrador, Lady, ambled to his side and looked up. She was tired with the weight of her coming pups, but devoted to her master. Although it was the smallest ship of the fleet, *'The Friendship'* deck was not so cluttered with equipment and barrells as her sister ships so there was plenty of room for dog and master to take walks on board. What the ship lacked in size however, she gained in speed and Meredith fully expected *'The Friendship'* to be one of the first to enter Botany Bay.

Midships, he came across Lieutenant Clark also enjoying an evening that augured a pleasant summer for England. The two men leaned against the rail and exchanged a few comments before they fell into a companiable silence. They listened to the gentle slap of cold currents against the hull, and it was as though nothing and nobody could be troubled on such a beautiful night. Eventually, Meredith adjusted his cape and expressed his intention to retire early.

"By the way, Clark," he said. "Would you care to have one of Lady's pups when the time comes?"

With a rare enthusiasm Clark said, "Well, thank you, sir. I would indeed."

Meredith gave a satisfied nod. "G'night, Clark."

Overcome by the unexpected thoughtulness, the First Lieutenant smiled into the moonlit sky when the Captain had disappeared immediately wishing it were possible to share the puppy with his beloved wife and son. "How much longer," he sighed, hoping his three-year old son would not forget him. "This waiting around for permission to sail is intolerable."

On his way back to his cabin, he frowned at the raised voices coming from the womens' prison and thundered on the bulkhead with his fist. There was an immediate slence, but he yelled anyway. "Enough of that noise, you creatures. Settle down in there."

In the gloom of the hold, Beth Thackery's carroty head nodded, and her Yorkshire twang whispered, "Ay, lad. You're asking for it. You're asking for it."

"Watcha reckon you can do about him then, Yorkie?" scoffed Cockney Liz.

"Something, anyway," grunted the redhead, with no plan to elaborate. "I'll cook his goose."

"Be careful, or he'll make a Yorkshire pudden out of you," emphasised the gypsy, and chains rattled as they kicked out at each other.

"Shut up," snarled Elizabeth Powley. "Ain't much any of us can do, not so long as they got us tied up like dogs."

They drifted into a silence that was broken only by intermittent whimpers from Susannah's baby and spasmodic coughing from Sara who, on her return to the female prison, had intrigued everyone with her description of Surgeon Arndell's sanctum.

"He's got a little kid in there, too, scrubbing the floor. And the bed was so clean." She said the last words with awe then screwed up her face. "But the whole place smells awful."

In the darkness, Powley found herself surprisingly pleased to hear about John Hart. That he would grow up to be as bad as most of the men she'd encountered was a forgone conclusion. It didn't seem possble to Elizabeth that the likes of Gant and the hair-hacking jailers at Newgate, could ever have been boys. John had regarded her with fear while they travelled from the prison in that draughty cart If someone had suggested that a small emotion had stirred in her when the driver's whip flicked the boy's cheek, she would have screeched a denial.

Susannah's baby grizzled. "You've gone soft in the brain since being cooped up with that brat," Elizabeth muttered to herself. She then stirred her mind with Sara's description of the Sick Bay. "Bet the Captain's got 'is own clean bed, too."

She heaved at the sleeping Liz Dudgeon with her rear and turned on her side, then gave in to weariness.

Meanwhile, in the male prison area, William Gant waited for slow, rhythmic breathing to come from Henry Cable, then he leaned into the next berth and clamped chained hands over Hart's mouth.

"One word, sprat," he said thickly, "and it'll be wif your last breath. Understand?"

John nodded and stared in horror at his tormentor. Once before in his young life he could remember the same vice-like grip and being made to look up into an ugly face. That time he had dared to hesitate after an instruction, and his uncle had repeatedly punched his twitching body. John's face knotted, waiting for the first blow. Instead, Gant's hairy grip relaxed. Moonlight filtered through the hatch and added an eerie glow to the convict's grimace as he bent lower and hissed in the boy's ear.

"Do as I say, and I might not throw yer overboard."

It didn't occur to the terrified lad to question the feasibility of the threat, and he nodded dumbly at Gant's brief instructions. The criminal leered and lay back into his own berth, but John Hart trembled for many hours. For the following three nights, Gant terrorised him while the other convicts slept.

Thomas Arndell was extremely observant and it didn't take him long to see that, having begun to respond to regular meals since embarkation, John looked haunted again. Some of the perkiness was gone and while sitting at his desk writing a report, Arndell studied the boy closely.

"Are you feeling unwell, Hart?"

"No, sir," lied the boy, unconvincingly.

"We can't have you working in here if something ails you, lad. You realise that, don't you?"

"Yes, sir . . . honest, sir . . . I'm all right, sir." As if to prove his words, Hart polished an already gleaming instrument industriously. Further questions were preempted by a knock on the door.

Henry Cable entered with the fresh water rations and he left the door ajar as instructed, so that the accompanying marine could wait outside.

"Afternoon, Cable," nodded the surgeon, then bent to his writing. Cable crossed to fill the doctor's copper and it took only a moment for John Hart to realised that no-one was watching him. He quickly opened a cupboard and stuffed a small bottle of brandy inside his shirt. He hurried towards the door saying, "I don't feel very well after all, sir. I'll go back to me bunk, if y'don't mind."

Henry moved faster and firmly closed the door before the boy could be seen by the soldier. "Put it back," he hissed. They both looked across to the surgeon whose keen eyes were riveted on John Hart's bulging shirt. The culprit dropped his head, but the tension was broken as the marine knocked sharply on the door.

"Are you all right, Mister Arndell, sir?"

"Yes," called the surgeon with an unwavering stare over his wire-rimmed spectacles. "I closed the door."

The two convicts stood still in what seemed an interminable silence, waiting for the wrath they were born to expect for such a crime.

Arndell spoke quietly. "Have I misjudged any spark of honesty you may possess, John?"

"He's only a boy, sir . . ." began Cable, but he was cut off with a perfunctory wave of the surgeon's hand.

"You realise I could have you flogged for this?"

Fear coursed through John's body and any bravado he might have possessed vanished in his tortured recollections of the carpenter's wounds. His face twisted, and his hand trembled violently as he withdrew the bottle and dropped it loudly onto the desk.

"Please, sir, not that." Tears spilled as he whimpered. "I didn't want to . . . it weren't my idea."

Henry Cable grasped the boy by the shoulders and spun him around roughly. Anger contorted the older convict's face and he shook the thin body as though it was his personal store of liquor that had been invaded.

"It was Gant, wasn't it? He made you . . ." Words lodged in John's throat and he hung his head low on his chest. "Speak up, y'little idiot . . ." Henry's flash of disappointed anger startled the surgeon.

"That's enough, Cable," he interrupted. "Go back to your duties. I'll handle this."

Henry picked up his water-bucket and swung open the door, with disgust written all over his face. "Come on, let's get on with it," he growled to the startled marine, and they left.

Arndell sat back in his chair, tapping the feathered quill against his pursed lips. Hart continued snivelling, with the all too familiar feeling of abandonment and despair.

"Was Cable right?" Unable to choose between the fear of Gant's threats and the agony of flogging, the little sweep began another kitten-like mewl. "Very well, then. You shall return to your berth in chains, until you decide to tell the truth."

The prospect was too much for the nine-year old, and he blubbered his story. "He keeps me awake most of the night, sir. Every time I nod off, he pushes at me with his foot until I wake up. Then he shows me a knife and says if I don't get 'im some more liquor, he'll part me froat!"

The older man watched the boy's quivering mouth and realised that the would-be murderer was not playing games. "Where did he get this knife, boy?"

"I dunno, sir, but 'e did have one, honest."

Arndell rose abruptly, then opened the cabin door. "Sergeant! Corporal . . . any one of you."

The men came running at urgency in his voice and John's terror imagined knotted rope slicing through the air against his bare back which made him cry again. The corporal clumped to a halt and glared at John, never doubting his guilt. He clamped the thin shoulders roughly and grated, "Come on, you brat."

"Stop!" commanded Arndell angrily. "I want you to go and search the male convicts' quarters for any weapons that may have been smuggled aboard. Bring your report to Captain Meredith's cabin." He turned irately to John and continued, "And stop your snivelling, boy. Come with me."

He propelled John towards Captain Meredith's cabin and spoke urgently. As he finished, the corporal entered, bearing a sliver of sharpened metal. Another soldier escorted a handcuffed William Gant, who had ground the broken shaft against the side of a coopered barrel until it became a lethal spike.

Captain Meredith's outrage surfaced. "What's this supposed to be?" He waved the weapon under Gant's nose. The uniformed Captain looked so tall and ferocious to the chimney sweep that tales of Jack and The Beanstalk his mother told him suddenly came alive.

Gant's face was a mask of hatred as he transfixed the boy. It had taken him many hours to doggedly hone the snapped ladle previously stolen from The Fox and Brush Inn on their journey from Newgate. Consumed with vengeful thoughts, Gant paid little attention to his accusers until the Captain's pronounced punishment was repeated.

"Do you hear, Gant? Fifty lashes."

Flooded with terror, John Hart almost fainted as the struggling and cursing convict was hustled away. "I'll get yer for this, sprat! You just wait . . ." The marine's rifle butt thudded into his spine and he buckled at the knees before being dragged away.

"Captain," said Thomas Arndell when the din was over. "With your permission I will keep Hart bedded down in the corner of the surgery in the future. Otherwise I don't think we can be sure of getting him to Botany Bay alive."

Meredith nodded in agreement, and as if to commiserate with John, Lady ambled over to nuzzle his hand.

On deck, two seamen lifted the main hatch and leaned it against the side of the ship's mast. They spread Gant's arms and bound his wrists to the timbers, then tore open his shirt revealing back muscles that were knotted in rage. Lieutenants Clark and Faddy had been ordered to supervise the punishment, and they climbed to the poop-deck where they could look down on the proceedings.

"What more can we expect," complained Clark. "We haven't even left Portsmouth yet, and already half the shipload deserves flogging."

Faddy agreed. "Seems as though the Captain has given up asking Major Ross to dole out punishment and we have to flog them ourselves. I suppose this will be the first of many."

"We should really..." Clark cut off and turned to the soldier testing the strip of leather against his knee before handing it to the brawny sailor assigned to the task of flogging the raging Gant. "Corporal, wait a moment."

Faddy wondered at his counterpart's motives, but said nothing.

"Get all the convicts on deck smartly," Clark bellowed. "They should witness this and know what they can expect if we keep having trouble." His order was duly carried out and the short Lieutenant stood rocking on his heels while he watched the prisoners assemble. "This is the only treatment they understand."

Again, Faddy said nothing. He was grateful that his opinionated colleague hadn't expected the civilian ladies on board to attend the flogging. A stiff breeze suddenly raced across the Harbour and ruffled the torn shirt hanging from Gant's back; he shuddered and fell silent as sheer terror overpowered his anger. He saw the soldier hand over the lash and the waiting seaman took his time flexing the leather-bound handle and his muscles. He swayed from side to side, waiting for the word to commence flogging.

The women were last to be led on deck, and above the grumbling, Elizabeth Powley yelled, "Well, well, well. Gotcha, 'ave they, Gant?"

"Is this yer lover boy, then?" asked the gypsy slyly.

"Shut yer face," Elizabeth spat.

"Garn," said Liz Dudgeon, adding in a loud voice, "his own muvver couldn't love 'im."

Liz's comment tickled the gypsy's humour and she cackled loudly.

"If you women don't stop your screeching, you'll all be getting the same treatment," shouted Clark. He waved angrily at the waiting sailor. "Carry on!"

Hardened to cruelty as many of them were, convicts and seamen alike found it difficult to ignore the revulsion in their stomachs as the knotted rope sizzled through the air. It cracked like a pistol shot before it bit deeply into the criminal's flesh.

"One . . ." called the ship's boy sitting astride a capstan. One of his duties was to count the strokes aloud.

Gant bit his lip, determined that his captors would not get satisfaction from his pain. But as blood oozed from the split skin, it spattered with the force of subsequent strokes and small whimpers could be heard from the weaker onlookers.

Again and again the leather flew and cracked. "Two . . . three . . .

A moan escaped Gant's throat and by the count of twenty, his agonised screams were tearing through the eardrums of those on deck. Many couldn't contain their sobs. Gant could also be heard below decks and while genteel ears were covered and small children were hugged protectively, the evening meal being prepared in the galley was stirred with undue vigour.

"Thirty . . . thirty one . . ." The ship's boy continued calling, and at the count of "Forty . . ." Gant fainted.

Still the sailor raised his sweating arm, but the strength and ardour had waned.

"Give no quarter," yelled Clark, and the call-boy turned and vomited, unable to cry out the remaining strokes.

Most of the other convicts had been staring at the deck after the first few blows, even though Clark kept admonishing them to raise their eyes. Susannah had buried her face into her baby. Mary hung her head with tears of revulsion coursing down her plump cheeks. Sara, still weak, fainted against Beth Thackery. Beth quickly supported her and together with Liz Dudgeon, sank to the deck grateful to have the grisly scene hidden from them behind the skirts of the other women. Only the gypsy and Elizabeth Powley stood implacable, their faces sculpted into a mask of hatred combined with satisfaction.

A deck hand had taken over the counting, and his final call could hardly be heard. "Fifty . . ."

The perspiring sailor turned towards the Lieutenants and touched his forehead with the whip. He had no breath to speak. The ensuing silence was disturbed only by the cry of wheeling gulls and the slap of water against the hull which made the timbers creak.

"Cut him down," ordered Faddy, anxious to get away from the terrible scene. "Take him to Mister Arndell."

"No!" interposed Clark, bristling with importance. "Take him below. He receives no attention."

Everyone watched in silence while the senior Lieutenant's orders were obeyed, and loathe to relinquish his command of the moment, Clark surveyed the gathered crowd. "Let that be a lesson to you all," he intoned. "Captain Meredith will not put up with any nonsense from you creatures. And neither will I."

CHAPTER 12

FIGHTING AND LOVING

A deckhand began to swab away Gant's blood while other sailors replaced the hatch-cover he'd been tied to. Made of solid oak, it resounded through the ship as it fell heavily into the recess, much as Gant's agony had filled 'The Friendship' with blood-curdling screams.

Lieutenant Faddy also left the deck, but Ralph Clark stood like a dictator while he watched the humbled convicts being returned to their prisons.

Elizabeth Powley drew level with the poop-deck and stared balefully at the shining boots planted firmly astride. She wondered why black boots symbolised authority when the feet inside them were no different to everyone else's. She was towards the end of the shuffling line of women convicts. The line stopped to enable them to climb down the ladder and Clark lifted his heels imperceptibly, calling out "Move it along, there!"

He did not see Elizabeth spit on his boots or grin as she continued shuffling forwards, her feline eyes slanted in satisfaction.

Having ensured all the convicts were under guard again, Clark went back to his cabin and began filling in his diary. The carpenter, Gilson, appeared in the doorway.

"Ah, Gilson. I want you to strengthen the meal bench in the female convicts' area while they're exercising tomorrow morning." Mournfully he added, "They damaged it while fighting again."

"Ay, sir." The gentle Devonshire accent rolled and he revealed malformed teeth that identified him as a country lad. He did not display the rough exterior of men who had either chosen or been forced into seamanship. He was the epitome of one who would be more at home on a farm. Despite his misleading looks and being born in Taunton, he had nevertheless spent his life serving on Plymouth ships. Portsmouth was a new world and he was still getting used to it.

It was fairly bright and breezy next morning when he lowered himself through the open hatchway to the womens's' prison. Above him he could hear the rhythmic accompaniment of chains as they tramped around '*The Friendship's*' small deck, and he took a moment to accustom his eyes to the gloom.

"Oh, it's you." A small voice from one of the lower bunks startled him as it continued, "How's your back?"

Peering closer, he observed Sara McCormick lying desperately pale with her blonde hair loose on the pillow. Her expressionless eyes seemed too large for her oval face.

"It's all right," Gilson answered, remembering the lashes he'd received on '*The Sirius*' for sharing his berth with this woman. "Why aren't you on deck with the others?"

"Do I look as if I could climb the steps?" There was no humour in the retort which was immediately followed with a bout of coughing.

Bill Gilson looked uncomfortable. "Can I get you a drink? Name's Sara, isn't it?"

She nodded weakly and closed her eyes. Gilson laid his tools on the bench and reached for the mug beneath her pillow, its normal place. He dipped it into the water container then knelt beside her. He raised her head and put her lips to the mug. She sipped gratefully and sighed.

"You should be in the sick-bay," he said. "Does Mister Arndell know how bad you are?" The sick girl didn't answer and Gilson lowered her to the pillow gently. "I'm supposed to get this bench fixed so I'd better get it done, before they come back. I'll try not to make too much dust."

He didn't think she'd heard him and he turned away to carry out his task. "Thank you," Sara whispered suddenly. "Didn't think there was anyone kind left. What's your name again?"

"Don't say you don't remember?" Bill flushed at his flippant remark and again turned away. He nailed a solid bar of timber to the underside of the bench were Elizabeth Powley had been tossed and slapped heartily by Elizabeth Barber. The two women had quarrelled over a lump of bread left, but this time Beth Thackery and Liz Dudgeon had been content to amuse themselves by goading the two combatants.

"Kill the bloody gypsy, Elizabeth," the Cockney had yelled.

"Ay—tek her by the throat and finish her," Beth had chuckled. The appearance of Lieutenant Faddy and a guard had put a quick end to the fight.

Bill Gilson worked efficiently trying to keep any disturbance to a minimum, but Sara seemed oblivious to this presence. He looked at her once and doubted that she would survive to see Botany Bay.

On deck meanwhile, Lieutenant Faddy was supervising the morning exercise and nodded briefly when a marine informed him that the carpenter was still working below. He sympathised with the 'nicer women' as he preferred to call those who were not prostitutes. With some of them guilty of no more than stealing bread to feed the family, they were kept below with their lewd counterparts. The atmosphere below deck was airless, rank with the acrid stench of vomit, sweat, and rotting bilge water. One of them had already made herself useful by laundering his shirts and stockings, and others willingly busied themselves mending and replacing buttons.

Faddy straightened his shoulders and addressed a nearby corporal. "Line the women up against the railing. It's a fine morning and I'm sure they will appreciate a little extra air."

"Begging your pardon, Lieutenant, but the men are already being brought up for their exercise session."

"That's all right, corporal. Just walk them up and down the other side of the deck."

Elizabeth Powley leaned against the ship's rail and through narrowed eyes she scanned the men's faces as they shuffled past. In her opinion most of them were no better than the vermin that invariably appeared in the sorts of places she'd been.

She had never really taken account of all the convicts in the men's area. Her main interest was in the sailors and marines who could exchange something worthwhile for her services. All at once her tall frame stiffened and a slow smile softened her face.

"Well, if it isn't me old mate, Patrick Daley." Instinctively she stepped forward a pace to wave to the one-time highway robber.

"Elizabeth, me darlin', what you doing here?" He raised manacled hands and blew her a kiss.

Lieutenant Faddy's reprimand was drowned by a furious yell from Elizabeth as the gypsy's foot suddenly swept her legs from under her. Elizabeth tumbled headlong into a nearby coil of rope and she scrambled to her feet clumsily. With murderous glints in her eyes, she glowered at the gypsy. "You bitch, I'll kill yer for that."

Before Faddy had time to signal the marines, Elizabeth flew at the cackling gypsy. The cackling changed to a screech when her opponent grabbed handfuls of her long black hair. Two soldiers grappled with the fighting women who were eventually separated and placed one on each end of the line.

Faddy sighed. "Get them below. If the carpenter hasn't finished tell him to do so tomorrow."

Patrick Daley gave a strange little bow as the women were led away and with a start, Beth Thackery observed a fleeting softness cross Powley's face.

In the four months they'd been aboard, Elizabeth's hair had regrown to hang attractively and the surgeon's order of regular ablutions was beginning to show its effect. Her skin along with that of the other women revealed an unexpected clarity.

"By 'eck,", Beth muttered. "She's soft on him."

Later that afternoon the still air between decks and the lazy dip of the anchored ship made the prisoners drowsy. Susannah Holmes slept contentedly now that she saw Henry every day. Mary Watkins crooned softly to the baby that meant so much to them. Gifted with the sweetness of tone in the Welsh manner, her voice lulled several others to sleep also. Elizabeth Barber, Liz Dudgeon, Sara McCormick were among them, although Sara often stirred fitfully and her pallor seemed more intense against the striped pillow ticking.

Seated opposite each other at the centre bench, Beth Thackery and Elizabeth Powley talked quietly.

"Who's Patrick thingummy when he's home, then? Not a bad lookin' lad, is 'e?" Beth asked her question with an ulterior motive. Having had to live by her wits all her twenty-two years, she knew the value of stored information. She escaped the gallows once by remembering that the magistrate trying her had a jealous wife, called Aisa. When he was about to pass the death sentence she'd called out, "Give my respect to Aisa, m'lud!" Flushing with the memory of how he'd come to divulge the information in Beth's bed one night, the judge had furiously ordered deportation for life.

Elizabeth, however, had accurately summed up her Yorkshire cohort weeks before and now looked evenly into Beth's startlingly blue eyes. After a few moments of thought whilst playing idly with the corner of a cloth used for cleaning their dishes, she explained.

"We did a couple of tricks together last year. Got on all right, we did."

"Did you love him?"

Elizabeth snapped loudly, "Nah! Don't believe in that tripe."

"Well then, . . . ?"

Beth's question disappeared into the noise of Elizabeth's fist thumped onto the bench. "That's enough. He's just another convict, d'yer hear?"

Their dozing compatriots stirred and Mary stopped crooning. From the top berth, Liz Dudgeon's Cockney voice grumbled, "Shut y'traps."

Elizabeth didn't move, but under her breath she said, "Ah . . . shut yer cake'ole, Dudgeon."

Sara McCormick began coughing and Beth prudently changed the subject. "Doesn't look good, that one. Think she'll mek it to Botany Bay?"

Elizabeth shrugged. "Who knows if any of us will?"

"The cook said we were supposed to sail yesterday," Beth continued. "Seems all the crews have started mucking up."

Again Elizabeth shrugged. "Who cares? I'm going to lay down. Ain't much else to do."

Beth watched with shrewd eyes as the tall woman clambered back into her berth. She concluded there was more to Patrick Daley than Elizabeth cared to admit.

Elizabeth Powley stretched back like a tabby cat flexing its muscles and making itself comfortable. Her eyes narrowed and an imperceptible smile lifted the corners of her mouth. The night of love she and Patrick had shared was not to be forgotten. He was the only man who ever undressed her with the finesse she'd attributed to the landed gentry with their women. Her smile soured as she recalled that most of the gentry were no better than drunken seaman and louts with her type. They would toss her to the bed then throw themselves onto her ravenously.

On the road to Salisbury village, she and Patrick shared pretty fine pickings from the coaches they'd waylaid. He was known as the Irish Highwayman. Especially to the whimpering females who stripped themselves of jewellery rather than their honour. To them he showed gallantry, but to the pompous and expostulating men he showed a ruthless disregard.

"Do you know who I am, you villain?"

"If the good Lord doesn't care about our names," Patrick would growl, "why then should I?"

Elizabeth could not put names to all the men who had taken or shared her favours but Patrick Daley was the only one from whom she had never accepted payment Patrick was different. He had lingered while untying her blouse string; his rough fingers had scraped deliciously across her nipples and within minutes she had been straining for closer contact with him, rather than lay back like an unconcerned observer. She squirmed with the secret memory she'd never share.

Lieutenant Clark stepped into the Captain's cabin and tipped his hat. "You sent for me, sir?"

"Doctor Arndell and I are going over to *'The Sirius.'* Meredith rose to his feet. "The Commodore has called a meeting, so I'll leave you in charge this afternoon."

"Yes, sir. I believe we sail soon?"

"Not soon enough, Clark. Much longer and we'll all start rotting."

"Just so, sir. What exactly is the hold-up?"

Meredith tugged at his buttoned jack and reached for his hat. "As far as I can understand, the seamen have refused to man the yards unless they are paid the wages due to them up to now. They also want permission to go ashore once more before we leave."

Clark shook his head, then the miserable man returned to his cabin determined to write another letter to his wife before they left Portsmouth Harbour.

CHAPTER 13

SET SAIL AT LAST

Lieutenant Ralph Clark sat at his cabin desk and dipped the feathered quill into the inkwell. He had already told his beloved wife about the many delays and shook his head from side to side as he continued to write.

"On consideration, my dearest Betsey, I can understand the seamen's' demands. They have been employed for seven months now, preparing for this journey; in all that time they have received nothing more than a few pence river pay and one month's advance. Because we shall be away so long, they should receive what they are due in order to furnish themselves with necessities at shore rates. Later on, they will have to pay exorbitant charges to the ship's masters for whatever they need. Anything to make this journey more comfortable really, as the Lord knows it is already unpleasant enough with these whores aboard. Never would I have believed that women could behave so. They are a disgrace to their kind."

Captain Meredith and the surgeon returned around five that evening. Although there was still a spring freshness in the breeze, the lengthening days held the sun brightly in the sky, playing hide-and-seek behind cottony clouds.

"Lieutenant Faddy." The Captain hailed the Second Lieutenant who was approaching. "Have all officers, crew and convicts brought on deck as smartly as possible. I wish to address them."

Meredith made his way to the poop deck as Faddy saluted, and Doctor Arndell climbed the steps behind him. Together they talked quietly while they waited for the ship's company to assemble. Francis Walton joined them and nodded in greeting.

"Good news, I hope, Captain Meredith?" The ship's master had a gravelly voice from barking orders to crews over many voyages.

Meredith nodded. "The Commodore and Major Ross have succeeded in settling this seamen's dispute at last. Apparently the recalcitrants have been sent ashore and replaced by the boatswain and ten men from the 'HMS Hyaena'.

"My crew knew better than to cause trouble," said Francis Walton ominously. 'HMS Hyaena . . . that's the ship that's going to escort us for a few leagues, isn't it?"

Again Meredith nodded as Lieutenant Clark joined them. "Ah, Lieutenant, you're the scribe amongst us. Before *Hyeana* leaves us again out there, I want you to collect any letters written for people in England by that time. We'll transfer them to her—she is going to bring them back for us."

Clark saluted lazily, and then as the officers continued chatting, he turned to watch *'The Friendship's'* ill-assorted complement congregate on deck. The nine marine-wives chattered together excitedly. Corporal Morgan's wife, now seven month pregnant, sat on the main hatch watching Margaret Stewart restrain her boisterous two-year old. Having soothed the lad who was the image of his father, she sat on the hatch also. "Isn't it exciting?"

The pale Mrs. Morgan answered fretfully, "I cannot really look forward to having my baby at sea, Margaret."

Margaret Stewart clucked sympathetically, and then she looked towards the female convicts being herded to one side of the deck. "I suppose they have even less to look forward to," she said. "How shabbily dressed some of them are. My husband tells me that some of their Government issued clothing still hasn't arrived."

Further conversation was interrupted by a drum-roll and the ensuing silence was broken only by the sea lapping against the hull. All eyes were on Captain Meredith as he stepped forward and put his hand on the rail in front of him.

"At first light tomorrow morning, on Thursday the 12th day of May, in this year of 1787, we shall set sail for the new colony. We have a long voyage ahead of us and one that will be made far more pleasant if there is little need for harsh discipline."

He stopped for the import of his words to take hold, his eyes coming to rest on Elizabeth Powley. She stared back dispassionately. Beside her, Sara gave a fitful cough and Meredith turned to Thomas Arndell with an unspoken command. The surgeon nodded and made a silent resolve to examine the sick girl as soon as possible.

"You convicts," Meredith continued, "should bear in mind that many have perished on the gallows for lesser offences than those committed by some of you. It is to be hoped that God will prevail on you to behave in a manner befitting His mercy."

He stopped again, vainly searching for some sign of contrition in the faces below him. "The Fleet Chaplain will come aboard shortly to offer prayers for a successful voyage. You may all remain on deck until after the service. God Save The King."

Nearly everybody gave the customary response. Only Liz Dudgeon heard Elizabeth Powley add . . ."and save the Captain for me."

That night, few slept in anticipation of the months ahead. Mixed emotions prevailed in cabins, hammocks and prison berths. The solemnity of their venture occupied most officers' minds, and the dread of unknown dangers caused even hardened criminals and prostitutes to lie quietly on their mattresses. They waited for the glimmer of light that would signal the beginning of a new life—or the end of it.

Susannah sat upright and gazed into the gloom while she rocked her son gently. Each prisoner had one ankle secured to the sleeping berth in readiness for the sailing, and the chains rattled as the women fidgeted against them.

"Can't you sleep, cariad?" Mary turned around and rubbed the baby's back.

"I'm wondering what it will be like?" Susannah whispered. "Henry says he's read that Botany Bay is very hot. I wonder if it is all jungle, like Africa? Or desert? Maybe it's got steep cliffs all around . . . oh, Mary—how will I climb cliffs with the baby?" She shuddered, picturing the Fleet dashed against towering cliffs while her son screamed in her arms and she vainly searched the boiling sea around her for sight of Henry.

"Hush now, Susannah," Mary soothed. "Try and get some sleep now, will you? Pray to God and ask for His blessing."

Through the gloom came Cockney Liz's voice. "Yus. We'll drink anything we're blest wiv." There was a chuckle and a nervous ripple from some of the berths, but Mary lifted her eyes and tutted.

An uncomfortable weight of fetid air was much more noticeable, charged as it was with combined expectancy and fear of the unknown. Every creak of the ship's timbers, every scrabble of rats foraging for dropped crumbs under the bench, every painfully drawn breath by Sara seemed amplified out of proportion. Sara had added fears, having been instructed to report to the Sick Bay in the morning, before they sailed.

Mary lay staring into the dark, remembering lessons that had been drummed into her early years each Sunday at the Noddfa Welsh Baptist Chapel. The Minister, soft in his approach to the sermon, ranted and reverberated by the end of the hour and always finished, "Survival in your darkest hour is assured, if only you will keep your faith."

Mary had already spent several hours praying but was no surer of her survival. So she began to think of her valley home. She recalled the laughter of miners' children as they clambered up the mountain-side to hunt for succulent wimberries below tough grasses and ferns. Hard stubble kept short by flocks of nimble sheep would stab into their bare feet, but none of the children seemed to care. Fingers and mouths were stained purple by the time the berry-hunters returned to their homes. They would clatter into the stone-floored cottage kitchens and pour their spoils into chipped enamel bowls. Soon smells of steaming fruit wafted from the ovens and they would crouch by the open fire. The cast-iron oven door was swung aside and golden crusted pies extracted with rivulets of purple juice across the pastry crusts. The memory drew saliva into Mary's mouth, and her eyes misted.

"Hey, Powley," called Beth Thackery quietly. "Do you reckon they will take the chains off afore we get there?"

"They'll have a couple of wet beds if they bleedin' well don't," came the reply.

* * *

In his cabin, Captain Meredith lay as much awake as the rest of the ship's complement. He listened to the gentle thud of ropes against furled sails that in just a few hours, would be free to billow and strain against the capricious May breezes. Already he could visualise men clambering about high in the riggings, responding to shouts and curses from Francis Walton. His heart skipped a little at the thought of the vastness of the seas that the intrepid fleet would challenge, with little more than Captain Cook's description of their destination.

As though aware of her master's unsettled frame of mind, the black bitch padded quietly to his bunk and nuzzled a cold nose under the fingers that twitched on the counterpane.

"Ah, Lady. We have all waited so long for the moment and now that it is here, I doubt that any of us are sleeping. All we can do is place ourselves in God's hands for He only knows what we are really facing." Meredith stroked the swollen dog at his side and as if by maternal instinct, her soft eyes lifted and with a moist tongue, she rasped inside his palm.

In the Surgery, Thomas Arndell crept towards his supply cupboard intent on not disturbing John Hart, who was curled in a tight ball beneath the table. He eased the hook from its hasp and reach inside for the brandy.

Hart stirred. "Is that you, sir?"

"Yes, lad" whispered the surgeon. "You're awake?"

There was a pause. "I'm a bit scared, sir."

"No doubt a lot of us are," said Arndell crouching down. "But you must think of it as more of an adventure. There are lots of boys in England who would like to sail the high seas, I'm thinking."

"Are you scared, sir?"

"No-one needs to be scared if they pray to God, like the Reverend said this evening."

"I prayed to God I weren't going, sir!"

Arndell hid a smile and ruffled the boy's hair before retiring to his cabin with the bottle.

CHAPTER 14

THE JOURNEY BEGINS

A light wind skipped across Portsmouth Harbour early next morning flapping the trousers of the busy crew as they scuttled to their stations. Captain Meredith, exhilarated despite his wakeful night, gazed at the majestic sails as they unfurled against the blue sky. They were awe-inspiring, except to the seamen who were battling to understand orders from the ship's Master, amongst all the frustrated confusion and frustrated curses.

The small fleet formed a truly wonderful sight as it carved a dignified path through the small boats that hastened like courtiers, making way for Royalty in a water palace. *'The Sirius'* led the parade, *'The Charlotte'* and *'The Friendship'* sailed proudly behind her and *'HMS Hyaena'* brought up the rear. Several other ships were to join the Fleet; they were to sail from Plymouth and join the main fleet in the Solent, a body of water between the mainland and the Isle of Wight. Not counting *'HMS Hyaena'* who was acting as escort, there were to be eleven ships altogether that would make the dangerous journey to a land unknown until now.

Around the deck of 'The Friendship' stood small groups of marines and their wives, some clutching their children resolutely, others waving handkerchiefs in a tearful farewell. Observers on the shore acknowledged them, but few realised they were watching a living page of history.

Meredith turned and beamed at the two officers at his side. "We're off at last, Lieutenants."

"God grant us a safe voyage, Cap'n," Faddy smiled tightly.

Ralph Clark did not answer. His eyes were fixed to the shoreline that was inching away from them like a great galleon. He watched the high escarpment of chalk that overlooked the Harbour from the North as it dwindled to a green hill. Portsmouth's Square Tower at the end of the main street glided past with the sun glinting off its dignified bay windows that had commanded a view over the sea-wall since 1495. Close to it was the Round Tower. It had discoloured granite walls and several sightseers stood waving from its flat roof. Clark sighed. "Would that I were standing there right now, with my darling wife and son. Promotion seems such a small recompense."

Below the deck in the male prisoners' quarters, there was an apprehensive silence. The ship's timbers creaked in the gentle Harbour swell, and the noises above could be likened to goading a ship of the desert into activity after being tethered for so long. Through each man's thoughts ran memories of what good things there had been, events that had led them to chains, and a great disquiet about the unknown chasms they were sailing into.

The increased lurch and dip of the wooden hull only served to intensify their fears of what lay ahead. One man, who's face reflected the apprehension of all, clung to the support beam between the sleeping berths. Tears streamed down his pale complexion, but only one saw fit to make any comment.

William Gant, still flinching when something touched his back, had not lost any of his sarcastic ways and grinned evilly. "Don't worry, matey," he said. "The way she's creakin' she'll fall apart afore we gets to the Isle of Wight!"

Nobody laughed.

Further along the men's prison, Henry Cable turned as his bunkmate spoke. "Wonder how long they'll keep us down here, Cable? Doubt if we'll get our exercise walk as long as they're all running around like cockerels in Covent Garden."

Henry shrugged. His thoughts were with Susannah and the child. Again he silently thanked his Maker and Mr. Simpson, the Humane Turnkey.

There was similar apprehension in the womens' prison. Some of them wept quietly; others lay staring at the timbers above them as though at any moment the churning sea would send her salted tongue probing into the holds and cabins and swallow the ship whole. One woman sat enfolding her young daughter, the maternal instinct as always transcending her own fear and trepidation.

In their corner berth, Mary sat close to Susannah whose soft eyes were fixed on the down cheeks of her baby. He snuggled against her, blissfully asleep. The even breath of complete innocence fluttered rhythmically with the rise and fall of the ship.

"Do you realise that he's the only one on board who is not leaving a thing behind?" asked Mary softly. Susannah seemed about to reply, but a broken sob from the bunk nearby distracted them. A frail woman whose bun-tied hair clung in damp wisps to her face was flushed with the effort to contain her dismay. Her sobs, silent at first, had broken the bounds of constraint and in an agony of separation, she began calling over the names of the husband and five children she had left behind on a Suffolk farm.

"Poor dab," said Mary, her voice heavy with empathy. "Just because she answered the magistrate back. Why, any mother would steal rather than see the little ones starve!"

The gypsy Elizabeth Barber, whose twitching hands betrayed her bravado, yelled at the crying woman. "Ah, shurrup!"

"Shurrup yourself," hissed Powley. Surprisingly, and perhaps indicative of the pervading tension, Barber glared but didn't reply.

'The Friendship' lurched deeper into the swell of the Solent as the fleet cleared Portsmouth Harbour, causing a few timid screams.

"For Gawd sakes—I feel bloody awful," yelled Cockney Liz.

"Stuff y'skirt in your mouth," laughed Beth. "At least we won't have t'listen to you, then."

The banter stopped as sweet tones of an old Welsh hymn began to flow from Mary Watkins. It was soft at first, as though she was drawing on her birthright to sing and was the only consolation she knew. The timbre of her notes strengthened into an inherited Celtic defiance, which silenced the bickering Elizabeths. It brought tears to many eyes but served to quieten the sobbing of the Suffolk farmer's wife.

From various shouts above decks, the passengers gathered that the other ships from Plymouth had now joined the fleet and they knew their compatriots were huddled in similar conditions.

* * *

By May 20th, the brave little Fleet had been at sea for eight days and Thomas Arndell had a constant stream of patients to his Sick Bay. The convicts, although now free of their leg shackles, were still handcuffed to their berths and had not been allowed on deck. Arndell made a twice-daily visit to the prison holds, a task he found increasingly abhorrent. Quite used to the stomach-lurching smell of vomit in the light and airy conditions of the Sick Bay, he found the vile and putrid odour below decks was almost unbearable. Combined with the smell of perspiration from fevered bodies confined in the atmosphere of rotting bilge-water, he found the stench caused more sickness than the ship's motion.

He'd taken a leaf from the book of many magistrates he knew and protected his offended nostrils with a handkerchief soaked in Lavender water. He'd begged the fragrance from Mrs. Morgan during one of her pregnancy checks.

John Hart, also afflicted with the seasickness that was rampant through the ship's personnel, lay moaning beneath the surgeon's table. Arndell bent and placed a wet flannel on the boy's forehead.

"There, young 'un," he soothed. "It will pass and probably never return."

"If I 'aven't gorn with it, sir . . ." Hart's reply was smothered by another mouthful of bile which burned from his aching stomach and Arndell moved a bowl closer.

"Have Faith, John" he said, and continued on his way.

In the women's quarters, Susannah lay trembling but she didn't dare move. Her hot forehead was pressed against the stanchion and beside her, Mary nursed little Henry who was crying lustily for his mother's milk.

"Can't you shut that bastard up?" shouted the gypsy. "Much more an' I'll chuck it overboard!" Far less affected by the ship's incessant rolling, Elizabeth Barber had made things even more intolerable by keeping up a stream of abuse. Elizabeth Powley and Beth Thackery were the only two females who seemed free of discomfort and they kept up their own diatribe of complaints to the doctor, the seamen, the marine guards—anyone who was foolish enough to venture into the prison.

"It smells like a filthy London sewer down 'ere." Elizabeth Powley spat on the floor at a marine guard's feet.

"Then you're in the right place, Powley, aincha?" The soldier grabbed her by the hair and she yelled as he forced her to her knees. Her hair had grown strongly in the ensuing weeks, but her earlier indignity had left its scar on her memory.

"Only the rats would come down here, then" she panted, trying to twist out of his grasp. "So that must mean you, too!"

The soldier let her go suddenly and jabbed the butt of his rifle into her shoulder. He made another swipe at her which, if it had connected, would have split her mouth. Instead, he whacked her rear as she scrambled back to her bunk and he laughed loudly at the muffled abuse Elizabeth uttered as her face sunk into a smelly pillow. Turning to leave for fresher air on deck, the soldier said nastily, "You're all mouth, Powley. Just a loud-mouthed slut!"

Elizabeth sat up and rubbed her behind while a stream of invectives followed the disappearing man.

"You tell 'em, Elizabeth," said Dudgeon. She was weary now that her vomiting bouts had eased.

"An' you shut yer face, too." Elizabeth was in no mood to speak with anyone.

On deck, the soldier was laughing cruelly as he gulped the salty wind that filled the ship's cheeks of spray-wet canvas. He was going off duty for a while and like all his compatriots, he welcomed the change of watch. It was midday and a shout from the crow's nest drew attention to a signal from Captain Phillips' ship, *'The Sirius'*.

All the ships were to come to anchor. Soon they were tossing like cumbersome tree trunks that had been felled in an overnight flood. Captain Meredith knew what the signal meant and quickly summoned the first officer to his cabin.

"Lieutenant Clark, prepare your collection of letters and reports. They are to be transferred to the *'Hyaena'* as she is going to leave us at this point."

"I have them ready, sir," said the pale Lieutenant. The voyage so far had not treated him kindly either, and he was glad to repair to his cabin to retrieve the package. His own letters were nothing but reports to his wife and friends of the abysmal degradations of sea-sickness he had suffered. These were made more lurid by the fact that Lady had chosen to sneak into his empty bunk during his many absences to spew over the side of the ship. She'd delivered herself of five spanking puppies. Only by allowing Clark first choice of Lady's offspring, and procuring the services of one of the healthier women to launder his bedding, was Captain Meredith able to placate him. The Labrador and her puppies had been transferred to the Captain's cabin, but Ralph Clark felt obliged to add a postscript on a letter to his London friend.

"It appears that not only are we expected to deal with the animals called convicts, we have to play wet-nurse to four-legged creatures as well! Further explanations in my next letter. It will be posted from Tenerife."

CHAPTER 15

SEASICKNESS TAKES OVER

Riding at anchor and waiting for *'HMS Hyaena'* to pick up their mail before she parted company with the fleet increased the discomfort below decks and shortened tempers more. Doctor Arndell administered what he could to the worst patients and resolved to make a request of Captain Meredith at the first opportunity. "Any method of fumigation that we can find should be utilised and put into operation immediately."

The urgency in his voice convinced Meredith of the need, and he set about giving orders to smoke out the various areas as soon as possible. None of the convicts had been allowed on deck as yet, so his orders were 'noted for later'.

Sara McCormick, who had quickly succumbed to the squalor, had been sent back to the Sick Bay and John Hart charged with watching over her. However, there was no fear of her creating trouble as her already weakened body was again racked by the debilitating cough.

The surgeon was presently visiting the marine-wives, especially to check on the well-being of the pregnant Mrs. Morgan. He was not to know then that his services were far more urgently required in the women's' prison. Trying to maintain a cheerful calm, he chatted to the wives and their children.

Meantime, Mary Watkins had found it increasingly difficult to placate the baby. Susannah bravely attempted to feed him but the incessant bobbing of the ship brought back the queasy giddiness, and she was obliged to withdraw her nipple. She handed little Henry back to Mary, and he objected loudly.

Elizabeth Barber, who had just filled her cup with water from the slopping copper, gave an eerie curse, turned, and tossed the water over the checkered shawl. "Shut that bleedin' kid up!"

Pandemonium set in. While Mary frantically brushed at the warm weave before the liquid could saturate the folds, she mouthed Welsh words that only she knew were obscenities. She managed to restrain Susannah's outrage but would have lost control of her own, except retribution was not to be hers.

"You bitch!" screamed Elizabeth Powley as she leapt from her bunk. She took the gypsy by surprise and like a wild tiger, she clawed at the cruel face. Blood spurted when her broken nails tore at the thin lower lip of Barber who yowled like an animal.

Liz Dudgeon sat up, enlivened by the action, and Beth scrambled from her berth yelling, "The murderous bitch attacked the baby."

Liz grabbed the opportunity to vent an old grudge on the gypsy, grabbed her metal cup from beneath her pillow and threw herself into the melee. Beth quickly lifted a ladle that had been left on the bench and the four Elizabeths fought in a confusion of flying arms, tearing clothes, bitten limbs and screams of abuse that percolated through to the deck above.

Marines came running, rattled down the stairway, and hoisted their rifles to their shoulders waiting for orders. Sergeant Steward took one glance and sent a curious seaman to fetch Thomas Arndell.

Three of the Elizabeths, as soon as they had heard the hatch being lifted, had rushed back to their berths and put on a pained expression. "It wasn't us," Beth lied. "We are all too sick to move."

Arndell came quickly down the ladder and gasped as he saw the woman lying face down and senseless. He rolled her over and bit his lip when he saw the battered features of the gypsy. "Good God, what happened?" He stared at the other prisoners but was met with a stony silence. "Sergeant, two men to carry this woman to the Sick Bay. Quickly, man!"

He looked around at the sullen faces once more and eventually spoke to Mary. "Well, Watkins?"

Before she had time to draw breath, Elizabeth Powley sat up on one elbow. Her hair was wet with perspiration and disheveled. "A terrible accident, Doctor. She says she feels giddy, gets up and crashes into the wooden upright there." Her eyes were slits as she continued, "And we was all too sick to help 'er."

Thomas Arndell felt rather than found proof of the conspiracy between the bribed marines who had broken up the fight and the prostitutes. And the hierarchy amongst the imprisoned women had been established long before they'd left Portsmouth's mother bank.

He shook his head and followed his latest patient up the ladder. Liz Dudgeon's slim shoulders trembled as she hid her grin with a pillow. Beth Thackery stayed facing the wall; she clutched at her blouse in case the doctor saw the firm breasts revealed when it was torn to the waist. Fear of Powley's wrath if contradicted overruled her modesty. An uneasy silence remained when the women were left alone, broken only by the hiss of seawater as the First Fleet resumed its voyage.

* * *

The following day, and feeling a lot better, John Hart accompanied the surgeon on his rounds. He'd survived his ordeal with nothing more than sips of water urged upon him and the doctor's soothing words. Lifetime bonds of a different sort were forged between the two, and John's determination to please his new friend and mentor was reinforced.

John's precocious youth was refreshing to Arndell and he nodded in approval as the boy walked lightly ahead of him to the men's prison. The ill-effects of the sea's motion were gradually abating and he found his attention required by only a few of the convicts. One of these was William Gant. Arndell measured the lecher's discomfort by the fact that he could not eat. Despite a jealous attempt to swallow his porridge rather than have it stolen from him, Gant's ration laid cold before him on the bench.

Henry Cable still felt a certain responsibility for John and greeted him warmly. "Hello, lad. You're feeling better, then?"

"Yus," was the succinct reply, "but I'm starvin'." He'd spotted the neglected bowl of porridge and licked his lips.

"If you wait," Arndell interposed sagely, "I'll see if I can get something warm from the cook's caboose for you. You don't want that."

"Yes I do," said John, and he grabbed a nearby ladle gleefully. With a gusto that can only be employed by the very young and hungry, he shovelled the porridge into his mouth. The clout and scrape of metal vibrated on Gant's nerves and while the other men laughed at the gobbling youth, he felt only a lurching nausea. He moved as if to wrest the bowl from John's hands but as he rose, he spewed onto his berth, and the men shouted abuses at him.

Hiding his amusement, Thomas Arndell gathered his medicine bag and nodded to the approaching marine private. "See that this mess is cleaned up by this man and inform me if there are any new cases of sickness. There's no need for more than a daily inspection, now."

Henry Cable leaned from his berth. "Mister Arndell, sir, would you . . . could you tell me is Susannah Holmes and . . . ?" He faltered, wondering if he had overstepped his bonds. But having heard nothing but rumors of sick women, children, soldiers and seamen, his usual caution had lessened.

"Quite well, now," answered Arndell. "Your son is a strong baby. You've no need to fret." He turned around and said, "Come along, Hart. You'll grind a hole through that dish."

In the Sick Bay, Elizabeth Barber had displayed a vindictive gypsy temper when she regained consciousness. One of her eyes was blacker than usual and blood had congealed on her lip. Her stream of invectives as Arndell applied iodine to the various bites and scratches on her body had caused him to threaten her with a dose of laudanum unless she calmed down. He finally sent out a request that the termagant be chained to her bed.

Sara McCormick on the other hand, provided quite a different problem. Now in a comatose state, her spasmodic breathing greatly concerned him. At dinner with Captain Meredith that evening, he reported the situation.

"She appears to have no will to live. I find the threat of death very disturbing despite my calling."

"My concern is that we support Captain Phillip's objectives implicitly," Meredith returned. He poured a glass each of their favourite Madeira wine. "I've no doubt that we shall lose some during the voyage, Doctor, but it would seem a little pointless to instruct you not to be concerned. Let's hope our losses are minimal—I have no liking for burials at sea. I know you will do your best."

'The Friendship' was now ploughing comfortably through smoother seas. On his way back to the surgery, Arndell stopped to gaze across the water to her sister ships. He wondered briefly how his counterparts were coping and if their Sick Bays were also fully occupied. Two small beds in each bay seemed inadequate on *'The Friendship'* already. He sighed and returned to his quarters.

He stopped to crouch below his examination bench and roused John Hart. "I am going to spend the night keeping an eye on the McCormick woman. If anyone requires me, fetch me immediately."

John nodded sleepily and settled back as Arndell proceeded to the small inner cabin. A low roofed area, it contained two tiny cots that had been painted white at his instructions. A white painted bench stood against one wall and on it was laid various surgical instruments covered with a white sheet. A tri-fold partition for screening births, deaths, and contagious patients stood around Sara and in the swaying lamp light, her face was cadaverous. Arndell quietly prepared his instruments to bleed the sick woman if the need arose.

Towards three in the morning, while the gypsy lay deep in the sleep of exhaustion, he removed the fever-hot towel from Sara's forehead. He wrung it out in a bowl of cold water to which he'd added a few drops of his precious lavender oil and gently laid it back. He frowned and searched for the weak pulse. For long moments he watched her bony chest remain deflated, then a rasping shudder engulfed her and she breathed again.

"She will have to be bled," he muttered. A lamp swung and squeaked with the incessant hiss of the ship's prow dipping into the waves, a low chorus to an early stillness. For as long as he could recall, this hour had been one where the whole of life hung by a thread, the hour when most deaths occurred and most babies were born. He removed his tailed coat and donned an apron that reeked of carbolic.

He carefully uncovered the metal bowl he'd prepared and wiped the tiny blade of a scalpel. Placing a thickness of cloth under Sara's limp arm, he fingered an area in the crook of her elbow. Her flesh parted easily under the pressure of the keen blade and for a while, he watched the red liquid ooze from her vein and jelly into a puddle in the bowl. Eventually he pressed his thumb onto the wound for a few moments in order to stem the bleeding, then he applied a bandage tightly. The procedure complete, and having cleaned the instruments away, the tired doctor poured himself a generous brandy. He replaced his coat after disposing of the apron, then he prepared to carry on with his vigil.

Sara remained almost lifeless and before long, the warmth of the brandy and the ship's motion brought its own oblivion to Arndell. His chin sagged onto his shirt, and his heavy eyes closed.

CHAPTER 16

JEALOUSY AND BRIBERY

Around seven the next morning, Thomas Arndell was startled awake by a tap on the Sick Bay door. "Yes, who is it?"

"Me, sir," came John's muffled reply. "If y'please, sir, Sergeant Stewart's here wif his wife and little boy."

Arndell looked quickly at the convict women. Barber was still sound asleep so he stooped over Sara. She was breathing more regularly now even though she was still unconscious. Satisfied, he fastened his shirt buttons and called, "Very well. I'm coming."

Margaret Stewart smiled as he entered the surgery. "The boy's a natural clown, Mister Arndell. What a shame he became a convict."

John Hart had been amusing the two-year old with grimaces and antics which would have done credit to a puppet on strings.

"A label he scarcely deserves, I'd say, Ma'am," Arndell agreed. "I must confess I find little to fault in his behavior." Despite his few hours sleep, Arndell was still tired and it showed in his voice. "Now, what's the trouble with young Charles?"

Margaret Stewart held her son while Arndell examined a small mother-worrying rash. Her husband stood back and addressed the Cockney sweep. "Did you have any brothers or sisters, m'boy?"

"Nah. I'm an orphaned." Still a little pale from his bout of sea-sickness, Hart stared up at the tall marine and wondered at the grandeur of his uniform. Unlike many of the other soldiers on board, Sergeant Stewart wore it smartly and his features didn't twist spitefully when he spoke.

"I trust you behaved for Mister Arndell?"

"Yes, sir."

Sergeant Stewart looked from his earnest face to that of his wife struggling to hold their son while she replaced his shirt. "Mister Arndell. Do you think the Captain would give permission for the boy here to play with Charles on some occasions? Now that he's beginning to run around, he's a handful for Margaret and it would help tire the child out if he had someone to play with."

Margaret Stewart straightened her brown gingham dress, then she looked happily at the doctor. "Oh, what a marvelous idea. Could you enquire for us, please, Mister Arndell?"

"Cripes!"

Arndell looked sternly in John's direction and the boy cringed a little. "I believe it would be healthy for both of them. I'll speak to the Captain later. Now, spread a little of this ointment on the rash every evening before the child is put to bed, and I'm sure you will find an improvement very quickly."

"Cor!" was the only comment Hart kept repeating, long after the Stewart family left.

A few hours later, having snatched some sleep while the boy kept an eye on Sara, Thomas Arndell authorised the returned of the subdued Elizabeth Barber to the women's prison. Pushed by the marine who accompanied her, she stumbled down the steps into the gloom and all eyes were turned on her. Notably, the cold and calculating eyes of Elizabeth Powley seemed to bore through to the gypsy's befuddled brain.

"Wotcher looking at?" Barber's words were slurred as she sank into her berth. Apart from her clumsy movements, she appeared to be unaffected by the bruises evident on her face and arms, but her hand often flicked to the discoloured swelling at her temple.

"I dunno," came the soft answer from Elizabeth Powley. She sat crossed-legged, her elbows on her knees and her strong jawbone cupped in her hands. In the charged atmosphere, Beth and Liz watched their self-appointed leader keenly, and they shuddered. Two two younger girls had drawn closer of late in that their aims and desires in life coincided. They intended to gain as much influence as possible with anybody aboard who could be of advantage to them. There was something strong yet protective in Powley's aloofness.

The gypsy was chained to her berth again as Lieutenant Clark had ordered all women should be. He had been placed in command temporarily when Captain Meredith succumbed to the sea-sickness, and he was always quick to use his power. The departing marine glanced at other shackles around women's ankles, then he climbed the steps and fastened the hatchway behind him. His footsteps died away and the two arch-enemies stared at each other. Liz and Beth watched fascinated. Within moment, like a tiger that's been stared out, she grunted and stretched back on her mattress. Smiles flickered across Beth and Liz's features but as Powley swivelled to them, they quickly turned away, unwilling to involve themselves in any challenge.

In the more pleasant area of *'The Friendship'*, Thomas Arndell approached the Captain's cabin and entered quietly. He smiled and placed his bag on the nearby desk when he saw Meredith was awake. "Good morning, Captain. How are we this morning?"

"Like the weather I'm glad to say," came the reply. "Very much improved. What can you report?"

Arndell related the ship's medical standing, including his need to quell Elizabeth Barber's irrational behaviour and the night's vigil over the dying Sara McCormick. He talked while making a perfunctory examination and declared Meredith much improved.

"I'm sure you will share a warming pot of tea, doctor," said Meredith whilst buttoning his shirt. The order was conveyed to the galley.

"I must admit I would prefer to see the convicts released from their chains, now," Arndell said wearily while they waited for the tea. "Some have quite badly chafed ankles, and I hardly think they are going to escape in the middle of the ocean."

"As a matter of fact," said Meredith sitting up gingerly. "A signal was received from Commodore Phillip to that effect some days ago, but I have felt so poorly up to now that I have ignored it."

Arndell gasped. "You mean . . . ?"

"We should be at the Canary Islands in a few days," the Captain nodded. "I'll attend to the matters outstanding then."

A seaman entered and laid a tray on the table. He poured two cups of tea then left. Meredith peered at the calendar on the wall beside him as he sipped. "First of the month. We seem to have made good time despite the sickness amongst the crew."

Arndell's reply was interrupted by anxious shouts and heavy marine-boots pounding. On deck, Lieutenant Faddy halted a running marine and demanded to know the cause of the sudden confusion.

"Fight, sir," panted the private. "In the seamen's quarters." Faddy nodded and followed to the ruckus.

"I'll kill you, Morris," yelled a nuggetty seaman called Lewis, his arms and legs flailing as he was pinned to the deck. "She's mine." His right eye was practically closed and resembled raw beef. He gave a mighty heave from his pelvis and tossed the leaner man sideways. Morris landed heavily, his cropped head spurting blood as it connected with the metal trunk standing against the bulkhead, and with a bull-like roar, Lewis launched himself again.

"That's enough!" yelled Faddy as Lewis pummelled the sagging body. Two marines separated the sailors. "Sergeant, 'cuff them and bring them outside." Turning smartly, Faddy made his way to the deck and stood near the main hatch-cover. He was always uncomfortable with these confrontations, nevertheless he was not shy of maintaining discipline. The ship's Master, Francis Walton, was quite happy for his crew to come under military jurisdiction as it added weight to his command. Faddy stood astride, gripping the lapels on his red jacket.

Thomas Arndell took a place beside him as he had been asked by Captain Meredith to investigate the disturbance. He nodded curtly to Faddy but made no attempt to participate, preferring to observe.

Hands secured behind their backs, the culprits stumbled on deck aided by prods from muskets behind them. Arndell started when he saw the congealing wound on Morris's skull, but he remained silent.

"Well, what have you to say for yourselves?" Faddy looked stern but neither of the men answered. "What was the fight about?"

"Women, I think, sir," one of the marines volunteered.

Faddy rounded on the sailors. "Is this true? Speak up one of you, or the consequences will be worse."

Lewis seemed more capable of speaking than his groggy opponent, despite being drunk himself. He fidgeted for a moment, then he slurred an answer. " 'Lizbeth Barber. 'E called 'er a skinny pole and a gypsy and kept saying that anybody could have 'er."

Faddy trying to contain his amazement said incredulously, "You mean to tell me that you were fighting over a whore?"

Arndell felt obliged to interrupt. "Just a minute. Weren't you one of the four men taken over to '*The Sirius*' for flogging?"

Lewis showed no remorse and nodded. For the press-ganged seaman, the women had been an unexpected bonus when he'd organised that first breakout in Portsmouth. Since then, besotted with the tall gypsy, he'd spent spare moments discovering hideaways in the ship. He knew she would exchange her favours at every opportunity.

Morris had discovered him in the sail-locker on one occasion, fumbling under Barber's skirt while she swigged the liquor. He'd been blackmailed ever since with threats of disclosure unless he would instruct the gypsy to share her favours with Morris. Lewis had finally broken, and the fight began.

Incensed by the men's silence, Arndell continued testily, "What's the matter with you people? Wasn't that beating on '*The Sirius*' enough of a lesson to you?"

"By the look of it," interjected Faddy, "they've given each other enough of a beating this time. Perhaps now they will learn from their stupidity." He squared his shoulders and addressed the sergeant nearby. "Put them both in solitary confinement for seven days, with short rations."

The still silent men were led away and the surgeon and lieutenant walked towards the Captain's cabin to report this latest ruckus. "No doubt this is only one of many similar incidents we shall endure," said Arndell.

Faddy stood aside to allow him to enter the Captain's cabin, then he proceeded to make his report. Captain Meredith had by this time dressed fully and, albeit a little unsteadily, made his way to his table while he listened. He merely nodded his approval of Faddy's actions, then he offered the two men a glass of Madeira wine.

Arndell shook his head as he accepted his glass. "I fear liquor will prove one of the greatest hazards, both during the voyage and in the new colony, Captain. Between the seamen and the allowance for the marines that Major Ross finally achieved, I can forsee it becoming one of the greatest bargaining powers amongst the lower classes."

"I agree," said Meredith staring into his drink. "A small portion like this is very beneficial to our health, but the lower classes seem to have no control over themselves."

Faddy said nothing, knowing that class distinction frequently gave rise to criticism and he, for one, was uncomfortable with it. The doctor and lieutenant emptied their glasses then they took their leave.

CHAPTER 17

BEING HAPPY IS PENALISED

While Lieutenant Faddy and Thomas Arndell enjoyed their glass of Madeira wine with Captain Meredith, the atmosphere down in the men's prison hold was one of pure boredom. Some of them slept fitfully, some chatted quietly, and others masturbated, much to the disgust of men like Henry Cable. The only one who seemed to have any life in him was Patrick Daley, Elizabeth Powley's one-time lover. He lay back in his berth with his strong arms behind his head and stared at the berth timbers above him. He hummed an Irish tune softly in rhythm with the sea's swell, his black curls sticking damply to his forehead. All around him men lay in total boredom. Some thought of nothing but how to escape their bonds, others contemplated their misfortune and wondered about their future.

Patrick was thinking he'd much rather be astride his magnificent stallion with flanks of the powerful horse glistening between his thighs. He could almost feel the wind whipping across the open plains and his leather jerkin slapping at his broad chest.

"Ah, Patrick, m'boy," he muttered sadly. "Those foine days are indeed ended. But maybe . . . when we gets there . . . maybe Elizabeth . . ." He sat up suddenly, aware of a thumping in his chest. "Begorra, Patrick, I tink you're in love wid the colleen!"

"Are you talking to yourself, Mick?" A fresh-faced rogue hung upside-down from the berth above and grinned. He gave an inverted wink, then he swung down to sit at Patrick's feet.

"I don't believe it," said the startled Irishman. "Why aren't you chained?"

"I wriggled out of them, didn't I? Easy, if y'knows how." The cheeky young convict gave a grin.

The other men slowly rose to their elbows, then they sat up and stared at the finely-built young man whose voluminous prison clothes seemed to float around his supple bones. As if to prove his freedom, he levered himself out of Daley's berth and gave an impromptu dance in the middle of the deck. His boots clumped on the boards and his arms flung from side to side as he gyrated much to the amazement and gradual amusement of his audience.

"Dah-de-de-diddle-da . . . howsat?" He stopped with one heel stretched out on the floor and his arms flung wide, like a circus entertainer. The young man's name was Tom Bennett and his face showed a medley of audacity and achievement. Involuntarily, the other men applauded.

"Look out!" came a warning cry from Henry Cable. "Here comes a scarlet beetle."

"Don't tell on me," warned Bennett. He scrambled back onto his berth then quickly draped the chain around his ankle before hiding his hands beneath the blanket. Stretched back on the pillow, he pretended to be asleep. Even the blackguard William Gant had enjoyed the spectacle, and with all the other men, he followed suit and closed his eyes. Each man had regarded the young man's freedom as a personal possession, and they hid their smiles as the unsuspecting marine passed through to the other end of the prison. Once there, he retrieved some rags he'd previously used for polishing his musket and then he returned to the foot of the ladder.

"Nice to see you all quiet for a change," he grated sarcastically, then he made his way back to the upper deck. Smothering their laughter, the men waited quietly for a while. The rhythmic hash of waves against the ship seemed to combine with their secret and it symbolised a victory over their circumstances.

"Come on, lad," said Daley eventually. "Give us another dance. They won't be coming near us for an hour or two now. Too busy lazing in d'sun."

Patrick began to chant a catchy Irish jig, and Bennett willingly entertained his fellow prisoners with leaps and pirouettes that, although no challenge to a ballerina, lifted the heart of every man who clapped to the Irishman's beat. As always, when frustration and deprivation is pushed aside for a while, any thought of caution faded into the background.

Lieutenant Ralph Clark had been clinging halfway down the ladder for moments, mesmerized. His screech of anger cut across the hilarity like a sword and two marines rushed to peer down the hatch, thinking their superior had fallen down the ladder. "You all right, sir?"

"Both of you, get down here!" Clark flung himself down the rest of the ladder and stood trembling with fury. His normally soulful eyes glittered like coals and his breath was erratic. Bennett slowly lowered his suspended leg as Clark's voice sliced through the tension like a blacksmith's hammer on hot metal.

"At first light in the morning, this prisoner is to receive seventy-five lashes!" The irrational punishment was pronounced as though 'seventy-five' was the most terrifying combination of syllables the little man could concoct. He breathed deeply again before continuing, "In the meantime, he is to be tied overnight to the pump on deck."

In the stunned silence that followed, the two marines rope-tied Bennett's hands and jostled him up the ladder. But not before he'd winked broadly at Patrick.

"Whatever's the matter with Bennett?" said Henry Cable irritably as the hatch was replaced. "Does he count on escaping from the pump overnight and jumping into the ocean?"

"Could that be any worse?" growled his bunkmate. "Maybe we'd all be better off if we pretended to be idiots."

"Then we'd all qualify to be Lieutenants," quipped Daley and all the men laughed shakily. "No doubt about it, though—the man was askin' for it."

"You're a bastard, you Irish Mick." Gant grated his teeth and rattled his chains.

Patrick Daley glared at the villain in the opposite berth, and his voice shook with fury. "Why don't you take his place, then? They wouldn't care. One man's back is the same as another to them. There's none of us does anyt'ing unless we're prepared to take the consequences."

Gant leered and made an obscene gesture. "Wrap yer rosary around yer neck and yank it tight, Irishman."

Patrick's heart thumped uncomfortably and his head spun in frustration at the callous laughter from some of the other men. "Just you watch every time you lay down, Gant," he threatened. "There might be a knife in y'r back!" The jangle of chains accompanied by raucous laughter increased at his words. This was a welcome break from the monotony they had been enduring up to now and they were making the most of it.

Patrick leaned back against the timbers behind him and tried to steady his breathing in an effort to submerge his temper. He wanted to smash into something—preferably the side of the ship, or William Gant's grinning face.

* * *

The following morning dawned with the promise of a fine day's sailing. The sheets billowed and flexed in the fair winds and dolphins were sighted off the starboard bow. Relief from the scourge of sea-sickness cheered everyone's spirit above decks. Pale but smiling, Captain Meredith appeared from his cabin and breathed the fresh air deeply. Lady, abandoning her maternal duties for a while, loped at his side with her teats engorged and tender.

Meredith's appreciation of the beautiful morning was soon engulfed by his responsibilities. The sight of the dismal Lieutenant Clark approaching him didn't help, but he tried to sound cheerful. "Good morning, Clark. You're on deck early."

Clark tipped his hat. "One of the men has to be flogged, sir."

Meredith's joi de vivre plummeted as Clark reported the previous afternoon's incident in the male convicts' quarters. In fact he only noticed that Clark had finished talking when the smaller man became agitated by his silence.

"Permission to carry on, sir?" Clark finally blurted.

A movement behind caused Meredith to turn and there he observed the shivering Bennett, bound securely to the ship's pump to one side of the main deck. He studied the lad who by this time showed no trace of his former exuberance. A night on deck with nothing but a thin shirt to cover his wiry body was taking its toll. Meredith turned to stare at Clark for a long moment, then he gave a small nod and walked to the poop deck.

The relieved Lieutenant turned and barked his orders to a nearby corporal. "Get the other men up on deck."

"There is no need for that, Lieutenant," interrupted Meredith pointedly. The silent battle of wills was short-lived and Clark countermanded his order before joining the Captain on the poop deck.

While Bennett was being prepared for flogging, Meredith quietly addressed Clark. "The surgeon tells me that the convicts below are still in chains. Why was my order yesterday ignored, Clark?"

The smaller man hesitated. It was evident that the Captain's annoyance was bubbling beneath the outer calm. He also knew that Meredith, when roused, was a formidable enemy.

"You had been so sick," Clark started whining. "Practically all my men were still very weak and even I was affected for several days." He listed the excuses like a truant schoolchild.

"That order," Meredith bristled, "originated from the Commodore himself. Do you realise that I could have you court-martialled for this?"

Antagonism crackled between the two men, Meredith knowing that Doctor Arndell would not reveal the time lapse between receiving the order and issuing it aboard *'The Friendship'*.

Clark didn't answer, thinking only how incongruous it would be to have his career besmirched by not releasing convicts from chains. He puffed defensively and stared at Meredith's coat buttons.

"In future, Lieutenant Clark, I wish to be the only officer to instigate flogging. In addition, I require that the surgeon be standing by." He turned on his heel to leave the poop-deck as the sergeant indicated all was ready. Meredith added, "See that my order is obeyed as soon as possible."

Clark saluted with a look of pure hatred, then he watched as his superior disappeared. He vowed that during that evening, he would write a letter to his Betsey Alicia with strict instructions that their son, Ralph, should never be allowed to go to sea. He turned back to the scene below him and ordered, "Fetch the surgeon."

Thomas Arndell steeled himself as he appeared. His chosen profession was dedicated to the repair of the human body, not its desecration. Flogging seemed the only method of controlling criminals, but he loathed the enthusiasm that invaded the lash-wielder. It occurred to him that by the time they reached Botany Bay, he would in all likelihood, have become inured to the sight of flesh being laid open. He doubted if he could ever condone it.

Bennett's screams percolated between decks. They'd stopped long before the rope ceased slashing at his flesh. Several heads were buried beneath striped pillows, sobs emanated from some of the female passengers but the men remained stoically silent. They had been spared the sight this time, but Gant's memory in particular, made him flinch with every stroke.

"That's enough, surely?" said Arndell angrily.

"Cut him down," Clark ordered.

The surgeon descended the steps quickly and bent to tend to the man's wounds. Then he straightened and glared at Clark. "I can do nothing. The man is dead."

CHAPTER 18

REST AT TENERIFE

A few hours later, Captain Meredith answered a tap on his door. Sergeant Stewart entered at his bidding and saluted. "Message from "*Sirius*", sir. Tenerife has been sighted."

Meredith nodded. "Has the man been buried?"

"Yes, sir. He was tossed overboard without ceremony. Lieutenant Clark said there was no time, although Mister Arndell protested."

"He should have sent for me," Meredith said. The remark wasn't in the slightest critical of his First Lieutenant, and his attitude was one of gratitude. Burials at sea were not his favourite chore.

"A further message, sir. Major Ross will be coming aboard shortly."

"Thank you, Sergeant. Ask Master Walton to hove to and notify me when Major Ross arrives." The affable soldier saluted and left smartly. Meredith sat back sighing. Lieutenant Ralph Clark's insubordination gnawed at his military training. The man deserved official reprimand. "Circumstances were difficult no doubt," he reasoned with himself. "Hopefully the man will not make a habit of this."

Major Ross arrived to interrupt his thoughts. Ross was also a short man, but more stockily built than Ralph Clark. In his inimitable style, he'd insisted on standing in the prow of the small boat that transferred from the "*The Sirius*" to each ship in turn. Once aboard, he ordered each surgeon to prepare a record of sickness since leaving Portsmouth and Plymouth. He also required the Captains to give a verbal report on the behaviour of the convicts and each one caused Ross to draw his thin lips a little tighter.

As soon as he boarded "*The Friendship*", he shook hands with Meredith and saluted the paraded marines. He jutted his chin and surveyed the ship. "You're travelling well," he said to Master Walton. "I believe you lost your topgallant mast a few days ago?"

"Ay, sir," grated the old seaman. "But we soon got up another."

Ross gave a satisfactory nod then accepted Captain Meredith's invitation to his cabin. Once there, he unbuttoned his jacket and accepted a glass of wine. "I've just left "*Scarborough*," he began. "Captain Shea asked me to pass along his regards to you. You are good friends, I believe?" Meredith nodded. "Seems he's had his share of events aboard, too. Four convicts punished a few days ago for slashing open another's calf, a woman convict gave birth to a girl, and Lieutenant Watts' goat dropped two kids." Meredith hid his smile at the grouping and determined to invite Captain Shea to dinner when they were anchored at Tenerife.

After another wine and small talk, Ross got to his feet and adjusted his uniform. "I'll inspect the convicts before I leave."

"Of course." James Meredith addressed Sergeant Stewart who was on duty outside as they left the cabin. "Women's prison first." The three men strode towards the forward hold and Stewart removed the hatch.

Elizabeth Powley sat up slowly as they descended and she brazenly challenged the men. "Hallo . . . wot 'ave we here, then? Braid and buttons, ay?"

"That's enough, Powley," said Stewart.

"He must be someone big," scoffed Liz Dudgeon, gaining courage from her bunkmate. "Even the nice Capt'n is here to hold his hand."

Beth and Liz laughed out loud when their cheeky comments made Major Ross glare. Meredith's slow fury began to burn and he knew he would have to exercise his authority or lose face with his superior.

"Hold your tongues, you shameless women. This is Major Ross." He made the announcement hoping it would quell the blatant taunting, but Liz Dudgeon, for one, was not so easily threatened.

"No wonder they took off our leg chains this morning. Come to take your pick, have yer, Major?"

Even Elizabeth Powley who had not wavered in her stare at Meredith, joined in the harsh laughter that followed Liz's taunt. The gypsy's cackle was the loudest, but it did not hide Liz's scream as she reeled from Ross's stinging blow across her mouth.

"Bastard!" she screeched, and she earned herself another slap.

"That's enough," yelled a furious Meredith as Sergeant Steward leveled his musket at the women. "This way, Major."

Shaken and white with anger, Ross stood his ground. He was trying to lay his tongue to an oath that wouldn't demean his position too badly but fit the event. Abruptly, he shouted, "Scum!"

Elizabeth Powley spat in his direction and with an evil gleam in her eyes called, "See you another time, ducky."

Ross had turned to follow Meredith and paused, his right foot raised on the ladder. Pointing a quivering finger at Elizabeth he shouted, "Put that woman back in irons for two days."

He continued to climb the steps, the prostitutes' laughter burning in his ears but once on deck, the explosive Major collected himself and saluted the reassembled guard on honour. However, he was spoiling to transfer his ire, and he turned to Meredith. "Do I understand from that woman's remark, Captain, that the chains have only just been removed?"

Meredith looked uncomfortable. In the melee, he had hoped that Dudgeon's revealing comment would pass unnoticed, but he had not allowed for Major Ross's keen intelligence. "Am I to understand that you did not receive Captain Phillip's order a few days ago?"

"I . . . er, we . . ." mumbled Meredith, wishing the Major would not speak so loudly. "There was a lot of sickness aboard, Major, myself included. I felt it wise not to implement the order immediately for the sake of safety." He was pleased with his quick thinking, especially as Ross appeared to accept his reason.

"In future, Captain," said Ross with steely import, "orders from the Commodore are to be carried out immediately when they are received. On this occasion I know Captain Phillip would regard your excuse with great leniency, but any further breach of regulations will be dealt with severely. Understand?"

Acutely aware of the marines lined along the deck, Captain Meredith joggled his hat and inwardly bristled. "Thank you, sir."

During mealtime that evening, there were heated discussions between soldiers and seamen alike. "Cor, Captain Meredith copped it from Major Ross, today," one said.

"Not like him to neglect his duty," said another. "But he'll get away with it, not like us lower classes." There was a general murmur of agreement but no more was said.

* * *

Next morning a huge mountain rose into view like an Egyptian monolith as the fleet approached Tenerife. It was the first sight of land since they had cleared the Isle of Wight at the Southern point of England and one most welcome to soldiers, sailors and convicts alike. The civilians aboard, nearly all wives and children accompanying their soldier husbands, had gathered early along the ships rail, thankful to see stability again. Fears of insecurity lessened as the ships anchored in the sunshine off Santa Cruz. Officers and men watched while Tenerife authorities rowed out to make a cursory check of each ship. Local fishermen and fruit vendors brought boatloads of produce they hoped to sell.

"The flagship did not give the customary gun salute to the port," remarked Lieutenant Faddy to Clark. They ambled along the deck observing the mouthwatering offerings below.

"No," answered Clark. "I believe it was considered there were too many casks of powder on the gun-deck to take the risk."

"Hmm," Faddy mused. "Hardly do to blow themselves out of the water, would it?"

Clark smiled wanly. He was clearly in the Captain's debt now that he had shouldered the entire blame for delaying Commodore Phillip's orders, but it gave him little comfort. His dolorous mood was not improved when Meredith hailed him from the poop-deck.

"Release any prisoners remaining in chains." Meredith was anxious to regain his absolute authority and saw no reason to inform his men that this was another directive from the Commodore.

"Supervise the exercise period, Lieutenant," Clark ordered, after acknowledging the Captain. He strode away and left the amiable Faddy watching the convicts, who gulped the freshness of the salted air as they climbed on deck.

"Bring them all up," ordered Meredith, who stood with his hands behind his back. "A little sunshine will not do any harm." Thomas Arndell appeared as he spoke, and they greeted each other warmly. "I see you also appreciate the sunshine, Doctor?"

Arndell had removed his coat and left it in his cabin. "I've no doubt we all appreciate it, Captain. Some need it more than others."

He nodded towards the frail Sara McCormick who sat wearily on the main hatch-cover. Her recovery had been slow and spasmodic, and Arndell expected her to relapse at any moment.

"How's the boy performing?" Meredith asked.

"Very well, James. By the way, Sergeant Stewart and his wife . . ."

His conversation was halted by a scuffle from behind the main gangway. Two marine privates, their arms twisted behind them by two other redcoats, were followed by the shorter figure of Lieutenant Clark. With smug indignation he was urging the group to assemble in front of Captain Meredith. He marched to the front of the marines and saluted the Captain and Doctor.

"I have just come across these men, sir. They were with two of the whores and behaving in a very unsoldierly manner."

His quaint report sent ripples of laugher around the convicts. Patrick Daley was standing near the grinning Elizabeth Powley and he leaned over to whisper in her ear. She nudged him familiarly.

Lewis and the gypsy stood behind the mainmast, obscured from the proceedings. They were content to surreptitiously share a bottle, which the seaman hid in his shirt between mouthfuls.

Further along, the two prostitutes involved with Clark's captives leaned nonchalantly against the ship's rail. Seizing his chance to challenge the Captain's authority again, Clark had ignored Beth Thackery and Liz Dudgeon who had lost no time in running away from the scuffle. Feigning disinterest, the two girls now leaned over the ship's rail and hassled the local vendors as they bobbed in their boats.

Meredith straightened his shoulders. He knew the marines had fewer tasks when they were in port, and he could well imagine the 'unsoldierly behaviour' to which Clark objected.

"Is this true?" Meredith thundered. The men nodded. "How do you expect discipline to be maintained over the convicts if you men are unable to control your lust? Animals have more self-control."

"That's it, Capt'n," yelled Elizabeth Powley, her hands clasped and resting on one hip. "Give it to 'em."

"Silence!" If Meredith had lost any standing with his subordinates over the Commodore's bungled order, he was determined to re-establish his command. The fact that Elizabeth stood laughing openly, incensed him more. He decided that he would leave no doubts about his authority. "At midday, you men are to receive twenty lashes each."

The errant soldiers were led away, and Cockney Liz poked out her tongue as they drew level. Beth Thackery winked broadly and said quietly, "Don't you worry, lads. We'll make it up to you."

Having left the poop-deck, and followed by the surgeon, Meredith paused outside his cabin. "Would you care to accompany me ashore after the flogging, Mister Arndell? It is His Majesty's birthday today, as I'm sure you know, and a celebration would not be frowned upon. Besides, I am sorely in need of relief from this whore-ship."

"I agree," said Arndell. "A good idea—if the soldiers do not require my attention."

The surgeon repaired to his Sick Bay and Meredith entered the small cabin that had already gained the familiarity of the comfortable home into which he had been born. He sat at his desk and stared at the quill he twirled in his firm hands. The prisoner Powley had an uncanny ability to remain in his mind, long after he'd faced her. He found himself fretting about the fact like a lion would consistently tongue an offending thorn.

An hour before midday, Major Ross boarded *'The Friendship"* again to get information regarding the supplies. In Meredith's cabin, he was told of the current disorder involving marines and he sent for the culprits. They were in irons below, waiting for their punishment.

The men were led into the Captain's cabin, and Major Ross eyed them sternly. "Well? What have you to say for yourselves?" The soldiers hung their heads and didn't answer. "I trust you aren't under the impression that these whores have been put aboard purely for your gratification? Where's your pride, men? You are members of one of His Majesty's finest brigade. Is this the way to celebrate his birthday?"

James Meredith stood staring out of his window, hands tightly gripped behind him as his superior countermanded the ordered punishment. Ross proceeded to give the soldiers a tongue-lashing instead. With a deepening frown, Meredith thought of Portsmouth. A bachelor's circle of friends, none of whom to his knowledge were backstabbers, was one of the important things he'd left behind.

CHAPTER 19

KING GEORGE III's BIRTHDAY

It was close on one o'clock by the time Major Ross left *'The Friendship'*. Meredith had already handed command to Lieutenant Ralph Clark in readiness for the evening's celebrations, and now he sat fondling Lady, whilst he waited for the surgeon to arrive. He glanced over to the box the carpenter, Gilson, had supplied for Lady's puppies. They mewled and crawled over each other, soft scraps of fur that lunged pink noses into the air as they searched for their mother. "Your little family looks well, Lady." The Labrador gave a pleasured sound as if she understood the compliment. Meredith nodded at the largest puppy; it was black and unmarked in any way. "We'll give that one to Lieutenant Clark, I think."

A knock heralded Thomas Arndell and Meredith bid him enter. He reached for his stiff hat as Arndell said, "A peaceful night, Captain?"

"Hopefully," Meredith answered. "And I hear that, as it is the King's birthday, there will be wine and fresh beef for everybody this evening."

"Pleasant news," smiled Arndell. "It's a pity that the convicts . . ."

"They are also to get this," interrupted Meredith. "Captain Phillip is nothing, if not humane. Shall we go?"

The two men began to perspire as they went on deck and prepared to climb down into the waiting jollyboat. Their clothing was most unsuitable for the Spanish sun. Thomas Arndell fingered the ruffle at his throat and admired the glistening physique of shirtless traders that bobbed in small boats around the fleet. He noticed the main produce seemed to consist of figs and pumpkins, and he was a little surprised at the lack of variety for this particular season. The jollyboat crew dipped their oars and with damp patches appearing on their own shirts, began rowing towards the shore.

In the restricted prison space, the closeness of hot bodies, albeit lightly clad compared to their guards, was taking an alarming toll of the convicts especially in the women's section. Sara had been the first to faint, followed by three others but no move was made to help them recover. Susannah had abandoned privacy beneath Mary's Welsh shawl and welcomed the release of her breast to feed little Henry.

Liz Dudgeon's pretty face was framed with dark locks of hair that clung to her wet skin and channeled the sweat into her eyes. "Gawd, it's hotter than bleedin' hell down 'ere."

"How would you know"? The gypsy scoffed, her olive skin greased like a basted fowl.

"Yea!" Elizabeth Powley snapped, wiping rivulets from her bared chest. "Only you would know that for sure, Barber, wouldn't you?"

"That's right," Beth chipped in, always ready to add her barb. "So shut, y'trap."

Sara stirred and moaned and Mary ignored her own discomfort to bathe the frail girl's forehead with a cloth wrung in the water barrel. It was impossible to keep the water cool below decks and therefore afforded little relief. Mary raised Sara's head gently and lifted the hair away from her clammy neck before laying her back against the moist pillow.

"Duw, Duw!" Mary said softly, calling on her God. "That girl doesn't look well at all to me."

Sergeant Stewart made a sudden appearance at the open hatchway, and called for their attention. "Everybody up on deck. Look smart, there!"

There were mixed groans of relief and disquiet as the women obeyed. Some pushed each other out of the way in order to clamber aloft first. Others were almost too weak to set foot on the rungs. But the alternative gave them strength, and aided by kinder women, they heaved themselves out of the fetid atmosphere.

Meredith had left strict orders with his two Lieutenants that the convicts were to be brought on deck while Clark and Faddy supervised. It was clear that they had no intention of remaining at the mercy of the blistering sun for any longer than was necessary.

"Carry on, Sergeant," instructed Clark. "Keep at least half a dozen men on deck with you at all times. Faddy, would you care for a lemonade?"

Faddy mused that he would care for something a little more bolstering, but accepted the offer anyway. Their uniforms were also designed for the English climate and at least below decks, they were allowed to dispense with the cloistering jackets. Few other passengers elected to stay below, however. Marine wives, seamen and convicts milled together. Some sat on coiled ropes or casks of water, and some leaned over the railing to watch the traders.

"You buy?" pleaded several. They held up large pumpkins with shiny green skins, and handfuls of tempting figs. "Da best in Espana. Pretty cheap, very good fruit."

Beth Thackery leaned over further and yelled, "How much, y'orrible Spanish Onion?"

"Pliss," came the reply. "We have no onions. Just figs. Bee-ootiful figs. See? They ripe and soft . . ."The Spaniard stroked the smooth green peel as though he was handling a new-born baby.

Beth laughed and a seaman moved to her side, slipped his arm around her waist and whispered into her carroty hair. "That's a bargain, luv," she said, and gave her familiar wink to nearby Liz Dudgeon.

The elated seaman tossed a few coins over the side into the boat and lowered a wooden bucket. The trader eagerly filled he bucket with figs, but not too generously. Beth helped her benefactor retrieve the bucket and both made their way aft to a secluded area behind the men's cooking caboose.

Mrs. Morgan and Margaret Stewart sat fanning themselves on a bench. Just over six weeks from full term, Mrs. Morgan tried to shield herself with a small blue parasol loaned to her by Margaret.

"You poor dear," sympathised the sergeant's wife. "Charles was born in July also, and I know how uncomfortable you must feel."

"I feel so nervous," nodded Mrs. Morgan. "This being our first child as well. But Mister Arndell assures me that everything is perfectly normal. I really can't wait to see the baby. It must be a boy for Mister Morgan, of course." She smiled with the doting patronage that every pregnant woman has for the child's father, and it softened her face. "Where is Charles now?"

CHAPTER 20

MORE JOY, TEARS AND FEARS

Margaret Stewart looked around instinctively, and then she smiled. "Oh, he's playing with John Hart, the boy from Mister Arndell's surgery."

Mrs. Morgan looked horrified. "Good Heavens, Mrs. Stewart, isn't he a . . . convict?"

"He is only a nine-year old boy, Mrs. Morgan," Margaret answered while smothering her amusement at the other woman's reaction. "He seems very reliable and it is such a rest for me."

"Of course." The reply was stilted. However, they soon warmed their conversation to the coming event.

Further along the deck, Elizabeth Powley and Patrick Daley leaned over the ship's rail while they talked quietly. One of the traders had tossed a molding orange at them earlier and Elizabeth watched as pieces of peel slipped from her fingers and disappeared into the slapping waves below. She tore at a juicy segment and passed it to Patrick before nibbling at one herself.

Patrick wiped his chin. "Had you thought anything about when we gets there, Elizabeth? My sentence is for seven years. What's yours?"

"The same," Elizabeth answered and spat orange pips into the water. "No, I'm going to wait till I gets there." Her steely eyes slid sideways, and she looked at his profile. "Why? Wot you got in mind, then?"

"Well, I was t'inking we could get together and maybe . . ." Patrick half turned and stroked her shoulder. "Maybe . . ."

"Maybe." Elizabeth's face softened. "Y'never knows your luck, d'you, Patrick?" She stood away from the rail. "Want to come for a walk?" A smile flickered with meaning that no full-blooded male ever misunderstood.

Nearby, Elizabeth Barber stretched back against a coil of rope and watched the pair. Her long legs protruded from the Government-issue skirt and she wiped the sweat away from inside her thighs. Her own liquor supplying seaman had been rounded up with several others and sent aloft to repair damaged rigging. She saw Daley's arm slip around Elizabeth's waist and her mouth worked vindictively as they disappeared.

"Wotcher up to, Barber?" Liz Dudgeon sauntered past just then, and laughed loudly. "Casting a spell, are yer?" Not waiting for a reply, Liz walked over to a soldier who leaned sloppily against the steps leading to the poop-deck. His uniform jacket was wide open, and Liz ran her fingers over his chest. "Doing anything, soldier?" He shrugged, tossed aside the orange he'd been eating and wandered away with her.

The gypsy's expression darkened as she moved over to the ship's rail, stood with her back to it and leaned on her elbows. She stared around at the idle seamen and a sullen anger glowed in her eyes as she gauged possible sources of liquor. She was sorely in need of a drink.

The afternoon wore on with the sun's heat beginning to shrink the deck timbers and tempers became frayed. The paleness of British skins disappeared beneath raw burns that reddened faces, shoulders, backs and knees. People squabbled for any vestige of shade around cabooses or beneath gangways and invariably the women convicts were pushed aside by the men.

Barber had regained her shelter beneath a ladder leading to the poop-deck and she was the loudest objector when the men grabbed her hair and yanked her from her refuge. A continuous stream of invectives continued from her mouth and her fingers twitched. Eventually, her noise diminished to mutterings about spells, rats and spiders.

The other three Elizabeths meantime, were well protected from the blistering sun as they used their only assets. Once sexual appetites had been sated however, the couples rolled apart and wiped at their sweat with anything handy. Beth discovered a seaman's discarded shirt in one corner and they tore it to pieces but the rags did little to mop up the bodily moistures.

Some hours later, Elizabeth Powley reappeared and Barber watched evilly as Patrick hugged her. Powley was her arch-enemy and was now wearing the smile of a recently fed tabby-cat. The lovers parted and as Elizabeth sauntered towards her, she yelled, "How much did you get that time, tiger?"

"Mind y'business," snapped the prostitute, instantly defensive.

Barber lunged at her and grabbed her blouse. She used her height advantage to throw Powley off balance and the deck resounded as the raw-boned girl landed heavily. But Elizabeth sprung lightly to her feet again and for moments, the two of them faced each other, swaying and coiled, ready to spring. An imperceptible movement of anticipation rippled around those watching, but the marine wives cringed and called for their children to return to protection.

Powley filled her mouth and her spittle slapped against Barber's face. With an inhuman screech, the gypsy launched herself and their bodies hit the deck as one. Each woman had a handful of the other's hair and they gouged, kicked, bit and scratched as they rolled.

"A threepenny-bit on the gypsy," yelled one soldier, grateful for the diversion.

"You're on," yelled another.

Alerted by the noise, Liz Dudgeon searched around the deck for Beth. She saw her friend and they nodded impishly. They ran towards the fighting women and threw themselves into the melee, not to assist Elizabeth Powley, but to seize another opportunity for vengeance on their old enemy.

Sergeant Stewart, who had been chatting to his wife, ran to the scene. He promptly ordered a nearby seaman to get a buck of seawater. Although not as cold at the English Channel water, when dashed onto the writhing women it brought gasps from them and shouts of laughter from the observers.

"I might have known," seethed Ralph Clark as he appeared on the scene. "Put them in irons—all four of them!"

Soaking wet and with salt stinging their open wounds, the four women were led away.

Sitting in the shade against the gunwale, Sara McCormick shut her eyes and leaned back as the disturbance faded. She seemed to be absorbing the sun's rays in an effort to live, but with painfully shallow breaths. Bill Gilson had removed his shirt as most of the seamen did in this climate, and he glanced down at the recumbent woman as he passed. He hesitated, and then crouched beside her. "Hello, Sara. Haven't seen you for a while."

Sara opened her eyes and regarded his slightly crooked smile. Apart from the surgeon, Gilson was the only person she felt at ease with. Most of the women shied away from her now, fearing her sickness to be contagious.

"Hello," she replied and closed her eyes again.

"Are you feeling better?" There was genuine concern in his country drawl. Sara's pale face and limp hair was an unspoken answer. "Do you still receive treatment?"

Sara's eyes opened as she nodded. Encouraged by his sympathy, a smile hovered around her lips. Lost for words however, she stared around the deck at the men and women. All ages, all classes, all captives in their own way, and the sight made her speak. "Funny how it only takes the one sun to warm us all, isn't it? Except I'm cold."

Bill stretched his legs, and then he sat beside her, acutely aware of a growing desire to touch and hold this frail creature. She spoke as if Life had already deserted her, leaving only a hollow shell. She shivered as the first small breeze of the afternoon skipped across the deck and tossed the riggings of the furled sails.

Gilson placed his broad hand timidly over hers, and smiled when she left it there. "Are you very cold?"

"Yes."

"Measuring 'er for a box, are you, Chippie?" William Gant's harsh laugh as he walked past them made Gilson start to his feet, but Sara restrained him.

"Take no notice," she murmured. "You'd think the fool would know they sew the dead bodies up in canvas."

Gilson stared at her, unable to fathom this wraith of a woman to whom Death was no dark enemy. He was a man of country hedges and fields, gentle cows, and Devonshire cream on a Sunday. His open nature could not comprehend that the almost ephemeral woman at his side had been branded a convict. They lapsed into comfortable conversation, and his description of his part of the homeland and his childhood, seemed to light a spark in Sara.

The sun had lost some of its heat by now and was slowly sinking towards the horizon. But the afternoon's languor refused to disappear. Neither soldiers, seamen nor convicts felt inclined to alter the state.

William Gant walked the length of the ship several times, and he decided to take a different route for the last tour. He assumed they would all be returned to the prison holds shortly. Rounding the men's cooking caboose, he came upon John Hart sitting with Margaret Stewart's son. The toddler was fascinated by the shadow pictures that fluttered against the wall when John twiddled his fingers.

"Look, Charlie," said the engrossed Hart. "There's a pretty butterfly." The child moved to grab at the shadow, but Gant startled him as he revealed himself.

"Well, well, well." The villain gave a sickening leer, grabbed John Hart's thin upper arm and dragged him to his feet. "If it ain't our lucky little chimney-sweep."

John's terror was obvious. "Mister Gant, sir, . . ."

"Oh, my dear . . . Mister Gant, is it? Cable's been teaching you airs and graces, too, has 'e?" His thick voice lowered and sounded ugly. "I owes you for a floggin', Hart."

He raised his other fist to slam into the boy's face and blood spurted from John's lip as it split against his teeth. A small moan from the semi-conscious boy was lost in the toddler's squeal of terror and the cry lifted in the afternoon breeze. Gant raised his boot and kicked Charles sideways along the deck as a protective rage cleared John Hart's brain. He lashed out at his captor's shins with his own boots. His pathetic defence both surprised and infuriated the ugly convict. Tightening his grip, Gant lifted the boy off his feet. He clamped his free hand around the slender throat and Hart's eyes began to bulge.

Charles scrambled to his feet and ran wailing towards his mother, although instinct already had her running towards his voice. She clasped her sobbing son and looked around wildly as Sergeant Stewart joined her.

"Where's John?" he queried angrily.

"I don't know," Margaret said in a trembling voice. "They were playing up the other end."

Thinking that John had hurt his son, and intent on revenge, Stewart signaled two soldiers as he ran. They were followed by many more alerted to the disturbance. Seamen, convicts, marines and their wives all ran, because John was well liked by everyone. Gant heard the feet thundering towards him, hesitated, and then he tossed the unconscious boy to the deck. But he was too late. Concerned people crashed around both sides of the caboose. The convict attempted to jump overboard but he was quickly overpowered.

"The boy," someone shouted. "Is he dead?"

"I 'ope he is," Gant raved hoarsely as he was handcuffed and led away.

"Oh, dear God," whispered Mrs. Morgan, crossing herself piously.

Henry Cable lifted John's limp body easily, his hatred and instinct for retaliation overwhelmed by concern for the boy. With the crowd fluttering in a sympathetic wave behind him, he carried his little friend towards the gangway leading down to the surgery.

"The Captain's coming aboard," came the shout. "Mister Arndell is with him."

Recognising the emergency immediately, Thomas Arndell hurried towards Cable and stopped him momentarily to examine the boy. "Quickly, there's no time to lose," he said, and then he led the way to the Sick Bay.

James Meredith listened briefly to details from Sergeant Stewart, and then allowed the soldier to accompany his distressed wife and son to their cabin. The afternoon foray ashore for fresh fruit and vegetables had not been very satisfactory, but he had enjoyed Arndell's company. He had returned refreshed, but his good humour did not extend to sanctioning attempted murder.

He ordered that Gant should be taken to his cabin, and that Clark and Faddy also present themselves there. Moments later he was seated behind his desk and signaled the two Lieutenants to stand at his side. James Meredith glowered at the unrepentant Gant who, despite the shackles securing his hands behind his back, managed to swagger.

"You are an unspeakable villain," Meredith began. "For this ghastly behaviour you deserve to be hanged, whether the boy dies or not. Do you hear me?"

Gant's stubbled face registered nothing but antagonism and Meredith was unable to control the rise in his tone as he continued. "Lieutenant Faddy, take some men with you and have this blackguard ferried over to '*The Sirius*'. Major Ross will no doubt take a stern view and execute the necessary punishment."

"The sprat asked for it," yelled Gant as he was bustled away. "You ain't going to hang me! You're nothing but lousy bastards, the lot o'yer!"

"The man's right," remarked Meredith angrily to Ralph Clark, as the criminal disappeared. "I'm not going to hang him. I've never hanged anyone in my entire career and I see no reason why that should change. Such final judgment should be left to the Major, or the Commodore."

A surprised Clark found himself agreeing with the Captain. He had been outraged at the incident too, especially as it had occurred during his command. The boy's vulnerability had caused him to be grateful yet again, that his own son had not accompanied him on the voyage. Any sign of capitulation towards his superior disappeared however, when James Meredith continued.

"I'd assumed you would keep a tighter discipline on board, Clark. Were your men not patrolling the deck? I don't want this sort of thing every time I leave the ship. I could punish you too, you realise?"

Clark opened his mouth to hotly refute Meredith's condemnation, but he realized in doing so he would probably have to account for his movements. The Captain, he decided quickly, did not need to know that he and Faddy had drifted into sleep below decks for most of the afternoon. So he saluted smartly and gave his assurance.

Later that evening, John Hart lay on one of the cots he normally helped to clean. He looked so small, with his pinched features practically as white as the pillowcase. Thomas Arndell watched him anxiously. His breathing had improved, but he hadn't regain consciousness.

A light tap at the Sick Bay door heralded a strained Margaret Stewart, carrying her son wrapped in a light blanket. "Mister Arndell, sir. I am sorry to bother you at this hour, but perhaps you would look at Charles?"

The portly surgeon nodded, touched Hart's forehead, and then led the way back into the surgery. "Lay him on the table there, Mrs. Stewart." He sucked in air sharply as the blanket fell away from the child's body. It revealed a purpling bruise that spread across Charles' right side. "What an animal that man is."

"Will Charles be all right, Mr. Arndell? I haven't set him on his feet since, so I don't know if he can stand."

Arndell proceeded to examine the little boy, who whimpered when the surgeon gingerly touched his ribs. "All right now, young 'un. I won't hurt."

"Are there any broken, Mister Arndell?" Margaret Stewart's hands fluttered to her mouth in anxiety.

"I think not," he said. "Children's bones are very supple, thank goodness. But the bruising will distress him, no doubt. Keep him as quiet as you can and the bruising will subside eventually. If he shows any signs of increasing pain, or develops any other symptoms, please send for me straight away. I'm going to give him a light sedative so that he can sleep this evening and I hope things will be a lot better in the morning." He measured out a small vial of liquid and put it to the boy's lips. "Good boy," he said as the medicine disappeared.

"Oh, thank you, Mister Arndell." With great relief she gathered her son to her and stroked a few curls from his forehead. She dropped a light kiss on him and he put his little arm around her neck and whimpered again. She began to rock Charles gently, and then asked, "How is John . . . er, young Hart?"

Arndell beckoned, and together they crept back into the Sick Bay just in time to see John regain consciousness. "Don't try to speak, lad," urged Arndell. "Your throat will be painful for a while. Look, here's Charles come to see you."

"Do as the doctor say, John," whispered Margaret. "And when you are fully recovered, you will be welcome to play with Charles again."

John Hart merely closed his eyes, but Arndell smiled and nodded.

* * *

Lieutenant Faddy returned from '*The Sirius*' having left Gant to the mercy of Major Ross. He climbed wearily aboard '*The Friendship*' and acknowledged the saluting marines. Before the Captain and Surgeon left that morning, they'd said that he and Clark would be welcome to dine with them later. "We'll celebrate His Majesty's birthday in style," Meredith had said. He made his way to the Captain's cabin with full intentions of excusing himself from the dinner, after he'd made his report. However, he was met halfway by a disgruntled Clark.

"The man is mad. Now he's ordered that any convict still in chains is to be released, as a mark of celebration for the King's birthday. What's more, they are all to get a special meal tonight. What's more, I've got to go and see to it! You can go and tell those disgusting criminals." Clark stumped away without waiting for Faddy's reply.

The usual twinkle was missing from Faddy as he sighed and signaled for two soldiers to accompany him to the convict holds. He did get some pleasure from making the announcement, impressing on the convicts that they should be forever grateful to His Royal Highness.

"What for?" challenged Elizabeth Powley. "Didn't do us any good when he was born, did it?"

Faddy left without replying.

The toffee-smell of roasting beef had already percolated down to the prison and strained juices into everyone's mouth. Elizabeth wiped her hand across hers, and then she gently touched her bruised eye.

"You'd be better off having your beef raw," said Liz Dudgeon beside her.

"What? And insult His Majesty?" chuckled Beth, who was clumsily sewing the torn blouse she still wore. Giving an exasperated sigh she pulled the garment over her hair, then yelled from inside as the dangling needle pricked her arm.

"Gawd. If the bleedin' King was here now," Dudgeon said, "I'd ask 'im for one of his fancy vests for you."

"Like as not," quipped the Yorkshire girl. "He's royalty. An' I'd only have to tek it off agen for his Majesty's pleasure!"

Despite themselves, the other women in the prison hold, tittered. In the corner berth Susannah watched her son as he gulped at her plentiful milk supply. Her thoughts wandered to John Hart's mother, and how heartbroken she would be if she could see her own son now. "God has a funny idea of mercy," she muttered.

Mary patted the shawl and said softly, "Oh, I wouldn't say that, love. We just have to believe that He knows what He is doing."

With something between disbelief and admiration for the Welsh girl's simple faith, Susannah looked searchingly at her friend. Her eyes then slid around to the other women. Four months of endless weeks had revealed their different personalities. Some she liked, others she loathed, but increasingly she'd become aware of the enviable bond she alone possessed.—That of mother and child.

During their meal that night, it was almost as though the succulent beef had demanded its own ruling that an uneasy truce should exist below decks. Even the four Elizabeths were content to lick their fingers until no trace of beef juices could be tasted. Then they mopped their dishes with their bread. Tired from the heat, their day's activities, and unusually replete, they spent the rest of the evening licking their wounds.

Lieutenant Faddy had not been able to avoid dining at the Captain's table, however, the evening had passed comfortably. The two Lieutenants left together and, as his cabin was a little further on than Ralph Clark's, he paused to comment on the day's events. "Major Ross wasted no time in deciding Gant's punishment when he heard the facts. I'm extremely grateful that the decision was not mine."

"My dear Lieutenant Faddy," replied Clark. "Promotion has always been my goal ever since I joined the Marines. However, in only this short time, I am beginning to wonder if my aspirations have been misguided. I volunteered for this voyage with promotion in mind, but if I had known the sort of villains and whores I'd have to deal with, I certainly would have had second thoughts."

The two men bade each other a good night. Before retiring, as was his habit, Clark kissed his gold locket. Then he opened his journal.

"Very hot today. Tempers short.

Convict William Gant accused and found guilty of

attempted murder by Major Ross

Hanged aboard 'The Sirius'

CHAPTER 21

THE LONG JOURNEY RESUMES

The fleet set sail again on the 10th June, 1787. Replenishing water supplies at Tenerife had taken longer than anticipated, and the disappointing availability of fresh vegetables worried Thomas Arndell. *'The Friendship'* dipped into the ocean swell as he stood on the poop-deck with Captain James Meredith. They had discussed the Commodore's meeting with all the physicians the day before.

"Captain Phillip is naturally disturbed about the possibility of an outbreak of scurvy. As indeed we all are," Arndell said apprehensively. He knew the terrible effects of scurvy and dreaded it happening.

Meredith nodded and watched the Tenerife shoreline recede, and he again admired the stupendous inland peak. But any feelings of adventure he'd had at the outset of this voyage were being eroded by the weight of his responsibility already. This was not helped by knowing that Major Ross had undoubtedly cast aspersions on his discipline. At the Commodore's meeting with the Captains, he felt that the lecture on maintaining tight control was mainly directed at him.

He turned away from the beautiful scene to look at Arndell. "Captain Phillip indicated that his purpose in stopping at Port Praya, before we start the long leg to Rio, is again a quest for fresh produce."

"Good," Arndell answered. "And as soon as possible, we must make the convicts assist the seamen to increase our supply of fresh fish. That, at least, will fortify everyone's diet."

Again Meredith nodded. "Well, I'm going below. I have many things to attend to." He omitted to mention to the surgeon that he also needed to rest a thickened head after dinner with Captain Shea aboard the "*Scarborough*" the night before. The two officers had been the best of friends since they attended the same training school, and both considered avoiding marriage was one of their finest achievements.

"Good Lord, man" Captain Shea had quipped. "Who needs a wife? At least you can slap a harlot in chains."

"My dog is the only Lady I shall be content with at my side," Meredith had replied and they drank yet another toast to bachelorhood.

Within three days, having sailed into increasingly squally winds but still with extremely high temperatures, Arndell found himself kept busy with renewed bouts of seasickness. John Hart was slowly recovering from his distressing event. Savage bruises on the side of his throat were slowly turning yellow, and, although his voiced remained husky, his chirpiness improved rapidly. Especially when he learned that the source of his deepest fear had been permanently removed. Propped up in the cot, he turned to Arndell who was cleaning his instruments on the other side of the Sick Bay.

"It feels awful rough out there, sir."

"Yes, it is."

"It's awful hot, sir."

"Try and lie still," said Arndell. "You will be less uncomfortable." He fluttered a white bench-cloth over his instruments, mopped his balding brow and polished his wire-rimmed spectacles. "In fact, I think I will do exactly the same myself as it appears to be quiet for a while."

He noticed that the mattress heat beneath John's thin body had brought an unhealthy flush to his face, and beads of sweat balanced on his forehead.

When he suggested that John might feel more comfortable with a book in his hands and with a normal bed under the surgery table, the boy eagerly climbed down.

"Can I have one of those with drawings in it?"

The surgeon gave John a meaningful stare and the boy added, "Please, sir?"

Arndell restrained his smile and reached for a medical tome. "Remember to take care of it, and wash your hands before you turn a page."

John was soon lost in its contents and oblivious to his surroundings.

* * *

It took six more days for the fleet to arrive at the Cape De Vere Islands, during which several prisoners had earned chains for stealing, insubordination, or fighting. The four Elizabeths numbered amongst them, of course. On one occasion, when Powley ordered Beth and Liz to steal the gypsy's bread ration while she lay in a drunken sleep, Liz had inadvertently nudged and wakened the woman, with dire consequences. Once more their shackles had been replaced, and their wrists were raw with the chafing by now.

"Thank Gawd for that," groaned Liz as the ship's motion eased in the calmer port waters. "Thought I was going to be sick again, then."

"I'll only thank God when we get there," muttered Beth, her red hair matted and limp.

"You'll be sorry," snapped Barber with her fingers twitching. "They don't like whores."

Elizabeth Powley's growl from the top berth was ominous. "Shut up, you lot."

They listened to the usual activity on deck as *'The Friendship'* dropped anchor. Together with her sister ships, she was to take on water from Port Praya. It was being used at an alarming rate on board.

Captain Meredith sat coatless at his desk, fanning himself with a piece of paper when Lieutenant Clark appeared at the open door. "You sent for me, Captain?"

"Yes, Clark. See that all convicts are taken on deck." He waved the paper in dismissal and added, "And release anyone else in irons. Let's hope the heat makes them too weary to misbehave."

Clark's familiar negative expression mirrored his doubts, but he acknowledged the order, thinking it an imposition that he and Faddy should have to supervise such an exercise when they would only be in port for a few hours.

The convicts roamed freely on deck, rubbing their wrists, stretching their limbs and taking deep gulps of fresh air. The drastic change between stifling gloom and virile sea freshness beneath the hot sun was more than many of them could take. Some huddled in shadows. Others stood motionless against the ship's rail for a few moments then sank to their knees, crying. Among the more hardy, Elizabeth Powley spotted Patrick Daley and headed his way.

"Elizabeth, m'darlin." The Irishman greeted her with his black curls clinging to his clammy face. He was breathless and strangely pale.

"Here, you all right?" Elizabeth quizzed, leading him into the shade.

"T"be sure, colleen. I never did like the heat. 'Tis a wonder them divils didn't leave us down there today. 'Tis as hot as hell."

Elizabeth grinned slyly and nudged him with her hip. "Are you too hot for me, too?"

"Even d'real hell couldn't make me that hot," he grinned back and they walked arm in arm, out of sight. Beth Thackery had been watching them with blue eyes laughing, and then she turned to link arms with Liz. They both leaned over the rail.

"Gawd, it's hot," said Liz, flapping her blouse away from her body. "Come on, Beth. Let's go and find them soldiers."

They wandered away and Elizabeth Barber smiled evilly, shading her eyes as she watched them go. A hatred born of *'Mercury"* days had welled in her brain during the previous weeks. Fed by constant irritations and taunts, it had prompted her to a plan of revenge. By sharing her favours between Lewis, her regular liquor supplier, and his shipmate, she'd persuaded both of them to waylay the two prostitutes and give them a beating.

Convicts and soldiers, marine-wives and off-duty seamen dozed in the trembling heat, lulled by the vessel's gentle movement. One or two strolled along the deck, other spoke quietly in small groups, as if the humidity weighted too heavily for them to lift their voices.

The gypsy sat atop a coil of rope and waited, with evil anticipation.

Deep in conversation and nearing a gangway that led below deck, Beth and Liz gave small shrieks as grasping hands clamped over their mouths from behind. Black and red hair tossed as they struggled like wildcats, but the two seamen overpowered them and dragged them below into a darkened area.

"If you makes another sound," Lewis hissed from behind Beth, "it's killin' you, we'll be. Not just giving you a good belting!"

Beth stopped struggling and stared at Liz, who had heard the promise. Then she closed one eye in a broad wink. Without warning, her lithe body crumpled to the ground and Lewis stumbled over her as he was thrown off balance. "Jesus Christ," he swore, "the bitch has fainted."

Taken off guard, the other sailor dropped his hands away from Liz and she tried not to let her shoulders shake with laughter as she knelt. She put her arm around Beth and the two liquor-soaked sailors were obviously unsure of what to do in such unexpected circumstances. Beth's eyes slowly opened. "Come now, lads," she said softly. "I'm sure we could find something nicer to do on this hot afternoon. What d'you think?"

Lewis was trying to clear his head and the other man stood with his jaw gaping. Beth and Liz scrambled to their feet and they chuckled as they slid soft arms around the sailors. "C'mon now, luv," whispered Beth into Lewis's ear. "I promise yer I'll be better than the gypsy."

Liz tossed her hair and rubbed her knee along the inside of the other man's thigh. He shuddered with lust and buried his face into her creamy neck. Both couples sagged at the knees and gradually lowered themselves to the floor. The women rained moist kisses over the men's faces and the men desperately fumbled beneath their skirts.

That evening, with all in readiness for weighing anchor at first light, *'The Friendship'* rang with laughter from the women's prison as Beth and Liz related their story about seducing their abductors. Seething with defeat in her berth, Barber swigged on a bottle of liquor that Lewis had sent, via the two whores, to placate her. The defeated men also sent her a promise of more liquor if she didn't cast a spell on them.

"There you are, you witch," taunted Beth. "We've done you a favour, instead."

Within twenty-four hours of leaving port, the fleet was becalmed. It was to be a long haul to Rio de Janeiro as it was, and this delay did nothing to cheer the voyagers. Captain Meredith lay undressed on his bunk. His two lieutenants succumbed to the intense and still heat, and did the same. In the Sick Bay, and in order to gain as much ventilation as he could, Thomas Arndell had opened all the doors and windows. John Hart dozed shirtless under the examination couch in the surgery and Arndell envied him. He had already removed his own coat and was gazing out to the motionless sea contemplating removing his shirt when a lethargic marine tapped on the door-frame.

"Excuse me, sir," he began, "but you're needed in the women's prison."

Arndell sighed and, electing not to replace his coat, followed the marine. "What's the problem, Corporal?"

"Several of them have fainted, sir. With the heat, I expect." he turned and added meaningfully, " . . . and McCormick hasn't regained consciousness yet!"

Arndell began to hurry. "Haven't they been allowed on deck?"

"No, sir," came the reply. "No-one's given any orders."

Arndell reeled at the heat and stench as he clambered into the gloom of the women's prison. A few of them were moaning and many tried to move the air by fanning their skirts.

"There's no air in here to move," Arndell growled. He raised his voice to the marine who had wisely stayed on deck. "Get to the Captain immediately. Advise him of the situation. And get someone to carry McCormick to the Sick Bay."

The fuming surgeon crossed to Sara and felt for a pulse. "Heat exhaustion," he muttered and crossed to wring cloths in water, before laying one on her forehead. He placed another over her chest as Sergeant Stewart appeared in the open hatchway.

"All you women on deck," he commanded. "There's two men standing by to get that one to the Sick Bay, Mister Arndell."

"Well, they're no good up there," said Arndell crossly. "Send them down here. Some of these women will be unable to climb the ladder unaided anyway. You go and see that the male prisoners are all right. I assume the Captain's released them, too?"

Steward affirmed this and disappeared as two reluctant soldiers descended into the fetid atmosphere. The more able women clambered aloft immediately, and the soldiers dragged others behind them without ceremony. Mary and Susannah had been so occupied dousing water over the baby that their own discomfort had been forced into the background. However, they eagerly joined in the exodus. Once on deck the convicts found the unbearable sun almost as distressing as their gloomy quarters. At least the air was fresher. Meredith had ordered Faddy to take watch, but it was obvious that none of the convicts had the energy to escape, even if there had been an opportunity.

By the following day, a light wind had risen and so had everyone's spirit. Sara was the only patient in the Sick Bay now that John Hart was much improved, and despite her weakness, she also brightened. So much so that Arndell felt he could leave the boy to watch over her.

Thomas Arndell was preparing to make his weekly inspection of the convicts' quarters when Lieutenant Clark appeared. He noted that the little man looked unusually cheerful. "Lieutenant—what can I do for you?"

"Mister Arndell, I wondered if you would like to join some of us in the Captain's cabin after dinner this evening? It's the third anniversary of my marriage tomorrow, and Captain Meredith has kindly agreed to my request that extra liquor rations be issued to the crew and marines."

Scarcely disguising his astonishment, Arndell accepted Clark's invitation, then he walked with him towards the main deck. "You and your good wife have a son, I believe?"

"This is so," smiled Clark, obviously pleased to discuss his family. "He's also named Ralph. I had thought I might name the puppy after him—one of Lady's, of course." Encouraged by the surgeon's nod of understanding, Clark went on. "But I've decided to name it Efford, in honour of my dear wife's family home."

"Efford?" queried Arndell.

"That's right," affirmed Clark.

"In that case, we'll have plenty to celebrate at the Captain's table tonight," said Arndell brightly "I'll look forward to it."

The two men went on their way, but their words brought a slow smile across Elizabeth Powley's face as, unobserved, she stood under the steps to the poop-deck. She had been sulking because Patrick Daley had not appeared today.

"Sounds like they'll all be pretty busy tonight," she muttered to herself. "Time for some fun, eh? Don't see why we can't get a bit of liquor, too. And I fancies a bit more grub, I does."

She eased herself from her hiding place and stretched luxuriously, enjoying the balmier drop in temperature. "See if I care, Daley."

Word soon went around the convicts that there would be no fear of discipline that evening. Clark plied everyone with Madeira wine or brandy, and mugs were beaten on the table in tempo with boisterous songs. No amount of persuasion, however, could get him to acknowledge the many toasts to Betsey Alicia in anything other than lemonade. Nevertheless, drunk with unaccustomed happiness, his responsibility for the convicts' behaviour was the furthest thing from his thoughts.

"Hark at them," scoffed Elizabeth Powley as the laughter and singing drifted through the ship. "Give them another hour and you can get a move on."

She addressed Liz Dudgeon, whose pixie face was alight with mischief. The Cockney had listened to the explicit instructions and licked her lips at the picture of the rewards. Then she hesitated. "What if I can't find, em?"

"Then you don't come back 'til you have, do you?" Powley stared levelly at her pretty berth mate. "You'll find someone, just so long as he's got plenty of food and liquor. And two mates."

A blurry voice hissed from the gypsy's berth. "Make that three, or I'll raise the alarm and rat on all of you."

"Gawd, she's with us again," taunted Liz, leaning over. "Find yer own bleedin' grog, gypsy." Barber lashed out but Dudgeon drew back sharply, spitting out "Bitch!"

Elizabeth Powley shrugged and uncrossed her legs. "We might as well. We don't want her spoiling the fun. Anyway, we know who she wants."

Enjoying the joke, Beth and Liz chorused, "Lewis!"

A ribald version of an old drinking song filtered into the prison and no-one came to secure the hatch over the women by nine o'clock. This told Elizabeth that the time was ripe. She nudged Liz towards the ladder and hissed to the rest of the women.

"If one of you is even thinking about yelling a warning, I'll scratch your eyes out." Her own glinted with a mixture of threat and anticipation but she need not have bothered. Most of the women were either too sleepy or too disinterested to concern themselves. Their sense of right and wrong had long ago been swallowed into the ocean as their debilitating journey continued.

Liz peeped over the top of the hatch, then she grinned to her compatriots. "Flat as pancakes out 'ere." She wasn't referring to the sea, even though the huge coin of a moon silvered a path across the gently undulating waves—lazy waves that occasionally broke and skipped white-lace over the surface. She hauled her trim body onto the deck and chucked a sleeping soldier under his chin. Gently removing a bottle from his hand, she took a swig, and before moving on muttered, "Ta ducks, but you're no good to me."

Within five minutes, she was clambering back into the hold. "I've set up Lewis," she said excitedly, and then she turned to Beth. "And our two soldier-boys."

"What about me," said Elizabeth, secretly hoping that Patrick was waiting.

"All the men are wandering around out there and there's nobody much to care wot we does. You can choose your own."

Liz's chuckle was lost in the mad scramble for the steps and Barber landed heavily when Elizabeth Powley pushed her aside. But the lure of liquor prevented anything more than a thick curse from the gypsy. Within moments, the four Elizabeths had disappeared. A pregnant silence fell over the other women as the temptation to follow suit began to take a hold. No one moved however, until Mary got to her feet. "Come on, cariad," she said to Susannah. "A little evening walk will do us all a power of good."

Her leadership was quickly followed and the women gulped the pleasure of warm night air as they clambered on deck. Disheveled guards slept on, and the one or two that did arouse were beyond caring. The groups soon became couples that drifted quietly into the shadows. Others found rope coils or casks to sit on, and a few leaned over the rail watching fascinated as the ship's wake slowly streamed by.

"Hello, my love," said Henry Cable, putting his arms around Susannah from behind. He kissed her neck. "I was going to come and get you." With a little cry of delight, Susannah snuggled back into his embrace, taking care not to crush their son who slept smooth and cherubic in the moonlight.

"Here," said Mary. "Give him to me. You have a little walk together." So saying, she lifted the baby from Susannah's arms and started crooning as she wandered away.

"Oh, Henry." Susannah melted into his strong arms as he drew her behind a cooking caboose. "I can't tell you how much I've wanted you to hold me."

"You don't have to," he replied thickly. "Oh, my Susannah." He stroked her hair and kissed her mouth as though she were made of spun sugar or could vanish into his dreams before he could fill his senses with her softness and make love to her.

CHAPTER 22

LOVE, DEATH AND A STORM

Long after the convicts had returned themselves to their berths, some of them lay smiling into the darkness. The gypsy had stopped vomiting in a drunken stupor. The silence was only broken by the ship's timbers as they strained against the waves, and the occasional flapping from sheets set full to catch the slightest breeze. Elizabeth Powley's expression was of stone. She had earlier laughed loudly at Thackery and Dudgeon's giggled tales of their exploits with their soldier-boys, and gained their admiration when she told them that she had seduced two marines. But her heart was heavy. She'd really spent the entire evening alone, thinking of Patrick.

When he'd not appeared on deck with his compatriots, Elizabeth had toyed with the idea of another man. Or maybe going down into the men's prison to see if Patrick was still there. Thoughts that he may have found another conquest made the queries stick in her throat when other men approached. Nor could she be bothered to flirt with any of them. She'd eventually shrugged off thoughts of the Irishman while she enjoyed bread and pork crackling she'd stolen from the cook's caboose. Only now did Patrick's grin return to haunt her, so much so that the smell of her surroundings became unnoticeable as her body yearned for the highway robber.

"Bleeding Mick," she muttered, and she closed her eyes.

* * *

By seven the next morning the endless sky had turned into a grey roof, which made the sea a heaving body of Indian ink. Tempers were miserable above and below decks. Those who had not imbibed were quickly demoralized by those who had, and the convicts' fleeting hour of freedom had only served to emphasise their plight.

Ralph Clark, in spite of the quick smile he gave the new puppy that snuggled in a box near his bunk, had also regained his depressed air. "What a way for any man to spend his third anniversary." He thrust his arms into his uniform jacket then bent to stroke the puppy. "If only my little Ralphy could play with you, Efford. If only my dearest Betsey . . . every day I miss them, but days like this are even more painful. I wish I'd never . . ."

He broke off, with tears misting his eyes. Then he shook himself and set his face. "You're a marine, Clark. You must think of your county and your duty." He adjusted his uniform and strode towards the main deck. He and the ship's Master were to discuss the rearrangement of some of the marine equipment on board. It was proving to be a hindrance to the seamen.

Sergeant Stewart had not drunk as much as some of his colleagues and moved alertly although obviously concerned. Clark heeded the man's look of concern and asked sharply, "What is it, Sergeant?"

"We'll have to get the surgeon, sir."

"Who's sick?" demanded Clark, annoyed at the interruption.

"It's about one of the male convicts, sir."

Clark gave his usual paranoid sigh. "Carry on, Sergeant."

Clark and Thomas Walton turned away and left the concerned marine to make his way to the Sick Bay. He had to knock several times loudly, before John Hart nervously opened the door.

"Mister Arndell, sir, ain't well," the boy volunteered. "He's asleep."

"I'll wake him," said Stewart, brushing past John. "This is serious."

"No need," said Arndell, struggling into his coat as he appeared. "I heard. Lead the way, Sergeant."

The two men hurried back on deck as Arndell asked, "Is it Charles?"

Stewart shook his head, and led the way to the men's prison. They clambered down the steps and Arndell saw that some of them were still asleep. Others sat quietly, or they nursed aching heads. Few were interested in the surgeon's presence.

"It's Daley, sir," said Stewart, pointing to the unconscious man.

"Yeah," someone snarled. "He's as drunk as a bishop."

Arndell examined Patrick. He lifted the Irishman's slack eyelids and felt the stone-cold forehead, and then he turned solemnly to Sergeant Stewart. "Notify the Captain," he said. "The man's dead."

Born of confusion and mortal fear, a strange silence settled over everyone as the news was passed around. Tenuous though their lives may have been, few were brave enough to be unaffected by the departure of a soul, especially one that had been part of their daily routine. While they watched Arndell make a few cursory preparations, their eyes filled with an inherent suspicion of each other. The surgeon had made no mention of a wound, nor had he vouchsafed any other reason for the man's death. Cable buried his head in his hands, Lewis mouthed questions to his bunkmate, and John Gilson faced the wall with an expression just as solid and inscrutable.

"Get the ship's sail maker," said Arndell when Stewart returned. "There's no reason why the man shouldn't have a decent burial as sea."

Cable raised his head and asked quietly, "Why did he die, sir? He was often in pain." Henry Cable was the only one brave enough to ask.

Arndell shook his head without replying and made his way up the ladder intent on protocol. He headed for Captain Meredith's cabin. He needed to deliver his report and complete the necessary paperwork. |"The convict Cable told me that Daley had complained pain on several occasions. It appears the man died of a sudden and massive heart stoppage."

Meredith sucked his teeth and his lips pursed as he made the required notation in the ship's log. "At least he will be spared the remainder of our journey, and God knows what awaits us at Botany Bay."

"You sound doubtful of Captain Cook's description of the place. He was very complimentary about its possibilities."

"At this moment," answered Meredith as he sat back. "I doubt most things. But it's a frame of mind I must control." Reaching out to the bottle on his desk, he added, "Perhaps a glass of Madeira wine would help. You will join me?"

Arndell nodded grimly.

Around mid-morning a marine clattered halfway down the ladder into the women's prison. Most of them looked apprehensively at the red-coat. They always feared the worst. The four Elizabeths stared defensively.

"Everybody on deck," he ordered. "They've got to bury a man."

The women looked at each other in a silent question, and followed the marine as he disappeared up the ladder. Their silence was broken by Elizabeth Powley who said sarcastically, "I wonder who's joining King Neptune? Not our lovely Captain, is it?"

"Hold yer tongue, Powley," snapped the marine as he waved his musket at her.

Elizabeth pulled an impish face when he turned, and they all assembled on the main deck. Susannah suddenly realized as she looked for Henry, that it could have been him. He was her security. Nothing could ever happen to him, surely? A swell of emotion filled her as she saw him, broad-shouldered and serious, with Bible in hand. He was standing beside the plank that was being held by two seamen. It supported a canvas-shrouded body, feet towards the ocean, in readiness for its final journey.

"Can't be one of the crew,' observed Liz Dudgeon. "He ain't been sewn through th'nose."

"Pity it's not him," said Beth, nodding towards Lieutenant Clark. Together with Lieutenant Faddy, he was climbing to the poop deck to stand beside Captain Meredith and Thomas Arndell. Of late, Clark had taken to victimizing Beth, especially since he'd overheard her referring to him as "Little Clarky."

A subdued murmur drifted through the gathered throng as they waited for all the officers to take their place. The murmur was the dead man's name being circulated. The whisper reached Beth and her eyes widened. She hesitated, looked for a long moment at Elizabeth Powley who was standing beside her, and then she passed along the information. The only visible reaction from Elizabeth was a hardened expression. Her mouth twitched, and then she turned and passed the message to Mary Watkins.

The disheveled gypsy nudged Elizabeth from behind and snorted, "Ha!"

Powley stood like stone.

The Captain's voice rang out, "Carry on, Cable."

Henry's voice floated above the creak of straining timbers as he read a simple text from the Bible. The words reminded men and women of all ranks that in death, everyone is equal. Elizabeth Powley's face was a mask and she seemed oblivious of the ceremony. Her life of deprivation and self-preservation had inured her to unexpected losses. She felt only the same cold deadening within her that she'd experienced long ago, when her small dog was strangled by a drunken labourer. The man had considered the dog had no right to yap when he was ravishing its mistress. Elizabeth briefly wondered at her inability to feel anything other than betrayal.

A woman and daughter in front were quietly sniffling. It was a sadness that overwhelms many people at funerals, irrespective of the departed's identity. A solemn hymn known by all was sung, and the querulous voices rose above the sound of sliding canvas as the sailors tilted the plank. Few heard the sea part to receive the corpse. There was a brief silence before Captain Meredith stepped forward. "You may all remain on deck."

The crew returned to their duties and people drifted away with no inclination to remain at the scene. Only Elizabeth Powley stood at the rail, staring down into the dark undulating water, while the breeze played with her hair. Her lips were tightly drawn and her shoulders were rigid as a great battle for control raged beneath her flimsy blouse. But her eyes remained dry.

Clark and Faddy acknowledged the Captain before they left, and Arndell stayed long enough to comment. "Such a healthy looking man, too. Well, I must get on."

Sobered by the occasion, Meredith stood watching Elizabeth. It hadn't taken long for her to be proved the ring-leader amongst the trouble-makers. It was as if her blatant stare the morning after the Newgate prisoners embarked, had been a challenge to his authority rather than to his manhood. Elizabeth felt his eyes on her and turned to repeat her challenge. He straightened his back and shivered, before leaving the deck.

Roberts, one of the four seamen who had broken through the bulkhead at the Mother bank months before, was aloft. He was affecting some repairs to the mainsail, and grinned towards the rugged man working alongside him. "Fine looking tart, that."

"Ay," the other answered, having been another culprit. "Fine night that was, too." They worked in silence for a few minutes, the heavy ropes grazing their hands. Roberts suddenly said, "You up for another one?"

"No thanks." His reply was vehement. "One flogging's enough for me." He paused before adding, "Mind you, we was daft last time. And we didn't even try to avoid trouble. We could try again, and do it proper like."

"What about the other two?" Roberts asked. "Betcha won't coax Gilson."

Later in the afternoon, they stopped the carpenter near the mainmast, and drew him to one side. "How about it, Gilson? We need you to make a proper job of it, this time. Fix it so's the tarts can come and go without being spotted." The lusty sailors tried hard but Gilson was not to be persuaded.

"Well, just keep your trap shut, then," Roberts growled. "If we gets caught we'll swear you was in it anyhow."

Refusing to be drawn the carpenter shrugged and continued on his way to build a crib for Mrs. Morgan's imminent baby. Nearing the prow, he came across Sara walking slowly on the arm of Mary Watkins. He hesitated, and then he drew Sara aside.

"Call me if you want me, cariad," said Mary, before continuing her walk alone.

"Sara," said Gilson. "I don't want you asking any questions, but I think you know how I feel about you?"

Sara studied his open face, and then a small frown creased her forehead. "What are you talking about?"

"Just that . . . well, I wouldn't like you to be persuaded . . . I mean . . . tell them you don't feel well, or something." Sarah's amazed reaction made him flush. "Just stay out of trouble. Will you promise me that, Sara?"

Something in his face halted her questions and she nodded silently, her pale lips parting in a brief smile.

Gilson squeezed her arm before he walked on. "I love you, Sara."

Sara watched him swing away jauntily and, for the first time, the colour that stained her fair complexion was not due to the state of her health.

Within a few hours, the winds turned to blow from the south-west. Hoarsely bellowed orders rang for the sheets to be set to accommodate the blustery wind and the sultry heat, that always accompanies a gathering storm, increased the discomfort. Huddled groups watched the lightning break through the grey canopy and split in a dazzling network. The sea grew angry and thunder rolled across the little fleet like an avalanche of boulders.

One of Lady's pups escaped the boatswain's pouch and was immediately swept overboard. Walton's barked command stopped the seaman trying to save the puppy and Faddy reacted quickly. He had no desire for unnecessary fatalities while he was in command so he barked his own order. "Everyone get below straight away!"

"Set as many casks as you can," shouted the ship's Master. He was well aware of the dangers of dehydration in equatorial heat, and that gave him two reasons to collect the rainwater. He could sell it to the marine's wives, who had been complaining for weeks about washing their hair in seawater.

The convicts were herded below and, rolling with the ship, they clung to benches and stanchions for dear life. Some prayed as the storm increased and others seemed unconcerned. But they all swore that if they did get to Botany Bay, they would never set to sea again.

Elizabeth Powley, whose silence since the morning's burial had not gone unnoticed, lay in her berth and stared at the deck above, a strange expression flitting across her face. The sound of crashing waves and creaking timbers grew and no-one heard her muttered words. "Go on, stir it up, Patrick Daley. They should have known better than to trust you to the deep."

Beth and Liz Dudgeon exchanged glances, recognizing the reason for Elizabeth's aloofness, but unable to guess her thoughts. Unable to stand the tension any longer, Liz prodded Powley in the ribs. "Here, guess wot that bastard, Roberts, is planning?" Elizabeth turned her head, but didn't answer. "Another Portsmouth," the Cockney girl persisted. "That's wot!"

Elizabeth sat up with a hardened expression, as though the news was a cold wave that dashed away memories and sorrows. "Right, I'm on. How about you, McCormick? You're looking a bit perkier these days."

Sara shook her head.

"Ah, c'mon!" taunted Liz. "Perhaps your chippy will be with them. Ooh, look . . . she's blushin'." Beth joined in the laughter. It was a strange laughter from all those nearby, mingled with fear for their lives in the tossing storm.

Elizabeth Barber lunged forward groggily from her berth, and stood swaying. Then she staggered back onto her mattress. "I'll be in it."

"You couldn't stop opening your mouth for grog long enough to open y'legs!" Beth's yelled taunt gave rise to ribald laughter that served to release the morning's tension. Shielding Susannah and her baby from the violent rise and fall of the ship, Mary silently cursed the whores as much as the storm.

Having buried her emotions, Elizabeth Powley clambered down from her berth and straddled the bench where they sat for meals. She clung to a stanchion and spoke to Beth. "When are they going to . . . ?"

"Search me," the Yorkshire girl interrupted. "Ask Liz—she knows all about it."

Liz leaned over precariously from her berth and said conspiratorially, "Going to wait their chance, they are. And we're not going anywhere, are we?"

The truth in her words tolled like a knell and they all rode out the storm in silence. It quickly blew itself out, leaving a humid blanket that seemed to thicken the air and lend it a tremendous weight. Elizabeth Powley clambered back to her berth and stretched out, making an unspoken vow never to let another man possess her, without he paid dearly.

A calmer week of boredom followed for officers, marines, convicts and crew. A small group of marine wives met each afternoon to play bridge, and the convicts and seamen tried to enliven the day's fishing by gambling on who would haul the greatest catch. Most of the female convicts tried to fill their day by washing clothes, or repairing torn shirts and missing button for the seaman. The sea and sky were so endless it was hard to believe the small fleet was making any headway. More than twenty-five days had elapsed since they'd left Tenerife, and it would take another month's sailing before they reached Rio de Janeiro.

Captain Meredith entered the Sick Bay where the surgeon was attending two crewmen who had been injured during the storm. He was obviously preoccupied but when Arndell looked up, he signaled the surgeon to carry on while he took a chair and waited.

A trusted convict had been assigned to the Sick Bay as an attendant, and Arndell instructed him to finish bandaging the broken arm he was working on. Turning back to James Meredith, he indicated the way back into his surgery. "A glass of brandy, Captain?"

"Thank you," nodded Meredith. "A pleasant change."

The two men seated themselves in the surgery and the golden liquid poured into two glasses. Arndell said, "I'm a little concerned about the water supply. Cable tells me that the Supply officers have become less than generous when handing out the bulk rations."

"That's true," answered Meredith as he accepted his glass. "As a matter of fact, I have just received a signal from the Commodore. He wants the water ration cut to three pints a day for each man. However, you'll be relieved to hear the surgeons and people in the Sick Bays are not to be restricted."

"I thought we'd be better off after the storm," Arndell said. "Mr. Walton seemed to be arranging conservation barrels."

"It didn't rain enough," said Meredith flatly.

"No," Arndell mused, and then he looked past Meredith to the door. "Yes, Hart? What is it?"

"Please sir," John said. "Henry Cable says I can 'ave a reading lesson." He looked guiltily at the imposing figure sitting opposite the surgeon. "If y'don't mind, sir."

"Yes, get along," nodded Arndell. He noted James Meredith's restrained amusement and added, "Worse than having a son."

Meredith finished his drink and was preparing to leave when Arndell remembered. "Was there something in particular you wanted, Captain?"

"Not really. Sometimes a person needs to talk with a friend." Arndell looked quizzical until Meredith turned back as he neared the door. "There's also been a message that Captain Shea on *Scarborough* is dangerously ill. Mortification of the Saliva Glands—whatever that means. Their surgeon doesn't expect him to live for more than an hour."

"Oh, good Lord," said Arndell. "He was a particular friend of yours wasn't he?"

"Still is," said Meredith, refusing to acknowledge the tragedy. "You must be quite familiar with man's mortality, Thomas. I'm afraid I . . ." His sentence was left unfinished and he left Arndell deep in thought. Although they were good friends, they rarely used each other's first name and Arndell realized how upset the Captain was.

Meredith walked slowly back t his cabin and was met by Sergeant Stewart, who had obviously been looking for him. "You're required on deck, sir. Some seamen have been caught cutting a door in the bulkhead again."

Meredith groaned. "The same men?" The Sergeant nodded. Inside his cabin, he found Roberts and two others standing handcuffed between two soldiers. They had been unable to persuade Gilson to join them, but the carpenter had not disclosed their plot. It was their clumsiness in attempting the carpentry themselves that had exposed them. An alert marine had passed near the bulkhead at the very moment when Roberts had allowed a saw to slip and jag at his thumb, and the convict cursed loudly. The wound was still bleeding and dripped slowly onto the cabin floor. An anger born of despondency surged in Meredith as he observed this, and he rose to his feet ominously behind his desk.

"I will not stand any more of this. I don't know which is worse—you, or the whores. Fifty lashes each immediately."

Ignoring the gasps of horror from the culprits, he turned away as they were led out. He stared through the window, inwardly fuming. It gave him no pleasure at that moment, to recall Lieutenant Clark's gloomy prediction. In fact, his only solace seemed to lie in the bottle of Madeira wine that stood enticingly on his table. Some hours later, suitably mollified, he sat staring at a letter he was trying to write. It occurred to him that the middle of the Atlantic Ocean was hardly the place to effect his resignation, and he tossed his quill onto the desk. He poured another glass, swirled the rich liquid and stared at the hypnotic movement, then he made a decision. "Sergeant!" Stewart appeared at the doorway. "Fetch the female prisoner, Powley."

CHAPTER 23

ELIZABETH POWLEY'S VICTORY

The floggings had been executed and everyone was still on deck, so he climbed up to the poop deck to scan the convicts. He saw Elizabeth standing alone by the ship's rail and looking out to sea. "Powley! The Captain wants you."

"I'll bet he does," muttered Elizabeth. She was vaguely surprised but too despondent to challenge the order. Sergeant Stewart climbed down the stairway to lead her below, and she grinned. "You too, ducky?"

"Enough of that," he snapped. Elizabeth walked ahead of him, her thin skirt flapping in the breeze. Stewart nudged her into Meredith's cabin. "Convict Powley, sir."

Meredith remained seated and as the marine left, he regarded the well-built woman. Defiance glittered in her green eyes as she held his gaze. "Elizabeth Powley. That is your name?" She stood swaying slightly with the ship's movement, but said nothing. "Speak up, woman. Is that your name?"

Elizabeth recognized the voice of alcohol and answered quietly, without passion or fear. "Yes."

Meredith bristled. "It seems to me that you are the ring-leader amongst those women."

"Wot? D'yer means all of 'em, Capt'n?" She could see feigned innocence infuriated him but was on guard immediately when he made an obvious effort to retain a hold on his temper. Her chin lifted slightly. "They all do as they likes."

James Meredith reached for the bottle on his desk, but he changed his mind. "I once asked all convicts to make harsh discipline unnecessary. Why do you see fit to challenge me?"

Elizabeth shrugged. "Why do you lot see fit to haul us to Botany?"

"God, woman! That's your own doing. Nothing to do with me . . . er, us. Do you think we enjoy being cooped up with a ship load of harlots, thieves and murderers?"

She knew he did not expect an answer, but watched him keenly as he relented and poured himself another Madeira wine. His hand shook, and Lady sidled over to lay her glossy head on his thigh. The faithful expression that only dogs seem to possess glowed from the soulful eyes, and he fondled her ears.

"Nice dog, that," volunteered Elizabeth, testing Meredith's unguarded moment.

"Too nice to be cooped up." Meredith drained his glass, apparently forgetting Elizabeth's presence.

The convict woman's shoulders softened imperceptibly and she leaned forward. The late afternoon sunshine glinted onto her tobacco colored hair and gave her eyes an arresting luminosity. "I could make things nicer."

Elizabeth realized that she could cause an immediate and violent reaction, but played her chance. The heavy wine had soaked into Meredith's senses as he stared into the empty glass. Receiving no answer, she eased around the large desk until she stood at his side. He lifted his head, rose uncertainly and Elizabeth placed her hand on his upper arm to steady him.

"Careful, ducky," she whispered. "Can't have the nice Capt'n falling now, can we?" Her face was level with his and, for a long moment, she stood still, careful not to taunt him. She moved slowly closer and recognizing the growing desire in his eyes, ran her tongue over her lips. Fighting down the urge to dig her nails into the flesh of his cheeks, she slid her left hand up his arm and the other rested lightly on his shoulder. Her right hand fingertips traced his jawbone until she cupped his chin and drew him down, before she pressed her mouth hungrily on his.

Meredith groaned, shuddered and he grabbed at her. But not quickly enough to stop Elizabeth's hand as it dropped to fondle his hardening crotch. Fire seared through his veins and with a strangled cry, he threw her to one side Taken off guard, Elizabeth sprawled on to the floor and Meredith headed for the door, turned the key, then he spun to face her. Her breasts rose and fell in an undeniable temptation and the smile on her lips was nothing short of wicked.

With a loud groan, Meredith tore off his coat, unhitched his trousers, and fell across her. Elizabeth rolled from under him, he turned over, and she used all her experience to tantalize him before allowing him to take her in a passion that released all his fears, frustrations and inhibitions.

A little later, while he was spread-eagled and asleep on the floor, Elizabeth got to her feet. She chuckled softly in her victory, knowing full well the extent of her power over the Captain in future. She swigged wine from the half empty bottle of Madeira, and then let herself quietly out of the door.

A few hours passed when a loud knocking thumped painfully into Meredith's brain. He groaned and clasped his head, then tentatively struggled to his feet. The knocking persisted and Meredith called angrily, "Stop that and wait a minute!"

"Captain Meredith, sir "came Clark's petulant voice. "There's a message from the *Scarborough,* sir."

"Yes, yes, "Meredith snarled as he scrambled into his uniform and ran his fingers through tousled hair. He sat at the desk and replace the bottle stopper before calling, "Well, come in!"

The little lieutenant bounced into the cabin and glanced around curiously, noticing the Captain's reddened complexion and the almost empty bottle.

"Message from the *Scarborough* sir. Captain Shea has taken a turn for the better, and is now expected to live." Clark was at a loss to understand the look of mortification that appeared on Meredith's face. He waited while his superior poured the last drop of Madeira for himself and drained the glass. "Captain?"

"Fetch Powley here to me."

"Powley? You mean the convict woman?"

"Ye Gods, man! How many Powley's are there on board?" He replaced the bottle stopper and stared into the empty glass. "And handcuff her."

Clark saw the folly of further questions and tipped his hat. He stumped his way along the deck aggressively, relaying the Captain's orders to a marine. He had no idea what Powley was guilty of this time, and was beyond caring.

Prodded by the marine with his musket, Elizabeth again stumbled into Meredith's cabin. He stood shaking with fury and dismissed the equally curious soldier.

"You're a glutton, aren't you?" Elizabeth goaded. Her breasts stood proud from having her hands shackled behind her and her face was alight with amusement and control over the man standing before her.

"Hold your tongue, you harlot," barked Meredith. He drew himself to his full height, stood with his feet astride and glared at the woman who had crossed the threshold of his authority, scarring him for life.

She taunted him, a tigress of lust and victory. "It's all right, he's gone. Are you afraid he's listening behind the door?"

"One word . . . breathe one word, you whore, and I'll have you mercilessly flogged and put in solitary confinement for the rest of the voyage. Do you understand?"

Although the officers had often threatened the women, none of them had been flogged. However, Meredith's anger and thunderous words would have brought a weaker character to her knees. Veins knotted in the side of his neck, and his voice reverberated through the low timbers.

Elizabeth threw back her head and laughed. "How do you know for sure that I haven't already told somebody? Go on then . . . how do you know?"

"Silence!" Like a finely muscled puma, he leaned on his desk and lowered his voice to a sinister growl. "Because bitches like you wouldn't share that sort of victory, in case others tried the same thing and succeeded. Then your imagined power would mean nothing."

The truth in his words stung Elizabeth and after a long silence, she spat on his uniform.

"Sergeant!" When the marine appeared, Meredith pointed a trembling finger at Elizabeth and bellowed, "Gag this woman. Bind her to the pump on deck, and leave her there until the morning."

The marine obeyed and, threatened if caught talking to her, almost everyone on board had gone about their business without a glance in Elizabeth's direction. John Hart hesitated when returning to the surgery from his reading less, but there was little friendship or contrition on the defiant gaze he encountered.

Elizabeth sat with her back to the pump and with her arms tied behind her. She tried to ease her aching jaw from the roughly administered gag and growled softly in her throat. The onset of darkness made the ship's superstructure seem eerie, and tales of sea-dwelling ghosts flitted through her brain as she rocked with the heavy swell of the sea during the night. She was hungry and thirsty and it felt as though her bones had worn through her flesh against the deck. She tried to ignore the long hours and occupied her mind with a rumor that had permeated through the women's prison that morning.

The chief surgeon, on a routine visit from *The Sirius*, had been overheard advising Captain Meredith of a plan. "It has been suggested—and the Commodore agrees—that some of the female labour be employed in domestic service once the colony has been established in Botany Bay. No doubt some of the women you have on board here would prove worthy of such assignments?"

Elizabeth closed her eyes against another spray of salt water that whipped over *The Friendship*'s gunwale and shook her hair. Droplets flicked into her eyes and stung more than her predicament. It occurred to her that she had never seen the need to scrub floors in her entire life, let alone learn to cook. However, it could prove to be an easy way to feather her nest in the new life. Contemplating the possibilities whiles away the sleepless hours but did nothing to lessen her discomfort and exhaustion.

Around four in the morning, chilled and disorientated, she roused. At first she groaned when trying to move her stiffened joints. Then she gave another decisive groan when she recognized the black boots standing beside her. Hatless and with his coat unbuttoned, Captain Meredith towered over her. "Well?"

Both knew the terms for her release and she had the instinctive reaction to spit at him again. It wasn't the gag that stopped her, however. She now had another goal, and it wouldn't be achieved in her present predicament. She nodded, and her eyes slitted as she watched him stride away.

More than an hour passed and a tropical sun sequined over the horizon, mantling the expansive ocean in gold. Gentle winds billowed the sails then slackened them, like a small boy playing with paper boats in a pond. They eventually became lazy, then stilled as though growing tired in the rapidly rising temperature.

"Rio's a long way off at this rate," grouched a seaman, pausing to talk to his mate.

"Yes," came the reply. "Most of us are out of sorts with this voyage already. All these land-lubbers hanging around the decks. At least casks and the likes, you can stow and forget until you gets there!"

"Or toss them overboard." One of them nodded towards Elizabeth and they both laughed before moving on.

Still half asleep, a disheveled marine yawned hugely as he approached Elizabeth. He bent and clumsily untied her from the pump, but he did not release her hands or remove the gag. She made animal noises and glared at him. "Righto, Powley, keep your shirt on. Captain says you can go back to the prison."

He made no attempt to assist Elizabeth to her feet, and only laughed when, after several attempts, she managed to lever herself up against the pump. Again she growled through her gag at him.

"Never fear, m'darlin'" he smirked. "I'll untie your hands when you're down there and you can take your own gag off. I'll scarper before then. Not having you spit at me." He was true to his word and left the prison hold quickly, with Elizabeth struggling to free the tightly knotted gag. Her frustrated efforts roused the other women.

"Well, boiling cat's eyes. She's back." Elizabeth Barber's cackle was husky and loaded with liquor fumes as she stirred lazily in her berth. Elizabeth finally removed the dirty rag and flexed her jaw. She reached across to scoop some water from the barrel.

"Shut yer ugly face, bitch!" There would be a while to wait for their morning oatmeal, so she clambered back into her bunk, disturbing Liz Dudgeon.

"Hullo, Powley," the Cockney snuffled. "Did yer have a good night?" Recollection flooded and she rolled over to face Elizabeth. "Wot was all that about, then?"

"Nothing."

"Y'mean the Capt'n just chose you out of spite?"

"Yeah," Elizabeth answered quietly. "Something like that. Go back to sleep."

"Cor," was Liz's only comment.

Elizabeth massaged her joints and allowed the perpetual hiss of swell against the ship to lull her. But her thoughts sank to the bottom of the sea where a laughing Irish face kept affirming its love for her.

CHAPTER 24

CRUELTY

Later that day during their deck exercise, Liz Dudgeon spoke angrily with Beth as they stood looking over the gunwale. "That bleedin' Capt'n needs taking down a peg or two. Gags her up for no reason, and then leaves her tied up all night. Gettin' too big for his boots, he is."

"Aye, they all are, lass," replied Beth as she turned around to lean back on her elbows. She winked broadly at one of her 'soldier boys' across the deck. "None of them is worth even a crust of Yorkshire's pudding, if y'ask me. I'm going for a walk." She wandered off with the soldiers following conspicuously in her wake.

Left to watch the waves dancing along the starboard timbers, Liz became aware of a burly marine grinning at her side. "How's me darlin' this morning?"

She looked to the blue skies and groaned. "I'm fed up, that's how. Fed up with your slimy grin and fed up telling' you to shove orf."

"I likes a woman with fight, I do," answered the marine. He was well known for beating a woman before he had his way. "Come on, Liz. How about it?"

"Look 'ere, you squirt," Liz turned and shouted. "I'm choosy, I is, and you just ain't worth me while." Being a big man, the term 'squirt' instantly caused a reaction and he raised his fist. But he swung into empty air as Liz ducked and stormed off. If Lieutenant Faddy hadn't appeared on deck at that moment and called him to duty, the irate soldier would have followed her. He had no choice but to glower at the petite figure of Liz as she strode between the main hatch and poop-deck.

"You wait, tart," he muttered. "I'll get me chance. We're a long way off from Botany Bay, yet."

He wasn't to know that his 'chance' was imminent. Flouncing past the gangway, Liz almost collided with Captain Meredith who had been unable to settle to his paperwork that morning.

"Ow! Why don't you look where you're going?" Her words snapped out before she had a chance to think, and then recognizing her enemy, she stood rubbing her elbow and grumbling.

"Hold your tongue, woman," barked Meredith, irritable from a poor night's sleep. "Stand aside."

With the sudden inspiration that now was an ideal opportunity to 'give 'im is come-uppance,' Liz stood her ground. Dwarfed by the big man, she lit her face with an impish grin and put her hands on her hips. "Why don't you make me?" Not recognizing Meredith's hesitation as an attempt to control his anger, she continued to taunt him. "I knows about Powley. And what you did to her. Why don't you pick on me this time?"

James Meredith was livid. He tried to find words but was plagued with the thought that despite her assurances, Elizabeth Powley had regaled the whole of the women's prison with her recent exploits. Liz Dudgeon enjoyed watching his discomfort and goaded him further.

"If you liked gagging Powley all night, how about you takin' me to your bed? You'll like that more, I promise."

Meredith exploded. "Corporal!" The soldier Liz had just snubbed came running. "Take this woman and put her in irons."

The notion that Elizabeth Powley had outwitted him became a firebrand in Meredith's brain. His ferocity was inflamed by Liz Dudgeon yelling a mouthful of abuse. "You bleedin' bastard! You filthy lousy scum . . ."

Meredith's voice roared above hers as he waved wildly at the soldier now restraining her. "And see that she's flogged. Twenty lashes."

Realising she'd gone too far, Liz's eyes widened as she screamed. "No! Oh, f'gawd's sake, no!" The evil grin on the soldier's face added to her terror and she struggled like a wild-cat. Given the chance she would willingly have jumped overboard.

Within the hour and standing on the poop-deck, Lieutenants Clark and Faddy prepared to oversee the flogging. All the other women prisoners were made to stand in front of the assembled convicts, and Liz's eye grew darker with fear as she was tied to the main-mast. The thin blouse she was wearing was torn from her back, and her terror turned to horror when she saw the snubbed marine take charge of the whip. He grinned maliciously as he flexed the rope in his hands and waited for the signal to begin.

"The Captain was trying to avoid flogging the women," remarked Faddy quietly to Clark. The smaller man rocked on his heels and smirked without answering. Glancing around the other convict's faces, Clark saw that Beth Thackery, despite being one of the shorter women, had positioned herself behind the tall gypsy.

"You there," he shouted. "Thackery." All eyes shifted to Clark, then to Beth and back again to the poop-deck. Clark waggled an imperious finger in Beth's direction. "Stand in front of that tall woman."

Beth hesitated then reluctantly obeyed. She sidled around Barber and heard the gypsy hiss and cackle softly. "Looks like your mop is a flag to the bull."

"I'd like t'see him tossed in the sea," Beth gritted back and stared at him with eyes full of hatred and vengeance.

"And stop muttering," added Clark.

"Aye, aye, Little-Clarky," Beth murmured without moving her lips, and then she lowered her eyes.

"And look at Dudgeon," Clark persisted making the most of his elevated position. "All of you, keep your eyes on that rope and remember at any time, any one of you could be standing there. Carry on, Corporal."

The Corporal had ignored his choice of mercy by adjusting its weight and loosening the knots at the ends. He had no intention of tempering his blows and revelled in dramatically raising the whip before he began flogging Liz's pale back. It quickly reddened as her screams pierced the silence of the other women. Their hands flew to their mouths and others clapped their hands to their ears but nothing could blot out the terrible sounds.

Beth tried to bite on her knuckles to stop herself from crying out, but blood was pouring over her fingers and tears were streaming down her face by the time five lashes had been laid on. The rope whistled through the air before raising another weal on Liz's back and in his surgery, Doctor Arndell shook his head sadly as he prepared the necessary dressings. Only Elizabeth Powley stood immobile in her ability to become as stone.

In his journal later that evening, Ralph Clark noted that, " . . . *he did not play with her but laid it home which I was very glad to see.*"

Doctor Arndell had done his best to ease Liz's pain. Use of a rope did not disintegrate the flesh as much as the leather whip used on the men, nevertheless painful wheals were hatched across Liz's back and her soft skin was raised in an angry mass. She was returned to the women's prison hold and lay on her face in her berth. She sobbed as Beth gently stroked her hair and no-one spoke with the disastrous knowledge that no woman was safe from any atrocity on board this ship.

Liz finally drifted into an exhausted sleep for a while, until the evening meal of fish, potatoes and peas was brought to the hold. It was apportioned into each woman's bowl and soon began disappearing. Beth roused her friend and asked gently, "Do you want yours?"

Liz raised her head and flinched as she replied, "They ain't going to starve me as well!"

She clambered down from her berth cautiously and joined her friend at the food bench. "Bad enough that your head's empty, let alone your guts," said

Barber, pushing Liz against the bulkhead. Knives of pain slashed once more across Liz's back but her yells were lost in those from Beth and Elizabeth Powley. Incensed by the callous gypsy's attack they launched themselves at her. Meals scattered over the floor as bowls were knocked from the bench and the other women hastily withdrew to the safety of their berths. Yelled curses filled the confined area and Susannah, who had been standing away from her berth, clasped her son tightly as she eased away from the fighting women.

In agony, Liz had clambered back into her berth while the other three continued to tear and bite at each other. They staggered heavily against mother and child and little Henry began to scream lustily. Infuriated, Mary shouted a string of Welsh abuse at the women who had now paused, but stood watching each other like tigers. With a cruel snarl, the gypsy turned and dragged her fingernails down Mary's cheek just as soldiers clattered down the steps to take charge. Lieutenant Faddy, having accompanied the marines, surveyed the three fighters. They stood panting like predators amongst the debris of fish and potatoes.

"Be quiet, woman," he barked at the still weeping Liz. Then he turned to the marines. "See that these three get down and clean up this mess before you put them in irons."

"What about the other women, sir? Looks like their rations are on the floor, too." The younger marine flushed, suddenly aware that it was not his duty to question an officer. Falteringly he added, "I only thought . . ."

Faddy's normally good humour had been worn down by the long voyage, and he snapped, "If they want to eat it, let them. They'll get no more tonight."

Susannah soothed the child as Faddy stomped back up the steps. Then she wrung out a cloth in the water barrel to place gently against her friend's stinging cheek. "Oh, Mary, what will become of us?"

"We'll get there, cariad," whispered Mary, dabbing again at her injury. "But I doubt if some of these will."

With three of the Elizabeths in irons and the other unable to rest on her back, an uneasy peace reigned in the female prison for over a week. In the male quarters, several men had also earned chains for stealing from each other, and one man was sentenced to solitary confinement for battering his bunk-mate unconscious over an unpaid gambling debt. However, Arndell had instigated removal of all chains by the Sunday, as he was concerned about the sores appearing on the convicts' wrists and ankles.

"I have ordered gunpowder to be set alight between the decks today while the convicts are exercising," he announced in Meredith's cabin late that afternoon. "Smoke fires and oil of tar seem to be important in maintaining good health."

Meredith nodded absently. His thoughts of late had begun to impinge on his responsibilities and, as the days passed, he'd become a victim of self-imposed guilt. The Fleet Chaplain was due to come aboard next morning. Meredith had already mustered what courage he could and was going to ask for a private interview with the cleric.

CHAPTER 25

SIGNS OF LIFE

The First Fleet Chaplain came aboard *The Friendship* on Sunday morning and held his weekly service. Before he started however, James Meredith quietly asked if he would hear a private confession in his cabin. The Chaplain nodded then proceeded as usual. Confessions were a regular part of his duty because he claimed to be one of all faiths, and when the service was over, he followed Captain Meredith into his cabin. He settled into a chair, his Bible clasped between two podgy hands that rested on an equally round stomach. James Meredith sat in the chair behind his desk and put his head in his hands.

"Well now, Captain," began the Chaplain. "How can I help you?" His voice was weary and his expression was resigned. He couldn't count the number of confessions he'd heard from people who inevitably committed the same sin only hours after his blessing.

Neither of the men spoke for a while, and then Captain Meredith raised his head, opened his eyes and jutted his chin. "I fear I've been guilty of gross misjudgment, sir. May I request a prayer of forgiveness?"

The cleric sighed heavily then he leaned forward and got to his feet. Meredith's head bowed again as one of the podgy hands was laid on his head, and the Chaplain began muttering words, but James wasn't listening. He had soon realized that, despite his fears and suspicions, Elizabeth Powley had not reneged on the terms of her release from the pump. There had been no sniggering or innuendoes from anyone on board. He had simply misconstrued Liz Dudgeon's taunts and the consequent flogging meant he had betrayed his inner man. Nevertheless, he saw no advantage in confessing to his drunken behaviour and conduct with Elizabeth Powley, not even to the Chaplain. He added a silent prayer of his own when, at the close of his blessing, the cleric ended with the question, "Indeed, Lord, which of us is qualified to judge? Amen!"

Satisfied that he had saved another soul, the Chaplain made his farewells and left *The Friendship*. The Captain lingered at his desk, his tortured mind reliving again the incident with Elizabeth Powley. He was lost in reverie when Doctor Arndell poked his head through the cabin door. "James, will you join me in a glass of wine in the surgery this evening?"

Meredith smiled sheepishly and nodded. He was about to say something but groaned instead. They were interrupted by the screams of women above decks. "Not again!"

Arndell backed away from the door to allow the Captain to exit. "It sounds serious" he said, and together they headed for the ruckus.

Convicts, seamen, marines and their wives, all crowded around the open hatch of the men's' prison, their raised voices creating a babble of noise.

"Make way there," cried Arndell as he struggled so see. "Whatever's happened?"

The stunned surgeon broke through the circle of people in time to see Henry Cable carry the limp body of Charles Stewart out of the hold. He knelt down when Henry laid the baby on the deck, and he spoke gruffly. "Stand back there, can't you? I can't . . ."

Meredith jostled a few out of the way and some did retreat at first. They soon strained forward again though, to see what the doctor was doing. They discussed animated versions of the incident to Meredith, while three of the marine wives attended to Margaret Stewart. The poor woman had fainted.

"The child lives," pronounced Arndell as he rose to his feet. "Quickly, Cable. Bring him to the Sick Bay." Intent on his patient, the doctor did not stop to ask the whereabouts of John Hart but hastened after Henry Cable. Captain Meredith, however, tried to make sense out of the many versions that assaulted his ears.

"They was playin' as nice as you likes," said one woman. "Next thing, he's gorn."

"They'll hang the boy for this," said another sagely. "Where is he?"

"Down there." Mrs. Morgan turned from the recovering Margaret to join in the conversation, and she pointed towards the hold. "Sergeant Stewart's with him."

"Poor Bill got hanged for nuffin," said a one-time cohort of William Gant. "That red-coat will just as likely murder the little brat, and he'll get away wiv it."

"It's such a shame," remarked a buxom convict to her daughter. "He's not a bad kid really, and the baby idolized 'im. Wonder why he did it?"

Down in the men's' prison area a grey-faced Sergeant Stewart prepared to climb the ladder onto the deck. He turned to glare at John Hart, who sat sniveling and trembling like an autumn leaf that is loathe to part company with its parent tree. Stewart could feel no compassion for the boy. "Keep an eye on him, private," he ordered. "He's to stay here until I send word."

Charles had been as a baby brother to John, and he loved playing hide-and-seek with him. He liked nothing better than to hear the baby's infectious chuckle when, with a comical face, he darted from behind the mast or a pile of rope.

"You'll likely get the rope for this," said the callous private, as though he could read the boy's thoughts. "That's what comes of trusting convicts."

It seemed hours before Stewart reappeared at the hatch and ordered that John be brought on deck. Thomas Arndell stood alongside an agitated and pale Margaret, who sat fanning herself from the intense afternoon sun. Most of the onlookers had wandered off to discuss the episode once they knew that Charles had survived the fall. He had escaped with slight concussion. Several of the marine wives and some of the convicts remained however, and at the back of them, stood Elizabeth Powley. Apart from the light red wheals around her mouth from the gag, her face was inscrutable.

John could hardly stand and looked fearfully at the assembly. He longed to see a friendly face, but even his mentor had an expression of great sadness.

"Now then, Hart," began Arndell. "What happened?"

"We saw it, sir," chipped in the buxom woman nodding at the girl with her. "I don't think he did it on purpose."

"No, he didn't . . ." began her daughter.

Arndell interrupted her. "Let the boy speak for himself."

The world seemed suddenly full of tall and portly adults to John Hart. Eyes stared at him from all quarters of the ship, and even the crewman looking down from the crow's nest appeared to form part of the kaleidoscope of accusers. His lip trembled, his head dropped onto his thin chest, and tears escaped into his nose causing him to sniff loudly. It seemed interminable minutes before he could mutter an answer. 'I d-didn't mean it, sir. Honest I didn't . . .'

"Oh yes 'e did," broke in Gant's belligerent ally. "I saw 'im push the kid."

"And me," said another of Gant's cronies.

"He didn't," argued the mother and daughter.

Commotion began to take over again, and it frightened John even more. He sniveled louder while wondering what the rough rope felt like when it tightened.

"Quiet, everyone," snapped Arndell loudly. The effect was immediate, none of the onlookers wanted to miss a moment of the drama. Arndell paused irately then turned to Sergeant Stewart who was comforting his wife. "When all is said and done, I cannot I imagine the boy had any reason to want to hurt your son. Quite the opposite, in fact."

There was a rumble of conflicting opinions followed by a small silence. Elizabeth Powley had stood to the rear of the crowd with no sign of the anger that rose within her. She remembered when she was seven years old and she had been accused of knifing the ruffian who had attacked her mother. She never found out what happened; only that his body was thrown into the Thames River and her mother never mentioned wielding the knife herself. Elizabeth had grown up with continuous insinuations and the recollection burned in her mind. She spoke firmly and clearly. "He tried to save the kid."

Everyone turned to stare in disbelief at her, but she stood resolute and tall. Margaret Stewart studied the faces of the two convicts. The man's eager condemnation of the boy could be truthful. The woman stood aloof with an unwavering gaze and displayed no real concern for anyone's welfare.

Uncertain, Margaret turned to look again at the accused boy. She hesitated, but could not find it in her to imagine his guilt. Did he have a motive? Had he, in his simple-mindedness, imagined that he would be adopted by them if Charles was dead? Which convict was really telling the truth?

She leaned forward and put out her shaking hand to lift John Hart's chin. "Did you? Did you honestly try to save Charles from falling into the hold?"

John Hart raised tearful eyes and struggled to find courage for words. They wouldn't come, so he nodded dumbly.

"Thank you," Margaret breathed then she hugged him. A mother's instinct had decided the question and Arndell looked with question to Stewart. He received a satisfied nod from the baby's father and, with obvious relief, the surgeon put a hand on Hart's shoulder.

"Come along then," he said quietly. "You can help look after Charles."

The crowd dissipated and the unsavory criminal approached Elizabeth Powley. Her chin lifted and her eyes narrowed, but she said nothing.

"Gettin' soft ain't you, Powley?" he growled. "Since when have you set up as the Old Bailey?"

"Wish I was," said Elizabeth with an icy voice. "Swine like you wouldn't escape the gallows, let alone get to Botany Bay."

He chuckled and rubbed his hand against her breast. "Well, I don't know what you got chained to the pump for, but it sure wasn't for being a lady." Elizabeth stood her ground and he nodded towards the men's' prison. "No one down there now. Want a toss?"

Elizabeth made as if to fill her mouth with saliva, but changed her mind and stalked away. Quite used to being rebuffed, the convict laughed and headed for his liquor supply. He had no trouble in acquiring the odd bottle for his indiscriminate services amongst the seaman.

A sudden call from the side of the ship attracted everyone's attention. "Look! Dolphins."

People crowded to look at the sleek muddy grey bodies that kept pace then cleaved forward several yards before they turned to swim alongside the tall ship again. They were like grey ballet dancers on a sun-drenched stage. All at once, from below the surface of the rolling waves, birdlike creatures glistened as they flew high into the air to escape from the large school of skip-jacks that chased them. Some landed on the deck and there were squeals of delight from the women and children.

"They're flying fish," explained a seaman.

Intrigued with the sight, no-one noticed Mrs. Morgan crumple with a taut expression squeezing her eyes closed. She reached out and touched Margaret Stewart who took one look at her and shouted for help. Sergeant Stewart sent a message ahead to Thomas Arndell then moved to assist the pregnant woman to the Sick Bay.

"We'll manage," said Margaret while she tucked her hand under Mrs. Morgan's arm. "Why don't you go and find Corporal Morgan. Tell him everything will be well."

Once the women reached the Sick Bay, Thomas Arndell hastily erected the screen around Mrs. Morgan who was moaning softly. Then he poked his head out of the screen to instruct John Hart to stay with Charles. The child was sleeping soundly in a cot the other end of the room.

"Oh, Margaret," cried the mother-to-be. "I'm so afraid. My baby wasn't supposed to come for another two weeks." She ended with a small shriek as the ship dipped steeply and her every sensation sharpened. "Is there something wrong, Margaret?"

"Of course not," soothed Mrs. Stewart as she prepared for a protracted vigil. "Babies know when they are ready to come, much more than we or the doctors can say. Don't be afraid. I'll stay right here with you."

Memories of her own childbirth came flooding in and Margaret stroked the perspiring woman's forehead. A strange quiet reigned over the ship once all the convicts had been herded below and as the day disappeared into darkness, the usual winds buffeted the brave ships of the fleet. They looked so small and vulnerable in the middle of the ocean with the waves increasing by the minute. By midnight the waves had escalated into a squall that tossed the brig ceaselessly.

Mrs. Morgan found it increasingly difficult to maintain her silence as she endured the pains of advanced labour. John Hart stared at the silhouettes thrown onto the screen around her, and from his mattress on the floor he suffered his second agony of the day. He cringed and tried to block his ears into his pillow as every moan from the labouring woman blended with the howling elements outside. The shadows seemed agitated one minute and frighteningly still the next. The surgeon and Margaret Stewart spoke in almost inaudible tones in between Mrs. Morgan's cries. John Hart's vivid imagination conjured up monstrous pictures of the woman's ordeal. Unable to sleep and overwhelmed by the day's traumatic events, he crept over to the cot where Charles lay sleeping then slid under the blanket to cuddle him.

For many hours he laid under the blanket gathering comfort from the small form beside him, but he shuddered as each cry from Mrs. Morgan gained in intensity. Margaret Stewart's familiar voice rose accordingly and she could now be plainly understood. "Everything is all right, Mrs. Morgan. It won't be long now. Just hold onto my hand and push when you have to."

Her words served to confuse and soothe John who wondered what the poor woman had to push. The woman's final cry, protracted and echoing, terrified him and he ducked beneath the blanket wondering how Charles could still sleep? Moments later he peeped over the blanket and watched the surgeon's silhouette straighten as a tiny mewl replaced the mother's sob of relief.

"Oh, my dear," said Margaret anxiously.

"Mrs. Morgan," Arndell said gently. You have a fine son. But I'm afraid your baby has a crippled leg."

The poor woman, in a mix of grief, release and happiness, let out a sound that remained with John Hart for many years after, and reinforced his fear of unknown mysteries.

CHAPTER 26

CROSSING THE LINE

During the next ten days or so, *The Friendship* sailed with her sister ships through an ocean of varied lights and moods. The swell continuously changed from a glassy blue-green eiderdown to a rough black-green blanket that tossed the brave fleet like corks.

Some days provided entertainment by dolphins and strange exotic creatures that swam closely. Many days were filled with fear and apprehension as equatorial winds, under morose skies, battered the ships.

There were those aboard who vowed they would never become used to the perpetual motion beneath their feet. Others found comfort in letting their thoughts wander far beyond the endless horizon that bobbed hypnotically. Nearing the Equator, which was marked only with Man's pen-line on a map, Captain Meredith began to worry about the food supplies.

"There are only five fowls and one pig left," reported the gloomy Lieutenant Clark one morning.

"In that case," Meredith said efficiently, "set more of the men to doubling the fish catch. We may grow tired of eating it, but before we get to Rio, we will be more than grateful for the ocean's bounty, I'm thinking."

Clark stood at ease in front of the Captain's desk. Since the acquisition of his puppy, Efford, an amicable tolerance had existed between the two men. The manner in which Clark doted on Efford gave the convicts many an opportunity to surreptitiously mock him. Nevertheless, he'd gained a reputation for mood-swings, so Meredith was surprised when he produced an Aesop smile. "The men caught a large she-shark yesterday," Clark said. "She had *thirty-seven* young ones in her!"

Meredith raised his eyebrows dutifully, and nodded. "Carry on, Lieutenant." He had little interest in events he considered trivial, nowadays. The voyage had outstripped his wildest imaginations as to the discomfort they would endure, and far from feeling boosted by his responsibility, he was jaded. His solace came increasingly from the bottle alongside him, and he was forever grateful that the Government had seen fit to supply plenty of fine liquor for Captains and officers alike. His main confidence relied on his friendship with Thomas Arndell.

He spent a moment daydreaming of earlier associations with virile officers whose zest for life had created many a raucous evening at the barracks in Portsmouth. He smiled absently at memories of the long table in the Marine Barracks dining hall, laden with food served on ornate silver platters. Silver candelabra always festooned the centre of the table and he remembered the huge silver goblets—each item from the regiment's collection over the years. He also recalled the mouthwatering fragrances as course after course of roast lamb, beef and pork were ceremoniously laid before the diners, and blew his nose loudly.

But it was not the remembered smells that caused him to reach for his lace-edged handkerchief. It was the whiff of sweating bodies and rotting bilge-water that often permeated between decks. He poured himself a Madeira wine, muttering "Something will have to be done shortly."

A few days passed before a signal was received from the flagship *Sirius* that Captain Shea was out of danger and progressing; the fleet was making good headway despite frequent periods of calm, and the quality and quantity of each fish catch had improved.

More than twenty convicts and crew on *The Friendship* tossed strong lines into the current daily and hardly minutes passed before someone hauled in a writhing gleam of silver with its mouth gaped. The plank that was used in sea-burials was put to good use as the shirtless and finely muscled seamen scraped and gutted the catch before it was tossed into large barrels. Some of the translucent flesh was for immediate consumption, some was preserved with salt against leaner harvests.

James Meredith was heartened and, with the ship's Master, Francis Walton, he agreed to preside over the almost obligatory ceremony when they crossed the Equator. A hay-fork was broken out of the bundle of fifty that lay in the cargo-hold, along with other items for use in the new colony. Most of the expected needs for colonizing Botany Bay, which included items such as horse-harnesses, squares of glass for windows, a portable canvas house, and a quantity of ladies' handkerchiefs were stowed aboard *The Supply*, but an overflow of items had been distributed into the fleet cargo-holds.

"Make sure that thing is returned," Master Walton warned the seaman, who had draped the prongs with fishnet and shells. The grinning man sat on a throne of piled rope and balanced a paper crown on his head.

James Meredith stood beside Walton as they watched the antics on the main deck below them. "The Commodore is hoping Botany Bay proves as fertile as the Americas." he said. "I know most of us are hoping and praying we get there safely, first."

Master Walton gave Meredith a wry look and said, "We'll get you there, Captain. Have no fear of that." He then automatically inspected the set of his sails. Having spent his life at sea since being press-ganged from Portsmouth's streets as a boy, his main concern was their arrival at their destination, not the new colony's survival.

Laughter from the deck claimed their attention. Those who joined in the fun and were crossing the Equator for the first time, paid due homage to King Neptune and were initiated into his kingdom. They were granted safe passage when the hay-fork touched their shoulders then it was used to signal those who had become previous subjects, to toss buckets of water over the kneeling newcomers.

"Hail, good King Neptune," they all spluttered, and jovially bowled each other over. Male and female convicts were also permitted to take part if they wished, but only the hardiest chose to do so. Among these were the four Elizabeths, and the gypsy in particular drew shouts of derision when she staggered to pledge her troth to the king of the oceans.

"They should throw a bucket of liquor over her," sneered Liz Dudgeon. "I bet she would even lick the deck."

"Look at her hands. Mebee she's trying to turn the water into liquor, too." Beth's comment drew more laughs, and even Elizabeth Powley allowed her face to soften into a smile that made her eyes glow.

The marine wives of course, were treated far more gently. They had to remove their shoes and walk in the spilled water, and then were allowed to curtsey to the 'king' while he touched their shoulders with his 'trident'.

Four days later, the fleet was again becalmed. Bored and frustrated, the voyagers sweltered under a noon sun that showed no more mercy on water than it does to souls lost in the world's arid deserts. Conventions were cast aside, together with clothing that was more suited to Northern hemisphere temperatures. Skirts were drawn up into bulky knots in an effort to cool sweat-dampened limbs; mothers fanned their naked and fretting babies constantly and the marines envied the seamen who were stripped to the waist.

The canvas sails of the tall ships, as though too weary to continue their struggle against Mother Nature, hung slack in the shimmering heat, and the air was oppressive. Several hours passed before a small breeze skipped across the surface and capriciously stirred the sails, like a child rousing its sleeping playmate. Everyone's spirits began to rise as the wind increased and with his Sick Bay unusually free of patients, a coatless Thomas Arndell strolled on the deck with John Hart.

"Will we ever get there, sir?" asked the boy. He had no comprehension of where 'there' was, only that it was land. And it seemed impossible to his young mind, that land could suddenly arise from the water, especially with the endless horizon that had surrounded them for months

"Of course," answered Arndell, but not with a lot of conviction. Brushing disturbing thoughts aside, he stopped to acknowledge Sergeant Stewart who sat chatting with the young mothers. Margaret and Mrs. Morgan were trying to hold parasols over themselves and their children but the lacey umbrellas shades were of little defence for their English complexions. "My goodness, you are all very sunburned," Arndell observed. "Come and see me if you need a soothing mixture."

Charles held out his arms to Hart, and Margaret smiled her approval as she gently handed her son to the boy. "No running around the deck, now."

Bidding the young mothers a good day, the surgeon continued alone along the main deck. He spotted Henry, Mary, and Susannah there, sitting together on casks and coiled rope. He wandered over to join them. "Keeping busy?" He nodded to Mary who carefully stitched another garment for the growing baby. Her round cheeks were flushed from the heat and she brushed away a wisp of hair.

"Nearly six months old now and look—fat as a cherub." Mary smiled indulgently at little Henry being tickled by his father.

Arndell pinched the baby's cheek gently. "You have been fortunate to be able to suckle him all this time, Susannah. He has a good hold onto life."

"He will need it," sighed Susannah, stroking the fine down on the baby's head. "Being branded as a convict's son isn't a very good start, is it?"

"Come now, Susannah," chided Henry. "Even God's son started poorly with everybody against him."

"A commendable thought, Cable," returned Arndell. "Hopefully the new colony will be a good start for . . ."

A harsh cackle broke into their conversation as Elizabeth Barber staggered from below. She fell against the main-mast and sank to the deck, where she swigged from an almost empty rum bottle. She drained it, then made an uncontrolled effort to stare belligerently at people stepping around her. Her eyes lighted on the surgeon and with a screech that would have done credit to a fourteenth-century witch, she tossed away the bottle and lumbered to her feet. Henry gathered his woman and baby protectively as the gypsy stumbled towards them. She pulled up with one hand on her hip and the other flickered a long finger at the surgeon.

"You," she slurred before hiccupping. "You're nothing but a lah-di-dahdy old bugger. I've been watching you . . . I know what's going on."

The onlookers were stunned into silence and their eyes flew from her saliva dribbling mouth to the surgeon. His own mouth was gaping like those of the daily catch.

"See him, the lousy bastard?" the gypsy screeched louder. "He's bloody mad for my body." As if to illustrate her point, and to the amusement of some of the watching seamen, she placed her large hands beneath equally large breasts and bounced them.

Arndell found his voice and got to his feet as two marines approached the drunken woman. "Bind her," he bellowed. "And one of you fetch the Captain immediately!"

Barber cackled again and ducked away from the remaining soldier. She suddenly gained enough control to climb onto the ship's rail, and stood there clinging to the rigging. The rising breeze snatched at her skirt and rippled her black hair, turning her into a swaying Romany Medusa.

"No boy-mad heathen is going t'get me," she yelled, her eyes glittering. Then she spotted John Hart who had run into view, drawn by the furor. "You be careful, little Johnny. Soon he'll be asking you to warm his bloody feet!"

The shocked watchers drew an audible breath and Barber threw back her head in a maniacal laugh. It changed to a screech as two more marines arrived and grabbed her skirt. They hauled her unceremoniously to the deck and she fought dementedly while they tried to subdue her. More people grouped at the sound of the scuffle, and they cheered as the soldiers eventually managed to cuff the squirming woman's hands behind her back

A slow smile spread across Elizabeth Powley's face. She was standing near the pump and had noticed Captain Meredith appear in time to hear the gypsy's disgusting accusation. He clambered to the poop deck and the two Lieutenants, who had also run to the scene, clambered to their station beside him.

"Hah!" continued Barber, panting like a she-devil. "Look at them up there like three bloody monkeys. They're just as bad. Wouldn't be surprised if them two red-coats don't sleep together."

"Enough!" thundered Meredith.

"You're just as bad," the gypsy yelled back. Then she turned to the crowd which was growing by the minute. "What d'you thinks the lousy animal does all day with that bloody black dog of his, anyway?"

"Flog her!" roared Meredith. His face was florid. "Now! Not the rope—the cat o' nine tails."

"How many, sir," called the ship's boy over the gasp of horror from the crowd. He took his position on the capstan and prepared to call the count.

"I'll tell you when to stop," was the ominous reply. Fury seethed through his senses. The gypsy's insubordination mocked his attempted discipline and her scurrilous accusations were verbal whip-lashes to him. "Within an inch of her life," he ranted. "There will be no more mercy."

CHAPTER 27

MORALS AND PUNISHMENT

Feeling as though they had been plunged into a nightmare, the marine wives gathered their children and hurried below. Any sensitivity they had come aboard with had been permanently assaulted. No-one would remain the same as they were when they'd .their cabin for a rest and Mrs. Morgan sobbed into Margaret's shoulder. "Oh, I want to go home. Whatever will become of us with those convicts at Botany Bay?|

Margaret looked through her own tears at their sleeping babies. "I really don't know, Mrs. Morgan. Mister Stewart has contracted for five years in the Colony. I think I will take our son home on the first ship I can."

The two women clung to each other, their lives and aspirations destroyed in a matter of months.

On the deck, the gypsy continued spouting her liquor-incensed filth at her captors, and Mister Arndell watched the preparations as if the burning sun had forced him to hallucinate. Her tattered blouse tore easily and was completely removed, revealing the breasts she'd brazenly flaunted at him earlier. Eventually tied to the main-mast after a great deal of resistance, Barber then twisted her half-naked body towards Captain Meredith. He was trembling with fury still, and his breathing was laboured.

"'Ere you are, nice Capt'n," Barber yelled, repeating her maniacal laugh. "Come and kiss my lovely feeders while you can."

She continued abusing everyone she could lay her vile tongue to, and none of the officers restrained the gathered convicts when they yelled back at her. "Serves y'right," shouted Beth. "You've bin asking for it since the *Mercury.*" Liz Dudgeon said nothing, memories of her own flogging stilling her tongue.

Elizabeth Powley stood watching the Captain. He had studiously ignored her since their encounter in his cabin but she knew there was now an intangible link between them. He could have her flogged just as mercilessly if he wished. It intrigued her to wonder if Meredith really trusted her capitulation at the pump, or was he plagued by her ability to destroy his last vestige of authority? 'Who's got the upper hand, here?' she asked herself. 'Which of us is brave enough to test the other's will-power?' She had to admit the tall man had given no outward sign of his feelings, also that she had no wish to endure the gypsy's fate.

A big marine with a square face pocked by boils, prepared to flog the gypsy. His shirtless muscles flexed as he snapped the whip to the deck in order to tighten its knotted strands. Then he turned to Meredith on the poop deck that was standing between his Lieutenants with the doctor. The Captain nodded, his eyes black with the anger that consumed him. Arndell had already decided there was no point in appealing to James' better reasoning and he stared at the culprit with no intention of helping her.

Raising the lethal whip again, the marine laid all of his sixteen-stone weight behind his downward assault and it sliced deeply into Barber's soft flesh. The strands of leather were long enough to wrap themselves around her ribs so she also had wounds opened up at the side of her breasts and blood trickled down her back and side. A feral growl emanated from the gypsy and she bit her bottom lip through. The cat-calling convicts were stunned into silence as the marine raised his arm again.

"One . . ." came the call from the ship's boy. He had counted out for many floggings, but this time he cringed as he waited to call 'two'.

Oblivious to the beauty of sails filling against azure skies, those that watched heard the woman scream as the hardened leather struck again and small pieces of her flesh scattered to the deck with her blood.

Arndell was normally sickened by the merciless slashing and destruction but revenge for the gypsy's false accusation of pedophilia dominated his sensitivities. He stood motionless and hardly breathing as he lent a mental energy to the marine's rippling muscles.

Dudgeon and Thacker sauntered away. Showing a complete lack of concern for the gypsy's agony adequately vindicated their need for revenge on the lying murderess.

Elizabeth Powley remained by the pump with her green eyes riveted to Meredith's stony expression. He listened to the monotonous count of three, four, five, seemingly devoid of emotion. The harlot's screeches pierced the suffocating heat, but he watched her back and breast beaten to a jellied mass. Her cries lessened, then ceased. He body hung like a newly-slaughtered animal.

And still the marine pounded . . .

" . . . fourteen . . ."

Filled with a sudden revulsion, Meredith raised his hand. A low moan punctured the traumatic silence. Barber had been roused to semi-consciousness by the unexpected cessation of blows.

"Tie her to the pump until further orders." Meredith's voice was still tight with anger. He looked across at the pale surgeon and added, "She is to receive no attention to her wounds."

The two Lieutenants, obviously uncomfortable at the scene, looked at each other but said nothing. Meredith stood his ground while he watched the gypsy being untied and dragged to the pump. With a small shock his gaze locked with Elizabeth Powley's as she stood near the pump. She stood aside to allow the marines to carry out their orders but did not look away from him. In an unspoken message, Meredith acknowledged his misconception of Dudgeon's taunts and the unwarranted punishment he'd meted out to her. But his eyes repeated his warning. Barber's distress was his affidavit. Elizabeth was obdurate, and she walked away.

Several hours later when the carnage had been swabbed away from the deck by seamen who might have vomited had they not been stronger men, the silence was sinister. No-one strolled around the ship; crew and marines huddled in groups whispering about the horrible event. Thomas Arndell stood gazing at the interminable waves lapping at the ship's side; he passed his hand across his eyes as if to obliterate the recent scenes, then he produced a large handkerchief and blew his nose loudly.

With the added pain of an unforgiving sun searing her torn flesh, the gypsy drifted in and out of consciousness, occasionally moaning. Despite himself and James Meredith's orders, he had laid clean rags over the woman's body in an effort to stop the bleeding.

She was scarcely aware of relief when the horizon swallowed the ball of fire, leaving a bloodstained sky that slowly gathered with storm clouds.

The brig began to dip into the rising seas, and darkness enveloped all but pools of swinging light from lanterns hung at strategic locations along the deck. Bursts of sea-spray glistened into the arcs of light and stung Barber's back. Piteous cries sprung from her cracked and bloodied lips. Thomas Arndell, who had gone back to his cabin, appeared in the gloom and approached her. He hesitated, and then he turned and disappeared into the blackness. Approaching Meredith's cabin he tapped gently on the door.

"Yes?"

The voice inside sounded angry and tired, and Arndell let himself in gingerly. "A word with you, please, James?"

"Of course. Do come in." Meredith waved the surgeon wearily to a wooden-armed chair opposite him, and reached for the decanter at his side. "Madeira, Thomas? I think we've traveled far enough to use Christian names, now."

The doctor accepted the proffered glass, studied the rich red liquid and then he sipped it gratefully. "Disgusting debacle, this afternoon," he grunted. "I am a generous man, as you know, James. But I'll never find it in me to forgive that woman.

Meredith nodded his agreement and refilled their glasses. "I pride myself on thinking that you and I have become good friends, Thomas."

"Indeed, we are."

"Then, may I ask your opinion about a matter that has been troubling me of late?"

A little surprised, Arndell waited while Meredith swung the wine gently and stared into its ruby depths, trying to clear his thoughts. He was evidently turning over the words in his mind, before burdening his friend any more.

"Men in our position," he began finally, "are heavily laden with responsibility. We're each beholden to our King and superiors. One must assume we have performed our duties satisfactorily, to have attained these roles."

Thomas Arndell looked perplexed. Where was this line of thought leading his friend? Something more than the afternoon's trauma was troubling him obviously, and the doctor felt it was beyond the cure of Madeira wine. He didn't reply immediately, searching for words to fill the need of his friend's meditations. After a small silence, he said, "I've always understood that His Majesty's Government does not allocate responsibility lightly. Each to his own qualifications." He felt that was an adequate answer without making his curiosity too evident.

However, he was not prepared for Meredith's reaction. The Captain seemed to come to life and thumped hard on his desk. "Exactly!"

Arndell jumped slightly, and tried to recall his words to see what 'exactly' had come through. He had no way of knowing of course, that Meredith was still smarting from the recent public rollicking he had received from Major Ross. Again there was silence; broken only by sounds that had by now become so familiar they were almost unnoticeable to those aboard. Arndell waited patiently while Meredith continued to star into his glass.

Finally, the surgeon felt compelled to ask. "What is it, James?"

Meredith raised troubled eyes. "I am beginning to doubt my abilities and my posting, Thomas. I am afraid my sense of duty is becoming warped. I have never had to handle insubordination to this degree. Am I becoming ruthless?"

"No," answered Arndell levelly, relieved that the problem was no more than a case of self-doubt. "We all have these thoughts at times, I can assure you. But one's duty must come before all."

The doctor observed that his approach to the situation was evidently what Meredith needed, and he prided himself on his wise and sensible counseling. For a white, they sat in a companionable silence, allowing themselves to be lulled by the fortification of good wine and the familiar creaking of the ship's timbers. *The Friendship* valiantly rode and tossed on the ocean with the bad weather that increased its squall by the minute. Arndell finally looked at the swinging lamp above and said, "Master Walton will be busy, no doubt. I trust the whore at the pump is not in the way."

The surgeon's presence was a warm mantle and Meredith mustered his returning confidence. Quietly, he said, "Have the woman returned below." His friend's expression was inscrutable, so he asked. "I suppose you have some concoction or other to treat the wounds?" Arndell nodded. "Very well, but see that she is tied to the pump every day."

"Very well, James," the doctor replied, and proceeded to empty his glass. He hesitated and then asked, "Is there anything else you wish to discuss?"

Meredith seemed about to say something then both men rose to their feet . . . Although Meredith had spoken of his doubts, Arndell sensed that there was a greater conflict torturing his friend. He stood a few seconds longer, albeit a little unsteadily, and then he left. Heralding a nearby soldier as he approached the woman at the pump, Arndell gave instructions that she should be taken to the Surgery where he would treat her wounds. Then she was to be returned to the women prisoner's hold.

Still half-naked and with her wounds beginning to crust on her skin, Barber was dragged to the Sick Bay moaning loudly, The moans turned to chilling screams when Arndell wiped her back with alcohol. Then she fainted. The soldier humped her back to the women's prison quarters and unceremoniously flung the unconscious body onto her berth.

The other women, who had fallen silent as soon as the hatch was removed, said nothing. They all looked at Barber, unsure whether she was dead or dying.

Having attended to the Captain's instructions, Arndell returned to the surgery and stood looking down on John Hart's sleeping form. John had thrived in the fresh air and sunshine so different from the sooty chimneys of his former days in London, and the doctor couldn't help but smile at the boy's beatific expression. Then he peered closer and noted the boy was clasping one of his medical books. "My, my, John Hart," he murmured while he gently extricated the heavy book. "I see your reading lessons are progressing."

CHAPTER 28

EFFORD

Elizabeth Powley eased herself from her berth. She was unable to sleep between the turbulence of sea-water crashing against the ship and the gypsy's loud moans. Having first retrieved the cup from beneath her striped pillow, she dipped it into the disturbed surface of the barrel and sipped the tepid water. She told herself that she would enjoy a drink of the Captain's liquor much better.

Beth Thackery joined her at the bench, and she did the same. She pulled a face at the taste of the stale water and tossed the remainder back into the barrel. She ran her hands through her springy hair. She had washed it in seawater that afternoon and it had dried to a stiff, red halo. Beth looked at Elizabeth, who now straddled the wooden seat which ran beside the bench. "Can't sleep?"

Elizabeth shrugged.

I wonder how much longer it will be a'fore we gets t'Rio."

Again Elizabeth shrugged.

"That flamin' Capt'n can go overboard," Beth persisted, and then she grinned. "Or he should aught to."

"Bet she's wishing they all would." Elizabeth indicated the gypsy with her cup. But there was no flicker of compassion in her voice.

"It wouldn't tek more than a shove to send Little-Clarky to King Neptune," affirmed Beth vehemently. "Ooh, how I hate that little twerp."

"I hate them all," said Elizabeth. "Most of them are all talk and trousers."

Beth giggled and then looked curiously at Elizabeth. Over the past few weeks, in fact, since Patrick died, Beth told herself, the tall woman had become strangely distant from everyone. More often than not she separated herself from the throng and stood alone, staring out to the sea. When they were on deck, Elizabeth seemed to have little interest in the men, and even avoided the women. Apparently, she preferred her own company.

"Here," said Beth, searching for conversation. "What did you have to go to the Capt'n for that time? You must have trod on his toes to end up gagged."

Elizabeth had no intention of revealing that she had done everything but tread on his toes. She offered no reply, but sunk her head onto her folded arms on the bench.

Astutely, Beth did not press her question. She crept back into her berth and merely remarked, "The wind's dying."

Unable to sleep herself for a while, Beth brooded about the supercilious Lieutenant. A slow smile crossed her face and she heaved over onto her side. Then she closed her eyes and drifted into the contented sleep of a child who has thought of a way to outwit its despotic nanny.

Three days had passed since Barber's outrageous outburst. It took an uncharacteristic effort, but Thomas Arndell felt obliged to speak to James Meredith about her festering wounds.

"The woman's blood is so saturated with alcohol; I fear it is incapable of combating the infection on its own. She should have something to counteract the pus."

Meredith was completing his morning ablutions, and he rinsed the gleaming blade. He mopped his newly shaven chin and looked sternly at Arndell through the small mirror hanging on the wall. "I'll respect your judgment that it is a medical necessity, Thomas. Nevertheless, after treatment, she is to remain tied to the pump."

Arndell agreed and left to fetch his bag from the surgery. John Hart was busily scraping down bench surfaces when the doctor entered, and he curtly instructed the boy to prepare the operating table. John's eyes rounded in question, but he said nothing. "I'm expecting Mrs. Morgan with her baby later this morning. Will you please ask her to wait for me?"

"Is the baby sick, sir?"

"Not exactly," replied Arndell. "Carry on now. I have to tend to the convict woman first. I will not be long."

John did as he was ordered. First he wiped his hands from the soapy water he'd been using, and then he spread a clean sheet on the narrow table. He began thinking about the mysterious illustrations he'd seen in the surgeon's book, and stopped to regard his prune-wrinkled hand. It was splotched with red from his pressure on the wooden handle of the scraper he dipped into the carbolic water. 'If we 'ave all them bones in there,' he pondered, 'why don't they tangle up when we closes our 'ands?' He flexed and opened his fist and watched as his knuckles moved and he silently challenged the hidden jigsaw to disintegrate. He flexed his hands faster and became so intrigued that a tap on the door startled him.

"Oh . . . . Mrs. Morgan. Mister Arndell said would you please wait for him, Mrs. Morgan." He darted to the wall. "Here's a chair for you . . ."

Mrs. Morgan shook her head nervously, and proceeded to pace the floor while she continuously patted the infant's back.

"Is 'e all right, Missus?" John's curiosity gave him courage. Having been a witness to the baby's first breath he felt his bravado was permissible. Despite her concern, the young mother couldn't help but be impressed with his earnest query.

"Thank you, John," she answered. "I hope he will be. I'm sure he will be, in Doctor Arndell's hands" She was convincing herself as much as the boy.

"Is it 'is leg?" John persisted. He recalled the surgeon mentioning that in time to come, the child would require special boots to be able to walk, but he couldn't imagine the need for this at such an early stage.

"No," said Mrs. Morgan. Then she timorously added, "I'm afraid Mister Arndell is going to have to part the skin. My son was born with webbed fingers and toes."

John had no idea what this meant but his eyes grew wide and he said, "Cor!"

Thomas Arndell returned at that moment, and as the group went into the Sick Bay, John again stared at wonder at his own hand.

By the following afternoon the fleet was sailing calmly but with good speed. The blistering sun heated the main deck boards until they were too uncomfortable to touch, and several of the convicts and seaman continuously sloshed them down with buckets of seawater. Other seamen languidly checked fishing lines and calked gaping timbers, and many passengers sought the shade afforded by sails that billowed before the hot breezes.

The gypsy was still tied to the pump, but the doctor had covered her well with lightweight cotton sheets. Still her olive skin was no match for the devastating effects of continuous exposure. Half conscious, she licked her cracked lips and begged piteously for drinks from the passing seamen or marines.

"How long is he going to leave her there? Until she's dead?" Lewis muttered his question and averted his eyes as he passed the woman who had kept him company. He continued with his duties, unable to equate the crime to the punishment. The woman he once admired was now a mumbling witch. "She asked for it, anyways," he said callously.

Lieutenant William Faddy wore nothing but his trousers as he wearily piled his belongings and bedding to one side of his small area below decks. A large bucket stood on the floor beside him. It contained oil of tar. He dipped a spatula of strong timber into the glutinous sludge and proceeded to apply it thickly between the planks of his berth.

"Of all the filthy animals . . ." he muttered, his disgust lending vigour to the task. I wouldn't be surprised if the whole shipload of bugs and cockroaches has left the rotting timbers and come to my bunk." He turned to dip the spatula again into the bucket and then straightened as footsteps approached.

"Good Lord, Faddy," exclaimed Clark peering in. "What on earth are you doing?"

"Trying to assure a good night's sleep," came the reply. "Look at the little buggers. Hundreds of them"

Clark watched while Faddy forced more of the black concoction between the planks. "There are pests all over the entire ship, but you do seem to have a goodly share." He grimaced towards the bucket. "Don't know what you can do if that doesn't work."

"I think I would rather sleep in a jolly-boat if it doesn't," replied Faddy. "Phoow! I don't know which smells the worst, dead cockroaches or this stuff."

Clark clucked sympathetically and went on his way to find a convict woman he knew was rather clever at a craft called macramé. Ever since sailors returning from African and Arabic ports had brought the intriguing craft home with them, articles of macramé had become highly fashionable in Britain. Clark held a skein of heavy white cotton in his hand. He had purchased it at their stop in Tenerife and now required a nightcap made. He wanted it similar to the nightcap he held in his other hand. Eventually, he found the woman he sought sitting on the main hatch-cover.

"I would like you to make me a nightcap by knotting this twine," he said. "This one is far too hot and keeps sliding off my head. But you may use it to copy the shape."

He was so intent on giving his instructions that he barely noticed Beth Thackery pass by. However, instead of staring at him with her usual blue-eyed insolence, she quickly thrust her hand into her skirt pocket and hurried on, as if to hide a booty.

That same evening, having taken dinner with Faddy and Arndell in Captain Meredith's Cabin, Ralph Clark repaired to his own sleeping berth. He completed his usual routine, climbed into his bed and laid back, murmuring his wife's name like a magical incantation. Perfunctory prayers said and before turning on his side to sleep, he glanced over to the box where Efford always curled his shiny black body.

"Efford!" No tail-wagging whimper greeted him. The box he had lined with soft rags was empty and still, resembling the cold void that gripped his chest.

"Efford? Here, boy." Clark rose quickly, and in his stockinged feet, he cajoled the puppy while he hunted in various nooks of his cabin, in case Efford had become trapped. He sometimes did when exploring dark areas, or chasing vermin. There was no sign of the animal. Clark pulled on his trousers and boots hastily, and started to scour the area in great agitation. He searched his berth and he visited neighboring berths, fully expecting to come across Effort playing with one of his litter-siblings. Frantically, Clark widened his search until he was convinced that he had covered every square inch of the ship.

He questioned almost everyone, but he was unable to locate his pet. Defeated, he lay awake most of the night, hoping in vain that Efford would miraculously reappear. He occupied the long hours by enumerating his misfortunes of late, and he rose in the morning totally depressed.

It was barely daylight when he made his way to Meredith who, although sympathetic, was realistic. "Of course, we must face the fact that he may have slipped overboard."

Clark could not accept this possibility. All day he prowled and prodded into corners, beneath tarps and canvasses and coils of rope, behind barrels, and even in the cook's caboose. He became more disconsolate by the hour. He ended the day weary and distraught, and decided to record his worst sadness of the voyage in his journal. He twirled the feathered quill thoughtfully before writing, and then a fleeting memory fixed a conclusion in his mind. Beth Thackery's unusual behaviour the previous even came searing back into his brain and he wrote feverishly.

Last evening, my delightful Efford went missing, and I have every
reason to think that one of the whores is the culprit. I have no doubt
however, that the Captain will refuse to share my opinion,
let alone pursue the matter. No doubt he would if it had happened to Lady.

CHAPTER 29

HUMAN NATURE

Five days had now passed since Barber's outburst. Clark had complained to everyone about everything, including Captain Meredith's lack of concern and discipline. He took extra care however, that his mutinous opinions were not overheard. On this morning, he had cornered Francis Walton, the Ship's Master, who didn't even attempt to disguise his disinterest in the little Lieutenant's tale of woe.

"I have more to concern me than a dog, Lieutenant," the seaman replied grumpily. "How long is that Captain of yours going to keep that woman there?" He gestured towards the barely conscious Barber, who was still secured to the ship's pump. "She is nothing but trouble and my crew objects roundly when ordered to do something near her, for fear she casts a spell on them."

Clark's expression became even gloomier and he promised to speak with Captain Meredith immediately. He clumped down the gangway towards Meredith's cabin. Even his footsteps sounded petulant and he was muttering to himself. "I curse the day I joined this misbegotten . . ."

"Yes, Clark. What is it?" Meredith sighed when he noted the Lieutenant's approach. It had become *de rigueur* for him to listen to a tirade of complaints, and it was certainly not the life of a fully-fledged Marine he had expected. 'I'm more like a mother hen,' he thought grimly as he prepared for the onslaught.

Having relayed Frances Walton's complaint, Clark whined on. "Master Walton has already disclaimed all responsibility if the whore dies. From the look of her, that is well within the realms of possibility." He couldn't resist the chance to reiterate his well-known opinion, and added, "How I wish we could be rid of . . ."

Thomas Arndell appeared in the doorway as Clark spoke, and excused his interruption. Noting Meredith's look of relief, he said, "I'm afraid it behooves me to report that Barber may lose her life if she is left in the sun much longer, Captain." Clark puffed himself up and wallowed in his words being substantiated—and by the doctor no less! Arndell continued, "Her wounds are burned and festered, and she has lapsed into unconsciousness again."

Meredith recognized that the surgeon was reporting from professional etiquette more than sympathy. Nevertheless, he hesitated. He was struggling to find an unbiased decision without being seen to bow to the wishes of his subordinates. Unable to, he ignored his Lieutenant and addressed the surgeon. "Very well, Mister Arndell, you may order the woman to be taken to the Sick Bay."

Arndell nodded and left to do the Captain's bidding, but unwilling to relinquish his audience, Clark continued with his mournful monologue. He complained because a convict washer-woman had lost several pairs of his stockings overboard. He objected strenuously about the language in songs that were being sung by Powley, Dudgeon and Thackery. He went on relentlessly and said, "They claim they are entertaining the fishermen. No doubt those songs have their place in ale-houses and brothels, but I do not see why decent people should have to suffer. Military or civilian."

He ran out of words for a moment and Meredith tried to be judicial. His instinct was to peremptorily dismiss the Lieutenant but his realisation that once they reached Botany Bay, Captain Arthur Phillip would need the support of every man, woman, and convict. He cleared this throat. "Exactly who have you received objections from, Clark?"

Clark bounced on his heels and then whined, "That's just it, sir. They are all enjoying the disgusting ribaldry."

Without betraying himself, Meredith bent to his paperwork. "Very well, Clark. I'll see to it. Will that be all?"

His self-esteem raised, Clark saluted sketchily and spoke loudly. "Yes, sir!"

Meredith nodded to his desk, and waved Clark away. He looked up however, when he became aware that the little man was scrutinizing Lady's box in the feeble hope that Efford had returned unnoticed to his mother. The loss of his dog had exacerbated Clark's misery and for that, the Captain was sorry. But he said nothing.

Clark strode purposefully towards the women's cooking caboose, to agitate about fish smells that were adding to the pungent odors already trapped there. He paused near the fuel for cooking supply. A pile of logs seemed a likely hiding place for a mischievous puppy, and as he bent to search, he heard voices coming from inside the caboose.

"So, what did they say?" Clark heard the cook stirring and banging the ladle on the side of the iron pot.

It was the small, quivering voice of Sara McCormick that answered. "Any more fish broth and they'll throw it and you overboard."

It was difficult to determine which of the women jumped the most when Clark bounced into the caboose. The cook's mouth gaped, and Sara turned a deathly pale as the enraged marine gesticulated at her.

"Is there no end to the insolence from you women?" he raved. "Would you be happy with nothing to eat at all? I said right at the beginning that you convicts were being treated like gentlefolk. None of you appreciate a thing . . ."

"B-but . . ." Sara tried to interpose.

"But, but! Your sort is all the same. You all deserve flogging!" Warming to the growing distress on Sara's face, Clark vented his discontent on the misunderstood girl. It was obvious that the cook had no intention of speaking on her behalf, and Sara shook miserably. The cook's version of a trouble-free voyage was one that required nothing of her but to prepare the foodstuffs supplied, and that she not be required to offer her opinion as a garnish.

Steam from the boiling pot filled the small area and it boiled Clark's temper even more. He leaned out of the caboose and summoned a nearby marine. "Put this woman in irons," he commanded. "And see that she stays in the women's quarters without deck exercise."

Sara burst into tears. She had merely stopped to chat with the cook, and was repeating the Yorkshire humour of Beth Thackery when Clark overheard her. But the real cause of her distress was the promise she and Bill Gilson had made to each other just the day before.

"I'm never going to get into trouble again," Bill had said.

"Nor me."

"And when we get to Botany Bay, and I make the request of the Chaplain, we must show him that we deserve to be allowed to marry."

Sara had melted into his arms.

Now, she was bound and led out onto the deck. Beth Thackery stood idly chatting to a sailor as they passed, and it was enough that Clark followed them to guess at another injustice being perpetrated.

"The bugger," breathed Beth. "I wish he had another dog."

A moment before the group disappeared into the women's prison area, Bill Gilson appeared. His eyes were full of pain as he stared at the woman he loved so deeply and Sara's tears well again. She strained with every fibre to cry out to him and protest her innocence, but Clark pushed her roughly towards the ladder. "Get a move on."

With the naiveté of a sensitive lover, Gilson hung his head and continued on his way. Only once before had he given his heart to a woman. She too, had betrayed his trust and left scars far worse than any he'd ever suffered from a misjudged chisel.

In the gloom below deck, Sara lay chained and sobbing into her pillow. She felt life's thrust drain from her and wished the endless see would rise in one great swallow, engulfing the ship so that would suffer no more. By the time all convicts were herded below that evening, she lay with her face turned to the ship's timbers, and barely moved.

"You all right, kid?" asked Elizabeth Powley gruffly. Sara didn't reply, so Elizabeth shrugged and ate her meal in silence.

By the end of the following day, without food or drink passing her lips, Sara's oval face had again become drawn. The spasmodic coughing bouts had returned during the night, and the dull strangeness was back in her eyes.

Mary Watkins tutted several times during the day, and shook her head. "Poor dab."

Depression that had begun with Barber's display hung over the ship and cast a gloom far deeper than that which accompanied the evening squalls. Although the sea-sickness was less prevalent, the disgruntled seamen argued over normal tasks such as deck-swabbing and sail-mending. Marines argued from boredom over trivial matters, like the number of red and gold trimmed drums that were piled ceremoniously at the foot of the grand staircase in the Portsmouth Headquarters. Officers found it difficult to concentrate on routine matters, and their procrastination gave rise to more anger among the soldiers. An inevitable cycle of frustration ensued.

Below decks, an uneasy peace reigned while the gypsy remained in the Sick Bay. Nevertheless, complaints were many and bitter against the continuing heat and stomach-wrenching odors of stale sweat, greasy hair, vermin and bilge. Tempers fluctuated far more than the suffocating temperature, and attending to swooning women and sunburned fishermen kept the surgeon busy.

Petty arguments abounded. Even Susannah and Mary snapped at each other over the baby's welfare. Liz Dudgeon and Beth Thackery appeared to have tired of their friendship, and Elizabeth Powley seemed incapable of a sustained conversion.

Beth flounced along the deck looking for company. She found it in her favourite 'soldier-boy' who was sitting with his back against the men's caboose, reading an old journal.

"Ee, lad," she exclaimed as she sat heavily beside him. "I didn't know you could understand lettering? What is y'name, anyway?"

He glanced up and grinned. "Hello, Beth. I thought you knew it. I'm John Parker."

"Pleased to meet you," said Beth in affected tones of formality. She held out her hand and they both dissolved into laughter. Private Parker shook her hand and he bent over to kiss her. Beth cuffed his chin gently and teased him. "And you a man of letters, too! Ooh, I'm h-onored, sir." Again they laughed.

"Oh, come off that high horse," John Parker said. "I suppose I was fortunate—my father employed a Governess before he fell into debt, and he went into Marshalsea Prison."

"I've heard o'that," Beth mused. "A debtor's prison, isn't it? Is he still there?"

Parker shook his head and tidily closed the journal. "He died the day before my Uncle Jack did. Then we discovered that Uncle Jack had bequeathed my father his fortune—bit too late, then. So my mother paid off the debts and sent me to a proper school. She's dead now, too."

"Was there any brass left?" asked the calculating Beth.

"Wouldn't you like to know," teased Parker.

"Mebee we could get together in Botany Bay?"

"What? And you a convict for seven years?"

"No harm done in thinking," shrugged Beth. "Here, have a fig." She plunged her hand into her skirt pocket and withdrew two decaying figs. They were all she had left of those the seaman had bought for her at Tenerife, in exchange for her favors.

"Can't you offer me anything better than that?"

Beth laughed and returned the figs to her pocket. Then she lifted her skirt. "Come on then, make it quick. It's too bloody hot to muck abaht."

Some time later she stood alone, leaning over the rail and eating the shrivelled figs. She stared mesmerized into the water that flowed relentlessly past the ship, and her memory drifted to her mother. She'd passed her own fortitude on to her daughter, and her favourite saying had been, "Where there's brass, there's a way out, lass."

"Wot you doin'?" Liz Dudgeon approached, pulling a strand of dark hair out of her eyes. "Bleedin' hot, ain't it?"

"Yeah." For a few moments they stood in uncomfortable silence before Beth spoke again. "Haven't had much to do with you lately. You ever thought about Botany?"

"Only that it's a bleedin' long way," grinned Liz, obviously pleased to renew their friendship.

"No, A'mean, when we gets there?"

"Stayin' alive, I suppose. And havin' fun. Why?"

"Oh . . . nothing."

Liz looked sideways at her *Mercury*-mate and knew better than to press the flash-tempered girl. Beneath her capricious nature lay a seething anger and impulsiveness that had led her to the York Assizes for snatching and stamping on a gentleman's hat. He'd passed a derogatory remark about her to his friend as she'd walked by. Deportation for wishing the magistrate an eventual rest in Hell sealed her fate.

The two girls had been chatting for nearly an hour, when a pained look crossed Beth's face. She grabbed at her middle and moaned. "Me guts is griping summat terrible."

Liz said nothing but stared as Beth doubled in pain. An unhealthy flush stained her cheeks and then quickly drained, leaving the Yorkshire girl desperately pale. A loud rumble emitted from her abdomen and she started towards their prison-hold and the latrine facilities. But she couldn't make it. She squatted behind casks piled to one side of the deck, and lifted her skirt for quite a different purpose this time. Groaning as her bowels knotted and emptied themselves, she vowed never to eat another fig as long as she lived. Not even if she was starving to death in the middle of the desert, she wouldn't.

The malodorous fumes of gastritis assailed Captain Meredith as he climbed to deck level just then. He clasped a handkerchief to his offended nose, and his eyes darted around for the culprit. He spotted her and above the handkerchief, his eyes flashed. Beth was unable to hide or stop Nature's course, so she grasped the folds of her skirt and covered her face.

"Thackery!" Meredith's booming roar was muffled. "What do you think you are doing?"

Liz Dudgeon leaned over the gunwale and rested her forehead on her hands. Her shoulders vibrated silently as she fought to stem her laughter. Others around her voiced their disgust in no uncertain manner.

"Oh, the filthy beggar," cried one of the marine wives, hurrying with her companions to leave the scene.

"Glad I said 'no' to her and her figs," remarked John Parker, ignoring what he'd said 'yes' to. He was on duty now, patrolling the cluttered deck with Corporal Morgan, and they ran to obey Meredith's summons.

"See that she cleans up that disgusting mess," expostulated Meredith to Parker. "Then clap her in irons."

Mortified and sulking and still in some discomfort later on, Beth sat manacled to her berth. The Captain's wrath had been much easier to bear than the laughter at her expense. Her nostrils flared at the raw memory of excreta she'd had to wash overboard before swabbing the deck with carbolic water provided by the surgeon.

The Friendship's complement discussed the event with varying degrees of appreciation after the meal was served that evening, and spirits had obviously been revived by the diversion.

"I don't consider it very funny, dear," Margaret Stewart reprimanded her amused husband. "The poor woman must have been in agony."

"How can you defend the slut, Margaret?" cried another soldier's wife. "I can see the new colony will be no improvement on London's squalor, with women like her on the loose." She spoke irrationally, as though convicts would be given their freedom once on dry land.

In the male convict quarters, ribald remarks by those who had been in the vicinity filled the air. The laughter was that of men grasping at anything to alleviate their suffering.

"The poor old Capt'n," smirked Gant's old crony, Lewis. "He's getting' it from North and South."

"What d'yer mean?" asked another man. "Did she start throwing it at 'im, then?"

Raucous laughter prompted many to try and outsmart the previous remark, providing fine entertainment to while away the hot night.

The female convicts retired to their berths that night, with fish-soup and bread slopping around in their stomachs. Few slept as tattered clothes clung to their perspiring bodies. Beth slept fitfully, disturbed occasionally by vague twinges in her bowels.

Mary and Susannah rested deep in the sleep of innocence, and Sara's only cognizance of life was a faint cough every ten minutes or so.

Lying beside the sleeping Liz, Elizabeth Powley fanned herself with her skirt. It only served to move the fetid air for a moment and as soon as her arms became tired, the claustrophobic atmosphere closed in like an old horsehair blanket that had been submerged in tepid water. An idea slowly filled her head and she grinned slyly in the dark. Softly, she began to moan. Her voice rose with each successive groan until Liz snuffled awake.

"Wassamarrer?"

Elizabeth didn't answer directly, merely moaned a little louder. Another disgruntled voice pierced the gloom and muttered, "Who's that? What's wrong?"

Elizabeth still didn't answer but groaned again, causing Liz to sit bolt upright. "Wot's up, Elizabeth? You all right?"

Seeing the tall girl's hands clasped to her head, Liz grew frightened and started to yell. "Oy, Sergeant! Corporal! Any bleedin' one o'yer will do!"

The hatch-cover was hastily removed by Corporal Morgan in order to investigate the disturbance, and he climbed down the ladder. 'What's going on here? What's all the noise about?"

"You better gets the surgeon," panicked Liz. "She looks bloody awful."

Thomas Arndell arrived five minutes later. He tried sleepily to reach up to the top berth to examine Elizabeth. Her moans and immovable grip on her forehead had not lessened. "I can't do a thing up here," he said testily, easing back to the floor. "Corporal, get a stretcher." As was his habit he bent to check on Sara at the same time, and shook his head. "And get one for this woman, too."

Elizabeth Powley continued her charade as she was humped unceremoniously into a Sick Bay cot. Adrenalin had created an authentic flush to her cheeks and Arndell suspected an apoplectic fit. He tried to cool her with water-soaked cloths then woke John Hart and instructed him to continue changing the cold compresses while he attended the more urgent problem of Sara.

Hart trembled at Elizabeth's apparent distress as he obeyed and he grew visibly relieved when she calmed down. Elizabeth gradually regained her normal breathing rate, but kept her eyes closed. By the time Arndell had bled Sara and bound the wound, John was carefully wiping the cooled brow of a dozing Elizabeth.

"I fink she's better now, sir," he said proudly. "She's not goin' to die, is she, sir?"

Arndell ruffled the boy's hair and answered with the weariness of good souls who care for others consistently. He was quite content that Elizabeth seemed much better and saw no point in examining the woman more closely at this late hour. "I think not, young Hart. I think not."

CHAPTER 30

LAND AT LAST

Doctor Arndell rose twice that night in order to check on his three patients, and he decided again to bleed Sara. Her condition continued to deteriorate and he found himself grateful that the other two women, Elizabeth Powley and Elizabeth Barber, needed no assistance. Powley was sleeping as peacefully as an innocent baby, and Barber remained semi-conscious on her stomach, saliva dribbling onto the pillow from her swollen and blistered lips.

August commenced the following day with a dawn that painted the sky in pastel water-colours. A light breeze skipped over the glistening ocean and there wasn't a cloud to mar the scene. It augured another day of good sailing. At dinner the previous evening, Captain Meredith had said that with good winds, the fleet should reach Rio in a day or so. There wasn't a soul on board who would not be straining against the shimmering horizon to catch their first glimpse of terra firma for many weeks.

Elizabeth Powley stirred, opened her eyes like a sleepy lioness, and shut them instantly when she remembered where she was. Not since she had played the part of a distraught robbery victim in order to let Patrick Daley creep up behind her would-be rescuer, had she enjoyed such deception. She became aware of a small figure approaching her cot and peered from beneath her eyelashes.

"Hullo, Hart," she whispered, remembering to continue her deception. "Where am I?"

"In the Sick Bay, miss. You was ever so sick last night."

His deference disturbed her and she closed her eyes fully again. Deceiving men had become her lifetime's occupation, but this fresh faced and youthful innocence was not so easy to cope with. She hoped that his concern would persuade him to retreat and let her sleep a little longer. Twice during the night she had roused and let a Cheshire smile lighten her face. The comfort beneath her kept her awake as she savored the unfamiliar luxury. No-one cramped her into a few inches, no-one snored, and no babies bleated for a midnight feed. Hart tapped her hand paternally in the way of the surgeon, and crept away.

Another hour passed and the gypsy moaned once or twice. But Elizabeth could hear nothing from Sara b behind the nearby screen. Neither surgeon nor the boy was present and a feline curiosity roused her to her elbow. She swung her long legs quietly over the side of the cot, and was about to get to her feet when John Hart reappeared.

"Cor!" he exclaimed. Pride lit his face and he ran excitedly into the doctor's room. "Mister Arndell! Mister Arndell, sir! She's better an' she's sitting up an' all!"

For a moment, more concerned for the desperately ill Sara, the surgeon was mystified by the boy's outburst. He knew John was always keen to excel in his duty and would report any developments, but he stood nonplussed at his excitement. Without waiting for a reply, John darted back into the Sick Bay waving at Arndell to follow. He entered warily and was confronted by a smoldering Elizabeth. She flounced to her feet, pushed her thick hair roughly into place and challenged the medical man with her eyes. Despite her bravado, she was confused. Never before had she experienced such genuine warmth from a virtual stranger, much less a gutter-snipe who'd been taught to wash his hands. For the life of her, she could not decide if she was flattered or angry.

"I'm all right now," she said haughtily. "I'll go back to me berth."

A low moan from Barber distracted Arndell and he quickly gave Hart orders to fetch a marine. "And tell him he has to take this woman back to the convict's hold."

He immediately crossed to the gypsy's cot. Still lying on her stomach, she moved stiffly and moaned again as she tried to raise herself and twist her head. A strange depth in her black eyes stared as she collapsed back onto the pillow, and this worried Arndell. There wasn't a great deal he could so, so while Elizabeth Powley watched with coldness in her expression, he made the gypsy comfortable. He then administered ointment to her back and lips and did so with less than his normal gentleness. Elizabeth smiled cruelly as a marine arrived to take her back to the prison.

Sara's condition was giving Arndell much more genuine concern. The repeated bleeding had done nothing but drain her, and she resembled a figure of wax. Limp and immobile, she looked as though at any moment, she would dissolve. She displayed no intention of clinging to life. Arndell stood looking down at her, unconsciously matching his breathing to the painfully slow rise and fall of the girl's chest.

"I'm going to lose her, I fear," he murmured sadly to himself. "Perhaps mortal power is no longer enough. God . . ." he addressed the swaying roof. "Your wishes for these poor people are somewhat obscure, and I am faced with an increasing sense of inadequacy. I wish I knew what to do. I am full of grave doubts."

All that day he fought for her life. He found it impossible t entrust her care to anyone else and barely left her bedside. John Hart brought him cups of tea which he swallowed without interest, and he snapped at the boy for saying he was afraid of the gypsy when he'd asked him to check on her.

The tropical heat depressed him, but not as much as the thought these there was very little likelihood of Sara surviving the night. The watch hanging from the chain at his waist told him the time was moving towards ten in the evening. He passed his hand across his forehead and eyes. "I must rest," he muttered, 'or I will not be able to help others who may need me."

He stood awkwardly and stretched the discomfort from his legs and shoulders. Then he moved into the Surgery to sit at his desk. Within minutes his eyes closed and his head rolled gently on his chest with the ship's movement. But his mind was active and brought distorted dreams of his youth and the high-flown ideals embedded in his Hippocratic Oath. A dark, overpowering figure loomed in his dream and reminded him in sepulchral tones that the ultimate decision of life over death, was not his. He jerked back to reality, and then he frowned at the perceived futility of his calling.

A small tap on his door made him press hard into his eyes as he answered. "Yes? What is it?"

The door eased open and the nervous figure of Bill Gilson peered into the room.

"Gilson! Can your problem not wait until the morning?" He spoke sharply then he noted the carpenter's concern. "Well, what is it?"

"If you please, sir," came the soft Devonshire drawl. "Could I enquire about Sara McCormick, sir?"

Something in the man's demeanor struck a clear chord with Arndell, and dejectedly he shook his head.

Gilson moved further into the room and his eyes widened. "You mean . . . Is she dead, sir?" His eyes filled with tears and a shocked finality blanched his face.

"All but," replied Arndell, and shook his head again.

Gilson struggled with the knot that blocked his throat and looked around the surgery. His chest heaved deeply and he seemed at a loss for his next move. "C-can I see her, Mister Arndell? Please, sir?"

Arndell studied the earnest man. He was normally averse to visitors in his Sick Bay and considered they were much more useful once his patient had been released. Not that there were visitors for the convicts most time. He thought deeply for less than a minute and then he rose and whispered to Gilson to follow him into the room where Sara lay immobile. Her fair hair was fanned out on the pillow and she looked ethereal. Her white lips were still and her expression blank. Arndell leaned over the girl fully expecting to see that life had expired. He then straightened at a feather-light draught of expended air, and he reached to the bedside for a small mirror. Placing it close to her lips, he shook his head as it remained clear. He looked back to Gilson whose jaw was set so rigidly there was no chance of a sob escaping. Doctor Arndell beckoned him closer. "A moment only."

Gilson moved to Sara's side and whispered her name before he touched the small, cold hand lightly. With supreme control, he again controlled the sob that welled from his chest. He leaned over and pressed his lips onto her blonde hair. "Sara, my sweetheart, my little maid. If there be a God like they keep telling me, I pray He will look after you. If only He would let me breathe for you . . . if we could have but one chance . . . oh, Sara." His sob could be contained no longer.

Visibly moved, Arndell led the crying man back into the surgery and sat him on a chair. "Life can be extremely hard, lad," he said, patting Bill's shoulder. "Had you planned to marry the woman?"

The carpenter threw back his sandy head, trying to stem the tears that flowed uncontrollably down his cheeks. He closed his eyes, and nodded.

Thomas Arndell laid sympathetic hand on the young man's shoulder and was lost for adequate words. In the midst of trials and degradations, the strong bond of love had triumphed again, only to be stripped away mercilessly and snapped like the stem of a crystal goblet. "Life can be extremely hard," he repeated.

After a while, Bill Gilson quietly left the surgery and made his way back to his hammock. He lay awake listening to the ship's timbers creak and the swell of the ocean surging alongside. He took a deep gulp of air, as though we were willing it to breathe life into the woman he loved. The doctor, meanwhile, sat at his desk and stared into space. The lamp flickering on the wall timbers lowered, and he silently made a note to refuel it at daylight, presuming it would last out until then. The darker the room became, the more isolated the doctor felt, and he muttered a prayer for himself and all who were enduring this monotonous voyage with him. The ocean's rush past the hull numbed his brain and he didn't realise that he'd dropped into sleep.

He woke with a start and peered into the gloom, unaware of how much time had passed since he last checked on his patients. He rose jerkily and made his way into the Sick Bay where he immediately saw Elizabeth Barber had not moved an iota. Automatically, he glanced at Sara McCormick and held his breath. An almost invisible rhythm pulsed at her throat. He crossed quickly and picked up the girl's hand to place it on her chest and yes, it was rising and falling almost imperceptibly. He crossed himself, and put the back of his hand on her white cheek. There was an undeniable hint of warmth under her skin. Her eyes flickered open but she didn't attempt to speak. Arndell was content to cover her hands with the blanket and he crept away, with lightness in his heart.

Early the following morning, having replenished the lamp's oil, he said to John Hart, "Mind you stay here, I'll only be a few moments." Still half asleep, John nodded and began to climb back into his breeches.

Arndell made his way to the women's prison and ordered the duty soldier to raise the hatch. He clambered down the wooden ladder and at the intrusion of sudden sunlight, the women began to wake. He ignored them all and made his way to the end of the hold, where Susannah Holmes cuddled her baby and Mary Watkins began to rouse.

"Watkins," he said quietly. "I want you to come with me to the Sick Bay."

Mary knew better than to question the order, and she straightened her voluminous black skirt as she prepared to follow the doctor. Susannah awoke, and Mary said, "It's all right, cariad. I won't be long." As she climbed the ladder, Mary realized she had no way of telling just how long she'd be or why she'd been summoned. But she trusted Doctor Arndell so was not unduly concerned. She followed him to the Sick Bay and said to John Hart, "Hello, cariad. You all right?"

A nod from the boy reassured her and she turned when Doctor Arndell spoke. He'd settled himself behind his desk and already had quill in hand to write his daily report to Captain Meredith. "Watkins," he began, "you are to post yourself at the side of Sara McCormick for as long as it takes her to get stable. John will supply you with whatever you need for her comfort, and he will get some breakfast for you."

Mary nodded, and went into the room where Elizabeth Barber now lay on her back, but her eyes were black and lifeless, and her fingers twitched as they lay on her chest. In the cot nearby, Sara's pitiful body lay fragile but warm, and the rise and fall of her breathing was now undeniable. Mary asked John for a cloth which she dabbed gently against the girl's face. John produced a stool where Mary sat, eyes glued to her charge. A little while later, she allowed herself to glance at the gypsy and shuddered at the sight. 'More like a Mari Lwyd than a gypsy,' she told herself.

She looked back to her charge, and recalled the Welsh event when she was much younger. A man from the village dressed up in a long white gown and a huge horse's head mask walked around the street. With a group of men following, he would visit every house and beg for bread. The legend held that if the Mari Lwyd received nothing, then you would have a year's bad luck. 'I knew I should have given him some,' she chided, recalling that her sentence was imposed just a few weeks later.

The sun very quickly heated the confined quarters below the decks every day and the atmosphere became stifling within a short while. Mary asked John to fetch her some cool water but instead of drinking it, she moistened and wrung the cloth before gently padding Sara's dampening face. Sara stirred and her eyes flickered recognition.

"There now, cariad," crooned the Welsh woman. "That's nice, isn't it? We'll soon be 'aving you much better now, won't we?" Mary's indomitable spirit helped her pray silently that she could somehow expend some of her own energy into the frail girl, but se had no intention of relaying her concern. A figure suddenly appeared in the doorway and she looked up with a start. "Duw mawr," she cursed softly. "You frightened the life out of me. How did you get in?"

Bill Gilson appeared not to hear her question and hugging himself as if to prevent his shadow startling Sara, he moved slowly to the foot of her cot. His presence flooded Sara's consciousness and she lifted her eyelids again. Pain crossed her face. For a long moment, the two young people filled their hearts with the vision of each other, Bill Gilson hardly daring to speak. Then the Devonshire drawl whispered, "Sara—my dearest Sara—I love you. Please live."

He didn't see the hot tears blue Sara's eyes as he stemmed his own, and turned before striding out. Neither did he hear the sympathetic click from Mary's tongue.

Mary's vigil ended the following day and she was returned to the women's prison, happily relating her news about Sara's much improved condition. And it was news that seemed to lighten the load of many of the women, including Beth Thackery. "Abaht time something right 'appened,' she declared as they all prepared for the breakfast meal. Bowls and cups were retrieved from beneath pillows, and most of them assembled alongside the eating bench.

Lieutenant Clark and a couple of marines assigned to doling out the breakfast came into the women's hold. Clark's mood was cantankerous as usual, as he'd already endured the men convicts' bad grace and grumbling about their rations. A thin copy of the oatmeal which was issued at the beginning of the voyage was ladled into the waiting bowls. Some women raised a few spoonfuls into their hungry mouths then pushed it aside. Their diminishing weight was another of Doctor Arndell's concerns. Other women, including Liz and Beth objected loudly to the unappetizing liquid.

"Gawd rest me soul," said Liz, "I wouldn't wash yer stockings in it," Liz said to Clark. He glared balefully, still dolorous from the loss of his puppy, Efford.

"By the look of his stockings," said Elizabeth Powley, "they already have been."

Beth rattled her chains and held her nose. "I didn't make as much stink as your stockings, Clarky."

"You'll not be allowed on deck until decorum returns," shouted the incensed Clark, impervious to the fact that most of the women would not understand the meaning of the word 'decorum'. His threat barely had any effect and his footsteps reverberated up the ladder while he again repeated his opinion that all the women deserved to be kept below decks for the rest of the voyage.

Beth rattled her chains disconsolately. You'd think they'd tek these things off. It's going t'be hot enough already."

"Ah, shut your belly-aching," snapped Elizabeth in a flash of her old self. "You're nothing but a mess o' shit."

And that was the beginning.

Sergeant Stewart looked into the hold to see what all the fuss was about again then made his way resignedly to the Captain's cabin. He nodded to Thomas Arndell as he entered and the surgeon stood tapping his wire-rims on his thumbnail. He was too tired to tolerate petty interruptions, especially at Stewart's opening remarks.

"They're at it again, Captain. Fighting like caged tigers. Do you want them on deck? Lieutenant Clark has all of the women confined to the hold, this morning."

Something stopped the weary Meredith from asking the Sergeant to explain. He had hoped to be at anchor by now, and the antics of a few habitual fighters seemed to him of the least importance. "No, Sergeant," he said, waving him away. "leave them and let them fight until they want to stop, if needs be."

Arndell clicked his teeth and breathed over the glass lens of his spectacles before he polished them. For him too, the past week had seemed what he imagined the final days of pregnancy to be for a woman—interminable.

"What about McCormick?" Meredith sighed.

"Well, she lives," said Arndell, carefully fitting the sire arms behind his ears. "Far beyond what I had expected. She appears to have regained some hold on life but I doubt if she will be well enough to be sent back to the prison for at least two weeks. Even if she does continue to progress."

Meredith grunted. "Women!"

"The other woman," said Arndell, refraining from using her name for fear of antagonizing the big man, "is out of danger. She is no longer sane, but I shall have her returned to the women's prison at the earliest possible moment."

Meredith inclined his head and he indicated the decanter of Madeira wine to Arndell. It had been refilled to its elegant stopper. Receiving an assent from the doctor, he poured two glasses and Arndell sat down.

"Halfway around the world," said James Meredith, "and spitefulness is the same. How far would you think a man would have to said, in order to escape it?"

"He couldn't," Arndell replied astutely and he drained his glass. Further philosophy was interrupted by Corporal Morgan.

"Land sighted, sir!"

Elation replaced their glum expressions with the resemblance of well-being, similar to that at the mother bank. They hurried on deck, their smiles broadening at the hearty cheers from everyone aboard. All were straining to absorb the sight of distant peaks and misty outlines as Rio hove into view.

"Release all the prisoners," Meredith called, unsure if there were any still below decks in chains, but the feeling of generosity added to his elation.

On *The Charlotte*, their nearest sister ship, Meredith observed the same frantic activity and excitement over her decks from stem to stern, and small bodies like suddenly disturbed ants, clambered high into the rigging and the men pointed towards the long-awaited sight.

Meredith turned to his friend and grinned. "What a lovely day it is, Mister Arndell."

"That it is, Captain. That it is."

CHAPTER 31

HENRY CABLE ESCAPES

Slicing through the crystal blue water, the fleet drew nearer to the welcome shore and Rio. Officers hastened below to put things in order for the expected visit by the Commodore's envoy. This was always the first event once at anchor, and Major Ross was usually accompanied by the Fleet Chaplain, who thanked the Lord for delivering each ship safely, thus far.

Captain Francis Walton, the ship's Master, pounded along the decks, checking the correct procedure for anchoring, and several sailors flinched under the whip of his tongue if their work fell short of his demands. "Don't know what I 'ate most," Lewis grinned to his cohort as they ritually unleashed anchor chains. "Coming in, or going out!"

"You talking about port or wimmin?" The crass humour earned no reprimand as most of the nearby passengers were frantically setting their own arrangements in place and were not listening. The convicts, men and women, had been secured in their prison holds and the hatches battened down. James Meredith had no intention of giving his charges an opportunity to escape.

Doctor Arndell and the two Lieutenants stood alongside him on the poop deck, observing the hive of activity on the deck below. "I hardly think anyone would be foolish enough to jump overboard and try to swim ashore, would you, Captain?" said the doctor.

"Who knows?" Meredith replied. "The sea looks inviting enough. We've not seen it as blue and clear as this before and I've no doubt that, with this temperature, the water is warm."

Arndell nodded in agreement as they all watched jolly boats being broken out and lowered into the inviting water. Two had already started to row over to *The Supply* in order to pick up Major Ross and the Chaplain. *The Supply*'s own small boats were getting ready to convey the Commodore, Arthur Phillip, and his *entourage* into the harbour at Rio. They were to take His Majesty King George III greetings to the ruling Spanish Governor and be feted by the carnival loving country.

"How long are we to be moored here, Captain?" Clark didn't seem to enjoy the thought that the Fleet's departure for the final leg of their voyage could be delayed.

"Depends on the Commodore," Meredith answered. "Could be days, could be weeks."

"Oh, no," moaned Clark under his breath. He turned aside to speak to Lieutenant Faddy quietly. "This journey has been long enough as it is."

Faddy hid a smile and nodded. Then he addressed Meredith. "What about the convicts, sir? Are they to stay below while we are in port?"

As if suddenly reminded of the human cargo, Meredith said quickly, "Of course not. The Commodore has ordered they must be released from their confines as soon as the mooring procedure is completed and Captain Walton is agreeable. We don't want them hindering the crew in their duties."

Ralph Clark's face fell; he rocked on his heels and stared back out to the ocean. Faddy nodded again and checked out the marines standing by the hatches, waiting for orders to release the prisoners. All ranks had reacted to the sight of land with the joy that could be expected after the unbearable days and long nights endured. Boredom flew away on the wings of sea-birds that circled constantly and one or two seamen found inspiration to break into bawdy sea-shanties.

Hark at that lot," said Liz Dudgeon. "We ain't got nuffin' to sing about!" She looked over to Beth and laughed. "Coo! You should see yor 'air all over like a rat's nest!"

Beth roughly patted her red thatch into place and pulled a face at her friend. Elizabeth Powley said nothing, aloof as always.

In the men's prison, the convicts were already perspiring but the relief of monotony prompted lively chatter and Henry Cable sat on his berth with one leg up under his chin. All convicts had been shackled to their berths during the approach to Rio and the flurry of dropping anchor then securing the ship was a noisy one. Opposite him, John Hart tried to peer through the ship's timbers but his leg chain restricted his movement.

"Do y'fink we'll gets to see it, Mister Cable, sir?"

"It doesn't do us any good to think, John. We just have to wait until something happens." Henry laid his forehead on his knee, his loins aching to see his beloved Susannah. Like everyone else on board, he had no conception of what was ahead for them and he tried to imagine Botany Bay. Was it a big place? Must be, he decided, if all the ships were to be anchored there. What food would they eat? Surely there must be some animals for meat, or vegetables to eat? "Always be fish," he muttered, but didn't relish the image of fish soup every day, while prisons were being built in Botany Bay.

Gradually the noise and scuffles above grew less and the brave vessels rocked at anchor. They proudly resembled worn mothers who rested awhile knowing their children were safe, if only for the moment. Then the order was given and the hatches removed, allowing a hot stream of sunshine into the cramped quarters. Two marines clattered down the ladder and proceeded to unchain the convicts. "Go on, up you gets," said one. "An' behave yourselves." The marine giving the order stood aside as the men scrambled to be first up the ladder and into the freedom of warm sea breezes and the gentle sway of the ship.

The women had been released at the same time, and Henry immediately found Susannah and their son. Mary was close behind them, and as usual, she held out her arms for the baby then proceeded to walk along the deck, crooning to him. Henry quickly drew Susannah into a shadowed area near the gangway and the two young people melted into each other hungrily.

John Hart ran immediately into the Sick Bay and Thomas Arndell ruffled the boy's hair. "Like some books to read?" he asked.

"Can I go and see them first, sir? Please, sir?" He was staring across the water to where hordes of South American natives rowed small boats from the shoreline, like sharks that had been lying in wait for an opportune moment. They broke into groups and surrounded their choice of the eleven ships at anchor calling and cajoling those on board to sample the local fruits and produce that almost weighed down their craft. It was soon obvious that the finely-muscled young men, who grinned with unbelievably white teeth, didn't intend selling the oranges they had. They were bait, and there were squeals of delight from the women and children as hundreds of the fleshy orange globes were tossed onto the decks.

On *The Friendship*, men and women, convicts and civilians, all were intent on collecting as much fruit as they could and such was the excitement that even squabbles ended in a friendly banter.

"Stay where you are, cariads," she called to Henry and Susannah. "I'll get some for you."

"No," shouted Susannah. "I'll come and have Henry—you can't hold him as well." She darted forward and rescued the child from Mary's arms then stood aside as bodies surged forward with hands up trying to pluck the lovely oranges from the air. Henry, meantime, had clambered onto the roof of the men's cooking caboose in an effort to see what was going on. The ship's boy whose job it was to count flogging strikes was leaping about, trying to get his own fruit. Henry glanced at him to say something about being careful, just as the lad missed his footing. With a loud scream, the boy disappeared over the side and catapulted into the water. Cable leaned over and saw his small body connect with the anchor-chain and without hesitation, he jumped to the deck. Pausing only to tear off his boots, he threw himself after the boy.

Margaret Stewart saw them both disappear under the clear waters and she screamed for her husband. The alarm struck a chill through the hearts of everyone. Sergeant Stewart acted immediately and yelled, "Man Overboard!"

"Convict trying to escape," Clark cried instantly, as pandemonium set in a rope ladder was tossed over the side just as Henry surfaced. He struggled to restrain the boy who was frantically splashing in terror, but he could only grasp a handful of his hair. Henry kept the boy's head above the water while the hubbub continued and he finally persuaded the survivor to take a hold of the dangling ladder. Anxious hands hauled the pair back on deck, and as always with the young, the lad proved most resilient. Apart from a soaking in the warm tropical water, and an impressive bruise appearing already on his thigh, the boy was none the worse for the scare.

Henry Cable followed the boy aboard, his wet hands burning as he gripped the ladder tightly. The clear sea-water glittered in the sun as it streamed from his red hair and his clothes moulded to his well-built body. His head leveled with the deck and immediately, he was seized by two marines. He was hauled to face Lieutenant Clark and stood breathing heavily, waiting for the onslaught.

"Tried to escape when everyone was thinking of the boy, weren't you, Cable? I wondered how long it would be. I knew one of you would try it." Clark was flushed wit heat and exasperation, and he gave Henry no chance to reply.

Susannah stood trembling violently as she drew their son closer, and her eyes flickered like a startled fawn, between Clark and the man she so dearly loved. The punier man of the two terrified her. She held her breath as he continued to rave.

"You realise what the penalty is, don't you, Cable? It only goes to prove that not one of you can be trusted." Clark glared around at the subdued crowd and rocked on his heels. He had never been able to prove what happened to his puppy, Efford, and now he believed he had irrefutable proof of the foolishness of trusting convicts. And he couldn't resist the urge to gloat. He gave the order, "Bring him to the Captain's cabin."

Henry's wrists were manacled before he was hustled behind Clark, who strode dictatorially towards the gangway. The pompous officer glanced behind to make sure his prisoner was in tow and with a satisfied smirk, he clambered down the steps.

Susannah watched until they all disappeared, then she burst into tears. Mary hurried over to comfort her friend. "That blight of Scarlet Fever!" Her voice was scathing. "He's no better than my old black sow back home."

James Meredith's humour plunged to new depths when Clark presented himself at his cabin door. The fact that he was never allowed to enjoy any short break to his weariness was always proven by the appearance of the little man. Long ago he had confided to Arndell that amongst the trials and tribulations of this voyage, his first Lieutenant was 'like an obstinate boil.'

"I actually saw this man jump ship, Captain," bounced Clark. "He was obviously trying to escape. I recommend the usual punishment, sir. *Thirty-seven* lashes at least!"

Clark's smug face challenged James Meredith. It was obvious that nothing less than an abject apology and loud commendations on his perspicacity would gratify the man and Meredith bristled.

"I see," he said with even control. "Cable, was that your intention?"

"Of course, he won't admit to that, sir," interposed Clark, visibly gloating. "But I, and everybody else, witnessed it."

Meredith pointedly ignored Clark and looked at Henry's face. It was diffused with anger. Four years in captivity had taught Henry that exploding temper gained nothing, if not further condemnation. Struggling valiantly, he held his tongue.

Clark accepted Henry's silence as an admission of guilt, and he stood like an inflated pigeon. "What did I say? Not a word to utter in his defence." Any hopes he'd had of arousing conviction was dashed by his next words. "I'm sure Major Ross would agree with my recommendation, Captain."

Meredith rose to tower formidably over the Lieutenant. Measuring his words carefully he boomed, "Clark! If this man had intended to escape, tell me why did he not strike out immediately for the shore? Why did he wait to be hauled aboard?"

Clark stood shocked then began to bluster but he could not form a cohesive answer—not that Meredith gave him much of a chance. He turned to Henry and demanded, "Cable—were you, or were you not, endeavoring to escape?"

"No, sir," Henry answered firmly.

Meredith's shoulders took a satisfied set. "Neither do I recommend that any of you try." He transferred his glare to the marine guarding Henry. "Take him back, Corporal."

The soldier led the convict away, leaving Clark speechless. Ignoring him, Meredith sat down at his desk again and prepared to make a journal entry. Without looking up, he said icily, "That is all, Lieutenant."

Ralph Clark almost saluted and then turned on his heel and stomped up the gangway. His battered ego blinded him to the people he brushed past and they turned to watch his figure furiously pounding towards his quarters. He didn't even notice the three women who were about to lift themselves tenderly from the prison hold. Discolorations covered their bodies and yet an indomitable spirit pervaded. Beth, who was at the top of the ladder, instinctively drew back and hissed, "Wait!"

Her eyes narrowed as she watched her arch-enemy disappear and none of the others heard her murmur, "Yap-yap!" What they did hear as she peered around the deck was, "'Righto. Misery's gone. Let's see if we can find the 'boys' and have some fun."

The day progressed quickly. There were sick reports to be transferred to Captain Phillip as well as fresh water and supplies to be obtained from the mainland, and sails to repair. In a frenzy of relief from motion under sail, many of the convicts worked industriously at regaining some sort of comfort. Several of the women stood with rolled sleeves and bared arms immersed in barrels of sea-water that had been hauled aboard. Clothes that belonged to marines and seamen formed malodorous piles at their feet as more people took advantage of their industry. It seemed as if there wouldn't be a dry sock, shirt or skirt on board within the hour. Cleaner rows of vests and stockings festooned the rail eventually and played like flags in the warm offshore breezes.

Almost like a huge emerald, Rio was suspended between a cloudless turquoise sky and an unbelievably cobalt ocean. The rugged outline of nearby hills and distant mountains shimmered as the heat increased and they created a picture of proud dominance. Exotic undergrowth that was visible against the shoreline consistently parted to reveal excited youngsters who were berry brown. The gleam of their brilliant teeth rivaled the flash of their dark laughing eyes. Other children chattered and pointed to the unusual group of tall ships, and still more cavorted in the gentle waves that licked their naked and glistening bodies with tongues of foam.

A wiry sailor on board, sitting impishly atop the capstan, suddenly produced a fiddle and he started to play music with such gusto that the washer-women found it contagious. They could not help but match his beat with their singing and the slap of clothes into water. And they turned in circular jigs as they wrung out the washing.

John Hart sat nearby with Charles Stewart between his knees. He held the baby's hands and helped him to clap in time with the music. Spirits lifted higher and the mouthwatering smells of freshly skinned oranges added a new fragrance to the air. Peel floated around the brig like bobbing nuggets of gold.

"'Ullo, miss," John called to Elizabeth Powley as she passed. "You feelin' better, are you?"

"I'm all right," she replied curtly and walked on to the end of the ship, Hart's awe and respect continued to disturb her and she found herself handling an unknown disquiet. She leaned against the men's caboose and faced out to sea, allowing the tropical warmth to soothe her bruises. But it seemed there was little that could explain or soothe the bruises she felt inside. Eventually, for the fact that her muscles seemed to set themselves into cement if she held her stance too long, she wandered towards the middle-deck. There she observed Thomas Arndell and James Meredith in conversation. She was unaware that they had been summoned to meet with the Commodore again, to give a verbal report on the state of their ship's provisions. They were also to discuss the convicts' behaviour—in particular, the four Elizabeths.

"Jolly-boat at the ready, sir."

Meredith and Arndell prepared to climb down the ship's ladder and Elizabeth melted into a nearby shadow. She pondered the reason for their departure but every occurrence like this prompted an opportunity for her, as it did Liz and Beth. She knew they were still enjoying themselves with their 'soldier boys'.

The fourth Elizabeth, Barber the gypsy, had now been returned to the prison hold but rarely went on deck anymore. And the faithful Lewis, albeit with his allegiance misplaced, made sure her supply of liquor was constant. They had an inexplicable bond that has long puzzled the romantics.

Elizabeth Powley stepped into the sunlight as the men settled into the jolly-boat and a seaman prepared to row them over to *The Supply*. Without knowing why and as though drawn by a primitive instinct, Meredith looked up towards her. He frowned as his eyes met those of the only woman aboard who had been able to breach his wall of authority. He turned away with distaste, knowing he lived in silent apprehension of her and waved at the sailor to begin rowing.

"See that those four are kept well away from each other," he warned a nearby soldier as they drew away, thereby successfully disguising his real concern.

CHAPTER 32

ELIZABETH POWLEY IS CONFUSED

By noon the next day, Rio had dressed itself in the gayest of tropical colours. Streamers and flags danced merrily in the breeze, strangely shaped plants tossed their glossy leaves gently and exotic frangipanis and hibiscus splashed colour in magnificent abandon. Inland, far beyond the vision of all those who had lived for almost six months in a perpetually undulating world, the South American jungles steamed and the Amazon River flowed. The entire area echoed to Nature's order in which all species are prey for another.

Small craft again circled the tall ships, their overloads of oranges and bananas leaving little room for their black-skinned and grinning owners. The happy men manipulated the bobbing fruit markets as though the hollowed tree-trunk was an extension of themselves. Their entire English vocabulary seemed to encompass just four words. "You buy? Me best!"

Hard at work in his cabin as a result of various instructions received at the previous day's meeting, Meredith paused to gaze out at the jewel-blue sky. It was obvious from reports that other Captains had similar problems with women prisoners, but he had received a fair share of sympathy from everyone, including the Commodore and Major Ross, when describing the antics of the four Elizabeths. Inevitably they were referred to as 'those four prostitutes' as though there were no other immoral women amongst the fleet.

"I doubt if one of them has an ounce of humility," he'd affirmed, "much less any conscience. Not even the one called Powley, and she seems the most intelligent one of them all."

He'd found himself slightly uncomfortable at the quizzical glance he'd received from Thomas Arndell at that point, but nothing was said. He sighed and returned to his paperwork. As if by instinct, Arndell appeared at the door right then and Meredith looked up to greet the doctor. "Come in, Thomas," he said briskly. He reached for the always present bottle of wine. "Will you take a glass?"

The surgeon sat heavily into a nearby chair and mopped his thin hair. "I think not, thank you, James. As a matter of fact, I just came to say that I've decided not to accompany you to Rio again this afternoon."

"As you wish," said Meredith. "Not feeling ill, I trust?"

"No, no, nothing of the sort. The fact of the matter is that the choice between accepting the Rio King's invitation and getting together with my medical colleagues has been extremely easy. I much prefer a discussion on the successful avoidance of scurvy to diplomatic small-chat about varying court fashions."

Meredith smiled at the comparison and replied affably, "And I would much prefer discussing court fashions to writing reports on convict behaviour, Thomas. I will leave Clark in charge and invite Faddy to accompany me, instead."

He pushed aside his papers and, after a small persuasion, Arndell agreed to a glass of Madeira wine. They talked amicably for a while then the surgeon prepared to leave. "By the way," he said, "the convict, McCormick." Meredith drained his glass and waited. "She seems to have shown a continued improvement but I have instructed Mary Watkins to sit with her in my absence. So that he isn't overcome with responsibility again, perhaps you would notify Lieutenant Clark that the Watkins woman has my permission to be in the Sick Bay?"

"Of course," agreed Meredith. "You seem to be waging a continuous battle for McCormick's life. Do you think she will arrive at Botany?"

"Who knows?" Arndell shrugged. "Although I feel she has more of a chance now that she's fighting a little of the battle on her own account. Her condition has improved amazingly since the carpenter's visit, but it is really too soon to tell."

Before long, Meredith and Faddy, together with several other officers accompanying the Commodore, Arthur Phillip, clambered onto the landing stage at the Rio shore to receive a tumultuous welcome. The crowds lining the route of the parade had skin tones that varied from the light golden tan of Europeans who had visited then stayed at the exotic destination, to the deep leather tan of Rio natives. The officials all wore spectacular uniforms supporting lots of gold braid, and the officials' wives and women stood like animated rainbows alongside their men. Lieutenant Faddy remarked quietly to James Meredith on the amazing number of beads they wore around their necks and all had colorful turbans and flowers in their hair.

The South American King had ordered that the court's best carriages made available to transport his English guests to the palace and the huge wheels glinted with gold decorations. The English guests stood aside and insisted the women occupy the magnificent transports first and with some other Captains and Lieutenants, Meredith and Faddy elected to stride behind the polished carriages. They had only taken a few steps before they were sorry they had been so courteous.

"You have to envy these people running around half naked," said Faddy, fingering his collar. "I trust it won't be as hot in Botany Bay or we'll have rows of swooning troops in these uniforms."

"The new colony will have many problems," answered the equally uncomfortable Meredith. "Let's hope that getting used to the heat will not be one of them."

* * *

Some hours later, while the sun hung lazily and the shimmering heat widened the cracks in the deck timbers, creating a further tar-seal job for crewman, the majority on board *The Friendship* took advantage of the relaxed discipline and lazed around the deck. Some of the women sheltered beneath parasols, others nursed children who were fretful in the suffocating heat and fanned them with whatever they could lay hands to. Pieces of linen from torn up sheets were employed as fans until that occupation in itself made the women hotter still. Sympathetic sailors had rigged a spare sail as a sunroof for all but the convicts, who were obliged to find for themselves whatever shade they could.

In the shade afforded by the main-mast, Henry Cable read to Susannah from a book he'd been loaned by the doctor, and their almost naked son stretched face down between them on the deck.

Beth and Liz Dudgeon were engrossed in low conversation with their 'soldier-boys', and an occasional impish laugh floated on the hot, still air. Elizabeth Powley stood with one hand thrust deep into her skirt pocket and the other gripped a taut rigging rope. She squinted against the brilliant sunlight and focused on the even horizon. The fathomless deep of the ocean they had crossed she likened to the vast emptiness in her heart. It echoed her desolation and loneliness and the razor-edged line seemed like a barrier to unknown adventures that might have been with the only man she had ever loved. She was also painfully unaccustomed to the confusion and hatred that was adding to her bitterness. The discomfit that arose from John Hart's deference and the satisfaction from seducing Captain Meredith played constantly on her mind. Her seduction of the big man had brought with it a persistent memory of his strong arms and powerful thrust. A new desire had been born in her loins and the fleeting instance of her own vulnerability refused to leave her. She mimicked her Cockney berth mate and muttered, "Bleedin' men."

* * *

In the small hours of the following morning a luminous moon spread a silver sheet calmly over the harbour. The gentle tide playfully made lace to trim Rio's sandy foreshore, and most passengers aboard *The Friendship* tossed in a fitful sleep because the temperature had not reduced. Elizabeth Powley stirred. She hovered between the welcome oblivion of sleep where no-one smelled of oppressive bodily ordure and the consciousness that something was disturbing her. Her sleep peeled away in layers then she focused on a noise that wafted across the water. Gradually she recognized the increasing strains of a bawdy drinking song.

She sat up and listened as the noise change to shouts of laughter and banter when one of the voices sang the wrong words. There were bumps and scraping sounds alongside then it became evident that the owners of those voices were trying to climb aboard *The Friendship*, not without some difficulty.

"Sshhh!" hissed Faddy, in a stage whisper that would have given William Shakespeare great pleasure. "Mustn't wake our little babies."

"Worse than that," Meredith's words were slurred. "We mustn't wake our little Ralphy." The two men leaned on each other for support and giggled like schoolgirls. Their hilarity was interrupted when the Captain spotted the recumbent figure of the surgeon stretched out on the main-hatch. In another stage-whisper Meredith called, "Arndell—are you dead?"

"Yes," giggled Faddy. "Dead drunk, the beggar."

"It would seem" said Meredith, manfully struggling to remain upright and enunciate at the same time, "that Scurvy is an inebriating subject. Disgushing!" He leaned on Faddy and raised a bottle to his lips. "To the King!" Most of the wine spilled down his already stained jacket.

"To bed," Faddy hiccupped. "To hell with the King."

Their uncertain footsteps clumped away and Elizabeth sneered into the darkness. "Drunk bastards. And they think they're better 'n us."

Two weeks passed. An occasional shower of warm rain provided the only break in days of tropical azure and waving palms. A hauntingly beautiful moon glided effortlessly in all her phases during the balmy nights and the sky resembled a cape of spangled black velvet. No-one complained at the stream of dinner invitations received from onshore by the officers. Rio's society matrons eagerly scrambled for the accolade of having entertained His British Majesty's First Fleet. Fine food and wine never tasted before, exotic fruits, Rio's most beautiful daughters, and its most grovelling servants were laid at the feet of the "fine gentlemen from across the sea."

It was almost a catastrophe to all involved when, early on the 20th September, 1787, with riggings repaired, water supplies stowed in casks and animals loaded for fresh meat, the signal was sent from the Commodore on *The Supply*. "Prepare to set sail at dawn's early tide."

It was not too early however, for a flotilla of small craft to follow. No longer plying their daily trade, but loaded with sorrowful South Americans, they trailed behind the majestic sailing ships as they headed out of Rio anchorage and back into the Pacific Ocean. When they gave up, their boats bobbed and dipped like restrained ponies pawing in a field, longing to join the main herd. They grew smaller then disappeared as the beautiful shoreline slid away.

The convicts had been secured below decks as was usual and they sat or lay on their small berths listening to the now familiar sounds of Captain Walton and his crew bustling and shouting almost unintelligible orders at each other.

" . . . and tighten that line on the main-mast there." Master Walton bawled at his men in that same gravelly voice and subordinates repeated or relayed his commands. "Never see such a slovenly lot in all me life." Captain Walton always had the last word.

The men glowered and hastily carried out their orders. In turn, they grumbled at each other and soon the breeze was filled with furious curses. Further along the deck Lieutenants Clark and Faddy stood at the ship's rail. They were waiting until the pandemonium was over before they began to carry out their own orders.

"Doesn't take very long to become used to the ocean's swell again, does it?" Faddy grimaced to Ralph Clark.

The smaller man shrugged and looked away. "I can't help wishing we were retracing our voyage back to Portsmouth. We are but halfway there, so I understand. I dread to think the rest of the voyage will be as troublesome as the months we've already endured. But it will, I am sure . . ."

"A little more than halfway," Faddy corrected. "Did you receive any mail while at Rio?"

Clark brightened. "Oh yes. I knew my dear Betsey Alicia would make sure there was a letter waiting for me. I'd had a dream that she was terribly ill the night before, but happily, her letter told me that she and our son were both well. I've left letters there to be taken back to England on the next ship that goes into Rio, of course, but how I wish . . ."

"Of course." Exasperated by the whine in his companion's voice, Faddy made to leave. "I'll see about getting the prisoners moving around the decks now everything's settled."

Mesmerised by the roll of waves past the ship, Clark seemed not to notice Faddy's departure and gazed dolefully into the swell as though conjuring pictures of happier days. However, he was not alone in his discontent—all ranks felt the same. Soldiers stood in groups and silently stared into the receding distance until Faddy called. "Release the prisoners, men." Their reverie broken, the soldiers dispersed towards the prison holds and lifted the hatch covers.

"Bout time, too." Lewis was the first to emerge into the sunlight. "Stinks like a sewer, dahn there."

The soldiers had given up reprimanding the convicts for any comments and ignored the man. The women were soon on deck and almost all passengers watched as South America's imposing landscape slowly disappeared over the horizon. Captain Francis Walton and his crew had seen it before, so carried on with their task of keeping *The Friendship* up with the other ten ships of the fleet. It was obvious by the way Walton surveyed the craft that he was extremely content to be back at sea again.

Seasickness returned to many of those on board almost immediately, and several of the weaker passengers were decidedly uncomfortable once more. The days dragged on and petty squabbles rumbled around the decks; the squabbles erupted into spiteful barbs ad sly attacks. Any fruit that hadn't been consumed soon rotted and this added to the objectionable odors that pervaded the ship. During each day there were few who elected to stay below even though the punishing sun's rays continued to burn bodies that had rarely known anything but cool and damp atmospheres. Complexions, except those of the experienced seamen, suffered from the effects of blistering sun, drying winds and salt spray that was whipped from the endless ocean.

Elizabeth Barber, having improved enough to be returned to the women's hold, was the only one below deck and she sat by the meal bench flickering her long fingers at unseen phantoms in the gloomy and fetid air. She kept glancing at the open hatchway with dull eyes as though waiting for someone, and did not flinch when Henry Cable appeared silhouetted in the sun. "You down there?" he called, and clattered down the wooden steps when she made an unintelligible sound.

He stood opposite her, swaying slightly with the ship's motion. "They said you wanted to speak to me," said Henry guardedly. He did not bother to elucidate who 'they' were.

The gypsy's voice was low and strained. "You can write, can't you?"

Henry nodded, curiosity curbing his tongue. Apart from protecting Susannah and the baby from her one afternoon, he'd only listened to Mary's lurid descriptions of this woman's behaviour. Other salacious tales from Lewis and his ilk had confirmed that she only had one method of trading for a bottle of liquor. And Henry had no intention of negotiating the same rate for use of his pen.

"I don't know what it is like for you men, but I reckon we have cause to complain," she said slowly. Henry was taken aback by her lucidity and too surprised to answer. "I reckon that this 'ere Capt'n Phillip should be told what it's like on 'ere. None of the other ships can be as bad."

Henry stared at her in disbelief. Her face twitched constantly and weird hollows in her cheeks served only to exaggerate the strong line of her Romany nose. In the months they had been at sea, she'd become an emaciated hag. There was little evidence of the imposing woman who had towered above the others, watching with an evil grin while men were mercilessly flogged. On one of her bare shoulders, angry wheals still festered and Henry couldn't guess when she'd washed last.

"What are you staring at?" she challenged.

"Nothin," Henry replied hastily. "What is it you want?"

"I want you to write a letter to his lordship Phillip and tell him what they are doing to me."

Henry stood silent, weighing her words. Their squalid conditions and lack of privacy had long bothered him, and the treatment of convicts like the dancing John Bennett still rankled. The young man had not deserved to lose his life in exchange for his high spirits. Barbs from the opinionated marines brought daily aggravations and, criminal or prostitute, they should have the right to speak up. Even at the Assizes, they allowed you that, he mused. Nevertheless, self-preservation made him hesitate.

Reading his mind, the gypsy leaned forward. "Don't worry, I'll not say who writted it for me. And you won't have to deliver it. My friend Lewis has agreed to do that."

Once strident and large as she had been, her voice was now husky and slurred. The continuous supply of liquor from Lewis who had allowed his distaste to be overcome by lust, had relentlessly blacked her eyes, deadened her senses and made her skin sallow. Henry turned his head away from her foul breath, inclined to refuse her request, and yet his affinity with all the other convicts held him.

"D'you hear what I say, Cable?"

Henry struggled with his conscience, and then he replied grudgingly, "All right." He could not let the occasion pass without some gain for himself. "But you never come near my son or his mother again."

"He'll be as my own," Barber answered slyly as Henry sat down to write. He wrote on a page of the journal he kept and carried on his person daily and when she'd finished dictating her message, he tore the page from the book and handed it to her. No other word passed between them and her usual cackle followed him as he quickly climbed out of the stinking hold, eager for fresh air and to be free of her.

CHAPTER 33

MEREDITH AND ARNDELL ARGUE

Captain Meredith and the surgeon dined together that evening, in an extremely dour mood. The general dejection aboard had obviously percolated to the officers' cook, and from the first spoonful of lukewarm soup to the burnt bread and partially cooked vegetables, Meredith had cause for complaint. Even Lady slunk away, showing no interest in scraps from her master's plate.

Arndell mopped his damp forehead and chin, enmeshed in his own discontent. "This damned heat is unbearable. I'll open the door, if I may." Without waiting for permission he rose and admitted a movement of hot air that did nothing to relieve the claustrophobic atmosphere. He glanced at the floor and bent suddenly. Then he straightened with a small wedge of wood in his hand. His face darkened uncharacteristically and he glared at Meredith. "What's this?"

"I saw it lying in your surgery," said Meredith offhandedly. "I decided it would be the ideal thing to keep the door open."

"Oh, did you?" Arndell sneered. "And am I to thank you for not asking my permission first? Gilson made that for me especially. There is precious little privacy aboard this accursed ship, but I would hope at least, that a man's possessions would be safe from his fellow officers."

"Come now, Thomas. An insignificant piece of wood . . . ?"

"Insignificant it may be to you, Captain, but I'm objecting to the principle involved." The irrational outburst crackled between the two friends and Meredith felt a matching retaliation rise in his chest.

"Arndell," he warned, rising to his feet. "You are becoming ridiculous."

"Ridiculous! Ridiculous! I'll have you know . . ."

"Captain? Mister Arndell? What is it?" Hearing the raised voices, Ralph Clark had hurried to investigate and now stood at the open door looking mortified.

Arndell was livid and jeered as he spoke. "Your Captain obviously sees his authority and discipline over thieving felons as having no bearing on his own conduct. The right of possession depends entirely on one's class, no doubt."

Clark's amazement robbed him of comment and he jumped like a startled mouse when Meredith banged his fist on his desk and knocked over the half-finished glass of wine.

"I'll thank you to take your damned 'possession', Mister Arndell," he emphasized nastily, "and leave my cabin."

The normally affable surgeon crimsoned with fury and sweat beaded his forehead. "Indeed I shall. And I'll thank you not to speak to me in future, unless it is with an apology!"

Meredith's eyes blazed and his fist struck at Arndell's arm knocking the offending wedge to the floor. "I have rarely witnessed such childish behavior in a man of your supposed standing. Get out!"

The livid surgeon bent to retrieve the wood and rammed it in his trouser pocket so hard that it tore the stitching. He mouthed like a fish as if to reply, then he burst out with "You bloody bastard!" He brushed past the pop-eyed Clark and stormed back to the Sick Bay.

"Yes, Clark?" Meredith continued to shout. "I suppose you also have one of your petty complaints. What is it this time?"

Clark snapped to attention looking as though his world had finally crumbled beyond redemption. "Er . . . no, sir. I merely came to, er . . ." he realized that to confess to his curiosity would inflame the big man even further and sought to find an alternative excuse for his presence. "I . . . You will recall that Major Ross seconded six of our good women convicts to *The Sirius* before we left Rio?" Meredith bristled at the memory but tolerated Clark to continue. "Well, I came to tell you that one of the women he sent to us in exchange . . ."

Meredith groaned. The replacement convicts were undoubtedly as bad as 'those four prostitutes' and the 'sympathy' shown undoubtedly was very shallow. "Out with it, man!"

Clark swallowed. 'She has requested permission to read a Psalm at tomorrow's Sunday service."

"Of course she can," Meredith exploded. "Dismiss!"

Clark did so readily, omitting to add that he had already refused the request. He was livid that the changeover of prisoners included the only one he could trust to clean his quarters and wash his linen. He scuttled down the passageway nursing confused emotion. He was amazed that his two superiors, supposedly good friends, should quarrel over such a trivial matter. And he was incensed that he now had to return to the women's prison to reverse his earlier decision. It seemed to him that all sanity must have been left on Rio's beautiful shoreline. His manner was not improved when he tripped over the top step onto the deck and barked his shin on the hard deck-timber.

"Remove the hatch," he growled to the night-watch marine. He rubbed his injured knee miserably then clumped halfway down the ladder. He balefully searched for the newcomer and when he saw her, he said, "You there. I have decided to show extreme kindness and allow you to read tomorrow."

He disappeared immediately and left the amazed women staring after him. Mary looked at Susannah and shrugged, while Elizabeth Powley lay back on her pillow in disgust. Liz shook her pretty head in mock concern and said, "Bleedin' 'ell. He's gorn off his head!"

"He didn't have far to go in the first place," said Beth sagely.

The woman Clark had addressed, who alone knew what he was talking about; put her head on one side like a quizzical puppy. "Is he always like that, then?"

"No, came Elizabeth Powley's cool voice. "That's his good side."

Inspired by the Twenty-Third Psalm the next morning, Mary added to the Sunday service by singing an old hymn. Her melodic voice rose above the sea as it crashed against the dipping prow, and the sweet tones filtered around the deck before being borne across the water like an escaping wood-pigeon.

The monotony of their voyage remained however, and the afternoon stretched on with cloudless skies becoming grey and still, as though colour, life, and interest had decided to tarry in Rio. A crewman hung onto the helm, with a marked disinterest in the ship's course. His blank eyes mirrored even less as he gazed beyond Lewis and ship's boy. They were sitting spread-legged on the deck, with the caulking pot between them. Halfheartedly, and between long discussions of Rio's female talent, they laid a tarry substance into fissures between the timbers.

"Wish we could have stayed there," said the boy.

"Why didn't you jump ship, then?"

"'Cos I'm hoping Botany Bay will be even better."

"Whipper snapper," Lewis scoffed. "You'll learn. Nuffin's better than what you've got."

The young lad wiped his face with his shirt and grinned with the indomitable spirit of youth. "Get away wiv yer!"

For want of patients to tend, and having nothing better to concern himself with, Thomas Arndell strolled around the ship. He nodded amiably to the faces that had become all too familiar over the past months. Most were beginning to show the strain of perpetual motion beneath their feet again, and he sighed. He rounded the men's cooking caboose then quickly retraced his steps when James Meredith appeared at the top of the gangway. The day after their altercation had brought with it a more moderate temperament and a modicum of embarrassment. He did not know that Meredith was of the same mind. Stubborn pride had prevented either man from breaking the silence between them.

James Meredith hailed two nearby sailors and instructed them to lower the jollyboat. They were to convey the papers he held in his hand to Major Ross on *The Sirius*. Lewis watched through lowered eyes. The note from Elizabeth Barber he had managed to smuggle into the Captain's cabin during the morning service. He had inserted the letter surreptitiously between large sheets of reports and all had been stuffed inside a large parchment wallet which was now being handed to the sailors.

"You'd better wait for replies," Meredith commanded them. "But get back before dark."

The gypsy had made a rare effort to go on deck, and watched keenly, although out of the Captain's sight. Lewis saw her and returned her nod before she wandered away as if still bearing the weight of the lash.

Susannah, who was strolling with Henry and their son, spoke furtively as Barber passed them. 'She reminds me of the hook-nosed cronies who wander through country towns and villages at home. They swing hand-woven baskets on their scrawny arms and tell your fortune, if you buy a bundle of hewn pegs."

"Did you ever have your fortune told, my love?"

"Yes," she answered. "I bought pegs once and . . ." Susannah glanced at the baby asleep in her arms. "She said I'd have a son and that he would look like his father."

"She was right, then," said Henry proudly.

Susannah remembered how Barber continually grumbled about little Henry's cries and her face clouded. 'But that woman is evil."

"Maybe," Henry soothed. "Try and always look for the good, my love."

Susannah shook her head. "I look only for survival."

With just enough light left to silhouette their own ship, the sailors returned from *The Sirius*. No sooner were they aboard and stowed the jollyboat, one of them headed for the Captain's cabin. He saluted as he was called to enter.

"Your replies, Captain. Major Ross asks that you attend to the one about Elizabeth Barber immediately."

Meredith looked at the man as though he had delivered the message in Spanish. "Elizabeth Barber? You mean, Powley, surely?"

By this time, Meredith had scanned the folded missives and found the one marked "Elizabeth Barber." He dismissed the sailor and opened it. The gypsy's outrageous behavior had been fully described at the last meeting with Ross, as well as that of Elizabeth Powley, Dudgeon and Thackery, and he could only imagine that the Commodore had decided to do something about it. His jaw dropped as he read.

We have received a letter of complaint from the convict, Elizabeth Barber. In it, she affirms that the conditions and treatment of prisoners in your charge demands investigation. Captain Phillip, very justly, has agreed to speak with the woman at midday tomorrow. Please see that she is conveyed to The Sirius. Suitably manacled, of course.

"Received a letter of complaint?" expostulated Meredith, conscious of the familiar threat to his authority. "I wasn't aware that there had been a 'letter of complaint'. I wasn't aware that she could even write." He tossed the note onto his desk wit the fleeting realisation that he knew very little about most of the prisoners. Only since his lapse with Elizabeth Powley, thereby exacerbating Major Ross's innuendoes, had he been plagued by thoughts of inadequacy. And yet he was determined that one transgression was not going to be allowed to blot his career.

He decided to send for Elizabeth Barber. He issued the command then sat back at his desk, twirling the black-tipped quill in his fingers. He pondered how he would deal with the convict woman without fuelling her complaints to the Commodore in the morning.

"Dammit! You try to be reasonable with these people . . . ' His mutterings reminded him of the explosive argument with Thomas Arndell and although Clark had been the only witness, he realized that any lapse of self-discipline could prove fatal for an officer. He decided that, despite his consistent whining, Ralph Clark could be relied upon to keep his counsel, albeit in fear of reprisal should the quarrel with Thomas Arndell become common knowledge.

When dealing with the convicts, however, Meredith knew that his every move and word could become fuel for revolt. There had been 'disturbing events' he commiserated with himself, but his fellow captains, by all accounts, had suffered just as much. The growing spectre of a convict revolt aboard *The Friendship* made him bang his fist onto his desk. Impulsively, he changed his mind about the interview with Barber.

He got to his feet and called, and Sergeant Stewart appeared. "The convict Barber is being brought here," he informed Stewart. "Waylay them and have her returned to the women's prison hold."

Stewart saluted, and Meredith knew the man had left to carry out his orders with curiosity drumming in his brain. It didn't concern him that the convict woman would wonder for the rest of the night, why she had not had to confront him.

Elizabeth Barber was informed of Captain Arthur Phillip's command the following morning, and it was a turn of events that apparently hadn't occurred to her. The jolly-boat was to be lowered around noon, and the gypsy sought out her liquor source to way-lay her qualms.

"It's what you wanted, innit?" said Lewis taking the bottle back from her. He swigged the fiery brew and handed it back to her. "You got those scars to show 'im."

The gypsy shook, then demurred. "Well, I didn't expect 'im to send for me."

"You just out and tell him, Romany," advised Lewis, secure in the knowledge that the task wasn't his. "Just speak up."

Barber tried to compose a speech to the Commodore, but her alcohol-befuddled brain refused to come to order. The harder she tried, the more difficult it became. So the more she drank.

A stiff breeze toyed with the sails and the general temper aboard was still not at its best by eleven o'clock. Burly sailors prepared the jollyboat and heaved on the line to swing it overboard. There was little liking for the job of plying between ships while they were underway, and the purpose of this jaunt brought even more grumbles from the crew.

"Shipping a rotten convict to talk wiv his Lordship. Whatever next?"

"I thought Major Ross said we weren't supposed to do this, unless it was absolutely necessary?" his cohort complained.

"Perhaps it was Cap'n Meredith's idea," put in another sailor. "Perhaps he's hoping Phillip will keep the gypsy over there."

"Perhaps we should do him a favour and throw 'er overboard on the way," chuckled the first sailor.

"Nah! She might put a curse on us," came the reply, "and turn us all into rats."

Elizabeth Powley was passing on her way to see the surgeon. Her tall frame was erect in the breeze and her green eye flashed sardonically. "Hah! That would be pretty hard to do. Even for her! Someone's done it already!"

She dodged the calloused palm that swiped at her and reached the top of the gangway just as James Meredith appeared from below. She stepped back, tilted her chin, and what threatened to be ugly turned into an impudent grin. Meredith brushed past her in silence and she watched him for a moment, acutely aware of disturbing and confused thoughts. A frown creased her face and she made to continue, then she hesitated. Descending the steps evidently created some sort of challenge that she was not inclined to take up, so she turned away and walked to the side of the ship. Her archenemy was being lowered into the jollyboat, and Elizabeth's lips curled into a sneer.

"She's not going to get very far like that. Look at her—drunk as a turnkey on pay night."

Her prognostication proved to be correct. Incoherent and unable to state her case, all that the gypsy achieved from officers aboard *The Sirius* was the threat of another flogging if she didn't stop being a nuisance.

CHAPTER 34

THE GALE

Two days passed and the fleet sailed into an equatorial gale that struck terror into the hearts of most land-lubbers on board. Replacing the sapphire skies and waves of water clear enough to see strange specimens of fish fathoms below the surface, were rolling grey clouds that were whipped into a frenzy by spiteful winds. The sea became a heaving cauldron of black water and rose in walls around the brave ships. It tossed them around like wooden casks over waterfalls and they shuddered with the force of each liquid boulder that crashed over their decks. Jibs split, masts snapped, and *The Friendship* lost her main topsail yard. For many hours the mountainous waves clawed at the decks and sent fingers of icy cold water into the holds. The watery fingers assumed a frantic and repetitive search into berths and corners, upsetting anything that dared to sit free, and they saturated anything or anyone who wasn't already soaked.

The fleet battled the gale's fury for three long days and nights. Water slopped against the lower berths and the passengers were reduced to prayers, tears, and the conviction that, at any moment, the sea would claim the fleet as surely as The Great Fire had destroyed London many years before.

Late into the fourth night, there was a momentary lull. King Neptune had paused to draw another breath, and when he let it go it drove water into the women's prison with such a fury that several were swept from their berths.

The buxom convict's daughter was thrown against a stanchion, and the ominous thud of her skull on the timber sounded like Satan striking a deadened gong in demand of a sacrificial maiden. The girl slumped back and her mother screamed.

Elizabeth Powley scrambled from her berth and shuddered as she lowered herself knee-deep into the cold water. She made her way laboriously towards the steps and climbed up to look through the hatch-cover. She yelled with a voice strengthened by a lifetime of self-preservation, b but another wave broke over the deck and she was washed down from the ladder. Undaunted, she made her way up again, and clung to the wet timber screaming abuse. Her sodden fingers waved through the hatch-cover like drowning worms. "One of you bastards up there—get the surgeon."

Miraculously, a crewman relayed her cry to Sergeant Stewart, who had been called on deck when the women's cooking caboose was washed overboard. Stewart scrambled to the Surgery door and braced himself against it as he yelled, "It's urgent, Mister Arndell. The girl does seem badly hurt."

Thomas Arndell grasped his bag and an unlit lantern. He struggled wit his waterproof cape and wrapped himself as best he could. A fervent prayer escaped his lips as he battled to the women's prison. At one point, he clung desperately to the superstructure, convinced that another step would see him washed overboard. Great determination and commitment eventually saw him reach the hatch and climb down when the marine removed the cover. He could not light the lamp and after several attempts he tossed it aside in exasperation before he waded towards the injured girl, trying to ignore the pitiful queries from the other women.

"Mister Arndell. What's going to happen?"

"Oh God," moaned another, "don't tell us we are going to die in this rat hole"

"Is the ship sinking?"

Elizabeth Powley listened to the din. Voices cursed everything from the weather to the King, colony and convicts. "No chance," she yelled, "The rats are still on board."

"Just keep on praying," advised Mary to anyone who cared to listen.

Cradling her inert daughter, the buxom woman kept her eyes riveted on the surgeon in a silent plea. Surely his presence and her willpower would breathe life into the only source of happiness she had left? She began to whimper. "Is she hurt bad, doctor?"

Arndell didn't answer, steadying himself to lift the girl's eyelids. Her head was nestled in her mother's already water-soaked lap, so no-one noticed the slow ooze from her split skull. Arndell drew on all his skill and knowledge, realizing it would be impossible to get her to his Sick Bay. He examined the point of impact on her head and valiantly showed no emotion as he laid her back in her mother's lap. He stayed at her side hoping she would somehow regain consciousness.

At two in the morning, her life slipped away.

The mother's grief was terrible to witness. Her soul-torn cries vied for intensity with the storm above decks. All the women were silenced by the tragedy and Arndell experienced the familiar cold hollow in his chest. It reminded him that he was merely a tool of the Great Healer.

The poor woman fainted, her dead daughter's head still resting in her lap and her sudden silence seemed to gradually reduce the raging fury that had stirred the sea's bowels. It was as though the storm had gained a startled conscience about its ferocity and with an eerie howl, it retreated from its devastation. The fleet slowly regained a bobbing control and many on board the eleven ships cried in relief.

A few moments later the mother stirred and moaned. Arndell straightened to look about. He nodded his approval as Mary moved to comfort the woman and only the gypsy made any sound. She was huddled in her sodden blanket and rocked back and fore. A weird sound wailed softly in her throat and she seemed hypnotised by the proximity of death. In the macabre silence around her she resembled the Machiavellian reputation of her Romany ancestors.

"The storm was 'er soul." she said thickly, pointing at the dead girl. "It was trying to escape this hell."

Arndell gave an involuntary shudder and deliberately ignored her. He tried to gently extract the incredulous mother from below the corpse. "Thackery, make room for this woman in your berth."

"Ay, c'mon, lass," said Beth gently. "There's no point in nursing her now. She's gone."

The woman dissolved into mournful sobs again and refused to give up her girl, at first. Then, while tears and empathy emanated from every berth and enveloped her in her grief, she finally released the limp form.

Arndell laid out the body and covered it with a blanket, realizing the sail maker would be far too busy helping to set the ship to rights, to be able to attend to a corpse. It occurred to him that he would have to report the death to Captain Meredith. The fury of the past four days had somehow highlighted the ludicrous argument they'd had over an insignificant piece of wood, and it jolted him to realise that he was concerned for his friend's safety.

"The girl's body will be removed as soon as possible," he said before leaving the prison hold. He addressed no-one in particular but waded through to the ladder. The water continued to slop around with the ship's movement, but he was more intent on finding the Captain.

"Well, you won't catch me sleepin' with the dead!" said Liz Dudgeon loudly. Death had loosened her tongue and she tried to assuage her fear with an assumed bravado.

Elizabeth Powley stirred and rammed her elbow into the Cockney's ribs. "Shut up. At least she won't have you to put up with any more."

"Ow!" Liz's jaw tightened as if to retaliate, then her face grew sullen and she turned away.

Elizabeth Powley settled back onto her pillow, listening to the mother's sobs and Beth's ineffective comfort. In the oppressive gloom she grew angry at the fate of women who had to endure the trials of childbirth and the responsibilities of motherhood.

Dawn broke across a peaceful sea that belied its recent fury. Sailors scuttled around the deck trying to repair the ravages and cursed Captain Meredith because he'd ordered that the convicts be allowed on deck early. A small group of them assembled among the debris of damaged cargo and rigging to listen as Henry Cable read the funeral service over the young girl. The mother leaned against Beth Thackery with a blank expression waxing her face and strain etched on all faces reflecting the rigours of the storm that had swept away all joys and benefits of their break in Rio.

Henry ended with his own prayer. "Oh, Lord. Thou hast seen fit to take this young girl's soul back to your Heaven. We ask that you ease the sorrow of her mother, and show mercy to we that remain. Amen."

Over a hundred voices echoed the spiritual reply as the canvas clad corpse slid along the tilted plank and disappeared over the side of the ship. The mother wailed and would have sunk to her knees if Beth and several others hadn't supported her and led her to the women's prison. There she was left to mourn alone.

Thomas Arndell had watched the simple ceremony from the poop deck with Meredith and his Lieutenants, and all prepared to leave as the convicts dispersed. The surgeon hesitated, and then placed his hand on James Meredith's shoulder and the big man turned. Their eyes met in a rekindled harmony, and yet an explicable sadness seemed permanently imprinted on Meredith's face. The two friends shook hands in silence, and then went about their business. Lieutenant William Faddy had also noticed the Captian's unhappiness and hurried after Thomas Arndell.

"Mister Arndell, sir!" The surgeon stopped in his tracks and turned to wait for the normally affable le marine. Faddy's voice lowered as he drew near. "The Captain . . . he seems, er . . . unduly affected by this morning's burial. Is he well?"

Arndell blew his nose loudly on a large handkerchief that still smelled vaguely of lavender. But his initial pride when King George had assigned him as Assistant Surgeon to the First Fleet, had long since been drowned in the fathoms of ocean they had covered. And yet, despite occasional doubts, there remained the deep satisfaction of his chosen calling. And it was a satisfaction that extended to all living things. He took a deep breath and spoke softly.

"Several animals were swept overboard during the storm. A couple of sheep, and a pig—and all the dogs. Including Lady."

Neither man felt he could say anything more, and with a brief nod, they parted. Arndell continued his way back to the surgery, stopping only to hail a nearby marine. "Fetch one of the trustee convicts to the Sick Bay. I'm going to need extra help to straighten things."

The marine clumped off and left Arndell to enter the surgery then on into the Sick Bay. He had secured Sara McCormick to her cot at the height of the gale.—he had no intention of losing her now. The fight for her life had been a long and distressing one and he found himself with a parental concern that she and her Devonshire man should enjoy a life together.

John Hart looked up as Arndell entered the Sick Bay. The boy's pallor showed his recent fears but the perkiness of youth stood him in good stead.

Arndell peered at the sleeping Sara McCormick. "Well, John. Have you been keeping an eye on our patient?"

"Yes, sir," the boy nodded eagerly. "She was a bit sick once, sir. But I saw to it." He added the last remark with a pride born of advancing experience. Arndell turned to hide his smile. He was about to comment when a tap on the door interrupted him.

Elizabeth Powley entered and he looked surprised. She was a mixture of arrogance and apprehension, almost as though merely stepping into the surgery constituted a supreme act of bravery.

"Yes, Powley?" He was wary of the trouble that seemed to hang at this tall woman's skirts like Irish leprechauns. She hesitated, fixing John Hart with a look that unbeknown to the boy, was a confirmation of the thoughts that had been churning in her mind for several weeks. Arndell was anxious to get one with his tasks, and didn't appreciate having his time wasted by pretentious illnesses. He rapped on the bench. "Out with it, Powley. Are you sickly?"

"No," she said softly. "I think I'm pregnant."

Unable to judge if the woman was trying to deceive him again, Arndell thought quickly. John Hart gazed at Elizabeth as though she had just announced her intention to jump overboard.

"Keep an eye on Sara, John," said Arndell grudgingly. "I've ordered a trustee to come and help you clean up. Make sure he returns my instruments to their proper place. We cannot afford any more confusion in here."

"Yes, sir," said John proudly, but he was unable to disguise his curiosity as the surgeon ushered Elizabeth out of the Sick Bay and back into the surgery.

"Get up on the examination bench, Powley," said Arndell abruptly. To his surprise, she said nothing and did as she was told. He completed his brief examination, and after a few pertinent questions he confirmed that she was indeed pregnant. He told her to sit up and entered a note in his journal. "Who is the father?"

"Dunno," Elizabeth shrugged. Neither did it unduly concern her evidently. In the past four months since they had left the mother bank, her sexual favors had been nothing more tan the usual exchange rate for extra rations, and sometimes liquor.

A few times she had actually pocketed coins—tied neatly into a square of brown sacking, the money weighed reassuringly in the depths of her ample skirt pockets. They were the bricks of her dream. Her own roof, her own door, and a life that was independent of men's lust.

Only two men had ever known an untaxed satisfaction with her. Patrick Daley, whose child she secretly hoped it was, and Captain James Meredith whom she'd seduced in his cabin before they'd been to Rio. His offspring she would gladly bear, if only to provide him with a continuous reminder of his weakness.

Arndell paused to take in the full import of Elizabeth's answer, and then rubbed his forehead. "How on earth are you going to survive in Botany Bay, with no man to provide for you and the child?"

Elizabeth's face was already softened by the usual and inexplicable glow of motherhood, and now it took on a satisfied smugness as John Hart re-entered the surgery. "I'll take him in," she said, nodding towards the mystified boy. "He can fetch and carry for me, when I'm in me labour-bed."

Arndell looked amazed. His confusion at the unpredictability of people of any age increased when he observed the pleasure that lit the boy's face. Despite trials and privations, life somehow found a way to continue, and the thought sobered him.

CHAPTER 35

THE LAST PORT

Skies regained their azure magnificence in the beautiful days that followed. Waves that rivaled the sparkle of crystal in the courts of Europe played around the little fleet. And for reasons that can only be explained by the throbs and rests of activity that move the planet, prostitution on *The Friendship* decreased. The exchange of liquor for gambling debts remained however, and there was more time spent in deep discussion or contemplation about the future.

The alcohol-addicted gypsy, however, was the exception, but the daily routines for the other Elizabeths were definitely changed. Beth and Liz, continually in the company of Parker and another marine, were often found discussing the unknown qualities of Botany Bay.

"Have y'thought any more about wot you gonna do with all that money when y'gets there?" Beth probed Parker. "I reckon we could gets a good business going after we serve our sentence."

"I'm not earning money by selling your talents," said Parker crossly. "If that's what you are thinking, you can . . ."

"Ee, lad! I'll forgotten how t'do it by the time they let me out of jail." Beth had it in mind that there were strong stone-walled jails waiting for them and they wouldn't have a chance to do anything for the seven years prison she'd been allocated.

Parker jabbed her gently and said, "We'll have to wait that seven years to see, won't we, m'Yorkshire lass?"

Liz Dudgeon grinned and said, "Anyway, wot else are y'good at?"

"Cookin'" retorted Beth, and this drew hoots of laughter.

Elizabeth Powley became withdrawn and often succumbed to the fears and mysteries of approaching motherhood. She spent many hours of her day sitting on a water-cask on deck staring out to the shimmering horizon. 'What did you leave here on my own for, Patrick?' she thought frequently, and fought to subdue the self-pity that arose on these occasions.

Sara McCormick's recovery had been swift with the highly effective medication of true love. She was soon sitting up in her narrow cot and worrying Arndell that she would be able to recuperate even quicker, if only he would allow her to sun herself on deck. It took little of Arndell's intelligence to recognise that Bill Gilson's attention would create even greater miracles than the sun, and he nodded his approval.

"I must confess," he said to Meredith later, "it is a great relief to be free of worries about the woman. I cannot see that she will do anything but improve from here on in."

"Good," smiled Meredith, in a particularly jovial mood. "Madeira wine?"

The fleet prepared to come to anchor at their last port of call before Botany Bay, on the 13th October 1787. Rio Gallagas lent an air of mystery and excitement as it rose into the swirling morning mists, largely because it heralded the end of the greater part of the voyage. Several ships swayed leisurely against the roll of the tide in the busy port, and people quickly became used to the fifteen-gun salute from the waterside fort whenever a vessel departed.

Captain Arthur Phillip's fleet had been anchored for three days when a Dutch ship set sail for England. Lieutenant Ralph Clark, of course, had made sure that with its cargo went several letters to his Betsey Alicia and other friends in London. He stood beside Thomas Arndell, and watched it sail majestically over the ocean they had recently covered.

"Would that I was on that Dutch vessel as well, Mister Arndell."

"No doubt everyone wishes that, Lieutenant Clark," Arndell replied sagely. "But we must try and make the best of things." He didn't look at the short officer, but kept regarding the French vessel that had anchored close that morning. "I've a mind to pay *The Gendarme* a visit later this afternoon, Lieutenant. Would you care to accompany me?"

"Why . . . yes, thank you, Mister Arndell. She is a fine ship and it would be a tremendous break from this boredom." Clark looked a different man when something had enthused him.

"Good," nodded Arndell. "I'm put to understand that she carries a fine brand of coffee at sixteen pounds a hundredweight. You might be able to obtain some of those expensive perfumes and spice too, for your good wife."

Clark's enthusiasm increased and he hurried away to make suitable arrangements for use of the jollyboat. The surgeon gave a sign of satisfaction and gazed around, noting the increasingly high spirits of passengers on board. John Hart cavorted like a mischievous elf sending Charles Stewart into paroxysms of laughter, and this n turn brought a smile to the face of Margaret Stewart. She sat alongside Mrs. Morgan, whose obviously thriving baby chuckled infectiously as his father tickled his stomach.

Susannah Holmes had been delighted when Mister Arndell confirmed a pregnancy for her, too. She strolled happily in the sunshine with her man, while Mary followed, cuddling the almost nine-month old Henry. Arndell smiled with the paternal attitude of a grandfather and proceeded to his cabin to make ready for the afternoon's plans. Life couldn't possibly be all bad, he decided, not with a lovely day like this to remember.

The visit to *The Gendarme* proved extremely interesting and worthwhile and both men returned to *The Friendship* replete with good wine, perfumes, spices, and for Thomas Arndell, a wealth of up to date medicate information from that ship's medical officer.

"Seems the medical world is progressing very fast," he said proudly to Captain Meredith during their usual evening meal. "The medical officer of that Dutch ship passed along the news to the medical officer on *The Gendarme* that The Medical Debating Society of Copenhagen has closed, but a Society of Medical Knowledge has opened. Very interesting development."

Meredith nodded in all the right places but showed no real interest in the doctor's enthusiasm. He was looking forward more to the arrival of an English ship that was expected. She would be carrying letters for the officers, crews, and convicts aboard the first fleet and he knew bonds with the home country would be strengthened. This in turn augured well for a more peaceful end to their voyage and trepidation about their arrival at Botany Bay would be eased.

H.M.S. Royalty arrived two days later and the expected letters were conveyed to the respective ships of the first fleet. Margaret Stewart wept softly on learning that her mother-in-law had died not three weeks after they had left. She touched her husband softly on the cheek. "Although I could not continue living with her, my love, we parted the greatest of fiends. And she adored Charles. If our next child is a girl, we shall name her Ellen, in memory of her grandmother."

Sergeant Stewart smiled at his wife's already swollen figure, but said nothing. He had been particularly close to his mother, but a man—let alone a marine—could not allow emotion to cloud his eyes.

Further along the deck, Henry Cable reread the letter he'd received from the Humane Turnkey, John Simpson. The last paragraph filled his heart with gratitude as he read it aloud to Susannah.

"On 20th May, the day I write this letter, I have sent you a parcel containing books and a few items Mrs. Simpson considered would be useful. We both trust Susannah and the baby are well, and that the new colony will not be too harsh on you all."

October continued with the fleet still at anchor and Meredith stood leaning over the rail around the poop deck. He recognized that October in this region had nowhere near the autumn delights he was used to in the Northern Hemisphere. He thought of Lady's love of dashing through a carpet of crackly leaves that had fallen from the trees. Clothed in a tremulous gold and russet, the oaks and beeches in parks would now be shading chrysanthemums in their glorious hues of yellow, white and tawny red.

His sad stillness caught Liz Dudgeon's eye as she walked along the deck with Elizabeth Powley and she nudged her companion in the ribs. "Wonder what's up with 'im? He looks like he's got all the worries in the world on 'is shoulders."

Elizabeth followed her gaze and half smiled. Since having her pregnancy confirmed, and having hugged the secret from the other women, she had lain awake on several nights. She often imagined her total victory if she could categorically announce Captain James Meredith as her baby's father. She turned away and said, "Leave him be. He could have more worries than that."

Liz Dudgeon looked at the strangely aloof Powley, and was surprised at her docility. Then she became aware of an overall beauty that she'd never notice before in her companion.

"Gawd blimey, Elizabeth! You 'aven't gorn soft on him, have yer?"

She received a rough shove for an answer, and it sent her sprawling against a coil of rope. She recovered herself quickly and flexed her knees, ready to fight. Elizabeth Powleys reaction had quickly dispelled her previous thoughts and she was instantly ready to defend herself. After all, anyone could make a mistake. To her amazement however, Elizabeth made a small sneering sound, then she walked off. "Well! Stripe me bleedin' pink!"

James Meredith's reverie had been broken by the scuffle and he too, stared after Elizabeth as she strode aft of the ship. He did so with more than a modicum of relief that there was not to be another fight to contend with. He was about to lean back on the rail and return to his meanderings when he noticed a jollyboat being launched over at *The Sirius*. Within minutes it headed in the direction of *The Friendship*.

"What's he coming here for?" he muttered, watching the familiar figure erect in the prow. "Why can't he leave me in peace?"

It only took a few more strokes of the oars to cross the distance between the two ships, but James Meredith made sure he was in position by the boarding ladder well before the jollyboat drew alongside. He stood patiently while the usual procedure of piping the officer aboard was carried out, then he greeted the visitor with no sign of his inner thoughts. 'Good day to you, Major Ross. This is an unexpected visit."

Ross acknowledged him perfunctorily, then added, "Brilliant day, Captain. Shall we go to your cabin? I have some arrangements to discuss with you."

Meredith nodded and led the way, and then he allowed Major Ross to descend the gangway ahead of him. Foreboding drew his brows together as he matched his superior's military stride, and he mentally prepared himself for more trouble. They had entered his cabin and closed the door before pleasantries were exchanged, and in a feeble attempt to delay what he was sure would be bad news, Meredith offered his visitor a glass of Madeira wine. He was mildly surprised when Major Ross accepted, but grew increasingly nervous as the conversation generalized around the weather, the state of the ships, supplies, and the convicts.

James was well aware that the tropical warmth and calmer waters had rekindled an ambience of well-being amongst the ship's complement, the women in particular. Corners and dark spaces were once again being used by whores and their conquests, from the boatswain to the lowliest marine private. A more willing group in defeat could not be found. And he dreaded the thought of having to command stricter discipline from his men. Be was basically a peaceful man. His wandering thoughts came back quickly to focus on what Major Ross was asking.

"Would you arrange for the convicts to be assembled on the deck before I leave, Meredith? I wish to speak to them. I feel it does no harm for them to realise that Captain Phillip and I are well aware of their behaviour."

Meredith groaned inwardly then called for a marine to carry out Major Ross's request.

About fifteen minutes later, he stood with Ross and both Lieutenants on the poop-deck. With feet planted astride, the four of them waited until the tattered men and women were hustled into position. The clothing issued by the Government at the outset of the voyage had been of extremely poor quality, and it was certainly showing its wear.

"What a motley bunch," murmured Ross with disgust.

"At least Mister Arndell has maintained their health," replied Meredith defensively. He took Major Ross's comment as a personal criticism. "I understand that we have been more effective than any other ship in that respect."

If he had hoped for some evidence of contrition from the Major, he was disappointed. However, Ross did acknowledge the surgeon with obvious deference as he joined them on the poop-deck at that moment. His position as a 'go-between' for the eleven ships and Captain Arthur Phillip had not been an easy one, but his determination for total discipline was resolute. It was apparent even now as he stepped forward to address the gathering.

Ninety-three convicts stood shoulder to shoulder, wary eyes fixed on the officials on the poop-deck. Some of the prisoners had kept very much to themselves, others had formed lifelong friendships. Then there was the ubiquitous band of rogues who had continued along their criminal paths. The normal hierarchy that evolves when groups of people are cloistered, was blatantly evident. The convicts moved imperceptibly towards their leader as they waited for Major Ross to begin.

Elizabeth Powley stood erect and defiant amongst the women, with Liz Dudgeon, Beth Thackery and even the crazed gypsy near her. Nevertheless, the scorn and vehemence in her face was somehow less bitter than it had been when they first gathered on deck at the Mother bank.

Ross eyed the gathering with contempt, and he enjoyed elongating the silence to the discomfort of his audience.

"Come on, me lad, let's get about it!" Beth murmured and she received a playful nudge from Liz Dudgeon.

Finally, Ross puffed himself up and began. "The Commodore and I have heard many reports about your behaviour. And not pleasant reports, I can assure you." He ranged his eyes over the obdurate faces and lifted his chin. Then he tugged officiously at his gold-buttoned jacket. A slight breeze flapped uniforms and convict rags alike, but it was gentle, as though preparing them for a shock.

Meredith shifted impatiently. He knew the Major was not averse to using such an occasion to impress all who had to listen to his eloquence. Then almost without bidding, a though flashed through his mind that there were times when all men were the equal of convicts—they seldom had little choice.

"Some of you," Ross continued, with a glare at the gypsy, "have had the audacity to complain about your treatment. I would remind you that your King and Government have done everything possible to be fair to you. They have supplied you with food, shelter, and transport. When you have each served your sentence in the new colony, it is hoped that you will take the opportunity you have been given by being spared the gallows, and make new lives for yourselves."

He continued to stare at the gypsy, but she leaned against the main-mast behind Elizabeth Powley, angrily studying the deck-boards and flickering her fingers as though she were willing them to disappear, and Ross with them. He paused again dramatically and Elizabeth Powley smiled to herself at the impatience she detected in Meredith. Their eyes met but few others noticed the diffused embarrassment that darkened the Captain's face, or the smugness on Elizabeth's. Minds had started to wander and everyone hoped desperately that Ross would not turn this into a long dissertation. His next words however, riveted their attention.

CHAPTER 36

UNEXPECTED CHANGE

Major Ross stood with a pugnacious set to his shoulders, as though preparing to defend himself at any moment. Not that he was afraid of the rabble in front of him, but he was very much aware of the number of people who stood challenging him. Nevertheless, he was enjoying his moment of superiority to everyone on board.

"The Commodore, Captain Arthur Phillip," he began, measuring his words, "has decided to take important steps to remedy and finally put an end to the lack of discipline on board this ship." Captain Meredith's face colored slightly taking the phrase as a personal affront. "The fleet will soon arrive at Botany Bay," Ross went on, "and it is the Commodore's intention to make the colony as self-sufficient as possible, in the shortest time possible."

Most of the listening convicts had no idea what "self-sufficient' meant and their imaginations began to riot. Did that mean the convicts would be expected to fend for themselves, without assistance from the Government? A low mutter rippled around Ross's audience but it was quickly silenced as he continued. "To this end, we will be loading this ship with a good starting stock of farm animals."

There was an audible gasp and Meredith's colour deepened. The doctor shook his head and the two Lieutenants glanced at each other in confusion.

Henry Cable glowered and muttered to his friend, Lovell, "Good God. Do we have to raise chickens in our berths now?" Lovell suppressed a grin and waited for the pedantic Major Ross to continue.

"In order to make room for the live-stock which will be taken on board shortly . . ." He paused and his stare was pompous, but that did nothing to impress his audience, "You will be moved for the rest of the voyage, onto other ships. That is all. Carry on, Meredith."

An icy waterfall of shock dashed over his listeners, and he immediately left the poop-deck to head for the jollyboat. Meredith quickly followed as an ominous rumble of chatter emanated from the convicts. "There will be further orders, I assume, Major Ross?" There was a tinge of sarcasm in Meredith's voice, and he gave a perfunctory salute as his superior climbed down the ladder. Either Ross did not hear it or he chose to ignore it, but he did not reply until he was standing like a statue at the prow of the jollyboat.

"Of course," Ross replied tetchily. "I will come aboard tomorrow and supervise the transfer of convicts myself."

Meredith watched for a short moment as the erect figure was rowed back toward *The Sirius* then he resumed his position on the poop-deck. The muttering had risen to a multitude of loud objections from the convicts, male and female. They made angry comments to those behind, in front and beside them, and their imaginations ran riot. If the other convict ships were as crowded as *The Friendship*, where would they fit in? And what would happen to those who could not be fitted in? The non-convict listeners voiced their forebodings about animal smells, animal faeces all over the decks, and the seamen declared they joined the navy to sail ships, not feed and clean pigs and goats.

Meredith glanced at his two Lieutenants and nodded. They acquired rifles from nearby soldiers and began to bang them on the rail of the poop-deck. Clark continually shouted, "Silence, you rabble!" But there was a hint of glee in his face as he realized his dearest wish was about to be granted. Lieutenant Faddy walked back and fore yelling, "Silence. We will have silence!" His main objection was the odour of wet straw and unclean animals that was a boyhood horror to him, when he visited his grandfather's farm in the Cotswold Mountains. When he mentioned his fear to Clark, the little man answered, "It can't be any worse than the smell we've had to put up with from this lot."

Eventually the crowd grew quieter, especially when they saw that the Captain was about to address them. Before he had a chance to say anything, however, Lewis called out, "Does we gets a choice of ship to go to, Captain?"

Susannah and Henry had been locked in a fearful embrace and searched Meredith's face for the answer.

"They won't send us onto different ships again, will they, Henry?" It was a statement she wanted confirmation of, rather a question. Henry tightened his arm around her shoulders. He wanted so much to give her that confirmation but experience had taught him never to take things for granted when officialdom was involved.

Meredith sensed the storm he was about to ride and changed his mind. "Everyone may stay on deck," he said and he turned to Ralph Clark. "Dismiss them, Lieutenant."

Clark obeyed, then he and Faddy retired to their cabins; Clark wanted to write the latest joyful news to Betsey Alicia and Faddy was intent on updating his journal. Only when all the officers had left the deck did the full realisation of Ross's announcement seem to register with the convicts. Sordid and smelly as the ship was, *The Friendship* was a symbol of fragile security to most of them and the thought of boarding another ship with unknown horrors set nerves trembling and tempers flying.

"Thank gawd I'll be rid o' you lot," said Elizabeth Powley to Beth and Liz. Liz put her thumb to her nose and Beth poked out her tongue. The gypsy went looking for Lewis.

Standing with Henry and a tearful Susannah, a concerned Mary Watkins gently rocked baby Henry and patted his back. Lovell had also joined them and voiced his thoughts. "I wonder which ship we will be sent to? I hope it is not one of them big ones. They don't sail as well as this one, I'm told. I suppose they have their own trustees, too. That'll be the end of our privileges, Henry."

Henry shrugged, but had much more on his mind than carting water and helping to issue provisions. His concern for Susannah and their baby was compounded now that she was pregnant again. Ye he knew he could not betray his fears.

"Don't you worry now, cariad," Mary chimed in. She had read his apprehension and tried to lighten his load. The fact that she could well be parted from them all hadn't entered her head. "They'll be all right with me, I promise you that," she said firmly.

Thomas Arndell had elected to walk among the prisoners, giving a word of comfort here, reassurance there, and he stopped at Henry's bidding. Henry recognized the surgeon as a reliable authority who could be trusted to listen, and he had made up his mind to ask him to intervene on behalf of his little family.

"I appreciate your feelings, Cable," the doctor said, shaking his head sadly. "However, I fear it will not be left to me or the Captain to compile the assignments. As a matter of face, Major Ross's announcement was the first I'd heard of the intention. And I somehow think the first Captain Meredith had heard of it, too."

"Henry . . ."

Susannah's wail troubled the surgeon, and he searched for some words of encouragement for the young couple. "Look here, Susannah. We are now into November and we shall be in Botany Bay in less than three months, God willing. You will then be together for the rest of your lives." He searched the distressed faces in front of him, and then smiled as he realized the import of his next words. "Also, on my last visit to *The Sirius,* a letter from Lord Sydney was handed over to the Commodore, by Captain Tench. It seems it was addressed to *The Charlotte* but arrived the day after we sailed. It was amongst the letters the English boat brought for us a few days ago."

Arndell recognized that he had caught their attention as the trio looked at him in mystified silence. Having diffused the trauma of the impending move, Arndell's smile widened. "You will be pleased to know that Lord

Sydney has authorized that you are to be married, immediately upon our arrival at the new colony."

Susannah caught her breath and her brown eyes welled with happiness as she gazed at the man she loved. Henry hugged her, and said, "Now do you believe that God is looking after us?" Susannah thrust her doubts aside and buried her head into his shoulder.

Mary dropped a light kiss on the baby's head and said, "Well, there you are, then, innit? Everything is going to be all right."

Thomas Arndell pinched the baby's plump cheek and earned a cherubic smile. "By the way, Mary," he said. "I intend to make a request of Captain Phillip who will, of course, be the Governor of the new colony. I wish that you be assigned to serve out your time as my housekeeper."

He didn't wait for a comment from the surprised Welsh woman, but the satisfaction in her face when she turned to look at her friends, was plain to see as he strode off.

"I'll come and see you often, cariads," she said, as though the next seven years had already passed. They hugged each other and for a moment forgot the coming trauma of being reassigned to another ship. The difficulties and privations they were to encounter in their new country would be tremendous they all knew, but the brief pleasure of this moment would never leave them.

Meredith, meanwhile, sat at his desk sipping Madeira and contemplating the morning's events. He did not enjoy the thought that his command would be over pigs and cows and a veritable barnyard of chickens, ducks and geese. He was convinced that would be the consignment of animals and he screwed up his nose as he gazed into his glass, as though the odours already filled the air. His mind continued to appraise the situation and he realized he wasn't at all sorry that this change would put an end to the promiscuity he'd had to deal with. Then he wondered if natural procreation, combined with the short gestation period of animals, would not present him with more problems. He imagined *The Friendship* arriving at Botany Bay like a floating farmyard. "A veritable Noah's Ark," he muttered and drained his glass. "Tchah!" he exclaimed.

"I don't relish commanding men who have become a mere platoon of animal midwives."

His angry thoughts were interrupted by Sergeant Stewart who entered hesitantly at his curt command. "Excuse me, Captain, but there are two of the women here requesting to speak with you."

"I've got no time to . . ." Meredith's normal composure regained control and he lifted a weary hand to the smart marine. "Oh, very well."

Stewart opened the door wider and allowed Liz Dudgeon and Beth Thackery to step inside. They were intimidated by the big man, who looked even bigger against the grandeur of his cabin, and they both stood nervous and silent. Beth folded her arms as if in protection, and Liz stood with her fists clenched deep inside her skirt pockets.

"Well, what is it?" Meredith attempted to sound interested, but failed. Now was not the time to be obligated to listen to a string of feminine complaints. His drumming fingers betrayed his thoughts.

Liz Dudgeon kept her eyes glued to the Captain's face, while Beth—assuming leadership of the deputation—cleared her throat. "It's like this, Cap'n . . ."

Meredith stiffened, but not because the Yorkshire accent riled him, but because it brought unsavory thoughts. To his mind, the women were uncontrollable. Particularly this one who had made no attempt to use the latrine facilities provided. His nose wrinkled at the memory.

Beth persisted gamely. "Well . . . seeing as 'ow we're all going t'be shifted—well, me 'n Liz here would like to ask . . ."

Only the knowledge that he would shortly be rid of these cursed women, (therefore the one who somehow personified all manner of challenges to him), stilled his tongue. But Beth suddenly lost courage and the silence became pregnant. Picking up Beth's lead, Liz blurted, "We want you to speak up for us to Capt'n Phillip. We knows a bloke who is going to set up an Inn in the new colony, and we wants to work our time as servants there."

James Meredith stared at the two women, trying to comprehend their request. He knew Captain Phillip's plan was to utilise women convicts as domestic workers throughout the colony, but hadn't envisaged volunteers, especially of this ilk. His question was guarded. "What man?"

Beth's confidence returned immediately and she took over from Liz. "His name is Parker—er, Mister Parker," she corrected, fearing any familiarity would weaken their case. "He's one of your marines—an' he's willing." She added the last few words defensively and saw a flash of derision cross Meredith's face. Hastening to give more information, she went on, "The lad's got his own brass. And there's another lad with him. An' we'd be doing all the work . . ."

She instinctively realized that no great impression was being laid on the Captain despite their intentions, and faltered. It had taken the two women much courage to make their plea, and now they felt as though the thin blouses were already being torn from their backs.

Meredith's deep voice boomed as he called for a marine. A mortified look passed between the Beth and Liz as a soldier appeared, and their crestfallen faces reflected the despondency that was a daily companion to the convicts.

"Take these women away," Meredith ordered.

Beth followed Liz through the narrow door as her sharp ears picked up Meredith's muttered comment behind her. But she gave no sign that she'd heard anything.

The marine herded them away and told them to rejoin the other convicts. "And don't cause trouble or Major Ross will hear about it!"

As soon as his back was turned, Liz began a mouthful of abuse about "bloody officers who think they're little tin gods . . ." Parker and the other 'soldier-boy' of the quartet crossed the deck towards them, and Liz continued her tirade. "You and your bleedin' ideas. Lousy Capt'n wouldn't even listen to us. I bet he's down there now, laughing 'is bleedin' head off."

The two men reeled. Parker looked at his colleague then to the irate Cockney girl, hardly understanding her meaning. Liz's chagrin loosened her tongue and she raved on.

"I bet he'll court-martial the both of you . . . cast you adrift . . . drum you out of the service . . ." Her fury only stopped when she had to draw breath.

"What are you going on about?" asked Parker, when he managed to get in a word.

"Getting us to ask if we could work for you . . . speaking up to the Capt'n because you was too scared . . ."

"What did he say?" interrupted the other marine incredulously.

"He said . . ." Liz carried on, but Beth got in quickly.

"He said, 'I'd better make a note of their request.'"

"Wot?"

"Aye."

"When?"

"As we got shoved out of his cabin," said Beth, chuckling at the look of amazement on Liz's face.

Parker began to smile and slipped his arm around Beth's waist. "You mean there's a chance . . . ?"

"What do you think?" said Beth, and her eyes twinkled.

Liz Dudgeon gave a victorious yell as the probability came home to her and she linked arms with her admirer.

Leaning alone against the mainmast, Elizabeth Powley watched them all walk away, lost in their animated conversation. She rested her hand instinctively on her stomach, and for the first time, became aware of how lonely she had been. A pleasurable flush warmed her cheeks when she let her thoughts dwell on the one thing that was now in her life. No-one else aboard knew except Thomas Arndell, of course. A wry grin appeared—she'd actually trusted him when he agreed that nobody else needs to know.

October 27th dawned brilliantly after a magnificent sunset the evening before. Officers, crew, and convicts had dined on fresh pork from the mainland. Mouthwatering fruit followed and the meal was washed down with clear water. For those who craved it, there was ample wine or rum.

Daylight filtered through hatches and windows and roused those who had drifted into eventual sleep. However, it did nothing but heighten the feeling of apprehension and expectation of changes planned. Convict men who had preferred not to grow a beard carried out their usual shave, and then they collected their belongings while they waited for the breakfast rations. In the women's hold there was a low chatter as they gathered their meager chattels in readiness.

Major Ross was to come aboard some time around mid-morning, with the lists of allocations to each ship. Each convict harbored his own thoughts and fears. Would the ship they were assigned to be less cramped than this one? *The Friendship* was one of the smallest ships, after all, and there surely should be more room in the berths? Was the food the same? Would they be allowed on deck as they had been over the past six months? Some even wondered if they would meet up with old acquaintances from Newgate Gaol or the hulks that were anchored on Portsmouth Harbour. Others dreaded the possibility.

Elizabeth Barber had employed her gypsy guile to obtain two full bottles of rum in case her supplies were interrupted. Muttering to herself she glanced over her shoulder and rolled the bottles surreptitiously in her blanket. She never spoke to the other women any more and none could admit to feeling sorry that she was about to drift out of their lives. Her ugly face and character had added yet more darkness to their voyage.

Susannah carefully folded the Welsh shawl that was too hot to use in this climate. Besides, it would carry her new baby when it arrived in the colony and she treasured Mary's gift. Despite the promise of the marriage she so dearly wanted however, she could not prevent her hands from trembling.

"Oh, Mary," she said softly. "This God we are supposed to worship has some very peculiar ways. Isn't it enough that he is sending us across the world? I don't think I could bear it if I am put on a different ship to you or Henry."

The possibility was too imminent for Mary to soothe away her young friend's fears. She put her arms around Susannah and quietly prayed.

In another section of the ship, Captain James Meredith completed his toilet and breakfast, and then he settled himself behind his desk. He had no reason to welcome the changes about to take place this day, and he drummed his fingers on the arm of his chair. He stared at the portrait of King George III on his wall and wondered what manner of misplaced loyalty persuaded a man to give away his security and happiness to embark on a venture such as this. He and his men were as much prisoners as those they were responsible for and he shifted uncomfortably in his chair.

Corporal Morgan tapped and entered the cabin when bid. "Major Ross is coming aboard, sir."

"He's early," Meredith grunted. "Very well, Corporal. Kindly notify Mister Arndell."

"Yes, sir. Lieutenants Clark and Faddy are already on deck."

Meredith nodded in dismissal and stood to button his jacket, before reaching for his hat. He glanced sadly into the corner—the loss of Lady had created a void for him. As he left his cabin he thought, *'There is nothing and nobody I can lay claim to any more.'*

John Hart looked ashen when Corporal Morgan appeared to summon the surgeon. He had already taken a tearful farewell of his new friend, Charles. The little boy's mother had held back her tears and promised that once they were settled in Botany Bay, she would see to it that Sergeant Stewart arranged for him to visit Charles occasionally.

Thomas Arndell adjusted his spectacles and acknowledged the summons to go on deck. He didn't relish the day ahead either, much less the remainder of the voyage. James Meredith had already voiced a jaundiced opinion that the doctor would need to scratch his memory for any veterinary knowledge he possessed in order to handle the new cargo.

"Right. Get along with you, boy." Arndell spoke brusquely, and then added to himself, *'why they can't leave you with me is beyond comprehension.'*

The convicts stood in silence as the officers arrived on deck. The boat bearing Major Ross bumped against *The Friendship's* side and Ross castigated the young seaman for poor seamanship. Tension grew as he clambered aboard and mounted the poop deck. He acknowledged Meredith and Arndell with the briefest of salutes, and then looked down to the main deck with amazement. "Why are all the men on deck?"

"I don't understand," said Meredith, exchanging an exasperated glance with Arndell.

Ross whirled around. "Surely I make myself clearly understood, Captain. I am asking you why the male convicts are assembled on deck?"

James Meredith stared levelly at the irascible Major, endeavoring to cover his tracks before he lost face yet again to his superior. "Has there been a change to the arrangements?"

"No," snapped Ross. "What gives you that impression?"

Meredith straightened his shoulders, signaling an end to his tether. "I understood Captain Phillip's intention yesterday, was to relocate the convicts . . ."

"I said the female convicts, man." Ross's bark could be heard all over the ship. "The women!"

Ralph Clark and William Faddy knew that denial was beyond their rank, but together with the ship's complement they could have confirmed that no such distinction had been made. James Meredith bristled with such controlled fury that it was left to Thomas Arndell to quietly correct Ross.

"Excuse me, Major," he began quietly. "But you made no mention that the arrangements applied to the women only."

The silence was explosive. Only the morning breeze playing a game of slap with canvas and cloth took no notice, and Ross struggled with the knowledge that Captain Phillip held the surgeon's word in great respect.

Ross thrust a list in Ralph Clark's hand and hissed, "Read that out, Lieutenant."

James Meredith fought desperately to control the smile that played around his mouth as Ross looked stoically ahead. The ego-boosting turn of events would forever be relished and he stood astride, with his hands clasped behind his back and an unspoken gratitude to his friend, Thomas Arndell.

Lieutenant Clark's thin voice called the names of the first four women on the list. They included the gypsy and these convicts were to be transferred to *The Lady Penrhyn*. That brought a satisfied grin to the faces of the other three Elizabeths.

Twelve women were to be transferred to *The Prince of Wales* and these included the woman still mourning her daughter, Beth Thackery, Liz Dudgeon and Sara McCormick.

"Ee, lass! That suits me," said Beth as she and Liz Dudgeon hugged.

Sara turned to search among the faces of the crew who stood behind the convicts. Her eggshell complexion had taken on a glow with the aid of fresh air and sunlight of late, and the undying love of her carpenter had also played its part. She saw him and smiled. Even the prospect of unknown hazards on *The Prince of Wales* ship for the next two or three months, couldn't entirely spoil her memories. The warm afternoons she'd spent lying in Bill Gilson's arms and the promises they'd made to each other filled her senses. Their eyes met and their hearts were full.

Clark read out several other names, then finished with, "Betty Dalton, Susannah Holmes, Mary Watkins and Elizabeth Powley, go to *The Charlotte*. Then he handed the lists back to Major Ross and stepped back with a smug expression and a rare smile. His dearest wishes had been granted.

Through clenched teeth, Ross muttered, "Proceed immediately, Captain." Another half-salute and he abruptly left the poop-deck. He didn't even wait for Meredith to accompany him to the jollyboat, nor did he acknowledge the usual piper who signaled his leaving the ship. Meredith watched the Major's erect figure as he was transferred back to *The Sirius* then turned and shook Arndell's hand. Words were unnecessary and together they watched as Lieutenants Clark and Faddy carried out the task of allocating the prisoners to jolly-boats that had rowed over from the different ships to fetch them.

Just as it was their turn to descend the rope ladder, Mary Watkins hugged baby Henry before turning to Susannah. "Seems we were destined to get to Botany Bay in *The Charlotte* after all, cariad."

Already well-rounded, Susannah nodded and looked at Henry Cable who had joined the little family that meant so much to him. He enveloped Susannah in his strong arms and slightly surprised at her new-found maturity, Susannah kissed him warmly. "Soon, we'll be married, Henry and I think I understand your love of God, now. I suppose we can be grateful to Him for allowing us to travel together this far."

Henry didn't answer, but his eyes grew moist as he kept a strong clasp on the two women until the moment before they were herded into the jollyboat.

The jollyboat from *The Prince of Wales* had already completed the transfer of one group of women and was now ready to take on another load. Beth Thackery and Liz Dudgeon kissed their 'soldier-boys' and cheerfully joked about their futures together.

"I've got mates over on that ship," said John Parker darkly. "So don't you even dare . . ."

"Never fear, lad," Beth chuckled as she stood in line." I knows which side me bread's buttered on."

"We ain't properly daft, y'know," called Liz, who was already down in the jollyboat. "We'll see yer in Botany Bay, ducks." Then she caught sight of Elizabeth Powley. As was her habit of late, she stood alone at the ship's rail, waiting for the jollyboat to return from *The Charlotte*.

'Friendship' had only been a word painted on the side of the brig until now. Yet the prostitutes knew that friendship had grown in the world that had been theirs for the past six months.

"Tata, Elizabeth," Liz called out. "See yer in the Bay."

"Ay, tek care, lass," waved Beth. Only the previous day had she guessed Elizabeth's condition, but she'd said nothing. "Let the luck of the Irish go wi' yer."

A smile flickered in acknowledgement of their farewell, and then Elizabeth turned to lean on the rail again. She didn't notice John Hart standing nearby. His relief when he'd realized that the men were to stay aboard was immense. He could stay with Arndell now and could think of no better place to be. But his light heart grew heavy again as he looked in Elizabeth's direction. He was far too young and immature to recognise the bond that had formed between him and the tall woman. Nevertheless, he felt bound to walk across the deck to her. "Er . . . Miss?"

Elizabeth turned lazily toward him. Few other people had ever called her 'Miss' and certainly no other child had ever penetrated Elizabeth's veneer. His face had become familiar and yet she would only be conscious of him when he was no longer there, trotting behind the surgeon. She noticed for the first time how small and slim he was. He carried more flesh on his bones that when they had left Newgate a lifetime ago, admittedly. Nevertheless, he would no doubt benefit a great deal from a roof over his head when they got to Botany Bay. And regular work to build his muscles.

John squirmed under her scrutiny. "Miss, I been finking a lot I 'ave."

His continued deference began to grate on Elizabeth, and it occurred to her that her son would learn how to speak up for himself. She would make certain that he stood tall, and broad-shouldered, and not be afraid of any man or woman. Just like his father. The fact that she wasn't sure of that man's identity didn't bother her. With a mother's instinct she would know when the baby was born. She straightened and looked down at John Hart. "What have you been 'finking' of, sprat?"

John swallowed visibly and looked up at her. Then a memory imprinted itself, one he would always retain. Of a finely-molded, panther-like creature, whose aloofness was accentuated by height. "I know you said I could come and work for you while you're abed, Miss, but . . . if you don't mind, Miss . . ."

"Oh, stop 'missin' me, sprat. What are you trying to say?"

John gulped, but stood firm. "I've decided I want to learn doctoring, and Mister Arndell, sir, said that if I really wanted to, he'd learn me."

"Hah!" said Elizabeth loudly as she turned away. "You learn doctoring? You'll never live that long where we're going. Well, get out of it, if that's what you want. Makes no difference to me."

John hesitated and regarded her straight back. His short life had been one where the decisions of others ruled, and now he was baffled. For the first time he's had to make his own choice, but he didn't have the conviction of maturity. Nevertheless, he took a deep breath and spoke quietly. "Good luck, Miss."

Elizabeth didn't reply as he walked away. She kept looking stoically at *The Charlotte*—no doubt there would be urchins over there she could make use of she decided. If she played her cards right when the fleet reached Botany Bay, she might even get one of those domestic jobs they were talking about. That would do, at least until her sentence was finished. Her green eyes were moist and a familiar cocoon closed around her. Then her heart leapt at the sudden flutter of life deep inside her womb.

'This baby will be here long before my time is served,' she thought. *'And who of them hobnobs will take on a pregnant servant?'*

"Aah . . . what the hell," she muttered to her embryo. "We'll manage." Elizabeth was to be the last woman to leave the ship. The convict called

Elizabeth Dalton and two more she hardly knew were ahead of her in the line and she straightened, ready for the coming challenges.

One the poop-deck, Thomas Arndell wiped his spectacles and fitted them back on carefully. "Well, James, I think I will go below and prepare my report for the Commodore's meeting of surgeons tomorrow."

"You will join me for dinner, Thomas?"

"Of course."

James Meredith was left standing alone. His equilibrium had returned, the male convicts had dispersed and the crew went back about their tasks. His good mood was revived and he refused to spoil it with thoughts of the exchange cargo. Major Ross had left no details, but he hoped there were a few dogs amongst the animals. Then his attention was drawn to the remaining women and in particular, Elizabeth Powley. He recalled Arndell's conversation the night before.

"I am preparing a report on all the women to give to *The Charlotte's* medical officer. We have three women pregnant. Susannah Holmes, another one whose name escapes me, and Elizabeth Powley."

Meredith remembered the tumultuous sensation that had momentarily stunned him and his attempt to hide it from the doctor. Whether Arndell had noticed, James was not sure, but he feigned disinterest as the doctor continued. "Powley is pregnant, but refuses to name the father."

James Meredith shuddered involuntarily. The revelation had stunned him, but as a true friend and conscientious surgeon, Thomas had asked no questions nor made any comment. He looked across to Elizabeth and an unbidden concern for her welfare gradually refused denial.

He watched her climb carefully into *The Charlotte's* boat; the raw and ragged inmate of Newgate Gaol had developed into an imposing woman who was perfectly capable of controlling her own destiny, and that of her unborn child.

Elizabeth felt his eyes on her but waited until the sailors began straining on the oars before she lifted her head and looked back at him. She smiled as he turned away abruptly, but each knew their paths would cross again in Botany Bay.—the end-

CHAPTER 37

EPILOGUE

The Four Elizabeths is not an historical record. It is an envisaged account of the lives, loves, trials and emotions of some of the one hundred and fifty people that voyaged on *The Friendship*. This sailing vessel was one of eleven that made up the First Fleet in 1787.

Much has been recorded and written about the First Fleet and this story is not an attempt to trivialise that memorable voyage. However, it occurred to me that Human nature made it inevitable that there were lighter moments. Friendships, partnerships, life-long loves and even laughter must have prevailed at some time during those eleven months.

Some of the characters and events are fact, others fictitious. But the reader is warned not to be too hasty in the judgement of which is which. Research provided some startling facts.

The four Elizabeths were the whores who formed the hard core of constant fighters on *The Friendship*. The crime and punishment of Elizabeth Barber is recorded in the published version of Lieutenant Ralph Clark's journal. And a letter of complaint was smuggled onto the Commodore's ship *Sirius*.

Convicts, crew, and marines, all shared the oranges thrown on board the vessels and the Officers of the First Fleet were entertained sumptuously by the King of Rio.

The celebration of King George III's birthday; Ralph Clark's Anniversary—even the argument about a piece of wood between Captain James Meredith and Surgeon Thomas Arndell is also on record. The child born web-footed; Lieutenant William Faddy's battle with bed-bugs—these are only some examples of why I commend the reader to retain an open mind.

Authorities did refuse to take Susannah Holmes' baby aboard and her marriage to Henry Cable is one of the first that took place in the new colony. They eventually had eleven children, and Henry Snr became a man of some authority in the new colony. The surname was recorded in several ways; Cable, Cabell and Kable. Descendants using the surname Kable are numbered in their hundreds now, as depicted in a Genealogy Chart completed in 1986 by Sydney resident, Mrs Kable-Thomas. Both Henry and Susannah now lie buried in St. Matthew's Church, in Windsor, NSW.

Thomas Arndell was also an eventual resident of Windsor. The kindly surgeon, a man of stature in the pioneering of the district, acquired the services of the convict Elizabeth (Betty) Dalton. She is mentioned towards the end of this story during the transfer of the women, and they eventually married.

Thomas and his Betty had a son named James Thomas, and all three now lie buried in St. Matthew's Churchyard, in Windsor.

Few records remain of the transfer of women prisoners to other ships and it is doubted that *The Friendship*'s listing of convicts was altered.

Beth Thackery lies buried in an obscure and disused churchyard in Tasmania. On the tiny headstone of her grave is the information that she was the first white woman to set foot on Australia's soil. Apparently, she convinced someone to piggy-back her ashore when the fleet was settled into Jackson Port, (now called Sydney).

And what happened to others like Elizabeth Powley, Captain James Meredith? Perhaps I'll tell you another story one day . . .

Lightning Source UK Ltd.
Milton Keynes UK
22 February 2011

167956UK00001B/25/P